ERNIE ADAMS

PRESIDENT'S
EYES ONLY

President's Eyes Only is a work of fiction. Names, characters, places, and incidents either are the product of the author's imagination or are used fictitiously. Any resemblance to any events or locales, or actual persons, living or dead, is entirely coincidental.

To my wife, Linda

my daughters, Nicole and Paige

and my grandkids, Caiden and Caleb

this is for you

PRESIDENT'S

EYES ONLY

LAS VEGAS, NEVADA

1976

Chapter 1

Sprawled naked on her king-size bed lay
Hollywood's newest rising star. Her voluptuous, twenty-one-
year-old body trembled, in mounting excitement, because
she knew, *she hoped,* as her lover's lips moved down her
body that it was finally going to happen.

A refreshing and much-needed cool breeze swept
unexpectedly through the open bedroom window of her
spacious Las Vegas home. She shivered, but not from the
breeze. The further down he went, the more her body
trembled in anticipation. She had never experienced oral
sex before, giving or receiving, but not by any fault of her
own. The young men she had been with in the past, in rural

Idaho – *boys*, she called them – just never swung that way, and she didn't care to pleasure them like that without reciprocation. But now was different. This guy was different. Daniel Carter was late thirties and all man. Her mind raced with nervous, delirious expectations as he continued moving downward. She felt his lips brush across her stomach and continue down past her navel. *He was going to do it.* She trembled as he nibbled lightly across her pubic hairs. Now his hands were on her legs spreading them apart. Where her thighs met, her engorged flesh ached in anticipation and she moaned out loud. When he paused to admire her, she impatiently threw her legs over his broad shoulders and pulled him closer. Her black skin glistened against his white body in the moonlit room.

She caught her breath when she felt his hot breath on her inner thighs. *Now,* she thought. *It was going to happen now.* Gwen Stapleton did not notice the doorknob to her bedroom slowly turning.

Gwen's lover gave her what she wanted – what he wanted, too. Daniel Carter had an overwhelming sexual fascination for black women. Actually, it was more of an obsession, and he detested obsessions. But that beautiful ebony skin was his Kryptonite; it made him weak, made him take stupid risks, made him careless. He knew it, but he still had to have it.

When Gwen felt his tongue slip into her folds for the first time, quakes pulsed through her soul. She grabbed the back of his head with both hands and shoved her hips into his face. Carter welcomed it, holding her there with a firm grip, and within seconds she was moaning uncontrollably. Carter didn't notice the doorknob turning either.

Gwen Stapleton's body began withering in erotic convulsions as Daniel Carter hungrily explored every inch of her. The sensation was so intense, she thought she might pass out.

In the midst of their passion, her bedroom door burst open with a thunderous crash, and an enormous, muscular man charged in bellowing like a crazed animal.

Even in the semi-darkness of the room, Daniel Carter easily recognized the seven-foot giant.

Gwen screamed as the intruder dove onto the bed.

Carter did something that totally surprised their attacker: he moved. Carter instinctively rolled to the floor as his innate drive for survival took over. It was time to end the pretense; his cover identity was blown. He was no longer Daniel Carter, the millionaire playboy. He was once again Johnny Davis, the senior ranking agent in D-Branch, the CIA's most covert black ops division.

Although the spymaster's sexual obsession for black women was real, it was now the furthest thing from his mind. Gwen's presence, even her safety, was at this point, of no concern to him. His only concern now was the giant. Johnny Davis knew that he had to kill Eddie Bowman before Eddie killed him. That's why they sent the blond giant after him. It was Eddie's kind of game.

But as Davis knelt there, a slow controlled smile crossed his lips. This was his kind of game, too.

Eddie Bowman sprang off the bed with a frustrated grunt, completely ignoring the naked woman upon it, and started after Johnny Davis again.

Davis did not have time to grab his gun from under the mattress, so with both hands, he seized the solid oak chair beside the vanity table and came up swinging. The chair cracked across the big man with tremendous force, splintering into several flying pieces.

Eddie grunted, staggered only once, then continued to

3

charge.

Davis tried to sidestep out of the way, but the big man lowered his massive shoulder and rammed into him with a hulking 380 pounds of muscle.

Davis felt like he had been hit by a train. Then they crashed into a mirrored wall. Glass exploded into the air and dozens of razor-sharp slivers sliced into his naked body. Davis cried out, arching his back away from the splintered glass ripping into his flesh.

Eddie shoved him back against the busted mirror and was all over him like a wild animal, crazy mad — grabbing, ripping, grunting, snorting, constantly attacking, never letting up for an instant.

Davis tried to fight the big man off, but Eddie was too strong and totally relentless.

Somehow, Davis managed to get his right hand on Eddie's throat, but that was a mistake.

Eddie grabbed Davis's wrist, twisted it over to expose the elbow and then pounded on it with a brutal forearm smash, shattering the fragile bone.

Johnny Davis screamed in agony as the bone cracked with a loud snap.

Eddie grabbed a handful of the agent's hair then viciously slammed the man's head repeatedly against the wall.

Explosions rattled Davis's brain with each impact, until finally, he dropped to his knees, nearly unconscious. While still dazed, he felt Eddie's hand on his face and then the inadvertent slip of a finger into his mouth. The spymaster bit down as hard as he could and felt bone crunch between his teeth.

Eddie let out a wail and jerked his finger free. And for the first time, since he entered the room, the big man took a backward step.

Johnny Davis staggered to his feet in an attempt to escape, but Eddie bellowed angrily and rammed into him again. Blood and mucus spurted from Davis's nostrils. The audible crack of ribs punctuated the thud of Davis's body being slammed into the wall again.

Gwen Stapleton was paralyzed with fear. Her mind raced everywhere and nowhere; she couldn't think. She couldn't catch a full breath. Her head grew lighter with every shallow inhale. But even in this cloud of confusion, she knew she had to do something. She had to save herself. She had to get out of there. Gwen moved nervously toward the edge of her bed, her eyes bulging in sheer terror, her heart pounding in her ears as the squeak from the bedsprings seemed to pierce the air with each movement she made.

Gwen feared the big man would hear her, but she didn't dare stop. When she reached the edge of her bed, she moved one foot toward the carpet. As she shifted her weight to the floor, the bed creaked its final relief.

Eddie Bowman abruptly turned and glared at her.

Gwen screamed hysterically and made a terrified dash for the door.

Eddie spun away from Davis, and with two long strides, he easily caught her from behind. He clamped one huge, calloused hand over her mouth, then gripped the back of her head, like a basketball, with the other. With one quick snap of his wrist, he broke her neck, then dropped her lifeless body to the floor. Eddie turned back to the spyman only to find himself staring down the long, dark barrel of a .44 magnum revolver.

Johnny Davis had managed to drag his broken body back to the bed and retrieved the gun he had tucked under the mattress.

Eddie inhaled sharply, noticeably shaken. His eyes darted around the room looking for some avenue of escape.

Johnny Davis tried to steady the big gun in his one good hand, but the damn thing felt like it weighed ten pounds. He squeezed off one round anyway. He missed. He couldn't hold it steady.

When the bullet struck the wall behind the big man, Eddie sprinted forward and snatched the gun from his victim's trembling hand.

Johnny Davis was confused when the big man let the gun drop to the floor. His confusion lasted only a moment; Eddie Bowman grabbed his head in a vice-like grip with both hands and squeezed. Immediately the pressure between Davis's ears was incredible. It felt like his skull was going to explode in a hydraulic press. Davis clawed wildly at Eddie's grip with his one good hand but to no avail. The big man's fingers were locked-in too tight.

Just when Davis thought he was going to die, he felt Eddie's hands loosen. *He still had a chance.*

The blond giant relaxed his grip only to shift his fingers to a better position. Eddie then jammed his oversized thumbs deep into the sockets of Davis's eyes, all the way in to the second knuckle.

Davis let out a horrific gurgling scream and thrashed about violently like a bass caught at the end of a fisherman's hook. It took several moments for his spasms to subside, and then, as if a light switch was turned off, life mercifully left Johnny Davis's broken body.

Eddie Bowman dropped his remains to the floor, but the big man's massive chest still heaved, as he glared down at the agent's corpse. The bastard died too quickly. Although still fuming, Eddie started to turn away but noticed the man's hollowed eye sockets staring up at him, seemingly taunting him, mocking him, challenging him. Eddie flew into a rage again at that perceived sign of disrespect and stomped on the dead man's skull. The sound of bone fracturing cracked the silence. Eddie's chest continued to heave, as he stood towering over the body, his eyes glazed in crazy. He started to stomp the man's skull again but did not. Instead, he took a reluctant step back, drew in a deep breath, and held the air in his lungs while he closed his eyes. After a few seconds, he rocked his head back and let the air out slowly, like a man enjoying a good cigarette. And with that exhale, his tensed muscles relaxed. Only then did the maddening rage within, retreat to that dark place in his mind where it loosely resided.

Eddie Bowman wiped the blood and slime off his hands onto the bedspread, as his cold black eyes swept across the room to where the woman's body lay. He lumbered over to her, then picked her up and flipped her onto his shoulder, like a sack of potatoes. He patted her on the behind and laughed as he carried her corpse away.

Chapter 2

At 11:30 a.m., a black '69 Corvette, in pampered cherry condition, raced westbound on Highway 8 toward San Diego's Mission Valley area. The dark-haired man behind the wheel maneuvered his Corvette through the usual rush hour traffic, with the decisive precision of a race car driver. His hazel eyes glanced down at the speedometer, then up to his rearview mirror, checking the lanes behind him for the California Highway Patrol, and other local law enforcement officers, who occasionally poached the freeways for easy speeding tickets. When Alexander Temple was fairly sure that he was not in the crosshairs of one of San Diego's Finest, he accelerated as much as he could, in the heavy traffic, cutting quickly in and out of lanes in the briefest of openings. He did not mind that annoyed drivers blasted him with their horns or gave him a middle finger salute. It was more important to him that he not be late.

After several minutes of negotiating through the rush hour traffic, Temple could see the five-story Delaware department store up ahead. He gradually merged into the far-right lane, took the Mission Center off-ramp, and drove toward Camino Del Rio North until he reached the parking lot, which he found was full of cars. He drove down three aisles before spotting an open parking space and was pleased to see that the cars on either side were squarely parked in their own spaces. Great — fewer chances of door dings. Temple drove just past the parking space so he could back in. He put the car in reverse and started to back up, but then slammed on his brakes. An older Cadillac pulled up behind him and turned into his intended spot. Temple laid on his horn, but the Cadillac continued into the parking space. Temple uttered an expletive then shoved the gear into drive. He didn't have time to argue his point, nor did he want to get into a possible altercation in the parking lot. As he drove off, he could see the Cadillac driver exit the car from his rearview mirror. She was an elderly woman with dark glasses, walking feebly with the assistance of a cane. A resigned smile crossed Temple's lips, then he drove toward the far end of the lot where there were plenty of available spaces. He parked, glanced at his watch again, then hurriedly walked toward the Delaware department store.

Just inside the glass doorway, a saleswoman squirted a fine mist of perfume into the air as customers walked in. It was an interesting way to advertise perfume, he thought, but damned annoying. The woman squirted the mist in his direction as he entered. Temple politely smiled, but did not slow his stride, as he continued toward the elevator.

As usual, the store was full of noontime shoppers. There were businessmen and women on extended lunch breaks, housewives on credit card sprees, kids who should have been in school, and no doubt one or two shoplifters. As he stepped into the elevator, Temple wondered how many of the shoppers were actually plainclothes CIA Security Protective Service Officers. Their job was not to arrest shoplifters but to safeguard the security of the clandestine black ops division secretly housed upstairs. It was a black site so secret that the SPS Officers assigned to protect its location didn't know what division they were safeguarding.

Temple pushed the button for the fourth floor, the highest level each elevator could go. Access to the fifth-floor employees' office area was by stairway only. However, unbeknownst to the store employees on the fifth floor, some of the uniformed security officers were actually SPS Officers placed there in case shoppers ventured too far from the public areas.

The elevator rose swiftly and silently, but just before it stopped on the fourth floor, Temple pressed the buttons on the selection panel in a coded sequence. This caused the elevator to bypass the fourth and fifth floor and continue up to a hidden sixth floor.

The elevator finally stopped with a gentle thud; however, the doors did not open. Temple put his opened hand on a flat decorative metallic plate, on the elevator wall, and made sure he was standing in the right spot when he announced himself. "Alexander Temple," he said.

A light flashed on his face. Two or three seconds later, the elevator door slid open.

Temple stepped out of the elevator and, as he occasionally did, considered his fate, had his fingerprints, voiceprint, facial recognition, and retinal scan not matched.

Temple continued down the long corridor toward the lone door at the other end. When he opened the door, Cathy Robinson was seated on the front edge of her desk looking through some papers in a folder. She was dressed conservatively in a peach-colored turtleneck sweater and a black knee-length skirt, with a matching cropped jacket. Cathy was a petite little thing, under five-feet tall. Her hair was short and straight and combed back. She was not wearing any makeup; she seldom did. With her youthful good looks, she didn't need to.

Upon entering the office, Temple noticed that Cathy was seated with her legs crossed, showing more skin than she intended. Cathy Robinson looked up as he walked in and adjusted her skirt appropriately.

"Hi, Al," Cathy said, smiling as she hopped off her desk.

"Hello, Cat," he replied.

Cathy Robinson was the boss's niece and personal assistant. She was only seventeen years old. It was common knowledge amongst the operatives in D-Branch that Lincoln Delaware's motivation for hiring a relative had nothing to do with nepotism. Cathy Robinson graduated from college with a master's degree at age fifteen, and two years later she had a doctorate degree. Cathy majored in government and political science and had an extremely high aptitude for world affairs. She also had a unique ability that Lincoln Delaware found immensely useful: a photographic memory. With only a glance, she could vividly recall any image she was ever exposed to almost instantly from memory.

Cathy Robinson nodded toward the boss's door. "He's been waiting for you," she said, regarding him with a secret infatuation. He was such a gorgeous man, she thought. Tall, strong, masculine body and hazel eyes to die for – how could she not be attracted to him? Even with all of her degrees and

11

genius IQ, around him, she still felt like a lovesick high schooler. She knew she would have to control that childish crush.

Temple glanced at his watch. "I still have almost fifteen minutes."

"Not anymore. He wants you in there right now."

"Sounds ominous. What's going on?"

"You know I can't talk about that."

"How about the old man's mood? You can at least tell me that."

"Stable. Now go on, get in there." She gave him a gentle shove toward the big oak door across from her desk.

"Yes, ma'am," Temple said playfully, as he headed toward Lincoln Delaware's office. As he reached for the doorknob, the door unexpectedly swung open. The woman walking out almost collided with him and looked up with a startled expression. Her lovely Victorian face was accentuated by thin, black-rimmed eyeglasses. Her long blonde hair was pulled back out of her face into a French weave. She was wearing a loose-fitting blouse, baggy pleated pants, and high heels.

As she walked past him toward Cathy Robinson's desk, he wondered who she was and why he felt a familiarity with her.

"Mr. Temple!" Lincoln Delaware's voice boomed out, "Have you forgotten the way to my office?"

"No, sir," Temple replied, clearing his voice, "I was just —"

"Don't bother explaining, just come in."

Temple walked into the lion's den, closing the door behind him. Although Delaware was seated behind his desk and there was an empty chair alongside it, Temple continued to stand as he studied the old spymaster who was busily arranging papers.

Delaware was a tall, thin man with cold, steely eyes. He must have been at least sixty, maybe sixty-five years old, but was in excellent physical condition. Normally, Lincoln Delaware was an immaculate dresser. Some would say he was even anal about it. But today was different. Delaware's silver hair was uncharacteristically unkempt. He was wearing a wrinkled white dress shirt, opened at the collar, no tie, with his sleeves rolled up to his elbows. He was unshaven and his eyes were puffy and strained. It looked as if he'd been up all night. Without looking up from his desk, Lincoln Delaware motioned with his hand for Temple to have a seat. Delaware finished arranging his papers, then made eye contact with the agent code-named, The Iceman. He did not waste time with polite greetings or small talk. It was not his way.

"Mr. Temple," he began, "we have a situation blue. Four days ago, a CIA analyst was killed. He was relieved of twelve microdots, code-named the Alpha Data, which contained highly classified information meant for the president's eyes only. The analyst's body was found a few hours later by the Las Vegas Police Department, stuffed in the trunk of a stolen car."

Delaware handed Temple a manila folder. Inside were several 8 x 10 glossy photographs with brief dossiers on the back. As Temple looked at the first photo, Delaware said, "That's the man who orchestrated the theft of the microdots. His name is Jim Donnetti. He owns and operates a gambling boat called *The Lucky Lady*. It's moored at the Lake Mead Marina just outside of Las Vegas."

Temple shook his head. "Never heard of him or the boat."

"Not surprising," said Delaware. "Jim Donnetti caters solely to high rollers and the super-rich, but behind his false veil of respectability, he's heavily involved in loansharking, drug dealing, prostitution, kiddy porn, murder, and now espionage. He intends to sell the microdots to any government making the highest bid."

"An auction?"

"That's right. But we have to stop that auction and recover or destroy the microdots before they go public."

"What about Donnetti?" Temple questioned. "Surely he's viewed the microdots by now and knows what's on them. Maybe others have too."

"We don't think so, at least not yet anyway. The data was heavily encrypted before it was stored on the microdots. He hasn't had the microdots long enough to crack the encryption. However, eventually he will, given enough time and the right cryptographer."

"So Donnetti's doing a blind auction?"

"No. He knows that the information on the microdots could change the balance of power in the world forever. But that's all he knows, and that's what he's selling — world domination."

"Is he right?"

"It's much more valuable than that," Delaware said, then tactfully changed the subject. "Those other photos you have, you should remember their faces."

Temple thumbed through the photos. "Professionals?" he asked.

"Yes. They're hired assassins that Donnetti brought in to keep bidding governments from stealing the microdots before he can auction them off."

"Is this all of them?"

"All we know about, but Donnetti has blood ties to the Mafia. We're confident he's not connected with family business, but we don't know for sure who else he's been talking to."

Delaware picked up a photograph from his desk that he intentionally did not include in the stack with the others. He glared at it first, then passed it to Temple. "Pay particular attention to this man. His name is Eddie Bowman. He's Donnetti's bodyguard and chauffeur."

Although the photograph of Eddie Bowman was only a bust shot, his awesome physical size was obvious. "He's a big one, isn't he," Temple commented.

"He's also a highly unstable murderous psychopath. He's not a professional like the others. He kills because he enjoys it. Watch out for him, Alex. He's a time bomb looking for a reason to explode."

"A guy this big is going to be hard to miss," Temple said.

"There's one final member of Donnetti's entourage," Delaware added, "but unfortunately we don't have a photo of him. In fact, we know very little about him — except that he works for us."

Temple leaned forward. "For us? For D-Branch?"

"We don't know for sure. What we do know is that he works inside American intelligence and uses the code name Maxwell."

"That's it?" Temple queried. "We don't have any other leads?"

"No, but we suspect that Maxwell's intel got one of my agents killed last night."

Temple frowned. "What happened?"

"I sent an operative to Las Vegas last night to recover the microdots. He was killed shortly after he arrived in town. His nude body was found severely beaten in the home of a movie actress. The police think that she was murdered too."

"They think?"

"Evidence points to it, but they haven't found her body yet."

"Since our agent was killed, that kind of narrows down what department Maxwell is working for, doesn't it?"

"Not necessarily. Maybe the killer was tracking the mission and our man got in the way. The real question is, who had access to mission intel and how many hands did it pass through before it got to us?"

Temple exhaled with apprehension. "So — they could be waiting for me too?"

"Let's hope not," Delaware said.

Temple considered his precarious predicament, but then simply asked, "Who got it last night?"

Delaware took a moment before answering. Then he finally said, "Johnny Davis."

The name hit Temple like a kick to the gut. Johnny Davis was the last name he had expected to hear. Davis had been the resident legend around D-Branch for years and, from what he had heard, deservedly so. His extraordinary analytical mind helped him complete more missions than anyone in the division. His superior fighting skills kept him alive. Now he was dead. Temple's mind wrestled with that revelation.

"We can mourn over Johnny later," Delaware interrupted. "Right now, this mission concerns us more." Lincoln Delaware took one of his favorite Don Diego cigars from the box on his desk and puffed it to life.

Temple gave the old spymaster a curious look. "How do you know I'm not Maxwell?"

Delaware blew a billow of smoke into the air. He didn't seem to care that Temple was not a smoker. As the smoke dissipated, he locked eyes with his newest agent and said with chilling certainty, "We know you're not."

Temple nodded. Delaware's certainty was understood. Had he not already passed some recent internal investigation; he would not have stepped off that elevator alive.

Delaware threw Temple another unexpected curve. "That woman you almost ran into on your way in here — she'll be going with you."

"She what?"

"You've got a partner on this one."

"We usually work alone."

"Not this time," Delaware replied.

"Is she with D-Branch?" Temple asked.

"No. She's still in training at the Farm."

"She's a Company trainee?" Temple blurted out in astonishment.

"Yes," Delaware said.

"And we're sending her on a mission — sir?"

"She was specifically requested. She has specialized training that we need."

"Specialized training?" Temple questioned.

"She's one of five recruit volunteers that the Company has been training in the use of a new experimental transmitter-receiver."

"Must be one hell of a system to send a trainee on a real mission."

"With Maxwell out there, our normal coded communications may be compromised."

"Who made the request?" Temple asked.

"The President of the United States made it. He wants to stay on top of this mission and wants the microdots given directly to him the moment they're recovered."

"Did you say *directly*, sir?"

Delaware glanced at the wall clock above the door. "In just under three hours, the president will be secretly flown into Las Vegas in a private plane. He wants to be on site for this one."

Temple stared at the old spymaster with increased curiosity and wondered, what was on the microdots. What was so sensitive that it compelled the President of the United States to slip secretly out of Washington to be on hand for its recovery.

Delaware continued, "The trainee knows nothing about D-Branch or our mission objective. She thinks we're regular CIA."

"Does she know about the president?"

"No. Her only responsibility is to receive and transmit intel. That's all she needs to know. Is that understood?"

"Yes, sir, I understand. But with Maxwell on the loose, does she have an exit strategy?"

"You won't let it come to that."

"But what if it does?"

"We'll take care of it," Delaware answered.

"How?" Temple asked.

"The experimental transmitter-receiver that she's been testing is surgically implanted inside her ear and throat. It's designed to avoid metal detection. Under x-ray, it looks like cartilage next to bone. So – if she gets caught, she only needs to activate the transmitter and tell us."

"And?" Temple prodded.

Delaware frowned at Temple's persistence but decided to tell him the truth. He stared at The Iceman, then said very deliberately, "We cannot allow anyone to compromise this mission. It's too important. If she gets caught, we will terminate her."

Temple displayed no outward reaction. He was not even surprised at Delaware's answer. The critically sensitive cases assigned to D-Branch all had catastrophic consequences for the United States, or its allies, if there was a mission failure. That's why D-Branch had a free hand to act. That's why they worked in the shadows, with no rules of law, no watchdog committees looking over their shoulders, no congressional oversight. Each agent understood what that unaccountability meant. The United States government would never negotiate for their release if they were captured, nor would they send a rescue team or even acknowledge that they existed. Because of that anonymity, D-Branch offered the government a very valuable commodity: plausible deniability.

Temple studied Delaware's face as he asked the old man the next question. "Who?"

"Not you," Delaware said. "If she is caught and calls for help, a high-frequency signal will be sent to the receiver implanted inside her ear. The receiver will overload and explode. It'll be instant."

Temple maintained his stoic expression. He understood, sometimes collateral damage was inevitable. He had no problem pulling the trigger himself when it was needed, and he slept just fine at night. He learned long ago, when he looked through the sights of his weapon, to only see a target, never a victim. It was just part of the job. And he always did his job. That's why they called him The Iceman. Still, Temple knew he couldn't let this trainee die just because she called for help. He was going to have to babysit her, keep her safe until this mission was over.

Temple changed the subject. "Any idea where Donnetti is keeping the microdots?"

"Possibly in his casino vault onboard *The Lucky Lady*."

"You think he'd be foolish enough to keep it there?"

"We don't know, but we have to find out."

Temple briefly considered a couple of possible scenarios but quickly dismissed both. An all-out tactical team assault could fail because the strike force might not be able to breach the vault before the microdots were moved. And dropping a high-altitude bomb on the boat would remove any means of verifying that the microdots were destroyed.

"So, what's the plan?" Temple asked.

"We need to make you relevant to Donnetti."

"How are we going to do that?"

"Win big in his casino. Break the damn bank if you have to."

"That'll definitely draw him out, but I'm not very good at casino games," Temple offered.

"You don't have to be. I have a card man coming in from out of town. He'll meet you in Las Vegas and teach you what you need to know."

"How will I know him?"

Delaware slightly smiled. "He'll know you. His code phrase will be, *I'm your insurance man.*" Delaware took a long drag on his Don Diego cigar then leaned across his desk and handed Temple a blue manila folder.

Temple knew the blue folder contained documents on his mission identity – all the usual stuff like a wallet, driver's license, credit cards, cash, family photos of people he was supposed to know, and a dossier on who he was going to be. When he looked back up at Delaware, the old spymaster was staring at him with an intense gaze.

"What?" Temple asked.

"The Grim Reaper is also on his way to Las Vegas," Delaware told him. "He's after the microdots, too."

Temple felt an anxious twinge in his stomach. "Is that confirmed?"

"It's confirmed," Delaware said.

Alexander Temple thought back to the one and only time that he had ever met the KGB's top assassin. Temple nearly died during that encounter. If their paths were to cross again in Las Vegas, The Grim Reaper would have the advantage.

The Soviet knew what he looked like, but he never saw the Soviet's face.

For over thirty years, The Grim Reaper had wreaked death and destruction all around the world, and amazingly, in all that time, no one had ever seen his face. No one who lived, that is. Many inside the intelligence community feared his brutal reputation. He was a stone-cold killer without conscience; collateral damage meant nothing to him. He was totally ruthless and utterly relentless.

Delaware took an ink pen from his shirt pocket and handed it to Temple. "This is a pen-camera," he said. "If you get the opportunity, take The Grim Reaper's picture and fax it to me. Directly to me, nobody else. Is that clear?"

"It's clear," Temple acknowledged.

The request, however, was not as clear as Temple assumed. He had no way of knowing that Delaware's request was strictly personal.

Temple put the ink pen in his pocket then gave Delaware a probing stare before asking the next obvious question. "What's on the microdots, sir?"

Delaware's eyes rose to meet Temple's stare, then he answered softly, "The truth."

Temple's eyes squinted. "I beg your pardon?"

Delaware said, "During my briefing, I was told that this was, need to know only and that you didn't need to know." The old man leaned back in his chair. "I disagreed. I told them that my agents need to know what they're risking their lives for. But I compromised and said that I would only tell you if you insisted." Delaware regarded his newest agent for a moment, then asked, "You are insisting, aren't you?"

Temple suppressed his grin. "I am," he said.

Delaware took a few seconds to collect his thoughts. Then he leaned onto his elbows and said, "Three months ago

NORAD tracked an object flying erratically at twenty thousand feet just south of Las Vegas. Before they could scramble planes, the object dropped out of the sky. Highway Patrol was first on the scene. Later they reported that a meteor had crashed in the desert just south of Barstow. The public and all news media were barred from the area, supposedly due to some danger of radiation. Within an hour, the entire area was sealed off by the FBI and over three hundred military personnel."

Temple felt a nervous rush of anxiety as he spoke his next words. "What did they really find out there?"

Delaware raised his cigar to his lips but did not take a puff as his thoughts wandered. Finally, he said, "They found an unidentified flying object."

Temple leaned forward in his chair as Delaware continued.

"It was a dome-shaped disc, about one hundred and twenty-four meters in diameter. It was emitting a brilliant orange glow and had opaque porthole-like windows in the upper portion of it. When they found this — craft, it was up on its side, partially buried in the ground. Strangely though, there was no structural damage to it. Not even a scratch."

An eerie, unsettling sensation rumbled in the pit of Temple's stomach.

Delaware went on, "For security reasons the craft was moved to a secret facility in Nevada."

Temple's voice was almost inaudible when he spoke, "Did they ever get inside of it?"

"Yes. It took them almost three weeks, but they finally managed to cut through one of the porthole-like windows."

"And found what?" Temple mumbled, his voice cracking, as he now sat on the edge of his chair.

Delaware stared at him for a moment, then said, "They

found four alien beings strapped in metallic chairs in a compartment that appeared to be the craft's flight bridge."

Temple's eyelids blinked wide; his body went numb in disbelief. He could not believe what he was hearing. Dozens of jumbled thoughts collided in his mind as he tried to process the unbelievable. When Temple finally spoke, he just barely got the words out. "What do they look like?"

Delaware's gaze dropped as he recalled the photograph he was shown earlier. When his eyes rejoined Temple's, the old spymaster simply answered, "not human."

Temple's incredulous gaze widened, anxious for a better description.

Delaware knew what Temple wanted, but carefully considered his next words, then coyly replied, "They have a head, a body, two arms, two legs – but definitely not humanoid."

Temple's anxiety rose. Clearly, the old man was holding back. Whether it was by choice or by order, he didn't know. And except for his own curiosity, it really didn't matter. The aliens were real. Intelligent beings from another world were here, on earth. We were not alone in this universe.

Delaware continued, "Unfortunately, they were all dead. We can't tell at this time if the crash killed them or if it was something else." Delaware shifted uncomfortably in his chair, then added, "There's something else. A fifth body was also found on board the craft. It was strapped on top of a metallic table in another compartment. That body was not alien. It was the deceased body of a human male. Pathologists guessed his age to be between thirty and forty." Delaware looked for Temple's reaction as he posed the next question, "Opens up several possibilities, doesn't it?"

Temple considered one horrifying possibility. "You think he was being taken somewhere to be experimented on?"

"Or," Delaware suggested, "they were bringing him back from somewhere — conditioned for who knows what."

"What's the spook group doing about this?" Temple questioned.

Delaware frowned. "The Alpha Group," he clarified, "is doing their investigation as we speak."

"How much of this information is on the microdots?"

"All of it, including photographs, laboratory results, site analyses, autopsy results, and some technical specifications on the craft's advanced technology and weaponry." Delaware leaned back in his chair. He was silent for a moment. Then he said, "Once your plane lands in Las Vegas, you'll have forty-eight hours before the auction. Get those microdots back for us, Alex." The old spymaster reached across his desk and pressed the speed dial on his phone. When Cathy Robinson answered, Lincoln Delaware said, "Send her back in now."

Chapter 3

When the blonde re-entered his office, Delaware said, "I believe you two know each other."

"Hello — Al," she offered tentatively, extending her hand, as she crossed the room toward him.

Temple stood and shook her hand, but it wasn't until he heard her diminutive southern drawl that he realized who she was. "Hello, Karen," he replied.

Karen looked genuinely surprised. "I didn't think you'd remember me. It's been a long time since high school."

If not for her distinctive voice, he would not have recognized her. She had changed so much. She was no longer the awkwardly shy schoolgirl sporting braces on her teeth. Nor was she the 200 pounder who had endured relentless teasing for her large breasts and chubby body. Now she appeared to be a confident, attractive young woman with an amazing body, who moved with self-assurance.

Delaware interrupted, "You two can reminisce later. Let's finish this up. You've both been briefed individually and know what's expected of you; however, I want to reiterate something right now so we won't have any mistakes later. Miss Kiley, your only responsibility is to receive and transmit information. Under no circumstances are you to be involved in anything else. Is that clear?"

"Quite clear, "she said.

"Are there any questions from either of you?" When no one responded, Delaware said, "See my secretary about your tickets and reservations."

Temple started for the door and Karen followed just a couple of paces behind. As she walked behind him, she couldn't help but notice his solid build. Even though he was wearing a loose-fitting dress shirt, she could still see that he had big powerful shoulders and a strong, broad back that tapered to a small waist. Even his long sleeves couldn't hide the massive arms underneath. Karen glanced down at his behind. *Great butt, too*, she thought with a sly smile.

Cathy Robinson noticed Karen's gaze, and deliberately broke her concentration. "Miss Kiley!"

Karen looked up, startled, and a little embarrassed that Cathy caught her staring at Temple's butt. She flashed Cathy a sheepish grin.

Cathy curtly ignored it and handed her an airline ticket. "Your flight leaves Lindbergh Field at seven-twenty this evening." Cathy turned to Temple. "Yours leaves at seven-thirty, Al."

"Thanks, Cat," he said.

Suppressing a frown, Temple turned to Karen Kiley. He

was not happy to see her. Her presence reminded him of a time in his life he tried never to think about. It had nothing to do with Karen. She was a decent person. But she was from an era in his life that was full of bad memories, including the one that changed his life forever. Temple seldom thought about his former life or the repeated nightmares that had thankfully stopped long ago. But now that someone from his past was here, all those submerged memories and feelings came rushing back.

Karen slyly stole glimpses of Temple as he moved about the room. He was such an attractive man. He always was, even during their school days. Back then, she had a secret crush on him but never pursued it, due to her insecurities. He was the most popular boy in school and she was considered one of the nerds. Worse, she was overweight: a social stigma that affected every facet of her high school life. At the time, she never dreamed that she would ever have a chance with him. She was quite surprised now that her long-ago emotions toward him were still there.

"So — Al," Karen asked, almost feeling sixteen again, "would you like to go somewhere for lunch before we pack for our flights?"

Cathy Robinson was shocked at Karen's suggestion. Temple was surprised too, but he reminded himself that she was still in training. "That would not be a good idea," he replied.

"You're sure?" Karen pressed.

Temple shook his head, "The reason we cannot do lunch, Miss Kiley, is not a matter of preference. We can't be seen together from this point forward. That's why we're traveling on different planes," he explained. "You never know who might be watching."

"Oh! I thought we were okay until we got to Las Vegas.

I didn't think —"

"No, you didn't," Temple bluntly cut her off.

Karen's cheeks flushed crimson and her ears burned hot with embarrassment. "Then I'll see you in Las Vegas," she snapped briskly before striding out of the office toward the elevator. Temple gave Cat a nod as he left in the same direction. As he stepped into the corridor, over his shoulder he saw Lincoln Delaware walk into Cathy Robinson's office, with his usual limp. Temple continued down the hallway, his thoughts lingering on his boss, the former master spy who was once called The Fisherman. According to some of the original operatives in D-Branch, The Fisherman was one of the most feared agents of his time. But something happened to him, at the height of his career, that turned his life around. Whatever that was, nobody talked about it. Still, Temple had come to the definite conclusion that Delaware remained an extremely dangerous man, quiet and deadly, like a black mamba snake, waiting for just the right time to strike. That kind of a man, Temple believed, was the most dangerous kind of all.

Temple caught up to Karen just as she reached the elevator. When the doors opened, he followed her in.

Karen sniped, "Shouldn't we be taking separate elevators?"

"We're not getting off together," he said, reaching over to the selection panel and pressing the buttons in a pre-designated sequence. The doors closed and the elevator started down.

From Karen's peripheral vision, she could see he was still staring at her. She looked up at him. "What?" she snapped.

"I don't mean to stare. I'm just surprised to see you here. In this line of work," he clarified.

"I could say the same thing about you," she retorted.

"Touché," he agreed.

"So, tell me," she probed, "how are you here? I thought you were dead, Michael Darrin?"

Temple's demeanor shifted suddenly. His jaw tightened, and his eyes turned cold and cruel. "Don't ever call me that again!" he snapped. "Not ever! My name is Alexander Temple. Remember that."

His harsh, almost threatening tone caught her totally off guard and frightened her. "Ok — alright — Al, whatever you want."

The elevator doors opened on the second floor and Temple got out. The doors closed again and opened on the first floor. Karen stepped off the elevator and others got on. She walked through the department store and continued out to her car. She was confused. What was Michael trying to hide and who was he hiding it from? She pondered now if the name Alexander Temple was a cover for something more sinister. *Maybe he was the double agent that Mr. Delaware was talking about.* Karen shook her head, quickly dismissing that theory. Mr. Delaware knew they went to high school together. He must've known that Michael was his real name. *So how is Michael still alive, and why did he change his name?*

During his drive home, Alexander Temple had a lot on his mind. At the top of his list: aliens. Even now he found it difficult to accept. It was just so incredible, so unbelievable. It was arguably the biggest discovery in the history of man and the fact that they could be dangerous was frightening. What concerned Temple, even more, was something Delaware only spoke briefly of. Temple believed that this subject, so briefly mentioned, was the focal point of this whole mission. It was the new technology and weaponry found in the downed flying saucer – that's what the government was most interested in. That's what this mission was all about: power. Whoever controlled this technology and weaponry controlled the world. Incredibly, the historic news of alien life was reduced to a footnote. As for the mission, it may already be compromised if the double agent Maxwell is identifying American agents to the enemy. Temple acknowledged the very real possibility that Jim Donnetti could already know he's coming. Then there was The Grim Reaper. Temple always knew the Soviet would eventually find him. And how do you defeat a legendary assassin who knows what you look like, but whose face you've never seen? How do you find him before he finds you? On top of all that, Temple was again burdened with the tragic memories from his childhood that had resurfaced due to Karen Kiley's unexpected appearance.

As Temple neared his home, he pushed his personal issues aside to refocus on the mission. It was time to go to work.

Chapter 4

Lincoln Delaware's big secret began in the winter of 1953. Washington D.C. was in an uproar. A CIA agent had defected to the Soviet Union with a fistful of Top-Secret information, concerning ongoing CIA operations, including the names of two CIA agents who had successfully infiltrated the KGB. One of those CIA agents was posing as an instructor at the KGB Marx-Engels School for spies near Moscow. The other agent had attained such prominence in the Kremlin that he had on several occasions visited the Soviet super-spy school known as VINNITSA.

The President of the United States promptly dispatched a message to the Director of the Central Intelligence Agency, instructing him to resolve this matter immediately. The president ended the message with the words, "Turn The Fisherman loose."

Inside the secret inner circles of the intelligence community, not much was known about the American spy they called The Fisherman, although he had attained almost legendary status. Even the specifics of his missions were so sensitive they were only known to a select few.

Rumors about his exploits ran the gambit from incredible to impossible. The only fact everyone agreed upon was his uncanny ability to survive in seemingly impossible conditions. Whether alone or leading a team, he always found a way to survive, no matter how hopeless or suicidal the mission. The fact that he never lost a team member perpetuated his mystique among his colleagues.

So, within the hour, Lincoln Delaware – The Fisherman, was onboard a commercial aircraft with a team of agents, heading to the Soviet Union, with orders to stop the defector by any means necessary.

The long flight went smoothly, arriving in Soviet airspace on time. As the plane began its gradual descent, Delaware stared through the small oval window and collected his thoughts. He then leaned back in his seat and waited for the plane to land.

After a relatively short time had passed, Delaware felt a sudden nervous twinge. He couldn't pinpoint why, but sensing something was wrong, he looked around the cabin at the multitude of faces. While scanning the cabin, it dawned on him. The *Seat Belt* sign was not on. The plane was obviously below ten thousand feet, but no stewardesses were walking the aisles to check that seat belts were fastened. Nor were eating utensils or food trays being collected in preparation for landing. Delaware stood up and made eye contact with his team. Each of them silently acknowledged his alert and started to move in his direction. Before they reached him, a loud crash at the rear of the plane thundered forward. The aircraft jolted violently and an abrupt whirlwind flooded the cabin. Hysterical confusion spread rapidly throughout the aircraft, as passengers yelled and cried; some were praying.

Delaware and his team rushed to the back of the plane to find the rear emergency door blown wide open. There was no other visible damage. The aircraft was still intact and there was no decompression of the cabin due to their lower altitude. Delaware tried to pull the emergency door closed, but the hinges were damaged from the force of the door slamming open.

As more frightened passengers gathered in the rear of the plane, Delaware tried to calm them, informing them that the aircraft was still structurally sound. As he sought to console them, he noticed something out the corner of his eye, through the open door. No one else saw it and he only got a glimpse of it, as it drifted out of view. Off in the distance, he saw a lone man floating away under a deployed parachute. Delaware yelled to his men, "Parachutist!" then bolted back up the aisle, pushing his way through the sea of bodies that had now gathered there. Delaware hoped he would not find what he feared. One of his team members remained by the rear exit door, while the rest of his team followed him up the aisle, with a dozen or so passengers in tow. When Delaware reached the flight cabin, he found the door ajar. He carefully pushed it open. The sight inside was worse than he thought. The pilot, still strapped in his chair, slumped forward across the control panel. There was a small bullet hole behind his right ear that shattered his forehead. The windshield in front of him was splattered with blood and brain matter. The co-pilot had also been shot, except he took it in the face –

probably when he turned and saw the killer entering the cockpit. There was one stewardess, dead on the floor. Her body was stuffed awkwardly in the corner by the navigator's chair. Since Delaware hadn't seen any other stewardesses, he guessed they were dead too. Probably dumped in one of the lavatories.

Delaware's eyes scanned the flight controls and instrument panels. They had been smashed and broken beyond repair. The parachutist made sure that no one else would be able to fly the plane after he bailed out.

One of the passengers, who had gathered outside the flight cabin door, ran back down the aisle screaming in a panicked frenzy. Total pandemonium erupted throughout the aircraft. More passengers scrambled to the cockpit. More ear-splitting screams rang out. Delaware made brief eye contact with his men. No words were spoken between them, but they all knew what they had to do and immediately went to work. The team pushed and shoved their way back down the aisle. One team member updated his partner who was standing post by the damaged rear door, while the others searched through the storage compartments for parachutes, although they didn't expect to find any. Delaware stared at all the terrified faces before him and, for the first time in his life, he did an impulsive thing. "I can fly this plane!" he yelled out. "Listen to me! I can fly this plane!"

The disposition of the passengers closest to the flight cabin quickly changed. Delaware saw glimmers of relief on their faces. "Go back to your seats!" Delaware shouted. "There are too many people up here. I can't stabilize the plane with so much weight upfront. Get back to your seats — hurry!"

The passengers rushed back to their seats. Nobody argued or questioned him. He was offering them something that they gravely needed — hope.

Delaware pulled the pilot from his chair and seated himself behind the maze of busted gauges and broken control levers. He had no idea how to fly an airplane. He put the headset on to see if the radio was working. It wasn't. He inhaled deeply, then gripped the control wheel and held on white-knuckle tight. Not being familiar with the aerodynamics of an airplane, he tugged back on the wheel assuming the plane would climb. It did not. Instead, the plane began to descend more rapidly.

Delaware gripped the wheel even tighter, his heart pounded hard against his chest, as the plane plummeted toward the ground out of control. Sweat rolled down his brow into his eyes, but Delaware didn't blink, as he glared at the controls and pulled the wheel back even more. The plane did not respond. Delaware frowned and pushed the wheel forward. Still no response. He scanned the busted control panels looking for something, anything that could help him. Nothing looked even vaguely familiar. In a frenzied panic, Delaware started pushing levers and flipping switches. Incredible pressure throbbed in his head, as his mind raced desperately for something, anything that would help these people. There had to be something. There was always something. Delaware's ordinarily logical, well-disciplined mind could not accept what was happening. Even as the ground rushed up to meet them, he could not believe that it would end like this. The aircraft started buffeting and shaking, then violently rolled to its right. Food trays, luggage, and personal carry-on items flew across the compartment. More screams roared throughout the cabin. Delaware continued wrestling with the wheel, his eyes bulging, his body taut, every nerve in his body strained. As they rapidly neared the ground, Delaware cursed aloud and jerked at the wheel one last time. Then, in that final terrifying moment, before the aircraft slammed into the ground, the screams aboard the plane were deafening.

Chapter 5

A team of surgeons used all the skills at their command to keep the lone survivor of Flight 213 alive. The doctors, however, held little hope that he would make it through the night. Miraculously though, by morning his condition had stabilized. Lincoln Delaware was alive but laid deathly still in a catatonic coma. After six months of no improvement, some talk of mercy killing came up at CIA headquarters. No discussion of what was best for Delaware was ever mentioned or even considered. The Fisherman's knowledge of CIA affairs is what they feared; he was far too vulnerable now to enemy capture. If he were to regain consciousness under enemy control, it would be disastrous. The idea, however, was eventually abandoned.

Lincoln Delaware remained among the living dead for nearly nine years. Then, on August 27, 1962, The Fisherman woke up and was immediately transferred to a military-controlled hospital. For the next thirty-nine months, he received the best medical care available, including major plastic and reconstruction surgery, speech therapy, and the most grueling physical therapy imaginable. Initially, his progress was slow. Time seemed to almost grind to a standstill. One day dragged into the next. Weeks rolled into agonizing months.

It took nearly two more years before he started to show any significant improvement. From that moment on, his medical care was accelerated and his already grueling therapy sessions were increased. Over the next thirteen months, he got progressively better, stronger, and more alert. Except for a partially paralyzed right leg that left him with a noticeable limp and some other moderate physical disabilities, he finally recovered sufficiently enough that discussion of a possible release date from the hospital began. Delaware's only other substantial injury was one not obvious to anyone but him, one that was more critical to him than the injury to his leg. That was his ability of total recall. Although he could no longer instantly retrieve any facts from memory, his mind was still sharp and his IQ still rated at genius.

On the day he was released from the hospital, two very young-looking CIA agents – "Kids," Delaware thought – met him at his bedside and walked with him to a public park across the street. The shorter of the two agents must have been new at this. He was trying hard to sound important, even walking with a slight swagger and lowering his voice two octaves when he spoke.

Delaware concluded that this agent was suffering from a little man complex. The other agent was quiet, but it was evident that he was listening and watching everything. He was much more professional than his diminutive partner.

Delaware cooperated and told them what he could remember about the incidents leading up to the plane crash that nearly killed him. The shorter agent wore a detached look on his face as Delaware told his story. When Delaware finished, the shorter one said, "You're a lucky man, Lincoln. You were the only survivor, and only heaven knows how you managed that, after falling 9000 feet out of the sky."

Delaware was not interested in casual conversation, so he got right to the point. "The man that bailed out of the plane, who was he?"

The shorter agent said, "He was a rookie spy in the KGB. Ever since pulling that little number on you, his stock has gone up considerably. He's become a really dangerous man. Sometimes he even makes his own people nervous." The shorter agent glanced at his partner then back to Delaware. "They call him *Smert's Kosoy*. In English, that means —"

Delaware cut him off, "The Grim Reaper."

"Yeah, that's right," the shorter agent said. "The Grim Reaper. The devil's messenger of death. The name fits the son-of-a-bitch well."

Delaware shook his head in bewilderment. "He sabotaged an entire aircraft just to keep us from completing our mission."

The taller agent finally spoke up, "He didn't know about your mission, sir."

That remark caught Delaware off guard and confusion registered on his reconstructed face.

The taller agent continued, "He was stalking *you*, Mr. Delaware. His sole purpose for being on that aircraft was to kill The Fisherman. Interrupting your mission was just coincidental."

The shorter agent misread Delaware's body language and assumed the old spymaster's pride was hurt. After all, he was the so-called legendary Fisherman. Hunting people down was supposed to be what the old man was good at. At least, that's what everybody always said. The shorter agent made a mental assessment of The Fisherman. He was not impressed.

Delaware was not at all concerned about his pride or reputation. The fact that all those people on the plane died because of his presence there was hard to hear.

The shorter agent cut in, "Since you've been — away, this Soviet has become the KGB's top assassin. The bastard's gotten so cocky he now leaves an orchid bloom behind as a calling card just so we'll know it was him. Since his attack on you, he's done other mass murders to affect a solo hit. He doesn't give a shit about collateral damage. And the Kremlin won't even acknowledge his existence. He's become somewhat of an embarrassment to them."

"Because of the collateral damage?" Delaware asked.

"Yes. He's been stepping on too many toes. Not just ours. The United Nations has been in an uproar over these mass murders. The Soviets still won't acknowledge his existence, nor have they reined him in. They don't want to alienate this guy, he's just too damn efficient."

"Sounds like he's out of control," Delaware said.

"Maybe so. I don't know. But believe me, this guy is as elusive as hell. For years, we've sent some of our best people over there to track him down. He's killed most of them. The others are just running around in circles trying to find him. I swear the man is like a ghost. He does his shit then disappears without a trace. To date, he's credited with twenty-seven significant kills against our country. Seven of them were top CIA agents — including The Fisherman."

That comment caught Delaware's attention. The shorter agent picked up on it and elaborated, "The agency put the word out that you died in that plane crash. Hell, they figured you were gonna die anyway, but just in case you didn't, they didn't want The Grim Reaper to make another run at you, or worse, turn you over to his people."

With calm restraint, Delaware asked, "What's being done about The Grim Reaper now?"

The shorter CIA man said wearily, "Right now — nothing. We don't know any more about his identity today than we did fifteen years ago when he sabotaged your plane. We thought — we hoped that maybe you could tell us what he looks like."

Delaware shook his head no. "All I saw was a figure dangling at the end of a parachute."

The taller agent nodded. "That's about what we figured."

"Dammit," the shorter agent barked in frustration, "We never get a break with this guy."

Delaware had been listening carefully to the inflection in the shorter agent's voice every time he spoke about the Soviet. There was fear in the little man's voice. It unsettled Delaware that an American agent was so easily intimidated, that the mere mention of The Grim Reaper's name frightened him.

Again, the shorter agent misinterpreted Delaware's look of concern and said, "Don't worry. You're safe. He won't find you. He thinks you're dead. After the plane crash, the official report was that nobody survived. The agency closed the file on The Fisherman years ago."

Delaware decided it was time. He asked if he could meet with the CIA director in person. It was a matter of national security.

The shorter agent puffed out his chest, "I speak for the director. Whatever you have to say, you can say to me. I'll pass it along."

Delaware spoke as politely as he could. "What I have to say, I have to say directly to the director. As I said, it's a matter of national security. I'm sure you understand."

The shorter agent's jaw tightened and he turned beet red. It angered him that this has-been old man was challenging his authority. He took one step toward Delaware, his eyes spitting daggers, "Now you listen to me —"

The taller agent cut his partner off before he made a complete ass of himself. "We understand, Mr. Delaware. I'll take your request to the director."

"What's your name, son?" Delaware asked the taller agent.

"Johnny Davis," he said.

Three months and eight days passed before Johnny Davis got back to him. A one-on-one meeting with the CIA director was scheduled. Delaware was flown to Washington at government expense, picked up at the airport in an official state car, and then driven directly to Langley. It had been a long time since Delaware had last been there.

The director seemed genuinely happy to meet the former agent known as The Fisherman. They briefly exchanged pleasantries and he thanked Delaware for his valued service to the country. Then the director shifted the conversation toward the business at hand. "So, what matter of national security did you want to discuss with me, Mr. Delaware?"

The Fisherman explained his idea for improving the effectiveness of American intelligence. It was a radical idea he had contemplated years before his plane crash. It was the formation of a new, truly clandestine division with no jurisdictional restraints. He expressed his dissatisfaction with the destructive direction he felt the CIA was heading, due to bureaucratic red tape and the scrutiny of investigative committees. Delaware laid out his plan in great detail. He explained every aspect of developing a new secret division within the CIA. A division that would handle the sensitive missions that governments wanted to avoid association with. He also told the director in order to ensure the level of secrecy needed for such a division, full autonomy was paramount, unlike the current CIA Special Operations Division, which was still subject to congressional and 303 Committee oversight. Delaware suggested only the president, his chief of staff, and the directors of the CIA and FBI know of its existence or have operational knowledge of its missions. Delaware emphasized that no one outside this special unit should be allowed to maintain files or track its missions. To further guarantee secrecy, there should be no records of funds or appropriations of any kind connected to this new division. The men and women who would work in this elite group would have to understand, with this type of autonomy comes great personal sacrifice, as they would be working in a division that, for all intents and purposes, did not exist. The United States Government would have to deny any knowledge of them or their actions if they were caught or killed. They would be completely on their own, so extraordinary people would have to be selected for this division.

The meeting lasted just over three hours. Every question, every conceivable problem broached by the director was answered, and some the director hadn't even considered were addressed. At the end of the meeting, the director suggested they meet again in two weeks. At that subsequent meeting, two other men, the director did not identify, also sat in on the meeting and took copious notes. A half dozen more meetings were scheduled, at the end of which the director acknowledged that he was intrigued by what Delaware had to say. Delaware stood up and extended his hand, "Thank you for listening to me. I hope it helps you."

The director did not stand up or extend his hand. "Mr. Delaware, you misunderstand."

Delaware returned a confused look.

"I liked your presentation," the director said. "What you said made sense. So much so, that I think The Fisherman would be the perfect man to run such a division."

Delaware was stunned. He hadn't considered running the division himself. "No, that wasn't my purpose for coming here. I'm not a manager. I'm a field agent. At least, I used to be."

The director said bluntly, "Your usefulness as a case officer is over. You must know that. But your worth to the intelligence community is invaluable. I've spoken to your doctors. Their reports on you have been very favorable. The ideas you laid out for a covert division are impressive. And, I think, needed. The president will have to approve it though, and there will be some legal issues to address first, but after all the procedural stuff is done and proper vetting is completed, I will present your plan to the president." He paused before adding, "With the caveat that you agree to head up the division."

Delaware sat back down. Thus, D-Branch was born at the highest level of secrecy.

It was decided early on to protect the president. Only the new director of D-Branch, and on occasion, the CIA director would ever communicate directly with the president about mission details. The existence of D-Branch would be passed on, from administration to administration, via a note left on the Oval Office desk by the outgoing president to the incoming president. The note would direct the new president to confer with the CIA director for details. This intricate process was designed to protect the president and to afford him plausible deniability. The note itself could never be used to prove proof of knowledge by the president. Several people in the West Wing had access to the Oval Office. If the note ever went public, the president could credibly claim that any one of them could have left a prank note on his desk — plausible deniability.

The big hurdle for Lincoln Delaware, as head of D-Branch, was to select the right agents to work in his secret division. It was a commonly known fact throughout the intelligence community that there is, or has been, at least one double agent or informer in nearly every government's intelligence force. For Lincoln Delaware, that was one too many. Getting the right operatives was the key. Delaware spent long hours going through agent files. He found that selecting the first agent was the hardest, but after three weeks of researching the background records of operatives in various American intelligence agencies, he chose a man from the CIA's Counter-Intelligence Division. The agent was a logical, analytical thinker, tough, resourceful, and a survivor. Delaware had only met the man once before but had immediate respect for him.

Now, years later, after having worked and bonded with this man, their relationship had grown into something more, a father-son relationship. That agent's name was Johnny Davis.

But now Johnny Davis was dead, brutally beaten to death in a private home in Las Vegas. Delaware first heard about it at 2:30 a.m. on the morning after his death. For several minutes he sat alone in his bedroom, in the dark. After reflecting on his loss, Delaware rose from his bed with conviction and hurriedly readied himself for work. Within the hour, he was pulling into the Delaware department store parking structure. Delaware entered the building through a private entrance and went directly to his office. A sealed white 9 x 12-inch folder sat on his desk waiting for him. He stared at the folder for a moment, before reaching for it, knowing what it was. Finally, he sat down and opened it and study the official police reports and crime scene photographs of the Johnny Davis murder. He received this copy of the official reports without the consent or knowledge of the Las Vegas Police Department. After briefly reviewing the documents, he dialed a phone number from memory. After three rings a sleepy female voice answered, "Hello?"

"I need you in the office now," he told her. "Contact Mr. Temple on your way in. I need him here at 12 pm. Also, call the CIA director. Tell him I'm going to need Miss Kiley after all."

"Yes, sir," Cathy Robinson said, sounding more alert now. "Is there anything else?"

"No." Delaware hung up then sank back in his cushioned chair. He thought about his division's newest agent, Alexander Temple, the spy code-named The Iceman. Temple was the last operative hired into D-Branch over two years ago, but in that short time, he had already gained the respect and awe from his fellow agents, men not easily impressed. To them, Temple had done what no other man had done before: he had tangled with the deadly Soviet assassin, The Grim Reaper, and had lived to talk about it. Lincoln Delaware, of course, knew that Temple was in-fact the second man to escape death from the dreaded Reaper. He had done so himself many years before, but his encounter left him crippled. Delaware closed his eyes and thought back to that awful day. Even now he sometimes had nightmares about it. He could still see the passengers' faces looking at him with hope. He could still hear their screams.

Delaware opened his eyes. He thought about the moment when he learned that The Grim Reaper was after the microdots, too. Delaware had always hoped to get another chance at the Soviet himself but realistically knew his time had come and gone. Now he would have to rely on his newest agent to finish the job for him. In a way, it was poetic justice that the only other man to survive The Grim Reaper's attack would be the man to have that final battle with him. Once again, it would be an old pro against the younger professional. Except, back when he was attacked by the Reaper, he was the old pro against the younger Soviet. Now it was reversed; The Grim Reaper was older and would be going up against The Iceman, a younger professional. Delaware's heavy eyelids closed again, as he laid his head back against the chair and contemplated the Soviet's demise. *Maybe soon the nightmares would end.*

Chapter 6

Alexander Temple gazed out the window of the jet aircraft as it lifted smoothly from the runway at San Diego's Lindbergh Field. As it soared out over the bay, Temple had an unobstructed view of the Pacific Ocean from his window seat. He watched the waves roll into the shore and smash against the rocks. In the distance, he could see a U.S. naval ship pulling into the bay, most likely heading for the 32nd Street naval base. The aircraft made a steep bank to the right and continued to climb through the clouds, as it doubled back across the city, until the clouds themselves looked like little puffs of smoke below them.

When the *Fasten Your Seatbelt* sign switched off, Temple unfastened his and considered what awaited him. Despite all the danger surrounding this mission, the most difficult reality to accept was the Alpha Data – the truth about UFOs. Despite being trained to expect the unexpected, the unbelievable, even the impossible, the secrets of the Alpha Data caught even him completely off guard. The truth was just so mind-boggling. It made him wonder about the full spectrum of government secrets jealously hidden, from the world, in the name of national security, secrets that only a select few knew about. As for the numbing revelation of alien life, he still had fears. *What are they capable of? Why are they here? What have we learned about the abductee found onboard? Was he operated on? And most importantly, are they a danger to us?* And Temple most certainly had questions about their advanced weaponry and technology. *What were their weapons capable of? And how did they cross space to get here?* Temple wondered if he would ever find out. It was a little frightening, not knowing.

A stewardess offered Temple a drink, interrupting his thoughts. He requested a rum and coke and drank it slowly, as he shifted his thoughts to what he had to do. This was a kill mission. It was not his first. During the office briefing when Delaware said, 'we have a situation blue,' Temple knew then that somebody had to die. After the meeting, he knew who. Donnetti was at the top of the list. He was a truly evil man and people had died because of his greed. His hired gunmen and that psycho bodyguard of his were also on the list. And then there was the Soviet assassin, The Grim Reaper. It was just his time. His murderous career had gone on long enough. Unfortunately, Temple would have to wait for the Soviet to make his move first, because Temple didn't know what he looked like. As for the microdots, the worry was not that alien life would be revealed. If he got the microdots back, there would be no proof. Anybody making claims of alien life would be looked upon as just another

UFO nut. The problem was the advanced weaponry and technology. That's what scared the shit out of everybody.

While considering his options, Temple's thoughts were interrupted again, this time by the prodding elbow of the child squirming in the middle seat beside him. The boy was oblivious to the annoyance he was causing as he scuffled with his younger brother seated in the aisle next to him. The child's mother, in the aisle seat across from them, made no attempt to control them. Eventually, one of the stewardesses gave the mother of the two boys a stern look. After that, the mother tried to get her kids to behave, by repeatedly threatening them with punishment if they didn't settle down – punishment that Temple knew they would never receive. The boys knew it, too. Each time their mother yelled at them, they would momentarily calm down, but then, in a matter of minutes, they would start up again full bore. Temple rested back in his seat and mentally tuned the boys out.

The remainder of the flight went relatively smoothly. When the jet touched down at McCarran Airport, Temple remained seated until the aircraft had come to a complete stop. He then stood up and collected his carry-on baggage and merged in with the others exiting the aircraft. Some passengers elected to remain seated to avoid those rushing to deplane. The moment Temple stepped into the terminal, his battle-honed instincts attuned to a higher level of alertness. With only a glance, he noted everything, without slowing his stride. It wasn't long before one face in the crowd caught his attention. He recognized it from a photograph he saw during the briefing in Delaware's office. The man's name was Jason Meats. He was one of Donnetti's hitmen. Looks like Donnetti was expecting him after all.

As Temple moved closer to the killer, he noticed something was off. Meats was standing in the waiting area for an incoming Boston flight and seemed unaware of Temple's presence. Temple walked to within four feet of him, then continued past him. Meats showed no sign of recognition. Apparently, Jason Meats was not looking for him. *Good*, Temple thought. Donnetti's people did not know he was coming, at least not yet. It also meant, if D-Branch had been penetrated, it was not yet complete. Temple positioned himself next to a concession stand and watched Meats from a distance. He toyed with the idea of killing the Indian now and getting it over with. He would no doubt have to deal with him later anyway.

After giving it some thought, Temple passed on the idea for the present. Killing Meats now would only alert Donnetti that an agent had slipped into Las Vegas. Temple turned and headed again for the baggage area, but wondered who the young Indian assassin was waiting for. After Temple collected his luggage, he slid into the first cab in line, in front of the airport, and told the driver to take him to the Golden Nugget Hotel.

###

Approximately thirty minutes before Alexander Temple arrived in Las Vegas, the man who ordered the death of Johnny Davis leaned lazily across the railing of his gambling boat, which he affectionately called *The Lucky Lady*. The massive 42,000 square foot vessel was the largest on Lake Mead's marina and required the building of a specially-constructed pier to accommodate it. As the boat's owner rested on his forearms, he watched the brilliant spectrum of colors illuminate the sky, as the sun slowly set in the west. It was so beautiful. Jim Donnetti loved beautiful things. He often spent time at that port side rail at sunset. It was his place of solitude. Donnetti watched the few remaining moments of sunset, as the sun, without fanfare, seemingly sank into the lake.

When it was gone, only then did the man behind him dare to speak. Eddie Bowman's voice was harsh and raspy even in whispered tones. "Mr. Donnetti, they're all waiting for you, sir."

Jim Donnetti turned his girth slowly and looked up at his bodyguard, a massive hulk of a man whose mere presence was frightening in itself. The big man's straight blond hair hung down to the base of his wide neck. He had a square jaw and granite features. He seldom smiled. When he did, his face twisted into something resembling a hideous mask. It was his eyes, though, that first caught your attention and sent freezing chills down your spine. They were death personified: black and dilated, with no life in them at all. Beyond his dead man stare was an angry, highly volatile, and unstable man. Only Jim Donnetti understood the man beneath and the secret to controlling him.

"Then we'd better go," Donnetti told him. "We don't want to keep them waiting."

As Eddie turned to lead the way, Donnetti glanced upward at the boat's dazzling array of deck lights, shining as a welcome beacon of invitation under the darkening skies of Nevada. The fat man beamed with pride then continued through the winding passageways behind his bodyguard. Along the way, he mused about Maxwell, his mole inside U.S. Intelligence. Donnetti found Maxwell's intel to be very reliable and beneficial, but he didn't like doing business with someone he only knew as a voice on the phone. He would have to change that arrangement.

Donnetti's first-ever meeting with Maxwell was arranged by his former CIA snitch Barry Gleason, just before Gleason was sent to prison. Barry Gleason used to be a long-time paid informant to Mafia Chieftain Don Carlo Baresi. As a personal favor to the Don, Gleason kept Donnetti informed on certain government activities that might affect his gaming business. After the Don's tragic death, Gleason became Donnetti's man in the CIA. It was a rewarding association for both of them, until Gleason was arrested by the FBI for espionage and sentenced to life in prison. After his conviction, Gleason got word to Donnetti that there was another government agent who, for the right price, would work with him. He gave Donnetti a phone number, a time, and the code-name Maxwell. Donnetti made the call. After their conversation, Maxwell was put on Donnetti's secret payroll but insisted on remaining just a voice on the telephone. Maxwell added it was not personal, just a matter of self-preservation. Donnetti detested working in the dark that way but knew he had no other choice for now.

Eddie Bowman led Donnetti into the conference room. An eerie hush consumed the room as they entered. Alvin Gutloff, one of the men in attendance, paid particular attention to Donnetti. The fat man had changed so much since they were first introduced. Gutloff noticed how Donnetti now moved with supreme confidence, with an aura that was all-powerful, all-commanding. He ruled his vast multimillion-dollar empire with self-assurance and was totally ruthless against anyone who opposed him.

Gutloff switched his attention to Donnetti's giant henchman. Eddie Bowman was relatively new to Donnetti's organization, perhaps as little as two years, yet there was a strange bond between them. Strange, because Eddie was not the kind of man to take orders or conform to rules. Yet oddly enough, he obeyed Donnetti without question. This blind obedience was a mystery, but nobody dared confront the fat man about it. As for Eddie – well, he was quite frankly considered homicidally insane. It was risky just saying good morning to him. Eddie had a fragile, unstable boiling point; almost anything could set him off. Even Alvin Gutloff, himself a professional hitman, made it a point to steer clear of the blond giant.

Donnetti sat down, in the big chair, at the head of the table. Eddie stayed by the door, his cold, dark eyes watching everything.

The conference room was a large one adorned with mahogany wood paneling. High above the conference table dangled a gigantic crystal chandelier, which sparkled in blue-white flashes, as the fluorescent lights in the room shined into it.

Donnetti glanced around the table at the four contract killers Gutloff had hired on his behalf to protect his auction. He was not pleased. There was a nigger, a lesbo, and a goddamned Injun. In an earlier meeting, Gutloff assured him that they were the best money could buy. He told Donnetti the black man was a methodical, relentless assassin who didn't believe in any of that black power crap. All he cared about was money. He'd kill his own mother, if the price was right.

Donnetti stared momentarily at the black assassin named, Nick Marlow. Marlow was wearing a custom-designed, black, two-button tuxedo, with a vest and black bow tie. His hair was short, his mustache neatly trimmed. He had a light complexion – no doubt a bastard baby, the product of ill-conceived mixed breeding.

Gutloff had also told Donnetti that Marlow was quite the ladies' man, but he only dated white women.

Donnetti projected a curt smile toward Marlow, when their eyes met, but he had already decided to have the black bastard killed when this was all over.

Sitting beside Nick Marlow was Edna Jean Case. She

probably would not have been a bad-looking woman if she fixed herself up, but according to Gutloff, she never did. Her dark brown hair was cut short, butch style, and her face had none of the softness in it that one expected in most women. Even before Gutloff volunteered it, Donnetti had already correctly guessed that Edna Jean Case was a lesbian.

"Don't let her appearance fool you," Gutloff told Donnetti in the earlier briefing. "She is as cold-blooded a killer as I have ever known."

Then there was the Indian, Jason Meats. He was the youngest of the group, in both age and experience, but make no mistake about it; he was already a killer. Allegedly, Meats had killed three men before he was eighteen years old, two of them in street fights. The third one had something to do with a dispute in a movie theater. Still, Gutloff saw potential in the Indian to be a professional, and took him on as a protégé, even inviting him along on his last four contracts for the experience. In Gutloff's professional opinion, Jason Meats, though a bit hot-tempered and wild, was as cool under pressure as anyone sitting at that table.

Donnetti studied the Indian. He was a full-blooded Sioux, his Indian ancestry evident in his features. He kept his long, straight, black hair tied back in a ponytail, and sported high cheekbones set in a well-tanned face. He was only twenty-three years old.

Also, at the big table, to Donnetti's right, was his personal lawyer and accountant, William C. Penrod. His presence was required at all such meetings for legal advice, but primarily his job was simply to keep Donnetti clear of the law.

William Penrod was a former deputy district attorney out of Los Angeles. He had a promising career but, to the dismay of his colleagues, he abruptly quit and went to work in the private sector. He had quickly grown tired of the pennies he made in the prosecutor's office. The private sector is where the money was. Penrod was not the idealistic fool that his colleagues were. He didn't give a damn about defending those unemployed derelicts who seemed to always be assigned to him. Money is what life was all about – he learned that long ago. Money and power. He had plenty of both working for Donnetti. The fact that Donnetti was a major criminal, with Mafia ties, didn't bother his conscience one bit.

When the fat man made eye contact with Penrod, the lawyer smiled a polite greeting to his boss. Donnetti acknowledged him with a nod but displayed no facial reaction. Donnetti didn't like Penrod much, but Penrod was doing a good job for him, legally speaking. Penrod also kept Donnetti informed on the goings-on around the boat – things that a man in Donnetti's position would never hear otherwise. Penrod was a good little snitch.

After eyeballing each of the hired guns, Jim Donnetti resigned himself to a simple reality, it was too late to make changes now. Maxwell had informed him earlier in the day that American and Soviet intelligence officers had already arrived in Las Vegas, to steal the microdots, before the auction. He had no choice now but to stick with the starting lineup. So, Donnetti withheld his displeasure and addressed the four killers, "If each of you will reach under the table, you'll find a folder taped underneath. These are your contracts. Inside you'll find a brief but detailed dossier on your man, along with three current photos of him. You'll also find the down payment that was agreed upon."

Jason Meats started to open his dossier but stopped, when he noticed nobody else opened theirs. Donnetti said evenly, "I want these contracts handled today. The sooner the better." After seeing a couple of raised eyebrows," Donnetti added, "I realize this is short notice, but I pay very well for the inconvenience." He let that sink in, then concluded, "Let Mr. Penrod know when you've completed your contracts. Any questions?"

When nobody responded, Donnetti crossed his hands on the table. "Then our business is concluded," he finished.

Everyone except Penrod stood up and headed for the door Eddie Bowman now held open. As Gutloff neared the door, Donnetti stopped him. "Just a moment, Gutloff."

"Yes, Mr. Donnetti?"

Donnetti waited until the others were gone, then grumbled, "Are you sure about them?"

"I'm sure."

"The Injun, too?"

"The Indian, too," Gutloff assured him.

Donnetti stared at him from across the table. "You'd better be."

Gutloff turned and headed for the door. He did not look back.

When he was gone, Donnetti fell back in his chair and let his mind wander. He and Gutloff went way back. He had always been able to count on Gutloff's skill set to get the job done. He hoped now he could rely on Gutloff's judgment as well. For Gutloff to take the Injun under his wing was out of character; he had always preferred working alone. This marked change in attitude bothered Donnetti. Perhaps the old gunman couldn't cut it anymore. Maybe he needed the Injun as a crutch. Whatever the reason, Donnetti didn't like it. Perhaps it was time he be replaced. Men like him were not hard to find. Donnetti had known men like him most of his life. His introduction to them came rather abruptly at the impressionable age of ten.

Chapter 7

As a child growing up in New York, young Donnetti wasn't quite sure what his father did for a living to earn so much money. Not until one day in the summer of '31, when two men wounded by gunfire, came to his house with expectations of hiding out from the police. They did not come bearing guns as enemies, but as friends in trouble. His father and mother welcomed them in. The strangers stayed two days and then were picked up by other men Donnetti did not know. After the men were gone, Donnetti approached his parents for an explanation.

His father stared at him for a long while, contemplating an answer. Finally, he decided it was time to tell his son the truth. "Those men are in organized crime. They are friends of ours."

"I don't understand," young Donnetti said, puzzled.

His father exhaled deeply, as if releasing all his guilt. He reached over and took his wife's hand in his as he explained, "It all started a long time ago. The truth is, I never really wanted to marry your mother. When I learned she was pregnant, I did a cowardly thing. I ran. I left town without a word. I found out later that her father, Mr. Baresi, was actually Don Carlo Baresi, one of the most powerful Mafia chieftains in New York. When he found out what I had done to his daughter, he sent men to find me. They did, about a week later. They would have killed me had it not been for your mother's pleading."

Donnetti's father put his arm around his wife, and she held on tight as he continued. "Despite the terrible wrong I had done to her, she still loved me. Still wanted me to be her husband. Of course, I had no choice, so I married her. Over the years, I learned to love her. I can't imagine life now without her. On our wedding day, Don Baresi assured me, if I ever abused his only daughter unnecessarily, I would die that same day. Then he hugged me, congratulated me, and gave me twenty thousand dollars in cash as a wedding gift. A week later, Don Baresi appointed me president of one of his legitimate, non-family connected companies. At your mother's request, Don Baresi agreed to become your godfather when you were born. So, my son, this is why we are friends with these men. But we are not gangsters. We are not part of that lifestyle. We live an innocent life. We don't take crooked money from her family. That wedding gift money that I accepted – I didn't have a choice. It would have been a sign of disrespect to refuse it."

Young Donnetti understood, and over time, came to know and understand the Mafia way. He was strangely drawn to it, impressed by the supreme authority his godfather commanded over other men. It was, in a way, terrifying, yet awesomely addicting. His godfather had the power to dare challenge God and country. That power was something that Donnetti would never forget.

The following year, Donnetti's father and mother were both tragically killed in an automobile accident caused by a drunken driver. The drunk driver, who didn't suffer even a scratch, was eventually convicted of manslaughter and sentenced to fifteen years in a state prison. The driver, however, never served one day of that verdict. Less than twenty-four hours after the sentencing, he was found dead in the city jail, his throat slashed so severely that he was nearly decapitated. His killer was never identified.

Don Baresi took young Donnetti into his home and raised him as one of his own, being careful not to involve him in the family business. It was his daughter's wish that her son not grow up under the family influence. She wanted her son to be what she called, "respectable."

Tragically, the Don agreed to his daughter's request on the night before she died. He felt obligated to honor it.

Don Baresi set up a generous trust fund for Donnetti that was to be turned over to him on his 21st birthday. He then set about the arduous task of guiding young Donnetti's life toward a respectable future.

During the years Donnetti lived under the Don's roof, he came to look upon Don Carlo Baresi as his father, and he respected no man more. When Donnetti reached the age of twenty-one, he had the urge, as do most young men, to break away from the nest and conquer the world. The Don did not try to stop him.

Donnetti headed west to California in the spring of 1940, followed closely by – unknown to him – a six-foot-five, 245-pound guardian angel, courtesy of Don Baresi.

Donnetti moved into an elegant but poorly managed hotel in West Hollywood. He traveled around the city, looking for a good business opportunity in which to put his money, but without much success. Two months later, he bought the little hotel he was staying in and promptly moved himself up to the penthouse. He took over hotel management, hired an entirely new staff and made several expensive renovations. Eight months later, his hotel was one of the busiest in the area, frequently visited by Hollywood celebrities and professional athletes. Donnetti had no idea that Don Baresi's influence was the major factor behind his hotel's sudden luminary status.

In the summer of '41, Donnetti heard that some men in Nevada were looking to sell their casino operation. Donnetti did some research. The men owned a small casino-hotel on Fremont Street in Downtown Las Vegas. The business regularly returned a substantial profit, but the owners were tired of the desert city and the gambling business. They wanted out so they could channel their money in other directions.

Donnetti had the good foresight to recognize a golden opportunity. Las Vegas was growing. Gambling was legal in that state. Nevada, he reasoned, was destined to become the big money market of the future, and Donnetti wanted to be part of that future. The prospect excited him. On that very next day, he headed to Las Vegas to make the casino owners an offer. Upon his arrival, he ran into the unexpected. The owners refused every offer he made; they simply would not do business with him. No explanation was provided. Jim Donnetti returned home dejected and confused. A couple of days later, he hopped on a flight to New York. He sorely needed advice and sought it from the most knowledgeable man he had ever known: his godfather.

The moment he stepped onto the Don's estate, he was ushered promptly into the great man's den. The Don sat comfortably on a long, heavily cushioned sofa, reading over the stock reports in the newspaper when Donnetti entered. A large smile lit up Don Baresi's aged face. Donnetti greeted him and paid his respects, as was customary. That evening after dinner they sat down to talk business.

"Godfather, I need some advice. I have tried to reason with these men in Nevada — to buy them out of a business they want to sell. I have offered them a fair price, even more than they have asked for, but still they refuse."

"Why do they refuse you?" the Don asked, already knowing the answer.

"After I left Las Vegas, I heard through the grapevine that they were not going to sell to me at any price — because I'm your godson."

Don Baresi's expression did not change. He was not concerned that these men in Nevada looked upon the Baresi family with little regard. Their respect meant nothing to him. What mattered was that his beloved godson had made them a reasonable offer, but was turned down by ignorant men for personal reasons. The Don quietly asked, "Are you positive this is what you want?"

"Yes sir, I am."

"What would you have me do?" the Don asked calmly, though he had already made up his mind, even before Donnetti walked into his den.

"Help me to negotiate with these men. You know much more about these matters than I do."

Don Baresi activated the intercom switch built into the arm of the sofa. "Send Gutloff in here," he commanded. The Don turned to Donnetti, "Stay here tonight. Tomorrow, fly back to Nevada. One of my representatives will accompany you with enough funds and influence to settle this matter."

A knock at the door punctuated his words, then Don Baresi's representative walked in. His dark features radiated a silent force that Donnetti found uncomfortable. The Don made the proper introductions, then said, "Gutloff will fly back with you to help you negotiate a deal."

Gutloff smiled politely at Donnetti, but there was no warmth in the gesture.

Donnetti was surprised to see this man was a non-Italian. The Don only employed Italians for the top positions in his organization. It perturbed him that the Don would assign something so important to a man who must have been a low-level employee.

The Don continued, "Get some sleep. And don't worry. You'll have what you want within the week."

Forty-eight hours later in a private room inside the Nevada casino that was up for sale, an emergency meeting was brought to order. In attendance were the four owners of the casino and three of their attorneys, along with Donnetti and his associate from New York.

Donnetti began, "Gentlemen, I have met with you before, and have offered you a very generous price for your business. A business, I understand, you are more than willing to sell at a lower price than I have already offered. But still you refuse me. So, let's cut to the chase. I am authorized by my people in New York to increase my last offer by twenty percent. My associate," Donnetti said, glancing back over his shoulder at Gutloff, "has the power to speak for my New York interest."

B.J. Duggan, the man who elected himself spokesman for the casino owners, stood up. "Mr. Donnetti, we have decided to be perfectly frank with you so that we can stop wasting each other's time. We know who you are. We have no intentions of ever selling our casino to you or any other pinko Mafia bastard like you. Now is that clear enough for you?"

Donnetti spoke with a calm reserve. "Mr. Duggan, I don't know where you get your information, but a mistake has been made. I am not, nor have I ever been involved in organized crime. I'm a businessman."

"I suppose that clown with you is a businessman, too," Duggan snapped sarcastically.

"My associate is here only to advise me and to assure any financial settlement that we agree on in this deal."

Duggan barked, "There is no deal. And here's a piece of advice on the house. If any of you sons-of-bitches try any of that gangland crap in Nevada, you'll find your asses rotting away in a federal penitentiary just like Capone did. Now you think about that." Duggan glanced around the table at the other owners, then said, "This meeting is adjourned."

Later that night, B. J. Duggan laid happily between the legs of a beautiful woman who was not his wife. Gutloff and Donnetti stood outside the door preparing to enter. Donnetti was not supposed to be there, but he followed Gutloff, then cornered him just inside the corridor on Duggan's floor, insisting he be allowed to see this thing through. Gutloff tried to talk him out of it, but Donnetti refused to leave. He was curious to see how Gutloff planned to handle this matter.

Gutloff had no choice. It was too late now to postpone what was going to happen. Arrangements had been made; the gears were in motion. It had to happen tonight.

Gutloff entered the room using a key and turned on the lights. Donnetti walked in behind him and stood quietly by the door. Duggan was sprawled naked across the bed under a tall platinum blonde who was energetically giving him a blowjob. Startled by Donnetti and Gutloff's entrance, Duggan abruptly sat up and began cursing profusely. The blonde was not surprised to see them. She simply climbed off the bed and hurriedly slipped back into her clothing.

"What the fuck is going on here?" Duggan snapped. "This bitch working for you?"

The blonde silently left the room without looking back. Gutloff moved quickly over to the bed and backhanded Duggan across the face. Duggan fell back on the pillow, his nose bleeding, a welt already forming under his eye. For the first time since they entered the room, Duggan looked afraid.

Jim Donnetti remained silent, curiously captivated.

Duggan wiped at the blood running from his nose and stared at Donnetti. "Have you gone mad? Do you know what kind of trouble —"

Gutloff pulled a leather blackjack, with a lead-filled tip, from his back pocket and smashed it against Duggan's head. It only took one blow to knock Duggan out cold.

Gutloff flipped a sawed-off shotgun from under his coat, then threw a length of rope on the floor. "Tie him to that chair," he told Donnetti.

Duggan woke suddenly to a splash of cold water in his face. As his eyes fluttered open and awareness trickled back into his body, he became distinctly aware of two things: he was tied to a chair, and there was something stuffed painfully tight inside his mouth, almost to the point of gagging. Focusing his eyes in front of him, he was startled at what he found. Pushed inside his mouth was the working end of a double-barreled shotgun.

Gutloff spoke to him in a low growl, "You should have taken the deal." Then Gutloff squeezed both triggers at once.

Jim Donnetti watched in stunned fascination as the next few seconds seemed to move in slow motion. *First, there was the deafening blast. Then the two front legs of the hardback chair Duggan was sitting on started to spill over backwards. Duggan's frightened eyes went blank. The muscles in his cheeks began to quiver, and blood spurted from his nostrils as the shotgun slugs tore through his brain. The back of his head exploded. Bits and pieces of Duggan's head – brain matter, skull fragments, and blood, spattered the floor behind him. One large chunk of skull slammed against the wall across the room and stuck fast. The chair that held Duggan's body captive hit the floor with a bounce, sliding four or five feet before coming to rest.*

Gutloff wiped the blood off the shotgun barrel onto Duggan's pants draped across the back of a chair. When Gutloff turned to Donnetti, he saw a faint smile on the young man's face that he did not understand.

The next day, B. J. Duggan's execution-style murder made front-page news. Duggan's widow, who inherited her late husband's shares in the casino, and the other three owners were suddenly anxious to sell to Donnetti. By 8 p.m. that night, Jim Donnetti was the sole owner of the hotel-casino. The former owners quietly left town during the dark of night. Alvin Gutloff flew back to New York to report to the Don. He didn't leave anything out, including Donnetti's presence at the murder scene.

One month later, Donnetti's guardian angel also flew back to New York, at the Don's request. The Don merely felt it was time.

The next time Jim Donnetti saw Alvin Gutloff was in October 1945. Don Carlo Baresi had decided to move into the Nevada gambling business on a trial basis. He was not yet convinced of the soundness of such a move but felt that, before going all-in on this new investment, an arrangement with his godson would simplify matters. If he went into Jim's casino, as a partner, he could better evaluate the business' potential. If the reports were favorable, he would branch out and buy up as much land as he could to build more casinos or lease the land out to other developers.

Jim Donnetti loved his godfather dearly, but he had no intentions of sharing his casino with anybody. After giving the matter some serious thought, Donnetti arrived at the only logical conclusion: Don Carlo Baresi had to die. It was strictly business; he learned that from the Don himself. Donnetti was well aware that killing a Don would not be an easy task, but after two weeks of careful consideration, he devised a workable plan. Donnetti contacted Alvin Gutloff, who impressed him as being not only capable of doing the job but loyal only to the almighty dollar.

Donnetti soon flew back to New York at the request of the Don himself. There was business to be discussed concerning their impending partnership. Since there was no hostility between the five New York families, only three of the Don's bodyguards accompanied him to the restaurant meeting. Before talking business, they ordered large meals and casually discussed family, friends and good times, laughing jovially all the while. The topic finally turned to business as they finished dinner. The Don lit a cigarette and leaned back in his seat. "I understand you are doing quite well in the casino business."

"There is a lot of money to be made there," Donnetti said, as he, too, lit a cigarette.

The Don continued, "I have been considering such a move myself, but I still have some reservations. I want to test the waters. What I propose is a limited partnership. I believe, with the gambling, the nightclubs, and the prostitution, a nice profit could be made."

Over the Don's shoulder, Donnetti saw Alvin Gutloff

stroll into the little restaurant. The Don and his three bodyguards glanced at Gutloff when he entered, but thought nothing of it. They recognized him and this was a favored hangout for the Baresi family.

Gutloff made casual, but deliberate eye contact with Donnetti and continued over to the bar.

Donnetti knew the shooter was ready, but he continued talking to the Don for a few moments longer. Then when Donnetti was ready, he abruptly scooted his chair back away from the table.

The Don flinched at the sudden move. Confusion crossed his face as he peered across the table at his godson.

"I love you," Donnetti told him, then dove for the floor.

For an instant, Don Baresi sat stunned. Then his eyes blinked wide in surprised disbelief and he tried to spin out of his chair. The Don's bodyguards instinctively reached for their guns but didn't yet know where the danger was coming from. By the time they saw Gutloff pull the Thompson submachine gun from under his coat, it was too late. He opened fire in full automatic mode, shooting everyone in the restaurant. The deafening noise of his weapon rapidly firing seemed to go on forever. When the shooting finally stopped and the air stood still, smoke permeated the room. Jim Donnetti stood up slowly, quite shaken. Even though he knew that this was going to happen, he still could not control his nervous shivers. Donnetti took a deep breath to calm himself, then looked down at the once all-powerful Don Carlo Baresi. The great man looked so undignified now, lying twisted on the dirty floor.

Gutloff turned to Donnetti. "You ready?"

Donnetti took another deep breath to steady his nerves. "I'm ready," he said.

Gutloff flicked the selector switch to semi-automatic,

then raised his machine gun and fired a single round. The bullet slammed into Donnetti's shoulder, spinning him partially around.

Feeling the hot lead burn into his flesh, Donnetti growled painfully through gritted teeth to keep from screaming. But before he could gather his wits or prepare himself, Gutloff fired another single round. Donnetti cried out in shock as the bullet tore into the meaty part of his left thigh. His knee quivered then buckled and he went down hard, moaning in excruciating pain. Instinctively Donnetti grabbed his wounded thigh, as blood gushed between his fingers. Almost immediately, he felt lightheaded. His breathing became labored and he couldn't catch his breath. Dizziness rapidly clouded his brain. Desperately he began sucking in air, trying to stay conscious. Then somewhere in the haze of his mind, he heard Gutloff say, "One more."

Through fuzzy vision, Donnetti could see the shadowy figure of the shooter moving around him, but he was too weak and lightheaded to focus. When the final bullet exploded from the barrel, Donnetti was already nearly unconscious, but he felt the sting of the bullet rip through the left side of his waistline and out his back. He made a deep grunting moan from the impact but made no other sound. Awareness of reality was slipping away fast. A moment later, he lapsed into unconsciousness with a shallow smile across his lips, thinking, *this was going to work*.

Donnetti had deduced that killing a Don was the most dangerous hit in the world to make, even more so than killing a United States president. When assassinating a president, there was a cushion between crime and punishment. The shooter had to traverse the legal system before guilt could be established. Evidence had to be gathered and processed. The shooter had to be arrested and tried in a court of law.

Witnesses and experts would have to testify. The prosecutor would have to try to convince a jury that the evidence and testimony presented proved his case. Then a judge or jury would determine guilt. If guilt was established, only then would the shooter be punished for his crime and sent to prison. This process could take months, even years. And then there were the endless appeals to protect the shooter's rights. Killing a Don, however, meant the immediate wrath of an entire Mafia family would descend on your ass for the rest of your short life. Hitmen would be paid to find you and kill you in the most painful way possible, and there would be no brilliant defense attorney or legal maneuvers to slow them down.

To pull off this hit on the Don, Donnetti knew that he needed the perfect alibi. And he had one. If he were found amongst the bodies, all shot up with the rest, who would ever suspect him? Taking three bullets was risky, but there was no other way.

Donnetti awoke, in a semi-conscious state, lying on a bed in the Don's home. Jenny Baresi, the Don's daughter, stood over him, her face swollen with grief. Suddenly her face lit up. She called to her brother, Antonio, who ran into the room looking relieved. He exclaimed his joy in Italian, then said somberly in English, "We thought we were going to lose you, too, Jim. You lost so much blood."

Donnetti had the presence of mind to stay in character and he blurted out, in his most concerned tone, "Is my godfather all right?"

"They've killed him," said Antonio. "They killed everybody in the restaurant. Only you survived."

"Oh my God, no!" Donnetti cried out. Then in Italian, Donnetti said a prayer for the soul of Don Carlo Baresi.

For the next three months, Donnetti ate at Don Baresi's

table, slept in the Don's home, and comforted the Don's wife and children while he recuperated from his own wounds. Antonio became the next Don, vowing to find his father's killers, though he was destined never to do so.

Donnetti eventually flew back to his growing empire in Nevada, where he was now king cobra, and on his way to becoming the most powerful man in the state, he hoped.

Gutloff subsequently became a free agent when Antonio refused to work with a non-Italian. Donnetti quickly put Gutloff on his payroll, but he was not considered a full-time employee and his name didn't appear on any pay sheets. Donnetti only used his services from time to time, over the years, but paid him a regular monthly salary to keep him on retainer.

Now, however, with the microdots at risk, this was one of those rare times that he needed Gutloff's services. He also needed others like him to help protect his auction. Originally, Donnetti learned from Maxwell where the microdots were being transferred from. Maxwell only knew that the microdots contained highly classified information meant for the president's eyes only, and had something to do with the development of advanced technology and weaponry. Donnetti believed that type of information could start a bidding frenzy worth millions.

Donnetti contacted Gutloff and told him he needed four shooters as soon as possible.

Chapter **8**

One hour after their meeting with Donnetti, the killers went out to fulfill their contracts. Nick Marlow sat in the back of a little coffee shop in downtown Las Vegas. While sipping his coffee, he quietly observed two CIA assets sitting on the far side of the room – the two he held contracts on. Marlow had followed them there and was waiting for the right opportunity to make his move. One was black, the other white. According to their dossiers, they were highly skilled assets who did wet work for the CIA: meaning, they were skilled assassins.

After watching them for some time, Nick Marlow concluded they were not only partners, but were the best of friends, by the way they interacted with each other and joked with the people around them. Marlow finished his coffee, then ordered another one. Before he had a chance to take a sip, the two assets started for the door. Marlow stood, pulled a five-dollar bill from a large roll of bills and placed it on the counter.

The two assets stopped short of the door, as the black guy said something to the waitress that made her laugh. The other asset, grinning, joined in on the conversation.

Marlow put the money roll back in his pocket and sat down again. From the corner of his eye, he caught a short stubby woman in her mid-forties watching him with great interest. When he turned and met her gaze, she got up and walked over to him. "You want some company?" she asked.

"What did you say?" Marlow asked, confused.

"Are you looking for a date?" she clarified.

Marlow's face turned cold, and he growled in a low rumble, "Get the hell away from me."

The woman giggled, then said apologetically, "Oh, I'm sorry. It's not with me. I've got some girls."

Across the room, Marlow saw the two assets walk out of the coffee shop. When he moved to follow them, the short, stubby woman continued her proposition. "Young, sexy, black, white, Asian, whatever you like."

With a frightening calm, Marlow said, "I told you to get the fuck away from me."

As Marlow started to step around her, she blocked his path and snapped, "Who the hell —"

Marlow grabbed her collar in one violent jerk, "You should have moved your fat ass when I told you." Then he shoved her backwards into a table. She crashed into it hard and fell to the floor, the table flipping over on top of her. No one in the coffee shop made a move to detain her attacker or to help her up. They watched like frightened children, too afraid to get involved. The few patrons that heard her proposition decided she was an obnoxious woman with a big mouth, and got what she deserved.

Marlow caught up to the assets and followed them, at a discreet distance, to a side street barbershop. He peeked into the window after they entered, and could see two barbers on duty, one of whom was a woman. The man was busily cutting somebody's hair; the woman stood alongside the second chair, with a magazine in her hand, talking to one of the assets. The white asset sat in her barber chair, while his partner claimed one of the metal fold-up chairs along the wall. Nick Marlow waited ten more minutes before walking into the barbershop.

"How long before I'm up?" Marlow inquired.

The male barber said, "I'll be ready for you in just a moment, sir."

"Good," Marlow replied. "I've got to get back to that craps table. I'm feeling really lucky tonight." Marlow continued over to the cigarette machine in the corner, with his back to them. The two assets began bantering back and forth with each other, and soon the entire shop was buzzing with conversation and laughter. Marlow pulled his Luger out of his shoulder holster and slowly screwed a silencer onto the end of the barrel. At first, nobody batted an eye when he turned around. The black CIA asset saw it first. "Gun!" he yelled and simultaneously reached under his jacket for his own .38 Smith & Wesson. Nick Marlow shot a bullet into the asset's forehead before his gun cleared the holster. Marlow then targeted the other asset, shooting him in the chest as he started to get out of the barber chair. The asset fell back into the seat with a groan. Marlow put the next round into his head. The female barber, standing behind her mortally wounded client, screamed hysterically as blood from his head wound splattered onto her face. The male barber stumbled backward into the wall in shock. His customer made a run for the door. Marlow shot the female barber in the face to stop her screaming, then swung the Luger around and put one bullet into the runner's back. When the man went down, Marlow put another round in the back of his head. Marlow then leveled his Luger toward the male barber, who threw his hands up in a desperate gesture to calm the shooter. "Don't shoot. For God's sake, don't shoot. Let's talk about this. What is it that you want?"

"No witnesses," said Marlow.

###

In one of the more elegant restaurants just off the strip, Alvin Gutloff stood by the cocktail bar sipping on a martini, as he watched Richard Henderson and his family enjoying a late supper in the dining room.

Richard Henderson, a news reporter for an east coast TV station, was in town on vacation. He and his family stepped off the plane only about an hour ago. From reading his dossier, Gutloff knew that Richard Henderson was actually a Soviet agent more commonly known in intelligence jargon as a "sleeper." A sleeper agent is a person secretly sent to a foreign country, sometimes even as a youngster, who then pretends to be a citizen of that country. That agent then leads a relatively normal life, until one day he is called upon to do a job of espionage for his native land. Henderson's real name was not mentioned in the dossier because it was an unimportant fact. The dossier did state that Henderson was part of a special three-man team, sent to Vegas to steal microdots from Donnetti before he auctioned them off. The dossier also pointed out that even Henderson's wife and kids didn't know that he was a Soviet citizen. They were just unwitting pawns to better fortify his cover.

Underneath Alvin Gutloff's long overcoat was a custom-made sling that held his favorite weapon, a double-barreled, sawed-off shotgun. For this hit, Gutloff decided to wear a disguise. He knew that gunning down a reporter was risky, especially one well-known like this TV anchorman. Witnesses tend to pay closer attention when the victim has celebrity status.

Gutloff finished his martini, then walked through the dining room, past the Henderson's table, to the vestibule containing a row of four telephone booths. Gutloff went into the last one and dialed the number to the booth next to him. The girl at the cashier's desk walked over to the phone that was ringing and answered it. After a brief conversation, she sat the phone down, then sent one of the waitresses over to the Henderson's table.

Henderson did not think the phone call unusual because he had orders to meet two other KGB men later that evening. This call was obviously a message from one of them. No one else knew he was in town. Henderson excused himself from the table, with the explanation to his family that the phone call was probably his boss trying to get him to work on some big story in town. He assured his wife that he would turn it down, whatever the offer. When Henderson stepped into the lobby, the cashier pointed to the phone booth where the call was waiting. He nodded at her, then opened the door to the booth and stepped in. Henderson was surprised to hear a steady buzz from the receiver. *The stupid little bitch must have pointed me to the wrong phone booth,* he seethed. From the corner of his eye, he saw movement to his right. As he turned toward it, he felt an immediate emptiness in the pit of his stomach.

Alvin Gutloff squeezed both barrels at once. The boom was ear-splitting. Shattered glass from the phone booths sprayed into the lobby and dining area. As confusion and panic erupted within the restaurant, Gutloff walked out the front door and slid into a waiting car. There was no need to check the victim's condition. The sight of Henderson's blood-soaked body, twisted and mangled between the glass and metal frame of the booth, was proof enough that his job was done.

###

At McCarran Airport, Gutloff's young protégé, Jason Meats, awaited the arrival of his victim, Rudolf Rosinsky. Rosinsky was a veteran in the assassination bureau of the KGB; killing was Rosinsky's primary function.

Meats positioned himself in the waiting area for Flight 411 from Boston. He had maintained a mental image of Rosinsky in his mind and was carefully studying the faces of passengers as they filed from the plane into the terminal. After about two dozen or so passengers plodded by, Meats spotted him.

Short, stocky, and powerfully built, Rosinsky walked very cautiously. His eyes moved furtively from side to side, taking in his surroundings. Meats followed him through the terminal, carefully measuring his steps so as not to get too close. He had already decided to make his move on Rosinsky after he arrived at his hotel. Rosinsky approached the men's room, paused to glance at his watch, then went inside. Meats waited by a magazine stand for him to come out. After ten minutes had passed, Meats considered the horrible possibility that perhaps Rosinsky had spotted him and had somehow given him the slip. Meats cautiously entered the bathroom. He saw Rosinsky at the sink washing his hands. Meats continued over to the urinal and pretended to relieve himself. He noted, when he entered the bathroom, that they were alone. *Maybe I should do the job here.*

Rosinsky was taking his sweet time washing his hands, so Meats zipped his pants back up and walked over to the full-length mirror next to the exit door. Just as Meats started digging through his pockets for a comb, Rosinsky quickly rushed up behind him. "Blink and I kill you," Rosinsky growled.

Meats felt a cylindrical object pressing against the base of his skull, so he stood perfectly still.

"Very good. I have your attention," Rosinsky said. "This pen gun at base of your skull has bullet ready to fire. Make wrong move and you die. Do you understand?"

Meats nodded his head once for yes.

Rosinsky pressed the pen gun tighter against Meats' head, "Say it," the Soviet ordered.

"I understand," Meats answered.

"This is good," Rosinsky said, then took one step back. "You turn and face me — slow."

Meats complied.

The Soviet continued, "Remove hand from pocket and tell me why you follow me?"

Meats glanced briefly at Rosinsky's weapon to note which hand he held it in. Then Meats pulled his hand from his pocket as ordered, but with it came a butterfly knife. He sliced upward in one fluid motion and cut a deep gash in Rosinsky's wrist, severing tendons and nerves. Rosinsky's eyes bulged in pain and surprise, but before he had a chance to scream or drop the pen gun from fingers no longer capable of holding it, Meats brought the razor-sharp knife back down across the Soviet's throat, slashing his jugular vein. Rosinsky toppled over like a falling tree, never making a sound. He was dead before his body hit the floor. Meats recovered the pen gun off the floor, put it in his pocket, and left the men's room. When he was safely outside of the airport, he checked the weapon and found it to be just an ink pen.

Edna Jean Case strode through the crowded lobby of the Sahara, one of the most luxurious hotel-casinos in Las Vegas. She rode the elevator up to the second floor, then walked to the end of the hallway and knocked on the last door on the right. The door opened to reveal a tall, dark-headed man wrapped only in a bath towel.

Edna gave him a quick, unimpressed once-over with her eyes. The man held his towel in place with one hand and gave her a gold room key with the other.

"His room is ready," the man told her. "He should be back in about twenty minutes."

"Is the telephone ready?" she asked while removing her overcoat, exposing the white maid's uniform underneath.

"It's ready. Whatever number they dial, it'll come through my equipment here." He took Edna's overcoat, then closed the door. Edna proceeded to the suite just down the hallway. The room belonged to a Soviet ambassador named Emil Pollikov. He was supposedly touring the United States, while on vacation, but was really a top Soviet spy sent to Las Vegas to meet with two other Soviet agents. Their mission objective: steal from Jim Donnetti, stolen government documents, before he could auction them off. Edna had no information on the other two spies, but Pollikov had successfully used his ambassador cover for many years. Pollikov's job here was to use the two unwitting FBI agents assigned to his security detail as his alibi. At some point during the evening, Pollikov would slip knockout drops into whatever the two FBI men were drinking. He would then slip out of his room to meet with his two accomplices. They would locate and steal the government documents using any force necessary, after which, Pollikov would sneak back into his room before the FBI agents woke up, too embarrassed to admit they had fallen asleep on the job.

Edna entered Pollikov's suite using the gold key, leaving the door open as maids always do, then headed for the bathroom. She knew that Pollikov always took cold showers before going to bed; it was the only thing he did with any regularity. Edna decided the bathroom is where she would take him out.

Edna checked the shower to confirm it was rigged not to work. Then she went into the bedroom and picked up the pillow on the left half of the bed. She removed the two-inch .38 caliber revolver from the pillowcase and checked to make sure the silencer was screwed on tight. Then she put it back inside the pillowcase and placed the pillow on the floor beside the bed. So far, so good. Edna laid down on the bed and waited. She didn't have to wait long before she heard voices entering the front room. Edna got up and pretended to busy herself with maidly chores.

One of the FBI men stepped into the bedroom with his gun drawn, but not pointed at her. He looked at the room and Edna carefully. "FBI," he said, flipping out his ID card. "What are you doing in here at this time of day?"

Edna stammered in rehearsed nervous embarrassment, "T-the morning girl got called away before cleaning your room. Some kind of trouble at home. In the confusion, your room got missed. N-nobody cleaned it. The house manager called up to apologize personally, but no one answered. He figured m-maybe I could clean it before you found out what had happened."

The FBI man walked around and did a cursory check of the suite, then yelled to his partner in the hall to bring Emil Pollikov in. The agent lowered his gun as Pollikov was ushered into the room. Then he corrected the maid, "It's not my room, miss. It's his." The second FBI man said, "I'll call downstairs and check her story."

The man on the other end of the line confirmed the same story the maid offered. "She checks out," the FBI man told his partner, who only now re-holstered his gun.

Emil Pollikov was not the least bit concerned about the alleged assassination threat against his life. It was his own people who started that rumor, forcing the United States to unknowingly supply him with an alibi.

Pollikov frowned, "You nearly scared this poor woman to death with your guns waving in the air." He turned to Edna, "I apologize to you for their rude behavior."

Edna, still playing her role, nodded politely. "I suppose they're just doing their job," she said.

"How much longer will you be?" one of the FBI men interrupted.

"Not long. I only have a little bit left."

"Why don't you just wrap it up now? We're in for the night," the lead FBI man told her.

"I'm done in the bedroom. The rest won't take more than five minutes or so."

"Alright," the FBI man sighed, "just hurry up."

"I'll be gone before you know it," Edna chirped, heading for the living room area. As she left the bedroom, she heard Emil Pollikov say, "Guess I'll take that shower now."

Pollikov retreated to the bathroom, closing the door behind him. The FBI agents joined Edna in the living room, but they both sat down. Edna continued feigning work, waiting for her opportunity. After a short time, Pollikov stormed back into the living room area. "This is just not my day!" he bellowed. "Every damn thing is going wrong. That dinner we had down the street tasted like shit. I lose my ass off at baccarat. My room isn't cleaned up. And now the fuckin' shower doesn't work!" Pollikov snatched the phone off the receiver, prepared to give housekeeping holy hell about the shower, when Edna interjected, "Excuse me, sir. Did you check the depressed nozzle adjuster on the side of the showerhead?"

"Depressed nozzle adjuster?" He flapped. "No," he admitted, with a slight grin of embarrassment, "I didn't."

Edna Jean Case said, "Let me have a look at it." She headed for the bathroom with Emil Pollikov following close behind. While walking through the bedroom, she picked the pillow up off the floor as if she were still tidying up, then continued into the bathroom. With her back to Pollikov, Edna slipped the gun out of the pillowcase. When she reached the shower stall, she turned and handed him the pillow. As he reached for it, she shoved the pillow against his face and forced him back to the wall. Before he could stop her, Edna jammed the gun into the soft cushioned pillow and pulled the trigger once. The silencer lowered the sound to a soft thud.

Emil Pollikov's legs went limp under him. Edna carefully lowered his body to the floor. She then repositioned the gun behind the pillow, before walking back into the living room. The two FBI men were sitting around the coffee table talking when she reentered the room. "Did you get it working?" one of them asked.

Edna tapped the trigger twice. Stuffing flew from the pillow as the bullets passed through it. Both agents took rounds in the chest. One of them died instantly. The other fell back across the sofa, breathing in pronounced gasps. Edna walked over to him and put the pillow over his face. Instinctively the agent turned his face away from the gun. Edna pressed the pillow firmly against the side of his head and shot him through the temple. After the shooting, she stuffed the gun in her waistband and pulled her shirt down over it, then she left the room and let the door lock shut behind her. As she headed down to her car, she wondered if the other shooters had fared as well on their contracts as she did on hers.

Chapter 9

Alexander Temple enjoyed the magnificent view of the Las Vegas Strip, from the back seat of a cab, as it drove slowly in heavy stop-and-go traffic along S Las Vegas Blvd. Temple was aware the driver deliberately took the slower, longer, scenic route to increase the trip meter. For most tourists, it would not have occurred to them that there was a quicker route downtown. Most tourists tended to be completely enamored by the dazzling light show along the strip.

Temple didn't mind the longer route. He really did enjoy the view. It was nearly dusk out, but excitement lingered in the air. This was the time of day when Las Vegas seemed to come alive. The big casinos on the Strip boastfully bragged their presence with brilliant exterior light displays and giant marquees advertising big-name talent. Along the sidewalk, people moved in clusters, some laughing, others drinking, all seemingly having a good time. Temple caught a glimpse of one particular woman, just before she disappeared into the crowd. She wore high heels and a black skirt, too short and too tight. Temple smiled. There was always one short black miniskirt in the crowd.

The cab eventually turned onto Fremont Street. Not to be outdone in grandeur were the smaller downtown casinos whose lights, when combined at night, lit up a section of Fremont Street like a morning's day. Fremont Street was the main drag in downtown Las Vegas, and it was the street most often shown in commercials about Sin City. Hundreds of tourists walked along that street, at all hours of the day and night, moving from casino to casino. For them, it was a magical town, a place where dreams were made, a place where they could forget their day-to-day problems and just have fun. Temple watched the multitudes of people enjoying themselves with family and friends. In a way, he envied them and their carefree lifestyle. They had what he would never have again — a normal life.

The cab pulled to a stop at the main entrance of the Golden Nugget Hotel Casino. Alexander Temple paid the driver, then registered at the front desk under his assigned mission name, Tom Briggs. The desk clerk assigned him a room on the second floor. Temple never accepted the first room offered, just in case it was a setup. He asked what rooms were available. The clerk started rattling off room numbers. Temple selected the fifth room mentioned, then asked the clerk if there were any messages for him, though he already knew there would be one from Karen Kiley. The clerk located the letter and gave it to him. It read: *Dinner at*

8:45 pm, third table on the left. Temple understood its real meaning. Karen's room number was near 845. The *third* table meant the third number, and *left* meant less than. Her room number was 842. Temple grinned. Looks like she was paying attention at the Farm. He took the elevator up to his room on the fourth floor. Once inside the room, he did a cursory check for monitoring devices. He did not expect to find any but went through the process as a matter of routine. When he was certain the room was clean, he laid his sports coat across the back of the chair by the desk. He unzipped his suitcase, removed the stack of clothing and two ball caps, then put them off to the side. Underneath was a secret compartment that contained his toys. His primary toy was a Walther PPK .380 ACP 7+1, with a custom-designed silencer. The knock against the .380 was that it didn't have stopping power, but Temple disagreed. You just have to hit your target in the right place. He pulled the loaded gun from its shoulder holster and checked the weapon to make sure it had not been tampered with. Since his life depended on it, he always made sure his toys were still working properly whenever they were out of his sight. Temple slid the Walther back into the holster. His other toy was a .357 double-barrel derringer. It was a very dependable little weapon and could drop a big man at twenty feet. Temple slid the derringer into the quick draw device designed specifically for it. The device was made to be worn on the forearm, under a long sleeve coat. When properly activated, the gun would slide silently into the hand, with smooth precision and quickness. Temple worked the slide action on the device to make sure it was not hanging up, then he fitted the apparatus on his forearm and pushed the slide back into the ready position.

Upstairs, Karen Kiley nervously paced her room. The anxiety was killing her. This was her first mission, her first time in the field. She felt like a real agent and wanted so much to do a good job; however small it might be. She considered herself lucky to be partnered on her first mission with someone she already knew. Maybe he'd let her do something important. She worried about the message she left for him at the front desk. *Would he understand it?* Of course he would, she decided. It was very basic crypto. Academy level stuff.

Although Karen Kiley was expecting Temple to come to her room, the knock at her door still startled her. She flinched sharply, but then quickly giggled in relief, realizing it must be him. Karen bolted for the door and opened it with a big smile.

Temple hurriedly walked in, closing the door behind him. "Never open your door without at least asking who's there," Temple warned.

His warning went right over her head. "So," Karen asked, her eyes full of excitement, "what's our first move?"

Temple ignored her enthusiasm. "I'm going to Donnetti's boat to have a look around."

"Good," she beamed grinning broadly. "So, I guess I'll meet you there. Don't worry, I'll be inconspicuous. Nobody will know we're together."

"You're not going," he said flatly.

Karen looked genuinely surprised. "Why not? You might need me — for communications."

"Do you remember your mission parameters?"

"I do. But Michael —"

Temple cut her off abruptly. "My name is Alexander Temple. How many fuckin' times do I have to tell you that?"

"I'm sorry," she mumbled, frightened by his angry outburst. "I didn't mean to call you that. I really didn't. It won't happen again."

Once the anger left his face, she said in a softer voice, "Let me go with you. I won't get in your way. I promise."

Temple shook his head. "I can't let you go."

Karen flashed a playful smile at him. "You know, if you want to send a status report, you may need me close by."

"No," Temple said with finality.

Karen frowned. "Why not? Is it because I called you — that name?"

"You'd better come to grips with reality, lady."

"What's that supposed to mean?"

"You act like this is a game. It's not. This is serious business, the kind that could get you killed."

"If you're trying to scare me —"

"You should be scared," Temple snapped. "These people I'm after are killers. Professional assassins. Besides protecting Donnetti's auction, they've also been hired to find and kill us. And there's a possibility they may already know who we are."

Karen's eyes widened in surprise. "What? You think they know who we are?" Then her eyes narrowed. "You knew about this before we left San Diego, didn't you?"

"Yes."

Karen was livid to have been kept in the dark but tried to speak calmly. "If they already know who we are, why are we even here?"

"It's our job," he said.

Karen shook her head. "This is crazy! We're just going to sit here until they come for us?"

Temple said coolly, "If it becomes necessary, I'll kill them all before that happens."

Karen looked at him with fear in her eyes. "You could do that? Kill in cold blood?"

Temple just stared at her. He couldn't believe the

nonsense coming out of her mouth.

Karen glared at him. "You talk about killing as if it means nothing to you."

Temple chose his next words carefully. "Taking a life is sometimes necessary in this business."

"What about arrest and prosecution?" she snapped.

Her reply told Temple everything he needed to know about his former friend from the past. She was totally clueless about how things worked in the business of espionage. Her ignorance made her dangerous. He had to straighten her out now before she got herself or someone around her killed, namely him. "I don't know what they're teaching at the Farm these days or why someone thought you'd be suited for this kind of work, but you're living in a fantasy world."

Karen gaped at him in stunned silence, as he continued, "In the real world of espionage, we deal with the worst of the worst; ruthless, merciless, sociopaths, religious extremists, and terrorists from countries all around the world. These people want to kill us. They want to destroy our country and our way of life. And they attack without conscience, pity, or fear. If you want to stay alive in *this* world, you need to get your head out of the clouds. You need to be as cold and as ruthless as your enemy. Let the police read them their rights. That's not what we do. We meet threats head-on with intellect, and sometimes brute force. If that means pulling the trigger, you do it, and you don't necessarily have to wait until your victim turns around." Temple saw her eyes widen in shock at what he was saying, so he pushed harder. "That's right, you shoot him in the back if you get the opportunity. And if you're *really* lucky, you might be able to sneak up on him and blow his brains out while he's still asleep. That's the reality of this business. We only have one rule here: never give your enemy a chance to kill you."

Karen Kiley could not believe what she was hearing. How could he have changed so much? How could he kill like that – like an animal?

Temple saw the revulsion in her eyes and he continued to press, "Yes, it's a dirty, rotten business, but that's the job. We *have* to win every fight. If you hesitate for a second, if you feel compassion for your enemy, he will exploit that weakness and he will kill you. It only takes a second to die."

Karen Kiley's voice shook, "You're not the same man that I knew back in school. What kind of emotionless animal have you become?"

"I'm the kind of animal you're going to have to become if you want to stay alive. You'd better think about that real hard right now, because you don't have much time left. On the day you graduate from the Farm, your life isn't yours anymore. It'll belong to the Company. And they will use it as *they* see fit. So, on graduation day, you'd better be ready to become an animal. A vicious flesh-eating animal if necessary. Think about that real hard, lady, because if you're not willing to kill," Temple snapped his fingers, "and I mean just like that, then I suggest you walk away from this business. Find yourself a nice respectable job or get married and have a couple of kids. Do something that'll give you a chance at a normal life."

Karen Kiley exhaled deeply and reflected in silence. Deep down she knew he was right. Karen remembered the lectures at the Farm about the use of deadly force, but she had convinced herself that she could do the job despite her aversion to taking a life. Academically, Karen was at the top of her class. She kept telling herself that everything else would fall into place. Now Karen realized she was just fooling herself. She *was* living in a fantasy world. This was not the glamorous profession she tried to make herself believe. It was a dirty, ugly business, and its agents were nothing more than glorified mercenaries. She could never be that cavalier about taking a human life. Karen looked away for a moment to keep from crying, then turned back to him and murmured, "I won't cause you any more trouble. I won't leave the hotel while you're gone. If anything, I'll just go downstairs to the casino restaurant, okay?"

"Room service would be better," he said. "Remember, they may be looking for us."

"And you're going to go to his boat anyway?" she asked in resigned disbelief.

"It's my job," he repeated, then glanced at his watch. "I have to go. Don't open the door for anybody except me."

"I won't," she agreed. When Temple was gone, she stood alone in the middle of the room and cried.

Chapter 10

Alexander Temple hopped into a taxi parked in front of the Golden Nugget Casino. The driver, an overweight Chaldean, was still eating a sandwich when Temple climbed into the back seat. A frown crept into the driver's puffy cheeks, as he awkwardly scrambled to put his half-eaten sandwich away. Temple noted the driver was so obese that it must have been a great chore for him to get into the driver's seat. No doubt, getting out of his cab to open the door for his passengers was a service he probably did not enjoy. That is if he ever did it at all.

"Where to, mister?" the driver asked over his shoulder, still annoyed by the rude intrusion on his snack break. It had been a busy night for the driver, one passenger after another.

All he wanted was a few lousy minutes to finish his fucking sandwich. When Temple replied, "The Lake Meade Marina," the cabby's frown stretched into a silly smile. The marina was at least forty miles away. The fare and tip he would get for a ride like that was well worth the interruption. During the drive, the cabby tried to engage Temple in conversation, but only received one-word responses. The cabby took the hint and drove the rest of the way in silence. So much for getting a big tip, he thought.

As they approached the marina the driver asked, "Any particular pier?"

"I'm looking for *The Lucky Lady*."

"Oh, you mean that big mother." The cabby turned his taxi around and smiled inwardly. He knew *The Lucky Lady* catered to high rollers. Maybe he was getting a big tip after all.

Up ahead, *The Lucky Lady* towered over the other boats moored at the marina. As they got closer, Temple could see two brows reaching up to *The Lucky Lady's* elevated deck, one forward and one aft. The aft brow was adorned with a string of white lights from top to bottom, leaving no doubt that was the stairway intended for the boat's guests. The forward brow was less noticeable and with only minimal lighting, possibly reserved for the crew and ship deliveries. The cab driver stopped at the head of the pier. "We're not allowed to drive onto the pier itself, sir," he explained politely, salivating at the thought of getting a huge tip.

Temple got out of the cab, paid the driver, and told him to keep the change. The driver glanced at the single bill and could not hide his Cheshire cat grin. "Thank you, sir," he babbled enthusiastically as his passenger walked away.

Temple scanned the giant vessel for possible escape routes as he approached. He also looked for security cameras and guard positions on and off the boat, but never slowed his stride. He walked up the aft brow to the quarterdeck and was greeted by the boat's welcoming committee. One was a young, attractive hostess wearing a long, flowing black evening gown, high heels, and a friendly smile. The other two greeters, muscular no-neck college jocks, wore black tuxedos. They were most likely not involved in Donnetti's illegal enterprises, as was probably the case with most of the boat's crew and support staff.

To the left of the quarterdeck, Temple observed a security guard's shack. Inside the tiny room were two-armed security guards. Both were pretty big boys. One kept his eyes glued on the quarterdeck and the other was eating a sandwich while watching a TV monitor.

The hostess escorted Temple just inside the casino entrance, then returned to her station on the quarterdeck. Temple surveyed the large gaming floor. There were several rows of blackjack and poker tables. Other areas were set aside for roulette and craps. Slot machines, however, occupied over half the floor space, which was typical in most casinos. Temple casually walked through the casino, his eyes busily taking everything in as he searched for the right person. After rounding the gaming floor twice, he spotted three bartenders busily mixing drinks and interacting with the customers sitting at the bar. Temple was especially interested in the black bartender; he just might be the one. Temple studied him from a distance. He had the beginnings of a potbelly, stood about five-foot-nine, had short hair and a receding hairline. He was flirting with one of the waitresses, a dark-haired beauty wearing a short, black, form-fitting dress, with a plunging neckline that flatteringly displayed her ample bosom. The bartender leaned forward and whispered something to her that made her giggle, then she playfully swatted his shoulder. The bartender grabbed her hand, and she squeezed his in a lingering touch. Then she wrote something down on a piece of paper and slipped it into his hand. As she walked off, his eyes trailed her admiringly.

The other two servers were busily mixing drinks at the far end of the bar, when Temple entered the lounge and sat at the bar next to the service station. Before Temple could order a drink, another waitress moved into the serving station and ordered several drinks from memory. She was also wearing a black, form-fitting dress with a plunging neckline. The black bartender quickly filled her orders and placed them on her tray. As she turned to leave, he winked at her, and she answered it with a smile full of private connotations. It was obvious they had been intimate before or would be soon. The bartender admired her as she walked away. Temple pretended to do the same, and both men exchanged approving glances. Alexander Temple had decided to use this man. Someone like him, who chased the ladies and considered himself a player, was sure to know things or know how to find out things.

"What'll you have, partner?" the bartender asked Temple.

With an impish grin, Temple nodded after the waitress. "Some of that might be nice," he joked, trying to build a rapport with this man, "but for now, I'll just have a rum and coke."

"Any particular label?"

"Do you have Appleton Estates?"

"We got everything," the bartender boasted.

Temple watched the bartender mix his drink and momentarily wondered if the pudgy man was the playboy he pretended to be, or if he was paying for their favors with money or drugs or both.

The bartender sat the drink in front of him. "Would you like to run a tab?"

"No, I'll just pay for it now." Temple put a fifty-dollar bill on the bar and told him to keep the change. The bartender's eyes squinted. He knew that something else was coming. Temple stood up and leaned in toward the bartender and whispered, "I hear there's a private game onboard in a couple of days. Any chance I can get in it?"

"No way, baby. That's strictly a private, invitation-only game. People come here from all around the country hoping to get in that game, and I mean people that's got bank, and they can't get in without an invite. There's nothing I can do for you, partner."

Temple took five, one-hundred-dollar bills from his wallet and placed them on the bar. "They'll want to check me out," Temple said. "My name is Tom Briggs. Do what you can for me. There's five more of these for you if you can do me some good."

The bartender took the money. "No promises, but I'll put the word out. How do I contact you?"

Before Temple could answer, he heard a sudden murmur of commotion behind him. He turned and saw that the commotion was due to the arrival of one man, an elderly fellow just about Lincoln Delaware's age. He was dressed casually in a pullover knit shirt and dark slacks. Following within arm's distance behind him were two barrel-chested men in dark suits, no doubt his bodyguards. Some of the casino patrons in the area seemed to recognize the elderly gentleman, and many followed him toward the roulette table.

"Who is he?" Temple asked the bartender.

"That's Mr. Clarence Melcher. He's an east coast billionaire. Made his money in real estate, I heard. Anyway, he's been coming to Las Vegas once a year for over two decades. Always goes to a different casino. You never know where he's gonna show up. He only plays roulette. Picks the same number every time. He bets a million bucks at forty-to-one odds. One game, one spin, win or lose, then he flies home."

"Has he ever won?"

"Never has, but he doesn't seem to mind. He's one cool dude, that old man."

Temple started to move closer to the roulette table when the bartender behind him called out, "You never did tell me how to contact you."

Temple looked back at him. "What's your name?"

"George Atkins," the bartender said, "and how do I get ahold of you?"

"I'll be around," Temple said, then he pressed his way through the crowd that had gathered around the roulette table.

As Clarence Melcher cleaned his eyeglasses with a handkerchief, he seemed unaware of the crowd his presence had created. Melcher then put a certified check for one million dollars on the table. The roulette croupier handed the check directly to the pit boss. The pit boss examined it and returned it to the roulette croupier, who then dropped it into the money chute in the table. The pit boss then gave the croupier a million-dollar chip, which he promptly placed on the table in front of Melcher. Without hesitation, Melcher put the chip on number eight. A few other players at the roulette table followed suit and also put chips on number eight. Melcher's aged, weary face showed no signs of sweat or nervousness, as the ball was tossed around the roulette track. Tension mounted while the ball whirled rapidly around the wheel. Then, as it gradually slowed, an almost eerie hush engulfed the area around the roulette table.

Melcher's eyes intently followed the ball around the track, but his expression remained relaxed and unemotional. As the ball spun slower, it bounced out of the track and onto the table. The anxiety around the room was intense. Temple even found himself rooting for the old man. Finally, the ball came to a stop — on number nine. Hushed murmurs shot around the table then spread throughout the casino. Melcher had lost again. It was so very close this time.

Alexander Temple studied Melcher's face. There was no emotion. No anger, no frustration, nothing. It was as if losing the money meant nothing to him at all. When Melcher stood up to leave, only then did he notice the crowd that had gathered. He shrugged his shoulders at the onlookers, then made his way through the casino, with his two bodyguards in tow. As the crowd around the roulette table dispersed, Temple headed for the exit door, too. There was nothing more he could do onboard at this point. During his previous walkthrough, he had already identified the plainclothes security guards and noted their areas of responsibility. He saw where the exit doors were located and the location of all of the CCTV surveillance monitors. Temple had also spotted fire alarm exits and employee-only access doors. And, he had planted the seed to get close to Donnetti, by making contact with the bartender. There was not much more to do until after he met with Delaware's card expert.

Temple returned to the Golden Nugget by cab and went back to his room to see if he had any unannounced visitors, but he did not go into the room. Instead, Temple glanced at the door as he walked by. The single strand of hair he placed across the edge of the door and the frame was still in place. Temple continued to the elevator, then rode it up to Karen Kiley's floor. When he reached her room, he stood to the side of the door, just in case someone else was waiting inside, ready to shoot through it. Temple knocked on the door. After a few moments, he heard Karen's voice inside the room some distance away from the door.

"Who is it?" Karen asked.

Temple heard fear in her voice. Something was wrong. "It's me," he said, then heard her make an excitable shriek. A second later he heard the door chain sliding off and then the door lock was released. Temple activated the quick draw device on his forearm and let the double-barreled derringer slide into his hand. The door swung partially open and stopped. The room was dark, the only light came from the bathroom. "Oh, Michael!" Karen gasped from behind the door. Her voice sounded more relieved than scared. Temple stepped inside the dimly lit room, reaching back, searching for the light switch. Karen pushed the door shut behind him, and immediately she was all over him, hugging him tightly. Her voice quivered, "Oh, thank God you're alive. I was so scared."

The moment Karen Kiley hugged him, Temple was aware that she was wrapped only in a bath towel. Her body was shivering violently as she pressed against him, and in her visibly panicked state, she had accidentally used his real name again. But that was not Temple's immediate concern. The darkness was. He found the light switch with his left hand and flicked it on.

Although Temple had his right arm around her back, Karen was not aware of the derringer in his hand. After scanning the room, he stepped back and held her at arm's length. She had obviously just stepped out of the shower. Her hair and body were still wet and dripping. The damp white towel wrapped snugly around her body did not cover much; her full breasts were barely contained, and the bottom of the towel hung well above her knees. Temple noticed, too, that her eyes were puffy and red. It looked as if she had been crying for some time. Temple slipped the derringer unnoticed into his front pants pocket.

"Why did you think something had happened to me?" he asked her.

Still trembling, Karen mumbled, "I heard about all those people being killed today! I didn't know if you were —"

"What people? Where?"

Karen looked confused. "Here," she said. "In Las Vegas. You mean you haven't heard about it?"

"No, I haven't. What happened?"

"It started about a half-hour after you left. I heard it on the local news. Five people were shot and killed in a barbershop not far from here. Shortly after that, two FBI agents and a third unidentified man were found murdered in a suite at the Sahara. Another guy was gunned down in a restaurant full of people. The police even found some guy dead in the men's room at the airport. His throat was cut." Karen paused briefly to catch her breath, then asked, "Al, what's going on?"

Temple gently squeezed her shoulders to calm her, then nudged her toward the bed where he encouraged her to sit down. When she sat on the side of the bed, the damp towel crept even higher up her thighs. Temple forced his eyes away from her well-muscled legs and sat down beside her. "Was it at McCarran Airport?" he asked.

"W-what?"

"The airport murder. Was it at McCarran Airport?"

"Ah — yes," she answered. "Why? Does that mean something?"

"When I arrived in Las Vegas, I saw one of Donnetti's men hanging around one of the boarding gates. He probably did the airport killing."

"And the other killings today – you think Donnetti is responsible for those, too?"

"That's my guess. Sounds like he's making his move on the opposition."

Karen shivered. "You think he knows about us?"

"I don't think so," Temple told her. *At least not yet*, he thought. "I walked past Donnetti's henchman at the airport and he didn't notice me. You must have walked right by him, too."

Karen shuddered at that revelation. It unnerved her knowing she had walked so close to death. It took her a moment to compose herself, then she finally admitted, "What you said before about this job not being right for me – you were right. I'm not cut out for this kind of work. I'm absolutely terrified right now."

Temple was glad she came to that conclusion. She definitely was not agent material, but he still needed her to complete her limited part in the mission. "What are you going to do?" he asked.

"I won't run out on you," she assured him, "but when this is over, I'm done. I'm resigning." Saying the words out loud made it real for her, and she felt as if a weight had been lifted off her shoulders. She didn't have to pretend anymore to be someone she was not. She could just be herself. Karen inhaled deeply and let the air out slowly, and for the first time since hearing about the murders, she was able to somewhat relax. It was then that she noticed her reflection in the dresser mirror and remembered she was only wrapped in a towel. She gripped the towel tighter, a reflex response at seeing herself practically naked. But in truth, she was not embarrassed. She felt the complete opposite. To her astonishment, with all of the death and imminent danger that surrounded them, she was feeling sexually aroused by his nearness and her nakedness. She tried not to look at him for fear he would know what she was thinking. This man had been her childhood crush. Back then she had the most sensual fantasies about him. Even now she remembered them in great detail. And now here she was — naked, wrapped only in a towel, sitting inches away from him. His gruff demeanor earlier didn't seem so important anymore.

Karen gripped the towel tighter and tried to push those lustful thoughts out of her mind. This was the wrong time and the wrong place. "Are you ready to make a progress report?" she blurted out, trying to shift away from her lurid thoughts.

"Now? Like this?" Temple questioned, giving her a glance up and down.

Karen pretended to not notice his glance. "Sure. Why not?" she replied, trying to sound confident. After all, they were both adults, both professionals. She certainly wasn't going to run out of the room to get dressed like a scared little girl.

"It won't be much of a report," Temple confessed, "but I'll give you what I got."

Karen Kiley activated the transmitter implanted inside her throat, with one hand, while still clutching the bath towel with the other.

Temple stole glimpses of her smooth muscular thighs, as the towel crept up her legs with each subtle movement she made.

Karen verbally repeated the progress report as he recited it to her, then she deactivated the transmitter by simply removing her hand from the activation spot on her throat. "What's next?" Karen asked.

"I've got to get Donnetti to invite me to sleep overnight aboard his boat."

"How are you going to do that?" she asked, squirming as her sexual desires mounted.

"I'm going to beat him in a high-stakes card game. He'll invite me to stay over so he can have a chance to win it back. At least, that's what the psychological profile on him indicates."

"You must be pretty good at cards."

"I will be," Temple assured her. When Karen momentarily looked away, he sneaked another peek at her magnificent breasts, now almost spilling out over the towel, but then looked away just as quickly.

"What if he starts digging into your background?" she questioned.

"That's what I'm counting on."

"I don't understand," she said.

"If he does a background check on me, he'll find only what we've planted there: that I'm a successful freelance writer, who recently sold a blockbuster novel and got an advance royalty check for a quarter of a million dollars. He'll also find out I'm a compulsive gambler — and I lose a lot."

"But you won't lose."

"No, I won't. As long as my card teacher knows his stuff." Temple stood up. "I'd better go," he said, afraid she might catch him looking at her. "I should get some rest. I'm expecting that card expert later tonight."

Karen then said with a big grin, "And when you're on a mission, you sleep when you can. See, I was learning something."

Temple smiled back at her, then started for the door.

Karen bit down on her lip. She felt utterly shameful because, for a moment, she almost asked him to stay.

Before Temple opened the door, he turned around and looked at her. She was still sitting there clutching the towel.

Their eyes lingered briefly. Temple wanted to go back and rip that damn towel off of her, but instead, he simply smiled and left her room.

Karen exhaled softly and stared at the door long after he was gone.

Temple returned to his room. Before opening his door, he checked again for signs of an intruder but found none. Temple spent the next forty-five minutes flipping through channels, watching the news about the Las Vegas massacres, as it was being called. Afterward, he laid down and tried to replay in his mind how the murders were carried out, but his thoughts were interrupted with visions from his past life. Karen Kiley's presence had sparked old memories from a time that he had not thought about for years. Now those buried memories were all coming back to him. His life had been a tragic one, on so many levels, even before the CIA blunder that sent him to prison for life, with no possibility of parole.

Chapter 11

It was in the summer of '51 that Alexander Temple was born. He was the youngest of three kids, only then his name was not Alexander Temple; it was Michael Darrin.

Young Michael and his two older sisters were children of a mixed marriage. His father, David, was a black man, who worked as a steelworker in Gary, Indiana. His white mother, Marie, was a stay-at-home mom, who formerly worked as a receptionist in a doctor's office. She was fired when her relationship with a black man was discovered. Their union was not an easy one during those turbulent times in America, but they stayed together through the adversity and made it work. They were a loving couple but disagreed bitterly on how to raise their only son.

His mother, Marie, was a pacifist, who did not like guns. She was even against the idea of her husband being so intimate with them, but there was nothing she could do about that. Her husband's fascination with guns was much too deep. She was determined to save little Michael from that evil. Marie believed firmly in nonviolence; she was going to teach Michael compassion, empathy, and love for his fellow man.

David Darrin did not share his wife's views on guns, nor did he believe that nonviolence was the way. As far as David was concerned, turning the other cheek merely gives your enemy a second chance to hit you. David was determined to teach his son how to protect himself.

Although David and Marie could not agree on the proper way to raise Michael, there was no disagreement on how to raise their two daughters, Becky and Sue. They agreed that their girls should be raised as proud, respectful young women with good educations. Due to the recent advances in civil rights and women's rights, they both believed their girls would one day do well in the workforce and not become dependent on some man. Keeping potential boyfriends at bay during both their daughters' formative years would be crucial.

As the Darrin children grew, each developed different and distinct personalities. Their eldest daughter, Becky, was energetic, full of spunk, very precocious and outspoken like her father. Other children in her 3rd-grade class tended to gravitate toward her. The middle child, Sue, was a shy 2nd grader who seemed content to not mingle much with others. Michael, still not in school, was not yet the target for parental control. But the years flew by quickly, and when Michael turned ten, David secretly began teaching his young son how to protect himself. David had been a street fighter in his younger years. By necessity, he taught himself to fight, when he was in high school, just to survive Gary's notorious east side. So, when David was alone with his son, he preached incessantly, "Never be afraid of a fight. Never fear any man. He may be bigger than you, stronger than you, and you may lose, but you don't run. A man who runs is not a man. He's a coward, and no damn good to anybody, especially himself. A quitter is also a coward. You don't ever quit in the middle of a fight, as long as conscious breath remains in your body. You keep fighting until you drop from exhaustion, then you get your ass back up and fight some more. Fight to win. Take crap from nobody. Be a man."

After nearly two years of intense – some might say, brutal – physical training, at the hands of his father, Michael Darrin learned to street fight. While teaching Michael to fight, David also started taking his son on regularly scheduled camping trips with the guys. In truth, those trips were actually hunting trips with the guys. Despite his wife's objections to guns, David firmly believed it was not only his obligation, but his right as a father to teach his son the use of firearms. He did not want his son growing up to be a sissy. Guns were a man's turf. He would not allow his son to grow up afraid to handle them.

Not long after the covert camping trips began, David was delighted to learn his son exhibited a real flair for firearms and was rapidly becoming an excellent marksman. He was proud of his boy. *A real chip off the old block*, David beamed. A man's son was his bid for immortality, the carrying on of his name. Watching a son grow into a man was almost like having a second chance at life. What father could ask for anything more?

Although young Michael's father's dominant influence left the greatest impression on him, Michael still grew into the son both his parents wanted. He had his father's two-fisted ways, but still, he had his mother's temperament, compassion, and patience.

The last hunting trip Michael was ever to go on, with his dad, occurred during spring break of his second year in junior high school. The three-day trip went well, and as usual, the target shooting garnered the most attention. Everyone was in awe of young Michael. At thirteen years old, he could already shoot as accurately as most of the men.

At the end of their hunting trip, the group drove back to Gary in a convoy of cars. David and Michael laughed and joked most of the way back. One by one, the cars dropped out of the convoy and went their separate ways. As David got closer to his own home, he looked at his son and smiled. Michael understood its meaning and returned it. *It was always nice to come home.* Suddenly, David stopped smiling. Michael did not yet know why, but a moment later he did. Parked along the curb, in front of their house, were about eight police cars. Several policemen had congregated on the front lawn. The front door to their house was open, with some of the cops casually walking in and out. David stomped on the brakes and threw the car into park. Forgetting about Michael, he jumped out of the car and ran past the policemen, who were milling around the yard. No one tried to stop him. They knew who he was. Michael followed his father into the house, at a distance. Once inside, the strangest feeling washed over Michael. It was eerie and unsettling.

More policemen stood in the hallway leading to his parents' bedroom, but Michael, standing in the living room, could not see what was going on in there. He saw his father push his way into the bedroom, past two officers who were insisting he not go in. A moment later, an unholy howl, vaguely resembling his father's voice, blasted his ears.

When the two officers looked away, Michael ran into the bedroom. There were so many people standing around, he could not see his dad. He was, however, acutely aware of a terrible rancid odor. After Michael squeezed by some of the men in the room, his eyes widened as they met the grisly sight before him. His sister, Becky, lay dead on his parents' bedroom floor, her dress pushed up around her waist. Her panties and bra had been torn off and lay on the carpet in a heap next to her. Blood stained the carpet between her thighs. More blood pooled on the floor under her head. Becky's eyes were still open, as though she were staring directly at Michael for help. The terrible suffering she had endured was still evident on her face. Michael felt suddenly nauseous, but nothing came up. He could hear a man somewhere in the room trying to console his father, who had completely broken down and was crying like a baby. Then suddenly his father yelled out in a panicked frenzy, "Where's my wife and Sue?"

Michael heard someone behind him say, "They weren't here when it happened, but your wife found the bod — found her this way. She took it pretty hard. Had to be sedated. Medics took her to the hospital for observation. Your other daughter went with her."

Michael closed his eyes tight and shook his head, trying to wake up from this hideous nightmare, but when he reopened them, the nightmare was still there. Bright camera flashes went off to his right. A man was taking a series of pictures of his sister from different angles. Michael noticed that everybody in the room was staring at Becky as she lay helplessly exposed to their prying eyes. None of them made any attempt to cover her up. Nobody showed her that courtesy. Michael bolted to his sister's aid, pulling her dress down as far as it could go. Almost immediately a strong hand grabbed him from behind.

"What the hell is this kid doing in here?" the voice boomed behind him.

"Get him the hell out of here," another voice yelled.

Michael felt himself being lifted off the floor and passed to another pair of hands. He struggled to break free but to no avail. As he was being carried out of the room, he heard someone else say, "Leave the kid alone. The dead girl is his sister."

"They're not done in there yet," the man holding him replied. "He'll mess up the crime scene. Besides, he shouldn't be in there anyway."

"Then take him to the kitchen and watch him," a different voice said.

In the kitchen, Michael was put in the corner, by the dinner table, and told by a large uniformed policeman, to sit down. Michael did what he was told and the large policeman sat beside him. For the first time since entering the house, Michael began to cry. He could not forget the way Becky looked, the way she stared up at him. It was horrible. Michael could feel his stomach churning and felt nauseous again. A moment later his stomach erupted and emptied all over the table and the large policeman.

Later that evening, Darrin drove Michael to the hospital where Marie and Sue had been taken. His sister was sitting in the waiting room alone when they arrived. Her eyes were red and puffy from crying. When she saw her father and brother, she ran to them, bursting into hysterical tears.

About an hour later, Marie Darrin was brought down to her family. They all rushed to embrace her, but Marie did not respond to them. Her movements were slow. She seemed confused, as though she were in a trance or still on medication.

David was concerned by her lethargic demeanor. "Are you alright?" he asked her.

Marie stared at him but did not speak right away. After a moment she said, "My baby is dead." David hugged his wife in an attempt to console her, but she began thrashing about violently trying to get away from him. When he didn't let her go, she started screaming. It was earsplitting, uncontrollable screaming. Michael was frightened to see his mother acting in such a manner, and he began crying again. Sue started crying, too, as she held Michael tightly in her arms to comfort him. A nurse standing nearby had already called for assistance. Two men wearing blue smocks rushed over and grabbed hold of Marie. David stepped back, trembling, as the two men struggled to hold onto Marie's flailing arms. A third man, wearing a white coat, sprinkled something in a handkerchief then held it under her nose. Marie continued to resist for a moment longer, then her body gradually went limp. The two men holding Marie up carried her away. The third man turned to David. "We're going to have to take her back upstairs."

"What's wrong with her?" David asked, looking scared and confused.

"She appears to be in shock. We need to run more tests."

"You gonna keep her overnight?" David asked.

"I think it would be advisable."

David sighed deeply. "Do what you can for her, doc."

"Why don't you go on home, Mr. Darrin? Your wife is going to be heavily sedated for the rest of the night. No sense in you hanging around here. Go home and take care of your kids. If there's any change, I'll call you."

Reluctantly, David Darrin took his children home.

###

Early the next morning, David got a call from the hospital. His wife's condition had gotten much worse. She had lost all reasoning. Her mind had so deeply submerged, due to her daughter's murder, they could no longer reach her. There was nothing else they could do for her. They recommended a mental health facility. David gathered his children and rushed back to the hospital, to find Marie sitting up in bed, staring at a blank wall, her eyes fixed and dilated. She showed no awareness of their presence. For two hours, she never spoke a word and never looked in their direction. Sue realized, after that visit, her mother needed more help than her family could provide. David resisted the idea of having his wife committed. He just couldn't do that to her. *There had to be something else they could do.*

It was then that Sue, always so shy and soft-spoken, came out of her shell, by necessity, and became the mainstay of the Darrin family. She was just seventeen years old. Her first challenge was to convince her father to commit his wife. She hated the thought of institutionalizing her mother, but she knew it was the best option for her mother and their family. Sue argued this point with her father for three days. Finally, she got him to reluctantly sign the papers to have his wife committed.

During the weeks and months that followed, both Sue and Michael noticed a gradual change in their father. He started drinking more at home. Eventually, David began staying out late at night on weekends and coming home drunk, but somehow managed to maintain his day job. He had become a functional alcoholic, but his addiction was growing worse. It wasn't long before he was coming home stumbling drunk every night. One evening he didn't come home at all. The next morning, his daughter found him on the front lawn, passed out. He had been brutally beaten. His face and scalp were a bloody mess and his right eye was swollen shut. Through rips in his tattered clothing, it was evident his body was badly bruised, too. Sue noticed his wedding band and wallet were missing, even his new steel-toed boots had been ripped off his feet.

It took David Darrin several weeks to recover from that beating. For his children, it was frightening and disheartening to see their father, once such a powerful man, now reduced to a hopeless alcoholic. Sue worked desperately to hold the family together, comforting her father through his recovery and continual drinking, while trying to raise Michael the right way, even though she was only four years his senior. It was not easy, but she never complained and never let either of them down.

Fourteen months later, the police called their home with news. They caught the man who raped and murdered Becky Darrin. David sighed in relief. Finally. Justice. On the day of the trial, the Darrin family was all present in court, except for Marie, who was still institutionalized.

That day, the courtroom was unusually crowded and buzzing with conversation. An eerie hush consumed everything, as two marshals escorted the accused murderer into the room. He was a black man of about David's age. He was dressed neatly in a green print shirt, pressed slacks, and well-shined shoes. His hair was immaculately trimmed. He looked too damn clean, David thought. Too decent. No doubt the idea of some smartass defense attorney. David's jaw tightened in anger. The animal was well disguised, but they could not hide his cruel face. The child murderer made no attempt to cover up his arrogant smile, as he was led into the courtroom. David slid forward in his chair as the animal, *the animal*, was led past his seat, still smiling. Subconsciously,

David's hand moved toward the gun tucked under his belt. He brought it to ensure that justice was done. There had been some talk in the news that, "Mr. Brown" had been illegally arrested. That his rights had been violated by an overly eager, inexperienced, rookie cop. And, because of that minor technical error, the slimy defense attorney was going to insist that the judge throw out his confession and drop all charges against his client.

It was for that reason David brought the gun. For justice. If the law would not do its duty, then he would be obliged to do it for them.

As David watched the son-of-a-bitch saunter into the courtroom, with that confident smile on his face, Davis felt his own hand close around the butt of the gun in his waistband. Justice. Nowadays only the crooks got justice. Nobody gave a rat's ass about the victim. Animals like Brown were turned loose on the public every day, because some college-educated idiot claimed his client's rights were violated. The more David thought about it, the more he believed the courts were going to let Brown go free. David concluded that was why Brown looked so confident. He knew it, too. That illegal arrest rumor wasn't just talk. The law was going to let him go, even though the police had his confession on tape. David thought about his beautiful daughter, Becky, raped and murdered and cold in her grave; his wife, hopelessly insane; and his family life, ruined, because he had been reduced to a drunken bum, out of his own weakness and grief. All of this because of that bastard, who now had the gall to *smile*.

David Darrin stood up, yanked the gun from his waistband and aimed it at Brown, whose smirk quickly turned into a slack gasp of cold fear. One of the marshals made a leaping dive for David, while the other one tried to push Brown to the floor, with the intent to use his own body as a shield. Both marshals were too late. At the top of his lungs, David yelled, "Noooooo!!" and fired as many rounds into Brown's body as he could before the marshal tackled him to the floor.

David Darrin was arrested. Three months later he was convicted of the premeditated murder of P.J. Brown, and sentenced to twenty years in prison.

Sue, now nineteen years old, was able to keep Michael out of foster homes by taking responsibility for him herself. She gave up on her dream to attend college and instead got a job at the same steel mill where her father used to work. It was a dirty, grimy, labor-intensive job, but the money was good. For Sue Darrin, that was all that mattered. She didn't care what kind of job it was as long as she made enough money to take care of herself and her brother.

Eventually, Michael began his first year at Roosevelt High School. During that year, he did not date or attend after school social functions. Instead, he helped with the family finances, by working part-time in the evenings at a fast-food restaurant. Also, during that first year at Roosevelt, Michael learned rather abruptly that fights on- and off-campus were a common occurrence. It wasn't long before he was singled out and attacked. But, thanks to his father's intensive and sometimes brutal training, Michael had become quite skilled at street fighting. So, when he was attacked, he quickly dispatched his attackers, but each decisive win brought other would-be toughs out of the woodwork to challenge the new kid at Roosevelt. One by one, Michael beat them all and consequently gained the unwanted reputation of being a formidable street fighter. Although his noted reputation decreased the frequency of attacks, the assaults continued sporadically throughout his high school days. During his senior year, Michael appeared on the radar of a violent street thug named Bo Day, a well-known and feared street fighter, who many considered insane because of his viciously brutal fighting style. Bo Day was expelled from Roosevelt two years earlier but still hung out near the campus to pick up impressionable girls and to beat up school jocks. Bo Day didn't like Michael solely because of Michael's reputation for being a tough guy. He had heard the rumors from other gangbangers that Michael was the best street fighter they'd ever seen. Bo Day wanted to prove them wrong, and he wanted to do it in a very public way. One day, Bo Day followed Michael when he left school, but waited until Michael walked in front of a popular school hangout, where there would be plenty of witnesses. That's when Bo Day made his move. He rushed up behind Michael, punching him in the back of his head. Michael went down hard but instinctively rolled onto his back to keep his attacker from mounting him from behind. Michael brought his arms up quickly, in a defensive posture, to protect against the fists he knew would come. Bo Day – older, taller, and stronger – was on top of Michael instantly, throwing blows at his head, which Michael blocked. It took Michael a few seconds to get his bearings, then he saw an opening. Michael jabbed his fingers into Bo Day's eyes with such force that his attacker's head violently snapped backward. Bo Day screamed and instinctively reached up to protect his eyes. Michael grabbed Bo Day's collar and pulled him in close, then punched him with an inverted fist to the throat. Bo Day grunted, then made a harsh gurgling sound, as he tried to catch a breath. Michael rolled his attacker over onto his back, then straddled him and beat him to unconsciousness. Michael raised his fist again to throw another punch, but paused, then lowered it. There was no need to hit him again. The fight was over. As Michael walked away, he smiled inwardly. *Guess I have some of my mother in me after all.*

Michael went on to graduate from Roosevelt High School, with a full-ride academic scholarship to UC Berkley but decided not to accept it. He didn't have time for more school. He needed to go out and get a good-paying job so he could better help with the finances. It was time Sue got a break. She had given so much of herself, being more of a mother than a sister. Getting a good job now, while Sue rested, was the least he could do. When he mentioned this to Sue, she blew up. "Michael Darrin, if you turn down that scholarship, I'll never speak to you again."

"But Sue — I just thought it was about time I started pulling more of the load around here, that's all."

"You can pull your weight by going to college. Get a good education and make me proud of you. Make mama and daddy proud of you."

Michael let that sink in, then said, "I can't run off to college. I need to stay here and help."

Sue put her hands on his shoulders. "Look, Michael, why do you think I'm busting my back trying to do everything that I can for you?" Without giving him a chance to answer, she continued, "Because I want more for you than what Daddy had. You've got too much going for you to end up in the steel mills." Sue squeezed his shoulders, "You're smart. You're going to be somebody important in this world. Be that person. Don't worry about me. I'm going to be just fine. Now make me proud and take your butt on to college, you hear."

Chapter 12

At his sister's insistence, Michael headed west to San Francisco and enrolled at UC Berkley when he was eighteen years old. His first year at Berkley was the hardest, because the college routine was so new to him. He wanted so much to do well, to justify his sister's sacrifice. Michael attended classes, studied during the day and worked part-time at night in a downtown drive-in restaurant. Again, he had little time for socializing. During his second year, things were different. He loosened up and enjoyed more of the college experience. He started participating in school activities and began to make friends — and enemies. The girls at Berkley liked him. He was a big, good-looking man who projected a quiet strength and was very approachable. But a select group of guys at the University did not like the way he moved in on *their* girls. These guys were the campus toughs, the ones you just did not mess with. There was only a handful of them, but they had a big following of would-be toughs and hangers-on, and Michael was their newest target.

When Michael heard about the threat, he went directly to the toughest guy in that group, and for the first time in his life, he instigated the fight. The confrontation lasted only seconds. Michael quickly beat the bully into submission, after which he had no more trouble at Berkley.

Toward the middle of his second year, he started dating a young black student named Connie Miller. Their relationship blossomed. Almost a year later they were in love and sharing an off-campus apartment. Secretly, Michael felt guilty knowing so much happiness while his family was still suffering so much. He wondered why he was the lucky one. Two weeks before Spring Break, he got a letter from his sister. They had been writing to each other regularly for the last three years, but never more than one letter per month, so this letter alarmed him. After reading it, he felt a rush of relief. He did not have to worry about his sister, Sue, anymore. In the letter, she wrote that she had been going steady with a guy named Jerry Teller. She had not mentioned him before because she wanted to be sure about him. Now she was. Jerry asked her to marry him. The wedding would be in six months and she wanted her baby brother to give her away. The rest of the four-page letter was about *"darling Jerry."* Michael had never known his sister to flatter a man that lavishly. Yeah, she was bragging heavily, but Michael didn't mind. It made him feel good. Sue was, probably for the first time in a long time, happy. Michael could not suppress the tears that rolled down his cheeks. He was so glad for his sister and called to congratulate her. During their talk, Sue put Jerry Teller on the phone. Michael was not surprised to learn that Jerry was there and was pleasantly impressed with their conversation. Teller sounded like a good man.

Two days before Michael was to go home for Spring Break, he was home alone. Connie had already flown home that morning to visit her parents. Michael was packing a few things for his trip when he heard a knock at the door. Michael opened it to find a tall, solidly-built, middle-aged man standing there sporting a military-style haircut and clothed in a dark suit, his eyes hidden behind dark sunglasses. When the man spoke, his face was expressionless. "Mr. Darrin?"

"Yes," Michael answered curiously.

"FBI," the man said, flipping his ID holder open to show an FBI identification card and badge.

It looked official, Michael thought, but then he'd never seen one before.

"May I come in?" the agent asked.

"What does the FBI want with me?"

"May I come in?" he repeated.

Michael stepped out of the doorway and extended a hand toward the couch.

The FBI man walked in and sat down.

Michael sat on a chair across from him.

"I'll come right to the point," the FBI man said. "It's not you we're interested in. It's George Vereen that we're after."

George Vereen was Michael's next-door neighbor. Vereen was not a friend, but he seemed polite enough when they met on campus a few times in passing. Vereen was a student at Berkley, but they shared no classes.

"What do you want with him?" Michael asked.

"Vereen's real name is Boris Ivanovich. His being at Berkley is no coincidence. Ivanovich is a Soviet spy. He was sent here by the Kremlin to recruit assets. His secondary mission is to stir up the radicals at Berkley and cause as much havoc as he can, by inciting student protests and racial riots. We know this, but we can't legally prove it."

Michael was stunned. "You sure you got the right guy?"

"We're sure."

Michael stared at the agent for a moment, then asked, "Why are you telling me this?"

The FBI man asked Michael to help his bureau set a trap for Ivanovich. He explained their plans for an elaborate trap and assured Michael, if he agreed to help, he would at no time be in any physical danger and that it would be of great service to his country.

"I'm leaving town in two days," Michael told him. "When would you need my help?"

"It's going to take us three days to set things up."

Michael shook his head. "I already have my flight booked. Don't know if I can book another flight with such short notice."

"You do this for us, we'll get you rebooked on whatever day you want."

Michael paced the room as he considered the offer. "Okay," Michael finally mumbled.

"You'll help us?" the FBI agent clarified.

"Yes."

The FBI agent stood up and extended his hand.

After shaking it, Michael asked, "By the way, what's your name?"

"Dickerson Allen," he said, then started for the door. As the agent reached for the doorknob, Michael asked curiously, "How do you know I won't tip off Vereen?"

"We've checked you out thoroughly," he replied with the same blank expression he had earlier. "We know you're an honorable man, Mr. Darrin." Then he opened the door and left.

Three days later, everything had been arranged. Per instructions, Michael invited George Vereen to his apartment for a friendly little get-together with a few of his college friends, who would in actuality be FBI agents.

"It's about time we got together," Vereen had told Michael over the phone. "There are some things I would like to discuss with you."

On the evening of the party, Michael paced. The FBI men were late. They were supposed to be there before Vereen arrived. *Where the hell were they*?

When Vereen arrived, there was still no sign of the cavalry. Michael mustered his composure and let Vereen in. For fifteen minutes, Michael kept him talking, but then something went wrong. Maybe it was something Michael said. Maybe there was nervousness in his voice. Whatever it was, the Soviet agent gave him an abrupt stare. "You son-of-a-bitch," Ivanovich cursed as he stood up and pulled a gun from under his shirt. The Soviet took one step back, then with his other hand, pulled a silencer from his pants pocket and slowly started screwing it onto the end of the gun barrel. "Who's on to me — and what do they know?" Ivanovich asked calmly, his Soviet accent more predominant now.

Michael knew it didn't matter how he answered the question. This man was going to kill him. That's why he was attaching the silencer. Michael saw the barrel of the gun point briefly away from him, as Ivanovich twisted the silencer on tight. In that instant, Michael bolted toward the Soviet. He knew he only had a fraction of a second. He prepared himself to hear the gun go off and to maybe take a bullet, but he was determined to reach the Soviet before he fired a well-aimed second round.

Somehow Michael got to Ivanovich before the gun went off. They fought a vicious battle for control of the weapon, both men aware the winner would live and the loser would die. During the struggle, they fell to the floor together, both still grappling for the weapon, but the fight stopped abruptly when the gun went off. The Soviet jerked away from Michael, then staggered to his feet, but immediately fell back to the floor with a bullet hole in his chest. Michael scrambled to his feet, the gun now in his hand, and stood over the Soviet. Ivanovich stared up at him, coughing blood, his eyes in total disbelief that this nobody just killed him. He died with that dumbfounded look still on his face.

Michael Darrin couldn't believe what had just happened. He had just killed a man. A moment ago, he was fighting a Soviet spy for his life. Still dazed, Michael just stood there in shock. He had been in many fights in his life, but this was the first time someone wanted to actually kill him. Behind him, Michael could hear some commotion. He turned and saw his living room curtain open and people were gathered outside the window looking in. A few moments later a campus cop ran in. Only then did Michael realize the difficult spot he was in. He had just killed a fellow student, and there was no FBI to speak on his behalf. When Michael told his incredible story about Dickerson Allen, it was thoroughly checked out. An FBI spokesman flatly denied any knowledge of Michael Darrin's "ridiculous story" and said, "it was obviously a desperate attempt on the defendant's part to escape due punishment."

Michael was arrested and charged with murder. During his trial, Michael's girlfriend, Connie Miller, sat in the courtroom confused and teary-eyed. Sitting next to her was Michael's sister, Sue Darrin, and her fiancé, Jerry Teller. Sue cried heavily through much of the trial and, toward its conclusion, she had completely broken down. Jerry had to help her walk out of the courtroom. Two days later, just before the reading of the verdict, Jerry Teller held Sue's trembling hand. The jury announced their decision. Guilty.

Connie's eyes flooded with tears and she instinctively yelled out his name. Friends, who had come with Connie, had to help her out of the courtroom. Sue sat stunned. Her eyes met Michael's in a lingering, disbelieving stare. He could see the pain and profound emptiness in her eyes, as if she were suddenly all alone. Michael felt sorrier for her than he did for himself. He had let her down. She had always tried so hard, worked so hard, to give him a chance in this world. She had forsaken her own life, her own happiness, to become mother and father to him when he needed it most. She had assumed the burden of leadership for the Darrin family, after the death of their sister, the imprisonment of their father, and their mother's institutionalization. And now, again, she had been unjustly burdened with another tragedy.

Teary-eyed, Michael sadly watched his sister as her physical condition rapidly deteriorated before his eyes. When the two marshals came to take him away, Michael gave Jerry Teller a pointed look and Jerry nodded back, indicating he would take care of her. Sue Darrin cried hysterically as she watched her baby brother being taken away.

One month later, during the sentencing phase, the judge rendered his verdict: life imprisonment with no possibility of parole.

Three days before Michael was to be shipped from the city jail to a state penitentiary – ironically, the same prison where his father was also doing time for murder – Dickerson Allen walked into the city jail. This time Allen identified himself as a corporate attorney, newly assigned to the Darrin case, and asked to speak to Michael. When Michael first saw him, a sudden rush of relief flushed through his body. He could not suppress the stupid grin stretching across his face. "Boy, am I glad to see you. I thought you guys had run out on me." Then Michael noticed Dickerson Allen was not smiling. Allen was also now wearing a mustache and goatee, too thick to have just grown it.

"We have a problem," Allen said pointedly.

Michael's happy feelings deflated like a balloon.

Allen continued, "Unfortunately, our hands are tied now."

"What the hell is that supposed to mean?" Michael snapped.

"The prep work we did on Ivanovich was illegally obtained. We couldn't testify at your trial, because how we gathered that intel and who gathered it would have been exposed in open court. That would have been one hell of a mess."

Michael blurted out, "What the fuck are you talking about? I'm in jail on a murder charge. In three days, they're sending me to a fuckin' penitentiary for life. What in the hell could be more messed up than that?"

"Look, Darrin, I told you I was sorry for —"

"Fuck all that!" Michael yelled. "All I want to know is what are you people going to do to fix this."

"Officially, there's nothing we can do."

Michael gripped the cell bars tighter and glared at Dickerson Allen. "You son-of-a-bitch. I got involved in this thing to help you guys out —"

Allen cut him off. "Simmer down. We haven't abandoned you. Why do you think I'm here?" Allen waited until Michael regained his composure, then continued, "We can help you — off the record. But, as we see it, you only have two options. Which one you choose is up to you."

Michael took a deep breath to calm down, then asked, "What are the options?"

"The obvious first choice is to do nothing. Go to prison. Maybe you can find a smart attorney who can get your conviction overturned on appeal."

Michael knew there was no way he could get his sentence overturned. He killed a man. There were witnesses at the scene. There was nobody to back up his claim of self-defense. And the FBI publicly called him a liar. "You said there were two options," Michael pressed.

"The second choice is a bit more radical." Allen studied Michael's facial reaction as he explained, "My department can arrange a jailbreak for you. After we get you out, we'll have to fake your death, give you a new identity, and set you up somewhere else."

Michael just stared back at him. That option caught him completely off guard. He didn't know what to say.

Allen stared intently at Michael. "You understand, this option means total separation from your life as you know it. You will never see or communicate with Connie Miller, or your sister, Sue, or your parents ever again. Everything you own in this world will have to be left behind. That's your second choice. It's that or prison. You decide."

Michael stood there dumbfounded. That was an impossible decision. How could he walk away from Connie, the girl he had hoped one day to marry? How could he let his family think he was dead, especially Sue? She had already suffered enough in her life, with all of the Darrin family tragedies. How could he do this to her? But — to go to prison, for the rest of his life, was equally inconceivable. Michael's thoughts were whirling on a collision course. Either option would devastate his loved ones and, from their point of view, he wasn't sure which one would be worse. Michael hated the FBI for putting him in this untenable situation.

"What's your decision?" Allen asked.

"How long do I have before you need an answer?"

"I need to know before I leave this cell."

Michael agonized over the pain either choice would bring to Connie and his family.

Dickerson Allen moved closer to the cell door. "This is a one-time offer," he added.

In the midst of the turmoil racking his brain, Michael had to face one tangible reality. He was going to lose his family no matter what decision he made. Maybe his quick death would be easier for them, in the long run, rather than them enduring his life sentence in prison.

"Get me out of here," Michael croaked with bitter remorse.

With no show of emotion, Dickerson Allen only nodded before leaving the cell. On the day Michael was to be transferred to the state penitentiary, Allen's people had the escape set so precisely, Michael was utterly amazed at the ease in which he got away. Duplicate cell keys were smuggled in to him; various diversions caused the deputies to be away from their stations in the section of the jail where he was being held. There was a car, fully gassed, with a key hidden above the sun visor, waiting conveniently in the alley behind the jail. Michael simply drove away. He met Dickerson Allen out of town, at a prearranged location. Allen told him his phony death had already been put into motion. "A few hours from now," Allen explained, "authorities will find your getaway car in Oakland, California. It'll be wrecked and burning in a ditch. The body inside will be so badly charred, a positive visual ID will be impossible."

"The body?" Michael questioned.

Allen stared back at him. "We did a little grave digging," he said. Then he forced a weak smile and added, "You don't think we went out and killed somebody, do you?"

Michael didn't know what to think. The FBI are the good guys. Right? Surely, they didn't kill somebody to make this escape plan work. But they did illegally break him out of jail. With a cautious stare, Michael curiously asked, "What about my fingerprints and dental records? Once the authorities check the corpse, they'll know the body in the car is not mine."

"Don't worry about it. That's already been handled."

"How?"

"Your fingerprints and dental records have been systematically expunged, everywhere, meaning they don't belong to you anymore. They've been transferred to the corpse in your getaway car. We're still working on your new records, but rest assured, there won't be any doubt the body in the burning car is yours."

Michael momentarily dwelled on the dire ramifications of his decision. Although he had agreed to this deception, now somehow, with the pending news of his death about to go public, this all seemed so hauntingly real, and wrong. Michael gazed into Allen's eyes. "What now?" Michael drearily asked, resigned to the fact that his life was no longer his own.

"Your new name is Joseph Johnson. You were born and raised in Philadelphia. The other particulars you'll need to know about your new life are in this dossier. On the last page, there is an unlisted bureau number. Don't call that number unless it's damn important." Allen passed the file to Michael. "Read it, then destroy it. This is your life now.

Good luck, Joseph Johnson."

Michael looked at him strangely when he heard the sound of that name used to address him, but he knew he'd better get used to it, because Michael Darrin was dead.

Chapter **13**

Three months later, the man who now called himself Joseph Johnson was on a troop transport heading to Vietnam as a private in the United States Army. He was livid when he found out the new life the FBI built for him was in the middle of a war zone. When he called the unlisted phone number located on the last page of the dossier, he was fuming mad. "You son-of-a-bitch. The deal we made was for a new life. You didn't say anything about going to Vietnam."

"The deal we made," Allen calmly reminded him, "did not specify what new life you would assume, just that you would be reborn — and you were. We lived up to our agreement. So get used to it JJ, you're in the Army now."

Johnson sat on the troop transport with clenched teeth. The bastards were so eager to make this happen they didn't even send him to boot camp. His enlistment paperwork and boot camp records were forgeries, just like his identity papers. The FBI fucked him good. They arranged his jailbreak, put him up in a Philly hotel for three months and now, here he is, on his way to Vietnam as an Army private with no training whatsoever. It was as if they were intentionally sending him there to die. He couldn't even blow the whistle on them. All he had waiting for him as Michael Darrin was a prison cell.

After being in the jungles of Vietnam for months, Joseph Johnson, like many of the GIs over there, learned to adapt to the harsh day-to-day frightening reality of war. But, with men dying and being maimed all around him, the foreboding feeling of death was always there. As Johnson became more hardened and jaded in his new life, he felt his mother's influence fading further away.

During his second year in country, he worked almost entirely on special assignments. His sergeant became aware of his marksmanship ability and passed the word up the chain. Eventually, Johnson was transferred to sniper school and later assigned to sniper detail in support of the ground troops. During most of his sniper missions, he worked closely with Army and Marine detachments. Occasionally, he would go out on special ops missions for high-value targets. On one such mission, he was assigned to an Army Ranger detachment in Dong Tam. He was supposed to meet the team in two days. He had plenty of time to spare, so he hopped into a jitney, just outside of the base and told the driver to drop him off in My Tho.

My Tho was the red-light district outside of Dong Tam. It was a dirty little town crammed with bars and hotels; the scent of weed and hash was so strong it burned the insides of your nose. Vendors sat on various corners selling something they called pork meat, but Johnson was acutely aware that there weren't many dogs roaming the streets in that neighborhood. Maybe there was no correlation. Maybe.

As Johnson walked down the street, old out-of-date American music blared from many of the bars. Bar whores gathered in the doorways. Some made offers of fantastic bedroom abilities. Others exposed their bodies in quick glimpses, to make their offers more tempting.

As Johnson walked past the bar named 'Pussy Galore', one of the girls in the doorway ran over and latched onto his arm and pulled him inside. The place was crowded with drunk soldiers. Cigarette smoke bloomed like a thick fog, blanketing much of the room. A female bartender was entertaining the eight or nine soldiers who lined the bar. She was holding the water dispenser gun in her right hand, while pumping her left hand slowly in a seductive manner, up and down the connected water line as if she were giving a man a handjob. Then she started pumping her left hand faster. As she did this, she shot spurts of water from the dispenser. The effect was amazingly suggestive, and the soldiers at the bar loudly expressed their appreciation by yelling an assortment of vulgarities. As an encore, she spurted several shots of water into her mouth, then licked her lips with her long tongue. The drunk soldiers at the bar loved it.

The jukebox in the corner was playing one of those songs strippers dance to, with the heavy repeating thud from a bass drum. The bar girl pulled Johnson in the direction of the crowd gathered around a small stage. She took him to a position where he could see over the heads of the others standing there. She wasn't about to let him go, though. Whatever money he was ready to spend, it was going to be hers.

On stage, Johnson could see an American GI weaving in a drunken stupor while trying to stand at attention. He was fully dressed in Army greens, but his fly was unzipped and his erect penis was out for all to see. Two naked Vietnamese girls were stroking and grabbing his erection, as they danced around him. After a few moments of this, the two girls pulled the GI down to the floor, then pushed him onto his back. Both girls then got back up and stood with their feet straddling his body and gyrated their hips above him. When the drumbeat slowed, the girl that stood above his hips squatted until she was taking in his erection. The other girl sat on his face and started grinding her hips.

The Vietnamese girl holding Johnson's arm reached around and grabbed a handful of his crotch. "You real horny," she said. "Come with me, I show you very good private show."

Johnson stepped back away from her and shook his head. "I'm a butterfly, you don't want me."

"Shit," she cursed. "Everybody butterfly. Nobody faithful. I no mind."

"No, little one. I've got a mean old lady. If she caught us together, she would hurt you bad," he lied.

"Don't worry 'bout her. I no scared. Let's go fuck."

Johnson pulled back again. "No, I'd better not." He left the Pussy Galore then proceeded down the street, bypassing the other titty bars. At the end of the block was one of the few bars in My Tho generally not frequented by bar girls. Johnson went inside and found it mostly empty. Four older sailors, in Navy whites, sat at the bar drinking. A few locals were sprinkled throughout the room and a woman sat alone at a table by the back wall.

Instead of his usual drink, Johnson ordered a beer at the bar, then he slid into a booth facing the door. As he took his first sip, he thought about his family in Gary. That life seemed so long ago. Johnson let his mind wander back for a moment, then he guzzled his drink down. As he did this, the woman sitting alone got up and walked by his table. She continued over to the jukebox and flipped through the song selections. It took her a few moments, but she eventually chose a sad romantic melody, Ooo Baby Baby, by Smokey Robinson and the Miracles. While the music played, she stood there and listened to the entire song. When it was over, she returned to her seat.

Johnson recognized the Vietnamese woman as she walked by. He had seen her before, in Saigon. She had a reputation there amongst the GIs. They called her the Sex-Machine. The talk was, she was a sexual freak. There was nothing she wouldn't do to please a man – or a woman, if the price was right. Johnson had never been with her, but he heard the wild stories.

Johnson watched her from across the room. She was not her usual self. She seemed sad and in deep thought. When Johnson saw her wipe away a tear with her index finger, he saw her in a different light. Not as the whore from Saigon, but as a woman with normal problems, who was unfortunately born into poverty, where prostitution was a way of life. Johnson walked over to her table to console her. "You look lonely sitting there alone. May I join you?"

She turned her head down and stared into her drink without a word. When Johnson sat down without an invitation, the Vietnamese woman frowned. "You no care 'bout me. You want some of this, I know," she said, pointing between her legs.

"What!" Johnson exclaimed, genuinely surprised.

"Don't bullshit me," she snapped. "I no baby san."

Joseph Johnson snapped back. "If that's what I wanted, why would I be in this place when all the willing women are right down the street? I just thought you might be lonely. Thought you needed somebody to talk to. Guess I thought wrong." Johnson stood up and started to walk back to his table.

The Vietnamese woman looked surprised when he turned to walk away, and at how easily he gave up. Maybe she was wrong about him. "Why you so mad for?" she called after him.

"I'm not mad."

"Then why you go way angry?"

"Look honey, I'm no baby san either. I know when I'm not wanted."

"Sorry," she whispered. "GI always hit on me. You sit down, ok?"

Johnson hesitated for a moment, then sat back down and stared into her sad eyes. She was trying hard to fight back tears. "Are you alright?" he asked.

"I am ok. I have much on my mind."

"What's your name?" he asked her.

"In Saigon, I called Sex Machine," she replied matter-of-factly. She was neither bragging nor embarrassed.

"I didn't ask you what you were called. I asked what your name was."

The remark caught her totally off guard and touched her deeply. He was the only man who had ever expressed interest in her as a person. She choked back her emotions, then responded almost shyly, "My name Ho Dinh Sing. What your name?"

"Everybody calls me JJ."

She looked at him with an impish grin. "I didn't ask you what everybody call you, I ask you for name."

They both got a big laugh out of that, then he told her his name was Joseph Johnson. They talked for about an hour. Their conversation was flowing and easy. Finally, Ho Dinh Sing stopped talking and stared at him with a curious gaze.

"What?" Johnson asked.

"Let's go my sister house. She not there," Sing said.

Johnson didn't immediately answer.

"You already got girlfriend?" she asked.

Johnson thought back to his former girlfriend and the life that he would never have again. Then he said, "No. No girlfriend."

"You very respectful soldier. We should go now," Ho Dinh Sing urged, then took his hand and led him outside. They got in a rickshaw at the corner and arrived at her sister's house within minutes. Johnson let her get undressed first, then he slowly and very cautiously slid his index finger into her vagina. It was not meant to sexually stimulate her, but to assure himself that it was safe. It was something he began doing after that terrible thing happened last year. His platoon had bested the Viet Cong in a two-hour firefight and had taken prisoners, one of whom surprisingly was a woman. In a wartime situation, when prisoners are captured in the field, no distinction is made between the sexes. Everyone must be searched immediately. Unfortunately, once the search began on the girl, things got out of hand. Sergeant Miller started fondling her body through her clothing as she stood helpless before the entire squad. The sergeant and three other soldiers dragged her off into the bush. The rest of the squad was shocked by the actions of their sergeant but were too afraid to interfere.

Seconds later an unholy scream erupted behind the

bushes. Sounded like it came from Sergeant Miller. A dozen rapid shots rang out after that, followed by panicked, horrified yells from the three soldiers.

As the yelling and screaming began, Johnson was just returning to camp from reconnaissance. He did not know about the assault on the girl. When the rest of the squad ran toward the screams with their guns drawn, Johnson followed them. What he saw behind the bushes turned his stomach. Sergeant Miller was dead, flat on his back in the dirt, blood everywhere. His pants were down around his ankles, his dick was cut into several slivers and he had bled profusely. The female prisoner was dead, too; she had been shot multiple times by the other three soldiers.

Johnson was later told about the assault on the woman and how medics had discovered a removable rubber cup full of razor blades inside her vagina. When the sergeant jammed his dick into his helpless victim, it was immediately slashed to pieces. The other three soldiers, waiting to rape her, were horrified at seeing Miller in the worst kind of pain. They panicked and shot her to death. Johnson never learned their judicial fate, but due to that incident, he wasn't going to take any chances. Before going any further with Ho Dinh Sing, he checked her first. Once he was satisfied that she was safe, he found out that night, the soldiers in Saigon had not exaggerated. She was insatiable.

Ho Dinh Sing was asleep when Johnson left in the morning to head back to base. When he dragged into his hooch, he saw a big ugly bastard lying fully dressed on his rack. It was his friend, Dalson. Johnson didn't know Dalson's first name. He never asked and Dalson never volunteered it. Dalson was a tough man, who always appeared to be combat-ready, but didn't talk much about his work as an Army Ranger. Maybe that's why they got along so well.

Johnson didn't talk much about his work as a sniper, either.

"What the hell are you doing on my rack?" Johnson yelled at him.

Dalson woke up immediately, with a deadly air of readiness that confirmed to Johnson that Dalson was a dangerously volatile man. Johnson made a mental note to never sneak up on Dalson again, ever.

"Easy, JJ," Dalson said, smiling now. Then he glanced around the hooch. "Nice digs. You snipers clearly get the best accommodations."

"Fortunes of war," Johnson said with a grin. Then Johnson stopped smiling and asked, "What's up, Dalson?"

Dalson got off the bed and stood close to Johnson. "They got a mission for you."

"They?" Johnson questioned.

"The CIA."

"The CIA? What do they have to do with this?"

"They're involved in everything over here."

"So, this is not a standard setup and support op."

"No, it's not. The target is a South Vietnamese official."

"I thought the South Vietnamese were on our side," Johnson interjected.

"They are. But Senator Tran Van Bao has been secretly working with the North

Vietnamese Government."

"The CIA is positive about that?" Johnson questioned.

"They have an informant."

"And they're just gonna take his word?"

"They put a tail on the senator and found out everything the informant said was true." Dalson glanced cautiously over his shoulder, then continued, "Later today, the senator will be in Saigon, secretly meeting with some North Vietnamese officials, to verbally pass on information the United States and South Vietnam would rather not have leaked. We have to stop him before that meeting."

"Where do we intercept him?" Johnson asked.

"Saigon. You'll be shooting from a room balcony at the President Hotel. At precisely 1600 hours, several things are going to happen. On the roof top patio of the President Hotel, two CIA agents, disguised as soldiers, will cause a diversion by taking potshots at each other. Other agents disguised as MPs will rush up and arrest them before the real military police get there. This diversion will also get the Vietnam National Police moving toward the President Hotel, too. While that is going on, a Vietnamese girl, the one who has been talking to the CIA, will lead the senator out onto an open patio roof just over a mile away. That's why they picked you: you've made that distance before. The question is, can you do it again?"

"I can do it," Johnson assured him.

"One more thing — they want you to shoot the girl too."

Johnson gave him a curious look, to which Dalson answered, "The CIA knows the girl is working both sides. They've known it for a long time, but because they knew it, they could control the outgoing information. Since some of the incoming stuff was good, like this Tran Van Bao intel, they kept her around."

"So why take her out now?" Johnson questioned.

"She wore out her usefulness. It was her intel to the NVA that got General Westrick killed last month."

"Yeah, I heard about that ambush," Johnson said. "Will they be alone on the roof?"

"No. The senator will be heavily guarded by South Vietnamese soldiers. They don't know about the senator, so they'll just be doing their job in trying to protect him. Your job is to take him out, and the girl, in that order. When you get to the President Hotel, there will be a room ready for you. Go out on the balcony and look east, northeast. Your target area is the only flat-top building, with an outdoor pool in that direction. Arrangements have also been made for the rooms around yours to be occupied by our people or vacant."

"When do we leave?" Johnson asked.

Dalson glanced at his watch. "Ten minutes."

After Dalson left, Johnson walked over to his footlocker and took out some extra .45 magazine clips and a lightweight, but heavy-duty, rifle case. The watertight case contained a modified .308 Remington, with a Redfield Accu-Trac 3x-9x – 40mm scope. Beside it lay a starlight scope, packed snugly in a custom foam interior. Johnson checked his .45 caliber sidearm, then grabbed his rifle case and went outside.

Dalson was waiting for him beside an M35 cargo truck, with a camouflage canvas cover. Eight Army Rangers were seated in the back of the truck. An Army grunt was standing next to Dalson. Johnson guessed he was the driver. After Johnson walked over to them, Dalson led the sniper off to the side and whispered, "There's something else. There's an ex-military advisor on base. He's a full bird colonel now and he wanted to hitch a ride with us to Saigon. I said no, but somebody pulled some strings. We gotta take him."

Johnson saw a colonel walking toward them, cradling an M16 under his right arm. "That him?" Johnson asked.

"Yeah, that's him. Colonel Richard Tomson."

Johnson already knew his name. Every American sniper in Vietnam knew him by sight. Colonel Richard Tomson was well known for his outspoken views, and he made it clear he didn't like snipers, theirs or ours. In the Colonel's opinion, all snipers were cowards.

Conversely, American snipers privately referred to him

as Colonel Dick.

The Colonel sneered at Johnson as he approached. Then he turned his attention to Dalson. He respected the Rangers. They were real men. Real soldiers. But the colonel was angry. They were leaving late because that damn sniper didn't get back to base on time. The colonel puffed his chest out and vented at Dalson, "He's here! Now let's get the hell out of here!"

Dalson ignored the Colonel's rudeness and simply asked, "You riding up front or in back?"

"I'll ride in back with the men," he said, then climbed in ahead of Johnson.

Dalson and the Army private seated themselves upfront, then drove slowly out of the protective gates and onto the asphalt road leading to the main highway. Everything was quiet except for the Colonel's mouth. He started rattling off about his knowledge of the Cong. No one was interested but, out of respect, they pretended to listen. After a while, Dalson rapped on the side of the truck. It was a signal to the men in the back that they were about to enter a stretch of road referred to as Ambush Alley. Everyone automatically rechecked their weapons. The Colonel was quiet now. They were all quiet — and ready.

After what seemed an endless stretch of road, Dalson hit the side of the truck with his hand again. At that signal, they all sat back and relaxed, but remained vigilant. The Colonel started up again. "I really didn't expect any trouble back there. I know how the V.C. think. They wouldn't dare —"

Just then, a Viet Cong soldier, loaded down with explosive charges, jumped into the back of the truck with them. The charges were wrapped around his chest like a vest. Before anybody could make a move for him, the little bastard pulled the detonator cord at his side.

Chapter 14

Everyone in the back of the truck drew into tiny balls, trying to protect their heads and bodies from the imminent explosion. The Ranger closest to the threat yelled, "bomb," and dove on top of the suicide bomber, tackling him to the floor. Everyone else waited, but the explosion never came. Slowly, cautiously, they uncoiled their bodies. The Viet Cong looked just as surprised as they did, then he tried to push his way out of the truck. The Rangers grabbed him and started removing the explosive charges from his body.

The truck made a sudden jerky stop. Dalson ran around to the back entrance, wondering what the commotion was all about. He was surprised to see the Viet Cong. "Where the hell did he come from?"

Colonel Tomson stood up and spat out, "The son-of-a-bitch jumped in just after we left Ambush Alley."

Dalson looked at the Viet Cong, then at his team, and said, "We can't take him with us."

Everybody in the truck knew what Dalson meant. Colonel Tomson blurted out, "Yeah, let's kill this gook and leave his body stinking on the side of the road for his buddies to find."

One of the Rangers cautioned Dalson, "Rules of engagement."

Dalson said, "This guy is a suicide bomber. As far as I'm concerned, the moment he jumped into the back of this truck, he was already a dead man."

"Hooah!" one of the Rangers chanted.

Dalson made eye contact with each of his team members, then returned to his seat in the front of the truck. Shortly after the truck started down the road, the sound of a .45 caliber revolver firing split the silence.

The remainder of the drive to Saigon was uneventful. When they arrived at the President Hotel, Colonel Tomson got out and walked off, without so much as a thank you.

Dalson told Johnson they would meet him there, at the curb, when it was over.

Johnson entered the hotel through the large double doors, retrieved his room key at the desk, then took the elevator to his room on the fourth floor. It was 1350 hours. He called the desk and asked for a wake-up call at 1530 hours, then he laid down fully dressed and went to sleep. The time went by quickly. It seemed like he had just gone to bed when he received the wake-up call. Johnson grabbed his case, stepped out onto his balcony and looked east, northeast. The building he was looking for wasn't hard to spot. Johnson assembled his sniper rifle, with the Redfield scope and mini tripod. He loaded the Remington with a full clip, though he didn't plan on using more than two rounds.

It was 1540 hours. Johnson assumed the prone position and swiveled his weapon on the tripod until he had the target area in his sights. He made some scope adjustments for range, wind, and drop, then zeroed in on people who were already lounging on the patio. At 1550 hours, the senator stepped out of the elevator and onto the patio. Clinging to his arm was a young Vietnamese woman dressed in a light pink mini dress and high boots. At a modest distance behind them were two, armed South Vietnamese soldiers.

Johnson decided to do a head shot on the senator. He knew, once he took the shot, the Vietnamese girl would be harder to take out. She would most likely start running along with everyone else on the rooftop, to make it look like she was not involved. Johnson moved his scope sight back to the woman and focused on her face, then abruptly backed his eye off the scope in disbelief. After the initial shock passed, he reacquired the target. It was her. Ho Dinh Sing. He had just spent the night with her. Now she was his secondary target. Johnson had to put last night out of his mind as he watched her through his scope, because now, he had to decide on the best way to kill her. After a quick assessment, Johnson decided on a triangle shot, between chin and nipples. If, however, she was running away, he'd go for upper center back. Johnson was ready. All that remained now was the green light to fire.

Ho Dinh Sing led the senator to the bar and ordered drinks, then they sat on poolside chairs. She made sure the senator was facing in the direction of the President Hotel. The two South Vietnamese soldiers took their positions near the senator.

Johnson adjusted the crisscross pattern in his scope on

the senator's forehead and waited. Approximately six minutes later, he heard the signal, as shots barked out on the roof above him. From that moment on, Johnson's movements were sheer instinct. His cheek stayed in firm contact with the stock of the weapon. Both eyes were open as he looked through the scope. His finger started to depress the trigger during the natural pause in breathing. The trigger pull was smooth and gradual enough to not upset the sight alignment. He was relaxed and trained not to react to the noise and recoil of the weapon.

As the rifle fired in his hands, Johnson knew the round would hit its target before the sound even reached the poolside attendees. Still, he kept his sights on the senator, until the bullet tore into his head. Johnson then pivoted his weapon on the tripod to reacquire his second target. As he had anticipated, pure pandemonium had erupted on the rooftop patio. Everybody there was scrambling to the elevator or diving for the floor. One of the South Vietnamese soldiers had flung his body across the senator's, not yet aware he was dead. The other soldier had his weapon out, but not sure where the shot came from.

Johnson found Ho Dinh Sing lying on the floor, looking just as terrified as everybody else. She was a good little actress. Johnson started his trigger pull but stopped when several people lying on the patio floor, including Ho Dinh Sing, made a dash for the elevator. Before she got lost in the crowd, Johnson pulled the trigger for the second time. The bullet dropped by the time it reached her, but still caught her in the right calf. Ho Dinh Sing went down hard, but nobody running for the elevator stopped to help her.

Ho Dinh Sing's face twisted in pain, as she clutched her calf, then stared back toward the President Hotel, with the most dumbfounded look on her face. Before she could formulate her next thought, Johnson's third bullet slammed into her face.

Through his scope, Johnson saw her head snap back as red mist exploded into the air. Johnson backed into his room and quickly broke down his weapon, carefully packing the pieces back in the case. He took the elevator down to the lobby. When he got outside, he saw Dalson and his men across the street, standing alongside two jeeps. As Johnson approached them, Dalson got behind the wheel of the trailing jeep and motioned for Johnson to sit up front with him.

When Johnson sat down, Dalson merely looked at him. Johnson returned his gaze with a nod.

The Ranger sitting behind Dalson saw the nod, and barked in a muffled voice, "HOOAH."

Johnson sank in his seat and clutched his rifle case tighter. He didn't feel like celebrating.

Johnson spent a total of four years in country, three years of which he served as a sniper. He learned, while in that position, to accept and even appreciate his role in this war. The way Johnson looked at his job was simple. He was not shooting helpless victims at long distance, he was shooting targets, state-sanctioned targets, and protecting his brothers in uniform at the same time. Due to his efficiency, and lack of outward emotion, one soldier called him an iceman. That moniker, The Iceman, stuck to him the remainder of his government-arranged enlistment. But now, with his military career almost over, it was time he started planning the next phase of his life. Johnson had mixed feelings about going back to the states. As Joseph Johnson, there was nowhere to go that was real. He couldn't go back to his former life either, because Michael Darrin was dead.

When he finally got his orders to go home, he left Vietnam without fanfare and arrived back in Philadelphia, where Dickerson Allen's people arranged for him to have a house, a bank account, and a life. After several weeks of being back in the world, Johnson had difficulty dialing back his heightened sense of readiness. Spending four years in a war zone, left him a bit on edge, and he had no outlet to make that transition easier. With no family, no friends, and no direction, Johnson gradually started drinking heavily and thinking about the soldiers still in harm's way. He also thought about his father, his mother, and his sister. He thought about Connie, too. The more he thought about his past life, the more he drank. After months of struggling to fit into his new life, he decided to call Dickerson Allen. He wanted to reenlist. There was nothing for him in Philadelphia. The only life he knew as Joseph Johnson was in Vietnam.

Allen promised to call him back in two hours, three at the most. Allen didn't do either. Instead, he showed up at Johnson's door three days later with a bombshell revelation. Allen admitted he was not with the FBI. He never was. He was actually a CIA officer in the Special Activities Division. He had lied to Johnson, ever since they first met, because the agency's mission to trap the Soviet dissident, on an American college campus, was illegally initiated despite being government-sanctioned. When young Michael Darrin killed the Soviet, they had to come up with plan B, and thus Joseph Johnson was born. But now, he'd been authorized to offer Johnson a much more fulfilling opportunity as a CIA agent. He would still have to go through spy training at Camp Peary, but with that training and his current skill set, he would be an enormous asset to the government.

Johnson felt completely blindsided. All this time he thought Allen was with the FBI, only to find out that he was a CIA officer. That was a lot to process. Angrily Johnson snapped, "How do I know you're not lying now? How do I know who the hell you really are?"

Dickerson Allen calmly replied, "Look in the phone book. Find the number for the CIA and call it." He handed Johnson a business card. "When they answer, just read the alpha-numeric code handwritten on the back of the card. They will transfer you to someone else who'll know that I'm here."

Johnson made the call, and the CIA ultimately confirmed Allen's identity. Johnson hung the phone up. "Now what?"

"It's up to you," Allen said. "You can take my new offer or stay here in Philly."

"I can't stay here," Johnson declared. "I'll take the deal."

"Alright. Just sit tight for a few days, until we can arrange your new identity."

"My what?" Johnson asked, surprised.

"We're going to have to kill Joseph Johnson off."

"What the hell for? Joseph Johnson isn't even a real person."

"That's true, but if you make it as an agent, and then get caught spying in a foreign country, the fact that you were a former Army sniper is going to be problematic for you."

Johnson nodded. "I see your point."

"What we need for you is an average background. Something that won't set off alarm bells if someone runs a background check on you."

"What happens to me if you kill off Johnson and I don't make it as an agent?"

"Don't worry. We won't get rid of Johnson until we know for sure that you made the cut. In the meantime, we'll arrange for you to receive an extended leave of absence from your job, so you can go into training."

Johnson stared hard at Allen. "Before I do this, you have to do something for me first."

"What's that?"

"I have to know how my family is doing."

Allen gave him a stern look. "That's not a good idea."

"I have to know," Johnson insisted.

"What if it's not good news?" Allen asked.

"Good or bad, I have to know. Don't worry. Either way, I won't do anything crazy."

"Alright," Allen said. "This one time."

Eight days later, as Johnson exited a neighborhood grocery store, a little man selling newspapers out front extended a paper toward him. Johnson shook his head no and started to step around him.

The little man said in a firm whisper, "Take it, Mr. Johnson."

Johnson stared guardedly at the man as he took the newspaper from him.

The little man turned away and continued selling papers to customers exiting the store.

Johnson felt something hidden between the pages. He cautiously glanced over his shoulders then took the newspaper to his car. Once inside, he flipped through the pages and found a sealed manila folder, containing a small stack of 8 by 10 photographs. The first photo was of his father dated one week ago. He was still in prison but looked bigger and more muscular than Johnson remembered. That was a good sign. It meant he was taking care of himself and back in survival mode. There were other inmates in the photo with him. They were muscular, like his dad, and appeared to be his friends. The next photo was dated two years after Johnson escaped from prison. It was taken at his sister Sue's wedding. Two years. He hoped the marriage delay wasn't because of him but feared that it was. In any case, she looked cheerful in the photo, like she had finally found happiness. The pleasure on her face brought tears of joy to Johnson's eyes and a broad smile across his lips. He almost felt like he was there, experiencing the magnificent day with them.

While admiring the wedding photo, his jaw suddenly dropped. One of the women in attendance was his mother. She was sitting in the front pew. She looked happy. She was no longer in a catatonic state. Life was back in her eyes and her face was aglow. Johnson's grin returned but disappeared, just as quickly, when he got to the final photograph. The picture was of another wedding. Connie Miller's wedding. The girl he had wanted to marry in college. Johnson took a moment and just stared at the photo. He knew it was inevitable that she would move on. He was happy for her but incredibly sad at the same time.

There was a note paperclipped to the photos. It simply read: DESTROY AFTER VIEWING. Johnson sat there in the parking lot relooking at all the photos several times before finally driving home. Once inside his house, he spent another half hour looking at the pictures, feeling joy at seeing the smiles on his family's faces. They were going to be alright, even his father. Hopefully, with a little luck, he'd get out early on good behavior.

Johnson burned the photographs inside a bowl in his back yard and let the ashes fly away with the wind. Now he had closure.

Three weeks later Johnson was sent to Camp Peary and the intensive year-and-a-half-long training began. All aspects of clandestine operations were taught with an emphasis on survival, evasion, resistance, and escape. Because of his prior service as an Army sniper, Johnson was fast-tracked through the shooting courses, after demonstrating his expertise with various weapons. Johnson was on track to graduate at the top of his class, but during his last few days of training, he was pulled out of class, publicly accused of some alleged impropriety, and fired.

In actuality, he was quietly transferred to a secret division deep inside the CIA called D-Branch. Once there, he endured another fourteen months of demanding division-specific training in hand-to-hand combat, mostly centering on Kali and Jujitsu. His instructors were surprised by this young street fighter's amazingly fast reflexes and excellent hand-eye coordination. They also found, due to Johnson's natural fighting instincts, he was able to master the martial arts techniques quicker than most. On the day Johnson completed the advanced division training, Dickerson Allen was there to meet him. "I knew you could do it," Allen told him, with his usual bland expression.

Joseph Johnson gave him an indifferent look, "So who am I supposed to be now?"

Allen nodded. "Your name is Alexander Temple. You're a fiction writer. Periodically, books will appear in your name." He handed Johnson a dossier on his new life. "Read it, learn it, destroy it. You know the routine."

Johnson grabbed hold of the folder, but Allen held onto it and stared intently at him. "One day your life may depend on you knowing every detail in this folder."

"I know," said Johnson, "I've done this before."

Allen released the folder and extended his hand, "Good luck, Alexander Temple."

###

Alexander Temple's first agency mission landed him dangerously close to the southeastern coastline of the Communist China province of Kwangtung. He was there on a contact and kill mission, except his contact was late. He had already been up in the mountains alone for four days, waiting. Last night it had rained. When it finally stopped early that morning, it left the trees and leaves damp and musty, and the ground wet. An occasional cold breeze swooped down out of the northern mountains and bit a chill into everything in its path. It was an unyielding environment, but he was trained to endure discomfort for extended periods. It didn't mean he had to like it, though. Temple rolled over on his side and propped himself up on one elbow, then slid his hand into his sleeping bag. He reassuringly touched his modified .308 caliber Remington that he had used while in 'Nam and the Walther PPK he grew particularly fond of during a special weapons review at the Farm. And there was one more weapon. This one, the weapons section insisted he carry, at least while he was on this mission. The gun was a double-barreled derringer, connected to a specially-designed contraption that held the derringer snuggly against the forearm. With the proper muscle movement, a slide would push the gun into your waiting hand. Temple had it on now. It was a good little weapon for emergencies.

As he checked his weapons, another cold breeze swooped through his government-issued sleeping bag, as if it were made of fishnet. Temple buried his massive frame deeper into his bedding. Where the hell was the guy he was there to meet? The resident CIA officer in Hong Kong, Peter Sawyer, should have contacted him days ago. But Sawyer never showed. Temple knew Sawyer was on a recon mission to locate the KGB assassin, The Grim Reaper, who was believed to be in the area. Maybe Sawyer found him. Maybe he found Sawyer. In any case, Temple didn't like not knowing if his cover was compromised. Temple shivered again, as another stiff breeze cut mercilessly through his sleeping bag. *Where the hell was Peter Sawyer?*

Suddenly, Temple's survival mode switched to full alert. There was a sound out there somewhere. It was such a familiar rustling of the leaves, so faint, an untrained ear would not have noticed it. But Temple did, and instinctively eased his hand inside the sleeping bag and pulled out his Walther PPK. He did not hear the sound again, but he knew somebody was there. He slipped out of the sleeping bag, grabbed his sniper rifle, then low crawled as quietly as he could, over to the giant oak and down into the ditch behind it, dug out four days ago just for this purpose. Temple waited and listened, but still nothing except the cold wind, the musty leaves, and insects crawling all over him. Twenty minutes passed, then Temple saw him, under the moonlit sky, as he cautiously entered the campground. The man's back was to him, but The Iceman could tell it wasn't Sawyer. This man was carrying a rifle with a scope attached, and Temple could also see the butt of a handgun sticking just above the beltline in the back of the man's pants.

Temple aimed his .308 caliber Remington at the man's back, then yelled to him, "Drop your rifle — and the gun in your waistband." After the man complied, Temple bellowed, "Now get your hands up and turn around slowly."

The little man turned and faced him, then said, in a strong Chinese accent, "Mary had a little lamb."

It was the correct code phrase that Peter Sawyer was supposed to say, but this Chinese man was not Peter Sawyer. To see what the little man would do next, Temple gave the counter phrase. "You like nursery rhymes?"

The little man then correctly said the follow-up phrase. "No. I like Mary."

To which Temple replied, "Everybody likes Mary."

Upon hearing the completed code phrase, the young Chinese man smiled broadly and dropped his hands.

Temple remained safely in the ditch; his rifle still aimed at the man. "Who the hell are you, and what happened to — the other guy?"

Speaking with no accent now the Chinese man said, "My name is Raymond Wong. I was Peter Sawyer's informant."

"Was?" Temple questioned.

Raymond Wong nervously kept his eyes on Temple's rifle as he continued, "Peter was killed three days ago. The man from the Kremlin discovered we were trailing him. He rigged a delayed bomb on Peter's apartment door. It almost got both of us, but Peter pushed me to safety. Before he died, he gave me the code phrase and told me to come up here and meet you."

Still crouched in the ditch, Temple asked, "If Sawyer died three days ago, why are you just now getting up here?"

"The man from the Kremlin is after me. I had to hide out. Make sure I lost him."

"Did you lose him?" Temple asked.

"Yeah, I lost him. I wouldn't have come up here if I hadn't given him the slip." Then Wong added with a nervous stammer, "P-Peter said I could trust you like I did him."

Temple remained in the ditch a moment longer, then cautiously climbed out and laid his rifle on top of his sleeping bag, but sat close to it. The Walther he stuck under his belt. He told Raymond Wong to have a seat. Wong sat across from him, near his own discarded weapons, but didn't reach for them. Still uneasy, Temple asked again, "You sure you got away clean?"

"I'm positive, Mr. —?"

Temple ignored his question and asked one of his own,

"Did you see the Soviet's face?"

"Yeah, we both did. Peter got photos, but they were probably destroyed in the explosion."

"If you saw this Soviet again, could you identify him?"

"I think so. Sure."

"Just in case we get separated, why don't you describe him to me, and tell me how you tracked him?" Temple figured he'd better get the information now before The Grim Reaper caught up with Wong.

"Sure, I'll tell you anything you want to know."

"First, let's talk about the Soviet. What does he look like?"

"He's a big man. Not as big as you, but older than —"

And that's when Temple heard it. Raymond Wong heard it, too, the metallic click somewhere out there in the darkness that meant it was too late. One of them was going to die. Temple started to dive for the ditch but didn't make it. The bullet creased his forehead and he fell to the ground hard, dizzy and disorientated. Temple heard another shot and saw Raymond Wong fall. As Temple crawled desperately toward the ditch, he heard footsteps running, getting closer. He fumbled for the Walther tucked under his belt, but by the time he got it out, The Grim Reaper was there. Temple felt the blunt force of a boot smashing into the side of his head, and he nearly passed out. He vaguely remembered dropping the gun but it seemed a disjointed thought.

Through blurred vision, Temple could see the Soviet standing over him, but could not make out his features. Temple extended his right hand up toward the Soviet, feigning a desperate grab for him. Then he flexed the muscles in his arm, to activate the gun slide fastened to his forearm. But it didn't work. The damn mechanism didn't push the derringer into his hand. *Dammit*! Temple's thoughts flowed with profanity. *Work, you son-of-a-bitch*! *You bastard son-of-a-bitch!*

Suddenly, as if his enraged thoughts helped, the derringer leaped into his hand. The unexpected appearance of the gun startled The Grim Reaper, and he automatically took a step back in survival reflex. The instant the derringer touched Temple's hand, he pulled the trigger. The bullet tore into the Soviet's right arm, he grunted and dropped his weapon. Although Temple could only see a shadowy figure backing away, he fired another round and heard the man groan as he was hit again. The Grim Reaper turned and ran back into the woods.

Struggling to stay conscious, Temple dragged himself to his sleeping bag, to retrieve his sniper rifle, then he crawled back into the ditch. His head was still spinning and his vision was worse than before. If the Soviet came back now, Temple knew he could not hold him off. Temple stayed conscious as long as he could, but finally passed out.

When Temple woke up it was light out. He guessed early dawn. Apparently, The Grim Reaper did not come back. The Soviet, no doubt, slipped back down the hill into Hong Kong to mend his wounds, to attack another day. Temple was confident that the Reaper would attack another day because the Soviet had no way of knowing that Temple didn't see his face. To remain the ghost he had been for over twenty years, the Soviet could not afford to let Temple live. As Temple climbed out of the ditch, his head still burned with pain and fever, from the bullet crease to his temple. When he got to his feet, he felt dizzy, but his vision had cleared somewhat. Temple moved over to Raymond Wong's body and hurriedly searched the man's remains for some clue to The Grim Reaper's identity or location. He didn't find anything that would help him, but he took Wong's wallet and hotel room key. Temple tossed Wong's rifle and the Grim Reaper's rifle into the ditch. He put his own sniper rifle back in its case and placed it in the ditch. He didn't want to chance carrying a rifle case into town, especially in his weakened condition. The handguns, however, were more concealable, and with The Grim Reaper out there somewhere, he needed something. He put his derringer in his pants pocket and the Walther under his belt. The holster and gun slide went into the ditch. He pushed some dirt and leaves over the weapons, then made his way down the mountain into Hong Kong. He broke into a pharmacy in Kowloon and stole some medical supplies, then made his way to Wong's hotel room. Immediately upon arriving, he called the temporary phone number provided for emergencies, then updated his superiors on the mission failure through coded conversation. Afterward, he rested there for a few days while recuperating from his injuries. When he was well enough to travel, he booked a flight home.

As the plane lifted high above the city, Temple gazed out the window at the magnificent skyline of Hong Kong. He knew somewhere down there a Soviet assassin was licking his wounds. He also knew that sooner or later; The Grim Reaper would come for him. When that day came, the Soviet would have the advantage, because he knew what Temple looked like, and Temple never saw his face.

Upon Temple's return to the states, his encounter with the notorious Grim Reaper had morphed to almost epic proportions. The fact that he lived through the battle and even put two bullets into the elusive Soviet assassin caused many of the senior agents to look upon him with awe and respect. To their knowledge, he had done what no one before him could. He survived. Rumors circulated that the rookie killed the legend with two bullets at close range. Others believed The Grim Reaper was possibly still out there biding his time. Temple believed the latter.

When Dickerson Allen heard of Temple's battle with The Grim Reaper, and how the younger agent had put two bullet holes into the Soviet, he remarked to a peer, "I guess The Grim Reaper expected another easy kill when he climbed up that mountainside in China." Allen paused to grin. "Bet that Russkie shit his pants when Godzilla showed up."

Dickerson Allen was well aware of Temple's particular skill set. He had followed his development since his college days. Whether it was with firearms or hand-to-hand combat, he knew the man now known as Alexander Temple was a very dangerous man. The nickname, Iceman, fit him well. Dickerson Allen was also certain of something else: one day The Grim Reaper and The Iceman would meet again.

Chapter 15

Temple's memories of his past life were interrupted by a knock on his Las Vegas hotel room door. He grabbed his PPK and called out through the door, "Who is it?"

A strangely familiar voice replied, "I'm your insurance man."

The code phrase was correct for his contact. Temple lowered his gun and opened the door. He was surprised to see his boss, Lincoln Delaware, standing there holding an attaché case. "What are you doing here?" Temple asked.

"Aren't you going to ask me in?"

Temple stepped aside, and noticed that Delaware walked in without a limp. Temple closed the door once he was inside, then brought his gun back up. "Who are you?"

"I'm Lincoln's brother, Carlton."

Temple had heard somewhere that Lincoln Delaware had an identical twin brother. And there was no mistaking the fact, these two men were identical in appearance and mannerisms. If not for Lincoln's bum leg, Temple would not have known this man wasn't Lincoln Delaware. Temple lowered his gun again. "What do you know about me and why I'm here?"

"I know you're a government agent working for my brother, and I'm supposed to teach you how to be a winning card player, in only a few short hours."

Temple put his gun away. "Then we'd better get started."

As Carlton seated himself at the coffee table, he added, "I also know your mark cheats." Carlton took several decks of cards from his attaché case and placed them on the table, each with different casino markings. "Do you know anything about poker?" Carlton asked.

"I've played some, but I'm no expert."

"You won't have to be."

"You know I have to win," Temple reminded him.

"You will. I'm going to teach you how to cheat and how to look out for cheats." Carlton picked up one deck of cards from the table. "Let's talk about these cards."

"Trick cards?" Temple asked.

"Some of them. I'll show you how they're marked later. Now — most professional card cheats, the really good ones, prefer to mark their own cards. Some use block-out ink, to slightly alter the design on the backs of some of the cards."

"Some of the cards?" Temple questioned.

"With this system, you only mark aces, kings, and queens. Just knowing where these cards are can make the difference." Carlton passed the deck to Temple. "Flip through these and keep your eyes on the back of the cards."

As Temple flipped through the cards, he could see the subtle changes.

Carlton handed him another deck. "These cards are also marked. Can you spot how?"

Temple flipped through the cards as he did before, pausing to examine a few of them more carefully. "If they're marked, I can't see it."

Carlton handed him a pair of glasses from the attaché case. "Take another look."

The glasses revealed big bold numbers and the card suit printed on the back of each card.

"In a real game, the card cheat won't wear glasses; he'll use special contact lenses."

Temple asked, "So, these invisible markings can only be seen with special lenses?"

"No. There are other ways, but we won't get into that now."

Temple grinned, "I guess the only way you can be sure the cards aren't marked is to bring the deck yourself."

"Wrong," Carlton said. "There are ways cards can be marked even in the middle of the game."

Temple gave him a curious look.

Carlton picked up another deck of cards and opened it. "Marking cards, while the game is in progress, is easier than you might think. During the normal course of a game, when you get cards that you want to use later, you simply mark them. Use your fingernail, or the sharp point of a ring to make an impression on the back of the card. You can even nick the edge of a card with your thumbnail, or just put a slight bend on the card. Anything that will make that card stand out but isn't overtly noticeable."

"I see what you mean," Temple nodded.

Carlton continued, "If you're ever asked to cut for a high card, check the deck first. Make sure none of the cards have been waxed. A waxed card becomes the slickest card in the pack and can be cut to by applying downward, sideways pressure on the deck." Carlton handed Temple a deck of cards. "The ace of spades has been waxed. Try to cut to it."

Temple pressed the deck as he was told, then cut the cards — to the ace of spades.

Carlton nodded, "See what I mean." Then he cautioned, "Watch out for shiny objects, placed on the table, that are capable of reflecting an image."

"Like a chrome cigarette lighter?" Temple suggested.

"Yes," Carlton agreed. "If a chrome cigarette lighter is placed on the table, in front of the dealer, you can read each card he deals out. But don't forget about nonreflecting objects, like a wood smoking pipe. There could be a tiny mirror hidden inside the chamber of the pipe."

Temple interjected, "Professional dealers deal cards out pretty fast. Even with a mirror, can cards be read that quickly?"

"Professional cheats do it all the time. You should also watch out for holdouts."

"What's that?"

"Some card players hold specific cards at the end of one game and then slip them back into the next game once they receive new cards."

"How can they hold cards without someone noticing?"

"Generally, players don't keep track of how many cards are discarded at the end of a game. They should." Carlton picked up another deck of cards and dealt out about a dozen cards into one pile, face down. He looked up at Temple. "What do you think about that?"

"About what?" Temple asked.

"Watch carefully." Carlton turned the top card in his hand face up. It was a four of clubs. Then he dealt off ten cards, but the four of clubs never moved from the top of the deck.

Temple smiled, "You're dealing seconds."

"And bottoms," Carlton volunteered, then continued to deal until the only card left in his hand was the four of clubs. "You're going to have to learn this, Mr. Temple — tonight."

"I only have a few hours."

"Let's hope that's enough," Carlton said.

"How do you know when a guy is dealing seconds and bottoms?"

"Watch his eyes. Most dealers don't look at the back of the cards as they deal. A card cheat, if he's reading the backs, will glance at each card until he spots the card he wants, then he'll hold that card back by second dealing to everyone until he can give that card to himself or his partner. Also, note the speed at which the cards are dealt, before and after the dealer gives himself a card. You may notice a pattern, as he slows the deal to read the backs. And watch out for flushes. It's the easiest winning hand to deal using seconds."

Temple nodded as Carlton expounded further, "Dealing bottoms and seconds takes a lot of practice. I'm only going to teach you how to deal seconds. It's easier."

"Easy works for me," Temple said.

"You ever hear of cold decking?" Carlton asked.

"No, I haven't."

"Cold decking," Carlton explained, "is when you secretly switch out an entire deck of cards, at the beginning of a game, while everyone is watching you. It can be accomplished in many ways, but I think deck hold-outs are going to be your best bet." Carlton put a small mechanical device on the table that looked similar to the derringer slide device that he sometimes wears.

"It looks — familiar. What is it?" Temple asked.

"It's called a deck hold-out. There are different kinds. Some can hold one to five cards. This one with the expandable arm can switch an entire deck. It's worn around the forearm under your coat sleeve. This cord at the bottom of the device runs along the inside of your pants to the cuff. Once connected, you activate it by extending your foot. The device extends the marked deck into your hand and retracts the original deck."

Temple was duly impressed by Carlton's expertise, but apprehensive about developing any proficiency himself with such a limited time frame.

"Well, that's it, Mr. Temple. Now let's get started. We've got a lot of work to do."

Chapter 16

By morning, Temple still did not feel comfortable with all the techniques Carlton had shown him. In fact, he felt rather inept, but – ready or not – he had no more time.

After Carlton was gone, Temple hid his guns inside the room. He wasn't going to need them just yet. He then collected some of the card equipment and went to Karen Kiley's room.

"Who is it?" she asked when he knocked at her door.

Good girl, Temple thought. "It's me," he said.

Karen opened the door, then hurriedly walked back to the TV to turn the volume down. The pullover nightshirt, she was wearing, hung down to her mid-thighs and teasingly embraced her curvaceous body.

Temple shifted his eyes away from the view, then reached back and pushed the door shut.

"So, what's the plan?" Karen asked, walking toward him.

Temple kept his eyes on hers. He didn't dare let them roam. "I stopped by to let you know I'm heading back to the boat. I'll have something to report when I get back."

"Did the man you were expecting ever show up?"

"Yes, he did."

Karen stared at him for a moment, then said, "I'll be glad when this mission is over."

"It will be, soon," he assured her, then added, "While I'm gone, I need you to do something for me."

"Sure, what do you need?"

"I'm going to need a car. But I don't want your name on the paperwork. Use my mission ID. Call the hotel concierge. Have him make the arrangements. Tell him to leave the car in the hotel parking lot. I'll pick it up when I come back."

"I'll take care of it," she said.

"Great. Then I'll see you later."

When he was gone, Karen whispered, "Be careful, Michael Darrin."

Temple, again caught a cab in front of the hotel. During the ride toward the marina, he mentally practiced the card techniques. The mission relied on him getting this part right.

All of a sudden there was a loud boom. The cab began vibrating violently, then spun out of control. Other cars around them swerved to avoid a collision. Temple held on tight. The driver stayed with the wheel, until the taxi came to a screeching halt in the middle of Boulder Highway.

"Dammit!" the cab driver cursed.

Temple sighed heavily, then he and the driver got out of the cab and saw the left front tire had blown out. Temple helped the driver push the cab to the side of the road.

"I'm in kind of a hurry," Temple told the driver. "Do you have a spare tire?"

"We don't carry spares," the driver told him, still breathing heavily from pushing the cab.

"How long will it take to get another cab out here?"

The driver checked with dispatch and was told that all of their cabs were busy at the moment, but one would be sent as soon as possible.

After forty-five minutes had passed, Temple started down the freeway with his thumb out.

"Hey, buddy," the driver yelled to him. "What about the money already totaled on the farebox?"

"You must be kidding," Temple snarled over his shoulder, then continued walking.

The traffic on Boulder Highway was busy that morning. Still, it took over twenty minutes before a green Ford Pinto pulled to the side of the road. Temple rushed over to the passenger side front door and opened it. From the angle where he stood, the driver's shapely legs were the first thing to meet his eyes. Her dress was actually not that short but was hiked up a bit because of her seated position. Temple lowered his head to see her face, and was momentarily stunned, but suppressed his look of surprise. This woman looked remarkably like Connie Miller, his fiancé from his former life. She was almost an identical twin. Even the style and length of her hair was the same. The only noticeable difference was her eyes. They did not have the same sparkle, the same pop that Connie's did. But then, this woman wasn't wearing any makeup. Could this woman be Connie?

The female driver pulled her dress down to a proper level, as she leaned toward the open passenger door. "Where're you headed mister?" she asked, showing no recognition of him.

Even her voice was Connie's. "Lake Mead Marina," he said.

"I'm driving by the Marina. Hop in."

Temple tried not to stare at her as he slid into the passenger seat, but he did steal glances. The resemblance was incredible, but this woman could not be Connie. She clearly didn't recognize him. He wondered who the hell she was. She certainly wasn't Connie's twin sister, because Connie was an only child. Still, sitting beside Connie's clone brought back a flood of memories.

The woman beside him broke the silence. "You were in for quite a walk," she said.

Temple shook off his stroll down memory lane. "Thank you," he said.

"W-what?" she asked, confused by his answer.

"For the ride," he clarified.

"Oh. Well, I was driving by the marina anyway. I couldn't just leave you stranded on the highway."

"I'm glad you didn't." Temple couldn't help but notice more similarities. Her mannerisms, her facial inflections, even the way she bit her lip was all Connie. He had to find out who she was. "So," he said probing, "do you live around here, Miss —?"

"Yolanda," she said. "And no, I don't live around here."

Temple had hoped she'd give her last name, but she didn't, and he damn sure couldn't ask her for it now, without sounding weird. But he continued probing, "Where're you from?"

"Seattle."

"Here on business or pleasure?"

"I'm here to visit my sister." She turned and gave him a look. "What about you?"

Temple's expression registered nothing, but his mind was racing. *Her sister? Nah. No way. Connie would not have lied to him about having a sister. The resemblance had to be just coincidental.* "My name is Tom," he said. "I'm here on vacation."

"Are you a gambler?"

"No. I play cards."

"What's the difference?" she asked, her eyes squinting.

"Technique and strategy," he said. "Gamblers are people who play games of chance, like slot machines and roulette. There's no skill involved in those games. People just hope they win."

Yolanda smiled at his narrow distinction of a gambler, but said nothing further.

The remainder of the drive was spent in silence, but Temple's thoughts were consumed with a mystery. *Who was she? How could she look so much like Connie? Why is she here now? What are the chances he would run into a clone of his ex-girlfriend, in the middle of a mission? Could it all be a coincidence?* Temple didn't believe in coincidences. However, in this case, maybe it didn't matter much who she was. Once she dropped him off at the marina, he would never see her again anyway. Maybe that was a good thing. She would have been too much of a distraction.

Yolanda finally pulled to a stop across the street from the marina. "We're here," she announced.

"Thank you again," Temple said, then got out of her car.

Yolanda politely smiled then drove away.

Temple watched her Pinto, until it was out of sight. Oddly, he felt an empty sensation in the pit of his stomach, as if he was losing Connie Miller all over again. It surprised him how the mere presence of this look-alike stranger affected him. Temple exhaled deeply, cleared his thoughts of the past, then started down the pier toward *The Lucky Lady Casino*.

After boarding the boat, Temple stood just inside the entryway and scanned the casino. Right away he spotted a couple of familiar faces playing blackjack. One was a famous comedian. Temple had seen him many times on the Tonight Show. He was a funny man on stage and told jokes nonstop. Everybody loved his humor. But now was different. He was not amusing or amused and was uncharacteristically crude. His usually jovial face was drawn in a frown and he blurted out foul, obscenities as he got one bad card after another.

It was, however, the other familiar face that interested Temple more. He had seen the face twice before: once in a dossier at headquarters, and again at the airport. It was the Indian assassin, Jason Meats. He was dressed rather impressively, in a flashy sort of way. His straight black hair was parted down the middle and tied in a ponytail in the back. A broad nose and high cheekbones accented his narrow, roughly sculpted face. He was, in a rugged sort of way, almost handsome, but he looked as though he had lived a life far beyond his years.

Alexander Temple moved closer to the table where Meats and the comedian were playing. The table limit was a minimum of one thousand to a maximum of twenty thousand, and every seat was taken. He would have to wait until one of the players vacated a seat. While waiting, he watched how the gamblers played their hands. The Indian was playing good blackjack, and he knew it, and his pompous, confident attitude annoyed the other high rollers. Each time he won a big-money bet, his arrogant antics were on full display, as he heckled the other players.

Temple noted the seating arrangement. The comedian

sat in the first chair and was making some terrible basic strategy mistakes, the dumbest was he continually split tens. In blackjack, this was a cardinal sin, even worse than trying to draw to an inside straight in poker. No wonder he was losing.

Next to the comedian sat a tall, thin man, wearing a white felt cowboy hat, with a six-inch brim. Wrapped around his neck was a white silk scarf, like Gene Autry used to wear in his western movies. Temple heard the cowboy exclaim the hat gave him luck. The other three players were unremarkable: a businessman in a baggy suit, a middle-aged woman, and an older man seated next to Jason Meats. Temple shifted his attention to the dealer, a young Mexican man, sporting a long handlebar mustache and a stone face. Temple watched him carefully as he shuffled and dealt the cards with great skill. He noticed the dealer was using the mechanic's grip, one popularly used by card cheats; however, the dealer didn't appear to be cheating. In this kind of game, it wasn't really necessary. The odds were always with the house.

Temple refocused on the Indian. He was still playing extremely well. Temple knew Meats was not reading luminous markings on the back of the cards, because Temple could not see any markings himself, with the special contact lens he was wearing. And as far as he could tell, there were no identifying marks on the cards to make them stand out. He concluded Meats was probably just a skilled blackjack player — or just very lucky. Either way, it was good this was an honest game. If the game was already rigged with a marked deck, the cheat would know the instant Temple switched the deck.

After nearly twenty minutes, the elderly gentleman, next to Meats, picked up his remaining chips and walked off, dejected. Temple took his seat, exchanging glances with everyone at the table – except for Jason Meats, who paid no particular attention to him. The dealer cupped the single deck of cards in his hand and waited until each player placed a bet. Temple was prepared to lose. His mission profile was that of a prolific gambler who lost a lot. He would play that role for a while. Later, after he lost a significant amount, he would wait until it was his turn to cut the cards. He would then switch out the entire deck and take the casino for as much as he could, as fast as he could. That should get Donnetti's attention.

For the next hour and a half, Temple intentionally lost the majority of his bets. When he figured he had lost enough, he started playing basic strategy. Hopefully, he'd win a few big bets, before he switched the deck. That way it would look like his luck was changing, before he cut the cards. Luckily, Temple did win the next three hands in a row.

Finally, the dealer placed the shuffled deck in front of Temple so he could cut the cards. The Iceman felt a nervous chill tingling through his body. What he was about to do required precise timing and every move had to be done exactly right. The entire mission rested on the next few seconds. Very casually, Temple reached for the deck with his right hand, and, simultaneously activated the hold-out device on his forearm. The marked deck slid under his hand into his palm. He covered the deck on the table with his open hand, as if to grab it, then pressed the bottom of the card device onto the original stack of cards. The device locked onto the casino cards, released the marked deck into his palm, and slid the original deck up his sleeve. Temple lifted his hand and left half of the marked deck on the table, then placed the other half of the marked deck beside it, as if he were cutting the cards. As he moved his hand away from the table, he wondered, *did I get away with it?* The entire switch took about three seconds. Alexander Temple casually glanced at the dealer and the other players. He saw no signs of recognition on their faces. The dealer stacked the two half decks together, then picked up the cards and began to deal.

Temple breathed a silent sigh of relief.

For the next hour, Temple won the majority of hands played. The games he lost were intentional to make his wins seem more random. During that hour, he incrementally increased his bet, until he was wagering the maximum twenty thousand per hand. By the end of the hour, he had amassed nearly seven hundred thousand and, as planned, it got the casino's attention.

The crowd standing around the table parted, like the Red Sea, as Big Jim Donnetti walked through the center in a commanding stride, trailed by his entourage. Donnetti stared at Temple and made no attempt to hide it. Nick Marlow, another familiar face from the mission briefing, followed closely behind Donnetti. There was an air of quality and refinement about Marlow, but Temple knew, beyond that well-designed façade, was a conscienceless, cold-blooded assassin.

Walking alongside Marlow was a tall, statuesque, Hispanic beauty, whom Temple did not recognize. Her eyes sparkled, when she spotted him, and their eyes locked in a lingering stare. Marlow saw the attraction and said something to her she ignored. Temple's eyes followed her through the crowd, watching her hips sway provocatively, with every step. It was neither a cheap jiggle nor something she knowingly did. It was, obviously, just the way she walked. She was one sexy woman, and Temple could tell, by the self-assured look on her face, she knew it. She had straight black hair that dropped to her shoulders and nicely trimmed bangs over her forehead. Her eyes were dark and piercing, her complexion moderately tanned. And oh, what a body. Built like the proverbial 'brick shithouse,' she easily stood six feet tall and was wearing a dark-colored jumpsuit that clung to her shapely body, like a second skin.

The last of Donnetti's entourage was a blond-haired, baby-faced man who wore thick horn-rimmed glasses and a suit too big for him. Temple didn't recognize him, either.

Donnetti took a position standing behind the comedian and gave the pit boss a look. The pit boss returned it and offered a shoulder shrug. The dealer dealt another round of cards, his own up card was a ten. The comedian got two tens, which he promptly split, and he placed an additional two-thousand dollar bet on the second ten. Two of the other players, at the table, made eye contact with each other and shook their heads at the man's foolish strategy. Jason Meats stared at the comedian incredulously. *What an idiot*, Meats thought.

The dealer hit the comedian's first ten with a two of clubs, face up. The comic tapped his index finger on the two of clubs.

Politely, the dealer asked, "Did you want a hit, sir?"

"Of course I want a hit!" the comedian spat angrily. "Why do you think I'm tapping this fuckin' card?"

Very patiently, the dealer said, "You're supposed to scrape your hold cards on the table, sir."

The comedian snatched up his cards and scraped them roughly on the table, in an exaggerated manner.

The dealer hit his twelve with an eight of hearts.

"YES!" the comedian exclaimed, giving a double fist pump.

The dealer shifted to the comedian's second split bet and hit the ten with another ten.

"FUCK YEAH!" the comic yelled, popping up out of his seat and thrusting his fist triumphantly in the air. Then he sat back down, with a smug look on his face, as if he had made the most remarkable double play.

In reality, it was one of the dumbest blackjack moves a player could make. He just got incredibly lucky. After that, the two players, to Temple's immediate right, both busted. The dealer scooped up their cards and chips, then turned to Temple.

Reading the back of the cards, Temple knew the next card to be dealt was a ten. It would bust his hand. Temple tucked his cards under his chips, indicating he did not want another card.

Jason Meats took the hit. For him, it was good strategy, since he already had fifteen and the dealer was showing ten. But even good basic strategy was not foolproof. The hit busted Meats' hand. The dealer flipped his own down card over, revealing a total of sixteen. Blackjack rules in Las Vegas state the house must hit sixteen and stand on seventeen. The dealer gave himself the mandatory hit, and it busted his hand.

Donnetti motioned for the pit boss to come over as the dealer paid the winners.

Temple read Donnetti's lips as he whispered to the pit boss, "*How much is he up?*" Temple could not read the response because the pit boss wasn't facing him. Donnetti whispered again, "*You've been changing dealers on this guy, right?*" Donnetti nodded at the answer, then his lips moved again, "*Have you tried a new deck?*"

Another round of cards was dealt to the players. Temple intentionally lost the next bet, totaling twenty thousand dollars, to keep the dealer from bringing in another deck of cards. Temple subsequently lost the next hand, too, and cursed softly in pretended frustration. He then decided it was time. He had the audience he wanted. Temple stared at his stack of winnings, as if trying to make up his mind, then he pushed one hundred thousand dollars' worth of chips into the betting position.

The dealer glanced down at the large stack of chips and then politely recited the standard line, "The table limit is twenty thousand, sir."

Temple frowned. "I thought this was a high-stakes gambling establishment."

The dealer glanced at the pit boss, who in turn looked at Donnetti.

Temple asked in defiance, "This is the world-famous *Lucky Lady* isn't it?"

The tall woman standing beside Nick Marlow found this brazen act bold and intriguing, and she started to circle the table, to get closer to Temple. Marlow roughly grabbed her arm, but the woman jerked away from him, then walked behind Temple's seat and placed both hands on the back of his chair.

The opulent scent of Opium perfume filled the air the moment she stood behind him. Her breast pressed against the back of his neck when she leaned forward, presumably to get a better view of the table. Temple doubted it was accidental.

Donnetti gave the pit boss a nod to take the one hundred thousand dollar bet. The pit boss told the dealer to accept it. Before the cards were dealt, a new dealer took over the game and brought a new deck of cards with him.

Temple quickly reevaluated his chances. Without the marked deck in the game, his odds of winning this bet were less than fifty percent. Maybe it didn't matter. His winnings so far were in the hundreds of thousands. Hopefully, if he lost this bet, he would still have enough of the casino's money to keep Donnetti interested.

The new dealer dealt the cards. Temple glanced at his. He had nineteen. A good hand. He tucked his cards under his chips. Other players took hits to improve their hands. Only Jason Meats busted. The dealer had a four showing. He hit his own hand repeatedly until his cards totaled twenty. Temple lost, but hoped he still had enough in the kitty, to keep Donnetti interested.

Nick Marlow started toward the Hispanic woman with rage in his eyes. He was going to beat the hell out of her right there in the middle of the casino floor, for her disrespect. Donnetti signaled for him to let it go. Marlow reluctantly stopped and nodded at the fat man, then glared across the table at the woman. He realized she was a wild party girl, but when the bitch was with him, she was his property, until *he* decided to let her go. That Mexican whore was going to pay for this disrespect. But he'd let it go — for now.

Temple told the dealer, "Color me up," and then placed all of his chips on the table. The dealer took his large stack of chips and converted them to a smaller stack of high-value chips, then pushed them back to him. Temple noticed, while collecting his chips, that Jim Donnetti was staring intently at him. *Good.* Temple had done all he could to entice the fat man. The next move was Donnetti's. Temple stood up and turned to leave, but the woman who had been standing behind his chair, was now blocking his path. Their faces were inches apart. Although a small crowd had gathered around the table, there was still room for her to back up. But she did not. She just stood there and smiled. Temple smiled back, then squeezed past her and headed toward the cashiers' window. Obviously, this woman was flirting with him. But why? Why was she deliberately angering Marlow? Temple considered the possibility that her flirtatious act was just that: an act. Maybe she was a spy sent to lure him into the same kind of trap that cost Johnny Davis his life. Or, maybe she was part of a team of con-artists, who had chosen him for their next mark. She could have been almost anybody, even the horny woman she appeared to be. Whatever her reason was, maybe he could use that dynamic against Marlow later.

Temple put his chips on the cashier's counter. The cashier counted them twice, then said, "How would you like this, sir?"

"A check would be nice," Temple said. It took almost ten minutes for the cashier to bring him the check. After collecting it, he started toward the exit door. As he neared it, he heard what he was waiting for: footsteps coming up behind him fast. He hoped it wasn't the tall woman.

"Just a minute, Mr. Briggs," a male voice called out.

Temple looked back and saw the blond-haired, baby-faced man, who had earlier accompanied Donnetti into the casino. He was approaching at a hurried pace. Despite his innocent appearance, Temple could tell this man was quite capable of handling himself in a fight. Temple feigned confusion, "Do we know each other?"

"No, we don't. But if you have a minute —"

"I'm kind of in a hurry," Temple lied.

"I understand you wanted to talk to the boat's owner?"

"Yes, I do," Temple replied, pretending to be more interested now.

"He can see you now, sir."

Temple smiled. The bartender must have passed his mission's name along to Donnetti, which means they've probably already had him checked out. So far so good. Despite the bartender mentioning his name, Temple was fairly certain his walking away with over half a million dollars of casino money, is what generated this meeting.

"Where is he?" Temple asked.

"In the lounge."

"Alright. Let's go see him."

The young man led Temple back through the casino, toward the lounge. Along the way, Temple nearly collided with another man, but both men quickly sidestepped, at the last moment, avoiding the collision. They both made eye contact then went separate ways. The man Temple almost collided with, instinctively thought to go for his gun, but instead, walked on by without showing any sign of recognition. He had quickly assessed that the American, surprisingly, but apparently, did not recognize him. The Grim Reaper picked a spot in the casino and watched the American from a distance. He would wait, take his time, observe, and when the time was right, the American would die.

Chapter 17

Only a few people were in the bar, when Temple was escorted in. A female bartender was standing at the service station waiting on drinks. Jim Donnetti sat alone in a corner booth. Two of his goons stood on either side of him. The other tables, in that part of the lounge, were empty.

The blond-headed man who had escorted Temple, made a motion with his hand for Temple to proceed alone. As Temple crossed the lounge toward Donnetti, the fat man's smile was courteous, though a bit chilled and impersonal. When Temple reached the table, Donnetti neither stood nor offered his hand in greeting.

"Have a seat," Donnetti said.

Temple slid into the booth, but did not care much for that seating arrangement because, it exposed his back to anyone entering the lounge.

Donnetti lit a cigar and puffed it to life. "You're a remarkable blackjack player, Mr. Briggs."

"To be perfectly honest with you, I'd have to say it was more luck than skill. Guess I just got lucky today."

Donnetti took a long drag on his cigar. "How's your luck at poker?"

Temple grinned. "Poker's my game."

"But you didn't play poker this morning?"

"Well, I figured I'd warm up with a little blackjack. When I started winning, I wasn't about to switch games with a lucky streak going."

Donnetti took another drag on his cigar. "My people tell me you're interested in my private game."

"I'm interested."

"I'm curious," Donnetti said, staring through squinted eyes. "How do you know about the games?"

"People talk. I listen. I'm an excellent listener."

"What else have you heard — about the games?"

"I heard the games were no limit."

"And you're still interested?"

"I'm still interested."

"Excellent. I'll tell the other players you'll be joining us. We play a series of games over five days. The first game is at midnight tomorrow, in my stateroom."

"I'll be there," Temple said. "I really do appreciate the invitation, but I'm a little surprised."

"Surprised?"

"Frankly, I didn't think I had much of a chance of getting an invite. The word is that your games cater to a very exclusive clientele. Why me?"

Donnetti stared at Temple in total amazement. "You won a great deal of money here today. I intend to win it back."

Temple feigned a playful smile. "All of it?"

Donnetti was not amused. "I intend to break you, Mr. Briggs. Isn't that what this is all about? Winning?"

Temple nodded, then stood up. "Then I'll see you tomorrow night."

"Are you leaving the boat?" Donnetti asked, with a hint of concern in his voice.

"I'm a little tired," Temple lied. "I've been up for almost 72 hours straight. I really should get some sleep."

Donnetti said, "We have plenty of vacant staterooms aboard *The Lucky Lady*. You're welcome to stay here. We always comp my private game players for the duration of the games."

Temple pretended not to be interested, but the invitation was exactly what he wanted. "I do appreciate your offer, but I don't think —"

Donnetti interrupted, "All of the other private players have accepted my hospitality. You might as well say yes because I won't take no for an answer."

Temple pretended to think it over. "Alright. I accept your hospitality."

"Good," Donnetti said. "I'll have one of my security people show you to your room."

"I'll have to see it when I get back."

"I thought you wanted to get some sleep?"

"There are a few personal items I have to get from my room downtown first."

"We can supply you with anything you need."

"I'm sure you can, but I really would feel more comfortable with my own things. You understand."

Donnetti hesitated, then said, "Then I'll see you tomorrow night."

"Oh — there is one thing you can do for me. I just got a check from your cashier. Would it be possible to keep it in your safe until the games start? I can cash it out then. I'd rather not carry it around."

"Certainly. That's actually a benefit we provide to all of my private game players."

"Great! I do have one other request."

"And what might that be?"

"Would it be possible for me to see the casino vault?" Temple patted his pocket where he had the check. "This is a lot of money. I'd just like to know that it's — safe."

"That won't be necessary," Donnetti said. "Your money won't be in the casino vault. It'll be in my personal safe. I never mix personal finances with casino money."

Temple faked a look of concern. "I don't mean any disrespect, but I have to ask. How secure is your personal safe?"

"Would you like to see it?"

"That would ease my concerns," Temple pretended. And perhaps he just got his first clue, provided the Alpha Data was on board. If Donnetti truly never mixed casino money with personal funds, the Alpha Data was most likely in his private safe, and not in the casino vault that was accessible to others on his staff.

Donnetti stood up. "Follow me. I'll give you a close-up look. I think you'll be impressed." Donnetti led Temple through the casino with his bodyguards close behind.

Watching from a position only a few feet away, The Grim Reaper followed the group, until they disappeared into the bowels of the boat. He sat at a slot machine near the door that they had entered, and waited. They would probably come back that same way.

Donnetti led Temple into the upper levels of the boat. Temple paid particular attention to the route they took. On deck level 3, they walked through a wide passageway stretching from port to starboard. The entire corridor was painted white, with large, red security markings stenciled along the bulkhead and deck which read: *Stop. This Is A Restricted Area. Authorized Personnel Only.*

At the far end of the corridor, was a single door on the starboard side, with the words *Keep Out* stenciled on it. When Donnetti opened the door, Temple was surprised to see it wasn't locked. He was even more amazed there didn't appear to be any security guards or surveillance cameras in this area. Perhaps Donnetti didn't want anybody to see what he was doing when he was up there.

Donnetti held the security door open as Temple entered. The corridor continued for twenty paces, then led to another door on the right. A wall phone, without a dial pad, was mounted just outside this door. Donnetti picked it up. "This is Jim Donnetti," he said into the receiver, then hung up and turned to Temple. "This phone is connected to a speech recognition system. As long as the voice speaking into this phone matches my prerecorded one, the security systems on the other side of this door will be deactivated, for a preset amount of time, before automatically rearming. If the voice doesn't match, the security systems remain activated."

Temple noted the voice recognition system was similar to the one used at D-Branch.

Donnetti took a small leather key case from his pocket. He selected the proper key from a set of five, then unlocked and opened the door. Temple followed him into a narrow corridor that led to another door, which was also locked. Before unlocking the second door, Donnetti pointed back to the door they had just entered. "You see that small round mirror affixed to the back of the door?"

"I see it," said Temple.

Donnetti continued, "When the system is armed, that mirror reflects a continuous light beam back into the photoelectric eye on the wall ahead of us. If that door is opened, the beam in the mirror is broken and the alarm is triggered."

Temple nodded. "Impressive."

"I doubt anyone will ever get this far though," Donnetti boasted. "They'd have to first get past the pick-proof deadbolt lock on that door." Donnetti selected another key from the leather case and unlocked the second door. Before opening it, he said, "Behind this door is an infrared light beam grid that covers the entire doorway in a tight crisscross pattern when the system is armed. Not even a cat could get through without setting off the alarm."

Donnetti opened the door to reveal another corridor. This one led to a closet with no door. Inside that closet, Temple could see a 4-foot, heavy-duty steel safe against the far wall.

Temple pretended to be awed. "You've got one hell of a system, Mr. Donnetti. I feel better now that I've seen it. I feel kind of ashamed now that I even asked."

"You were perfectly right in asking. I should have offered this tour upfront."

"No harm done," Temple said.

"So, Mr. Briggs, how much will you be leaving with us?"

Temple handed Donnetti the check.

Donnetti snapped his fingers and one of his security guards handed him a receipt book. Donnetti wrote the receipt for five hundred and fifty thousand dollars and gave it to

Temple. "You'll have to wait back there, by the phone, while I put this in the safe," he said.

"Sure. No problem."

One of the security guards led him back to the wall phone.

Damnit! Temple thought, he had hoped to get a look inside the safe. Just a peek, to give him some idea of what he was going to find when he returned later that night to break in. He had already figured out how to defeat Donnetti's security system. What gave him some cause for concern was the unknown security systems Donnetti surely omitted talking about.

Donnetti rejoined them, and they headed back to the casino in silence. When they reached the gaming floor, Donnetti asked, "Have you made arrangements yet for your ride into town?"

"No, but I'll just catch a cab."

"Nonsense. You're one of my special guests, remember. I'll have my chauffeur give you a ride into town. He'll bring you back, too."

"Thank you. I do appreciate the ride, but I won't need your man to bring me back. My hotel has a rental car waiting for me."

"Alright. Just tell my driver where to drop you off." Donnetti turned and peered intently into the crowd of gamblers.

Temple saw who caught Donnetti's eye. Eddie Bowman had just entered the casino from the street entrance. He looked even bigger in person. Temple also noted the casual confirmation nod between the two men.

"I'll be back in a moment," Donnetti said, then he joined Eddie in the middle of the casino floor. The two men spoke briefly. At one point, both of them looked back at Temple.

They spoke some more, then Eddie turned and headed back off the boat.

Temple wondered where Eddie was coming from. And that nod between them, what was that all about? It appeared to be more than just a mere greeting.

Donnetti rejoined Temple. "That man I just spoke with will drive you to your hotel. He's parked at the foot of the brow." Donnetti extended his hand, "I'll see you tomorrow night."

"Looking forward to some good games," Temple replied, shaking his hand.

"When you get back here, tell the security man at the boarding brow who you are. He'll direct you to your room." With that said, Donnetti walked away and his bodyguards followed.

As Temple walked down the brow toward the pier, he could see Eddie Bowman standing beside a sleek, black, 10-pack limousine. The back door was open, beckoning him. Temple smiled politely at Eddie as he approached the limo.

The big man ignored the friendly gesture.

Temple slid into the back seat and Eddie forcefully slammed the door shut behind him.

When Eddie got behind the steering wheel, the entire vehicle rocked from his massive weight. Eddie looked back through the rearview mirror at his passenger. "Where to?"

"The Golden Nugget," Temple told him.

Standing at the end of the dock, The Grim Reaper watched them drive off, then he slipped into the back seat of one of the waiting cabs. "Follow that limousine," he told the driver, "but not too close," he cautioned.

Eddie Bowman drove like a maniac, well above the posted speed, and cut in and out of traffic with no regard for other cars on the road. The Iceman didn't complain. What was the point? He read the bio on Eddie Bowman and knew he was insane. Instead, Temple patted the empty spot on his right side where he normally carried his gun. Too bad he didn't have it. Eddie was perhaps the most unpredictable of Donnetti's hired killers. Temple knew, before this mission was over, he was going to have to kill Eddie before Eddie killed him. Now would have been the perfect time. All he needed was a simple ruse to get Eddie to pull off to the side of the road; then one bullet to the back of his head and a body dump in the desert. Problem solved. Unfortunately, he was not carrying his gun, and this had to be a quick, clean kill. Temple had ruled out trying to physically overpower him. He could tell at a glance, Eddie would not go down easy, and in this business, you don't risk an entire mission over who wins in a fistfight.

There was a time in his life when he would have taken Eddie head-on, and damn the consequences. But not here. Not today. Now it was all about the mission. His priority was to recover the microdots and protect the secret. He would just have to wait for a better opportunity to deal with Eddie. So, for now, the big man had a reprieve.

Eddie Bowman continued his reckless, aggressive driving into downtown Las Vegas. When the green traffic light ahead turned yellow, he started to slow down. Then he saw a police car waiting at the intersection, for the cross traffic to go. Eddie smiled in defiance, then accelerated, speeding toward the intersection and crossing the limit line just after the light turned red. The police car did not give pursuit. The cab following them was forced to slam on its brakes and stop at the red light.

The stretch limousine continued racing through the streets of Las Vegas, then made a sharp turn onto Fremont Street and finally came to a screeching halt in front of the

Golden Nugget Casino Hotel. Temple got out on the street side and walked up to the driver's door. He had to stand there a moment before Eddie reluctantly rolled down his window.

Eddie continued looking straight ahead as Temple spoke.

"I won't need you for the return trip," Temple told him, "but tell Mr. Donnetti that I appreciated —"

Eddie drove away from the curb, burning rubber, leaving his passenger in mid-sentence.

Temple watched the limousine speed away. He wondered why Donnetti ever hired someone so unstable. Eddie Bowman was definitely a prime candidate for the psych ward. But even more puzzling, why would Eddie, a man whose record showed he was a perennial loner, totally undisciplined, brutally sadistic, and negative toward authority of any kind – why would such a man submit to Donnetti's will? Temple thought back to when Donnetti spoke to Eddie aboard *The Lucky Lady*. Eddie seemed almost docile; his head bowed as he listened. What could Donnetti possibly have on him to keep him in line? Temple shrugged his shoulders, then headed into the Golden Nugget Hotel. It was time he made a progress report to Karen Kiley.

Chapter 18

Temple walked back into the Golden Nugget Hotel Casino and knocked on Karen's door. No one answered. He waited a moment then knocked again. Still nothing. *Where the hell was she?* She had promised to stay in her room. Temple wondered if Karen ignored his advice and left to make car rental arrangements on her own. He hoped that was it – that she had merely broken her promise to stay in her room. He didn't want to consider the other possibility. Temple stared at her door, tempted to kick the damn thing open, but knew security would be all over him within a matter of minutes. He had to get in there, without alerting security. Temple spotted the housekeeping cart down the hall. That was his way in. He walked over to the cleaning cart in front of an open bedroom door. From the hallway, he could see the maid in the room busily going about her duties. Temple called to her, "Excuse me, miss."

The maid walked toward him. "Yes, sir?"

"I won't need my room cleaned today, but I could use some bath towels. Room 842."

"Yes sir, right away."

Temple nodded and walked off, but waited around the corner, out of view. After ten minutes, he heard a room door close. He peeked around the wall and saw the maid heading toward Karen's room carrying bath towels. Temple waited until she started to unlock the door, then hurriedly walked up behind her, just as she pushed the door open. The maid, startled at suddenly seeing him standing behind her, giggled in nervous embarrassment.

"I forgot my car keys," Temple lied, then apologized for scaring her.

The maid handed him the towels. "Is four enough?" she asked.

"Four is fine," he said.

The maid smiled, then went back to her duties.

Temple entered Karen's room with caution, his eyes carefully examining everything. Nothing looked out of place. The bed was made. Karen's clothing was still in the closet on hangers. He checked the bathroom. She wasn't there. Temple had to consider the very real possibility that Karen Kiley's identity was compromised and Donnetti's people had her. And, if that was true, she was as good as dead. Either by Donnetti's order, or by the CIA, who would have remotely detonated the electronic receiver in her ear, the moment she called for help. Temple shook his head in regret for her situation. Karen never should have been sent on a mission. She wasn't ready. She eventually came to that same conclusion herself and was ready to quit. He hoped, when this was all over, she would still have that option. Either way, he had no options. He had to complete the mission. If in fact she was grabbed, he hoped she didn't give him up.

Temple left Karen's room and took the stairs down to his floor. He considered the possibility that one of Donnetti's assassins might be inside his room waiting for him. Temple removed the do not disturb sign from his doorknob, then cautiously opened the door. His room had not been cleaned by housekeeping. His personal items were where he left them. He went over to the nightstand and picked up the only thing that should not have been there: an envelope. He flipped it over and saw his mission's name written on it. He could feel a small solid object inside. He opened it and found a one-page letter and a key. The letter was from Karen Kiley. It read:

> *Sorry darling, but I had to leave the hotel to make arrangements for your rental car. I know you told me to let the concierge handle it, but I felt it was safer if I made the arrangements personally rather than having the hotel do it for me, as that might draw attention to our association. But don't worry, everything went smoothly. I used my fake I.D. and credit card to rent the car, so there's no way the car can be linked back to me, or you. I even went there in disguise. Smart, huh? Anyway, the car is parked in the hotel parking garage, 3rd floor, under the name Alice Parker. It's a blue Chevy Nova, license plate number GSH129. It's a plain-looking car. Very inconspicuous. You can thank me later (I'm smiling). If you are wondering how I got into your room, I picked the lock. By the way, lock picking was one of*

my best subjects in training.

You know, maybe there's a chance for me in this business after all. (Smile) I'm only kidding. You opened my eyes to a lot of things, and I do thank you for that. I'm heading back to my room now. See you when you get back.

Karen

Temple frowned. Damnit! Didn't those people teach her anything at the Farm? You don't leave incriminating notes lying around for anybody to read. Temple ripped the note into small pieces then flushed them down the toilet. How could she have done such a stupid thing? Even someone still in training should have known better than that. What a fool thing to do.

Although Temple was fuming mad over the note she left, his real anger stemmed from something else. She said she was heading back to her room. She wasn't there. Somebody must have grabbed her. If it was Donnetti, she's dead. If she called the CIA for help, she's dead. They would have remotely detonated that communications stuff in her head. Either way, she never had a chance. Temple hated to think about that being her fate. He had promised himself he would keep her safe. She didn't deserve to end this way. Temple had seen death and been around it most of his life. Ever since his sister was brutally murdered. He had accepted the fact that one day he might have a violent death too. And if he did, so be it. But it wasn't what he wanted for Karen Kiley. She was an innocent. Temple took a moment to reflect on this loss. Then he pushed his emotions to the side, as he'd always done, and focused on the job at hand. He retrieved his suitcase from the bedroom closet. He packed a few personal items so his reason for coming back to the Golden Nugget would look legitimate. He rolled his guns up in a bath towel. The card devices he wrapped in a separate towel. Temple took the towels and the suitcase down to the parking garage. Along the way, he scanned for Karen Kiley but didn't really expect to see her.

In the far north corner of the garage, Temple located the Nova. He placed the guns and card devices on the floor, behind the driver's seat; the suitcase went on top of the front passenger seat. He drove out of the parking garage and merged in with the heavy downtown traffic. Before getting on the freeway, he made a brief stop at a hardware store. He bought two small round mirrors, a roll of masking tape, and a two-cell flashlight, then he continued on to the marina.

Chapter **19**

Yesterday, before Karen Kiley went missing, Jim Donnetti was waiting anxiously across town, in his stateroom, aboard *The Lucky Lady*. He had showered earlier and was resting comfortably on his bed, dressed only in a robe. Donnetti was expecting a visitor. Actually, he was expecting a stranger, but in exactly twenty-three minutes he knew a girl fitting his requested specifications would be ushered into his stateroom.

Earlier in the week, Donnetti had met with a man, who recruits most of the talent for a well-known local escort service. Donnetti made arrangements with that man to provide him with just the right girl. He had called upon this man before and had never been disappointed. Because this man knew what he liked, Donnetti was confident she would be at the tender age of sixteen or seventeen, and most importantly, she would be a virgin. Donnetti harbored no guilt feelings about having sex with these girls. He believed most of them were trying to get laid by the time they were thirteen, anyway. So why shouldn't he get his? He saw no logical reason for those inexperienced schoolboys to get the first crack at those precious, young things. Those young boys couldn't possibly know how to appreciate the precious gift of a virgin. So sweet. So pure. Unviolated by man. Fresh as the day they were born. Besides, the way he figured it, he was doing them a favor; they needed a man of experience to guide them into womanhood. Not many men were willing to break in a virgin. *The fools*.

As Donnetti began to spin wild fantasies about what would take place once his guest arrived, the telephone rang, interrupting his thoughts. *Dammit*! Donnetti cursed, annoyed at the intrusion on his privacy. He hoped the call was not an emergency requiring his immediate attention. He had other plans. Donnetti picked up the phone and snapped, "This better be important!"

A voice familiar only to Donnetti said, "More trouble is coming your way."

"What kind of trouble?" Donnetti asked Maxwell.

"I just found out two more American agents are en route to Vegas. One of them is a CIA agent. Her name is Karen Kiley. She's some kind of specialist."

"What kind of specialist?"

"I don't know."

"And the other one?" Donnetti asked.

"I'm still checking," said Maxwell.

"What does that mean?" Donnetti asked.

After a short, awkward silence, Maxwell said, "I can't

identify the second agent. I've checked and rechecked every available source open to me, but I haven't turned up anything. It's like he doesn't exist."

"Are you sure there *is* a second agent?" Donnetti questioned.

"I'm sure. That much has been confirmed."

"What does that suggest to you?"

Maxwell said, "It suggests the impossible. That within American Intelligence, there is a subdivision so highly secretive its existence is virtually unknown, even to top U.S. officials. And *that*, I can assure you, is impossible."

"Clearly," Donnetti said, "it is not."

"No American intelligence organization commands that level of secrecy, not to my contacts."

"The question is," Donnetti challenged, "what are you doing about it?"

"As I said, I'm still checking."

Donnetti interjected, "You do understand this will change our financial agreement."

"I don't see why it should. This new development is something I had no control over. In our line of work, Mr. Donnetti, I'm sure you are aware, there is always a margin of error in any operation."

"I understand perfectly. But I pay for results, not promises. You told me you could identify every agent coming my way. That's what I'm paying for."

There was a moment of silence, then Maxwell said, "You'll get your money's worth."

"Good," said Donnetti.

"By the way," Maxwell added, pretending it was merely an afterthought, "once this mystery agent is captured, I know people who would be very interested in interrogating him. They would pay most generously for that opportunity. If your people could take him alive —"

"Capture him?" Donnetti blurted out in total amazement. "What the fuck are you talking about? I have no intentions of capturing him. If we catch any government agents snooping around here, they'll be killed instantly. I don't leave loose ends."

"I suppose that would be the wise thing to do — under normal circumstances. But, if this agent exists, he is no ordinary spy. It might prove valuable, to both of us, if these people I know have the opportunity to question him. You could always dispose of him later."

Donnetti shook his head, growing bored with the conversation. "Let's understand each other, Maxwell. The moment this mystery man shows his face in Las Vegas, he's dead. No games. No interrogation. No chances to escape. I kill him before he kills me. It's as simple as that. Now — do we understand each other?"

"We understand each other," Maxwell acknowledged.

Donnetti hung up.

Maxwell knew that wasn't the end of it. This mystery agent had to be found and interrogated. It was imperative they learn everything about him that they could before Donnetti sent his freak, Eddie Bowman, to kill him, just like he did with that other unidentified agent in the actress's home. When that first unknown spy showed up, Maxwell thought it only an anomaly. The emergence of another unidentified spy suggested the existence of much more, perhaps even a secret faction of government operatives, sanctioned and hidden inside American Intelligence. Maxwell had always believed that level of secrecy was impossible, until now.

Jim Donnetti dialed a local number, after hanging up on Maxwell. He wanted these two spies found as soon as possible. The phone was answered on the first ring, "Goodman Detective Agency, Mr. Goodman speaking."

"It's me," Donnetti said.

Goodman's demeanor perked up when he recognized the voice, "Yes sir, Mr. Donnetti. What can I do for you?"

"I've got a rush job for you. There is a woman on her way to Las Vegas named Karen Kiley. She may be using an alias, and may already be here. I want her found right away. I'm also interested in anybody she might be traveling with or contacts while she's here."

"Do you have a picture of her?"

"No."

"Is she flying in?"

"I don't know."

"You said she might already be here?"

"That is a possibility."

"Do you know anything else about this woman that might help me?"

"No. But when you find her don't make contact. Just report to me. Do a good job on this one and there'll be a bonus for you."

Goodman knew perfectly well what working for Donnetti meant. Whomever this unfortunate woman is, she was destined to suddenly disappear, as had the others before her. Goodman had convinced himself it was not his concern. His finding a person for a client was perfectly legal. Whatever his client decided to do with that information afterwards was not his business. "I'll find her," Goodman assured him.

Just then, there was a gentle knock at Donnetti's door. Donnetti stared at the door, then hurriedly said into the phone, "Then I'll hear from you soon," and hung up. "Come in," Donnetti said.

A young girl was ushered into his room, and the door closed behind her. Donnetti struggled to get his bulk to a seated position on the bed. Then he smiled at her. She was, as he knew she would be. Young. Cute. No taller than five-foot-four inches. Her complexion was smooth and clear and she wore no makeup. And her eyes were large and full of innocence.

As she stood before him, she shyly wiped a strand of hair from her face and wondered, if she could pull this off, pretending to be 16 years old.

Very nice, Donnetti thought as he continued to visually survey the goods. She had a fine little body, too, and wore a cute halter top with a short, loose-fitting skirt that exposed a teasing amount of her shapely legs, her most appealing physical asset.

Donnetti patted a spot on the bed to his right.

The girl approached timidly, then sat beside him.

Donnetti placed his sweaty palm on her knee, then moved his hand slowly to her inner thigh and boorishly squeezed the meaty flesh. As he did this, his breathing became heavier and more erratic. In little time, his hand moved under her skirt, until he found the spot.

Having been thoroughly coached, the girl knew, once his hand touched her down there, it was time. She faked a few moans and spread her legs, to give his fingers more access, just as she was instructed to do by the man who brought her there. It was like following a script. Depending on the client's actions, there were specific things she was told to do. She was not supposed to tell him her real age, which was nineteen, because she was told he liked younger teens. Being a virgin, however, was true. That was something that could not be faked.

When he removed his fingers, she slid off the bed and

followed the script, by taking all of her clothing off, slowly.

Donnetti dropped his robe and stretched out on the bed. The young woman hid her revulsion, as she got back on the bed and laid beside this grotesquely fat old man. Donnetti began fondling her small breasts. Then in a spastic frenzy, he started hungrily kissing her young virgin body all over, as if she were food to a starving man. Her pleasure was not his concern. It was all about him.

After defiling every crevice of her young body, he backed away and sat on the edge of the bed; his massive belly nearly completely covering his penis. Donnetti pointed to a spot on the floor in front of him.

The girl followed the script. She climbed off the bed, bowed her head submissively, and dropped to her knees. She had been told he could not get an erection without this. She took his limp manhood into her mouth and almost gagged; he was so sweaty and smelly. After only a few moments of this, she was momentarily relieved when he obtained an erection and pulled it back out of her mouth. But she was nauseated, because she knew what was coming next.

Donnetti moved his considerable girth to a kneeling position in the middle of the bed and glared down at her, still on her knees beside the bed.

The young woman got back on the bed again, this time on her knees with her back to him. She leaned over onto her forearms, leaving her hips up. She buried her face into a pillow, bit down on her lip, and waited for his assault.

The fat man grabbed her hips roughly and shoved himself inside of her without regard for her inexperience. It was brutal and fast, and over in less than twenty seconds. Afterward, Donnetti was totally winded. He collapsed on the bed trying to catch his breath as if he had just run a marathon.

The girl laid on her side, with her back to him, and stared

across the room at a single spot on the wall. She was in considerable pain. The fat man had not been gentle with her, during those few seconds. It felt like her insides had been ripped, but she dare not cry or complain in any way. She had been warned not to show this man any displeasure and not to leave until he dismissed her.

Ten minutes later, when his loud snoring broke the silence, she cried silent tears. Now she would have to wait until he woke up, before she could go home. The one hundred dollars she was paid didn't seem so important anymore.

Chapter 20

Donnetti abruptly woke to the annoying sound of his telephone. Instinctively, he glanced toward the empty half of his bed. He had sent the girl packing late last night, when he woke up to take a piss. She was a great little piece of ass, but he had no desire to ever see her again. She was no longer virgin pure.

Groggily, he reached for the phone. He hoped it was the Goodman Detective Agency calling with news about the two American spies.

The voice on the other end of the phone said, "This is Burnett. I hate to disturb you, but I think this may be important."

Burnett was Donnetti's casino floor manager. He was

fiercely loyal, very ambitious, and willing to step outside the law for Donnetti, if asked. Burnett was a good man to have around.

"What is it?" Donnetti asked.

"A man walked into your casino yesterday evening, said his name was Tom Briggs. He was inquiring about your private games. He wants a seat at the table."

"Tom Briggs, you said?"

"Yes, sir. I would have brought it to your attention then, but you were — ah, busy. This guy, Briggs, talked to one of your evening bartenders, George Atkins. According to Atkins, this guy appeared to be a big spender. He even invited us to run a security check on him. What do you think, boss?"

"I'll get back to you," Donnetti said, then hung up and dialed the Goodman Agency. The recorded voice of Goodman's secretary stated that Mr. Goodman was out of the office, but the caller could leave a message at the dial tone. Donnetti hung up, then dialed Goodman's home. The phone rang several times before an annoyed, sleepy voice answered. "Yeah, what is it?"

"It's me."

The voice on the phone perked up, "Yes sir, Mr. Donnetti, what can I do for you?"

"Do you have anything for me yet?"

"Nothing substantial, but I do have a few leads I'm working on."

"You do know this is time sensitive?" Donnetti reminded him.

"I'm getting up right now, sir. I'll do a good job for you, Mr. Donnetti."

"I know you will."

Goodman was expecting Donnetti to hang up. When he

did not, Goodman asked, "Is there anything else, sir?"

"Yes. I need some information – all you can get on a man who says his name is Tom Briggs. He's in Las Vegas now. I'll have my security people get you a photo of him off the boat's surveillance cameras."

"Alright, sir. I'll start on it as soon as I wrap up the Kiley investigation."

"No. Both investigations are time-sensitive. Do you understand?"

"Yes, sir," Goodman answered.

Donnetti hung up, then laid back down. About an hour later, he dragged himself out of bed, shaved, showered, and had a full breakfast brought to his room. As he was eating, he received another phone call.

"This is Goodman," the voice on the phone said. "I've got info on Tom Briggs."

"That was fast."

"You did say it was time-sensitive."

"What do you have?" Donnetti asked.

"I verified the photo of Mr. Briggs, from your security camera, with a picture of him on the jacket cover of a book he just wrote. From the jacket cover, I got his resident state. With that, I went through back channels and got a copy of his driver's license. He is who he says he is."

"Good work, but does he have the funds to play in a high-stakes game?"

"He's got a half dozen paperback novels already published. Made about one hundred thousand dollars total, on those six. His newest book went hardback a couple of months ago. It was an instant blockbuster."

"So, he's got money?"

"Yes. With the lucrative hardback book deal he got, plus the money he was paid for the paperback rights, and the money he will get on a pending movie deal already in discussion — I'd say he's worth somewhere in the high seven figures."

"Now you've got my interest," Donnetti said.

Goodman continued, "It seems Mr. Briggs is a compulsive gambler. He's played in some of the finest casinos in the United States. But he's a lousy gambler. He's built up quite a lot of debt."

"How much debt?"

"Nothing he can't handle now, with his latest book deal."

"How much?"

"I don't have an exact figure, but it's well over one million dollars."

"Thank you, Mr. Goodman. I appreciate your prompt response on this matter. I'm confident I can expect the same promptness on the Kiley investigation."

"I will be in touch with you soon, sir," said Goodman, feeling confident in his investigative ability, unaware the information he uncovered on Tom Briggs was all intentionally made available to him.

Donnetti dialed an internal phone number onboard the boat. When Burnett answered on the first ring, Donnetti said, "Let me know when Briggs returns to the boat."

"You intend to invite him into the games, sir?" Burnett asked.

"Of course not. But it wouldn't hurt to keep an eye on him. Besides, if he's as lousy at gambling as Goodman says, we should entice him to do his gambling aboard *The Lucky Lady*."

"Consider it done, Mr. Donnetti." Burnett already knew he had the perfect enticement to keep Briggs gambling onboard: Victoria Rodriguez. She was the boat's unofficial hostess. Donnetti paid her a stipend, off the books, to be —

available. She was the perfect vixen. Tall. Statuesque. And a real freak in the sheets. Burnett could personally vouch for her unique talents.

Shortly after twelve noon, Donnetti received another phone call from the Goodman Detective Agency. "We found Ms. Kiley."

"Where is she?" Donnetti asked.

"The Golden Nugget, room 842."

"Is she alone?"

"Yes, she's alone."

"Any visitors?

"Not that we know of."

"Alright. Thank you, Mr. Goodman." Donnetti hung up, then dialed a number from memory.

"Hello," Alvin Gutloff answered.

"This is Jim. I have a job for you. Her name is Karen Kiley." After briefing Gutloff on what he wanted, Jim Donnetti headed down to the pizza parlor aboard his boat. He ordered a whole pizza, with all the trimmings, and ate it all himself.

Standing outside the pizza parlor, Donnetti's casino floor manager, Burnett, waited patiently for Donnetti to finish eating, then he approached the table. "Mr. Donnetti, you wanted to know when Tom Briggs returned. He's in the casino now, playing blackjack."

"How's he doing?"

Burnett smiled, "He's losing."

"Let's keep him comfortable then. Make sure nobody bothers him. Have the most beautiful waitresses make regular rounds to his table. Keep him drinking if possible, but don't pressure him. As long as he's losing, let him."

"Yes, sir."

Donnetti headed back to his stateroom to finish working

on some paperwork. As soon as he arrived, he saw that he had a missed phone call. He returned the call and his lawyer, William Penrod, answered. "You asked me to let you know when the show was ready to start."

"Now?" Donnetti asked.

"As soon as you get here, sir."

"I'm on my way." Donnetti headed upstairs to the room behind the green door. Donnetti had ordered that the door be painted green, after viewing a private screening of the X-rated movie *Behind the Green Door*. He thought the idea humorous and appropriate, since this room was only used for special parties. When Donnetti got to the green door, he opened it and went in. The door was never locked. The staff understood it was forbidden to go beyond the green door, unless permission was granted by Donnetti himself, and that unauthorized intruders would be dealt with severely.

Another man was also heading toward the green door, but he did not have an invitation. He had a plan. George Atkins, the bartender who Temple spoke to earlier, had a message for Donnetti and had taken it upon himself to deliver it personally. He was supposed to let Burnett deliver the news about Briggs' return to the boat, but Atkins saw this information as an opportunity. Why should he be a mere lackey for the floor manager? After all, Briggs had initially approached him about getting into Donnetti's inner circle. Why should the floor manager get whatever appreciation this information would bring? Even if Burnett had already spoken to Donnetti about Briggs, at least Donnetti would know where the information actually came from. Who knows – maybe out of gratitude for steering him onto a big spender, the fat bastard might be willing to pay some kind of bonus. Even if that chubby asshole was not so inclined, Atkins figured he could still benefit. He would, at least, be noticed as more than just another bartender. And, if he was really lucky, he might even get invited behind the green door. Atkins had heard all the titillating gossip about what goes on in the party room, and he wanted to be a part of it. Atkins excitedly quickened his pace, as he recalled some of the stories of gang bangs and orgies.

As George Atkins knocked on the green door, he felt a charge of erotic excitement rush through his limbs. When the door swung open, George Atkins' enthusiasm went limp. Crippling fear flushed through his body, as he looked up into the cold, black eyes of Eddie Bowman.

"What the fuck do you want?" Eddie growled, glaring down at him.

For a horrifying moment, Atkins couldn't speak. The giant scared the shit out of him. The big man's volatile, unstable temper was well known amongst the crew. Everybody walked lightly around him. Atkins didn't want to say anything that would set him off more than he already was. When the blond giant took a step toward him, Atkins blurted out, "I-I have a m-m-message for M-Mr. Donnetti."

"What's the message?" Eddie snarled.

Atkins felt the words choking in his throat, but he forced them out. "I-It's a p-private matter – sir. It's important."

Eddie stared down at Atkins for a moment. Then the big man backed into the room and said, "Wait here," and slammed the door shut in Atkins's face.

George Atkins breathed a nervous sigh. He had never known anyone so utterly frightening.

When the door reopened, the big man didn't say a word but stepped aside for Atkins to enter, but only left him a small space in which to squeeze by.

Atkins shivered fearfully as he stared at the small opening. Now what? He was too afraid to press forward and too scared to ask the big man to back up. Atkins was terrified that Eddie might take either one as a challenge. Atkins next thought was to just walk away. Then he thought again about getting on Donnetti's good side, by passing on information about Briggs.

With nervous hesitation, Atkins made his decision and pressed forward. The blond giant never gave an inch.

After a few horrifying seconds, Atkins emerged on the other side, sweating profusely and trembling uncontrollably. He exhaled heavily several times to calm himself but was too afraid to turn around.

Suddenly the door behind him slammed shut. Atkins made a startled whimper and turned toward the noise. To his surprise and absolute relief, Eddie Bowman was gone. A flush of embarrassment washed over him, and he immediately looked around to see if anyone had noticed his cowardice. Atkins was relieved to see nobody was paying him any attention. He was also disappointed. Only a few people were sitting on a three-sectional couch, in the middle of a large room, talking with their backs to him. A handful of others were standing behind it. The room was not well lit and rather plainly decorated. There were no naked pictures of women on the walls. No X rated videos playing from wall monitors. No naked people running around. Atkins had expected to walk into Sodom and Gomorrah and various forms of debauchery. Instead, everybody appeared to be dressed, well mannered, and in conversation. It was not what he expected to see behind the green door.

After his initial disappointment, it dawned on him, the people were not just milling around the sofa; they were watching something he could not see, because he was behind the couch, several feet away. As Atkins walked closer to the sofa, he could smell the strong scent of marijuana.

Surprisingly, he had not noticed it before. When he got to the back of the couch, he could see what they were all looking at: a naked man and woman were engaged in intercourse, on the floor, in front of the sofa. The woman was so tiny, she could barely be seen underneath him. Only her legs and arms, wrapped around his body, were visible. Atkins could hear her moaning softly and grunting, as the man pounded his hips into her. It was only when the woman's head peeked around her partner's shoulder that George Atkins saw her face, and his jaw dropped. He couldn't believe it was her, the new bar back from the cocktail lounge on his shift. At work, she was so strait-laced, very shy, and always dressed conservatively, very prim and proper. She never showed any of the male bartenders any attention and only socialized minimally at work. Atkins had assumed she was a stuck-up little dyke. But now, after watching her, he realized how wrong he was.

At one point, the girl on the floor looked up and recognized Atkins. She did not look embarrassed or surprised to see him. Instead, she held his stare, as she continued whipping her hips aggressively, stroke for stroke with her partner.

The spectators in the room plunged into total silence, as the couple began bumping and grinding in a fevered frenzy. Atkins had all but forgotten his reason for being there until he heard a faint voice in his subconscious mind. Then, realizing someone was talking to him, Atkins abruptly turned toward the voice and saw Donnetti glaring at him from the couch. "I said, are you the one with the important message for me?"

Atkins nodded nervously. "Ah, yes — I am — I do, Mr. Donnetti."

"What's so important that you had to disturb me here?"

Atkins glanced at the other guest, then he leaned close to Donnetti and whispered, "It's about that man, Tom Briggs."

Donnetti gave Atkins a probing look, "Who the hell are you, anyway?"

"G-George Atkins, sir. I work —"

"You're the bartender," Donnetti cut in.

Atkins was surprised Mr. Donnetti knew him by name. He had to wonder if that was a good thing or a bad thing. It wasn't until the lawyer, William Penrod, leaned over and whispered into Donnetti's ear that Atkins even noticed the little snitch was even there. Penrod did not attempt to conceal the fact that he was telling Donnetti something about Atkins.

Anxious again, Atkins wondered what gossip Penrod was spreading now. When Penrod finished, Donnetti rose from the sofa and glanced at Atkins. "Let's continue this conversation in my office."

As Donnetti circled the couch and headed toward the door, Atkins sneaked one last look at the couple on the floor. They were fucking like rabbits in heat.

When Atkins turned to follow Donnetti, he noticed two other familiar faces on the couch. One he knew only as a special guest of Donnetti's. His name was Nick Marlow. The other familiar face belonged to that cock hound, Victoria Rodriguez. She was snuggled against Marlow, his right arm casually draped over her shoulder. Her hand was on his crotch, rubbing his manhood through his pants.

Jim Donnetti made a motion with his hand, for Penrod to come along. The three of them left the room in single file. Atkins had wanted to glance back one last time at the couple on the floor, but decided against it, since that snitch Penrod was right behind him.

After a short walk, the trio entered the boss's office. Donnetti sat down on the cushioned chair behind his desk. Penrod sat on a hardback chair against the wall behind Atkins, who remained standing. Although there were seats on both sides of the fat man's desk, neither was offered to him.

Donnetti regarded the bartender with cold contempt. Penrod had informed him that Atkins had been sleeping with two of the white cocktail waitresses, who worked his shift and that he had been stealing money from the cash register to finance his philandering.

For the theft, Donnetti had decided to make a public example of the bartender. He would be fired from his tip heavy bartending job and transferred to custodial duty, cleaning toilets, until his debt was paid. He could not allow someone to steal from him and get away with it. It set a dangerous precedent and had to be discouraged.

That other matter, however, Donnetti considered an even bigger crime. More than that, he considered it an abomination that this black bastard would dare stick his prick into a white woman, even one trampy enough to sell it to him. Donnetti took it personally because both those tramps worked for him. For that blatant act of disrespect, the bartender would receive some major hospital time – that is, after he spent four months, in humiliation, scrubbing toilets.

"So," Donnetti began, "what information do you have on this fellow, Tom Briggs?"

"I heard that you wanted to be informed when this guy returned to the boat."

"I did," Donnetti acknowledged.

"Well, he's back," Atkins said with an exuberant smile. "He's in the casino playing blackjack right now."

Donnetti leaned forward in his chair, waiting for more.

When nothing else was offered, Donnetti frowned, in obvious annoyance, "that's it?"

Atkins's smile faded quickly.

"You disturbed me for that?" Donnetti growled.

Noticing the fat man's displeasure, Atkins tried to clean it up. "You did say that you wanted this information immediately, didn't you, sir?"

"You were told to report to the floor manager?"

Atkins' mind stumbled for an answer, a lie, anything that would get him out of what had quickly become an uncomfortable situation. Atkins then blurted out, "I was going to go to the floor manager, sir, but I decided —"

"You decided!" Donnetti snarled. "You are not paid to make something as complex as a decision, bartender. You are paid to mix drinks."

"Yes sir, Mr. Donnetti. In the future, I'll go to the floor manager." Atkins turned to leave.

"Bartender, we do have another matter to discuss."

"Another matter, sir?"

"Isn't there something else you want to tell me?"

"I'm not sure what you mean, sir."

"So, you're a liar *and* a thief."

Atkins stood silently, with his head bowed, as Donnetti reprimanded him for the theft of the money. Donnetti assured him the police would not be brought into this matter, so long as Atkins didn't try to leave Nevada, before his financial obligation was paid off.

Donnetti held no false illusions that he would get all of his money back in four months, nor was he ever planning on reporting this incident to the police. Donnetti believed his own power was absolute. Whatever needed to be done to set things right, he would order it done himself. He only mentioned the police to divert Atkins' fear of him. He did not want Atkins running off just yet, which was also the reason Donnetti carefully omitted mentioning anything about the white girls. Had he shown his displeasure there, Atkins would have most definitely made a run for it – Donnetti was sure of that. Nothing could send a black man running faster than him getting caught screwing a white woman. But as long as Atkins only had the police to fear, he would stay put. Donnetti had no doubt though, that if Atkins chose to run, he would be found, given time, but why make an easy job difficult by sending the rabbit running?

Donnetti rested back in his chair again. "Now get the hell out of my office."

As Atkins headed toward the door, Donnetti added, "You'll be contacted later today about your new job."

Once Atkins was gone, Donnetti turned to Penrod. "Let me know when his four months are up."

"I'll let you know sir," said Penrod.

Chapter 21

An ill-fated breakdown in intelligence gathering resulted in the events that led to Karen Kiley's expedited disappearance. Maxwell, incorrectly believing that Karen Kiley was a highly skilled special agent, relayed that information to Donnetti, who, in turn, made decisions based on that faulty intel.

Before her disappearance, Karen had just driven back to the Golden Nugget Hotel Casino in the rental car she had procured for Michael. But then, he wasn't using his birth name anymore. Now, he was called Alexander. She was still confused as to how that name change came about. She preferred Michael, although she would never call him that again, to his face. Anyway, Michael had warned her to let the hotel concierge make the rental car arrangements, but she decided, it was safer for mission security if she did it herself. Karen parked the rental car in the casino guest parking area, then walked back through the casino toward the elevator. She heard a commotion to her left and saw a woman jumping for joy in the keno lounge, waving a keno ticket high above her head. Others, around the woman, congratulated her and gave her high-fives. Karen started to walk over there but decided against it. She had promised Michael that she would stay in her room and had already broken that promise, even though she did it to keep Michael's identity safe.

Karen continued toward the elevator wondering how Michael was doing and hoped he was alright.

The elevator doors opened and a couple of people got out. Karen stepped into an empty elevator and pushed the button to Michael's floor. When she got to his room, she picked the lock on his door within seconds and left a note for him inside. Afterward, she went back to her room, kicked her shoes off, and turned the television on out of habit, with no serious thought of watching it. She sat on her bed still thinking about Michael. The mystery of Michael Darrin nagged at her. How was he even alive? She vividly remembered the day he died. His body was found severely burned in a car crash. She remembered how so many people cried at his funeral. But Michael wasn't dead. Who died that day? Where had Michael been all these years? Why did he change his name? Karen sat pondering the mystery and wondering if she'd ever learn the truth.

After a while, Karen stood up and headed toward the bathroom to touch up her makeup. She wanted to look pretty when Michael came back. A curt smile crossed her lips, as she thought about yesterday. When she was wrapped only in a towel, she could tell that Michael was attracted to her.

Karen's smile widened as she walked into the bathroom fantasizing about the possibilities.

As she walked past the bathroom door, Alvin Gutloff stepped out from behind it and grabbed her in a sleeper hold, with his bicep and forearm pressed against the sides of her throat, cutting off the oxygen to her brain. His free hand went behind her head and pushed forward to increase the pressure on her carotid arteries. Karen tried to resist but passed out quickly. Even after her body went limp, Gotloff maintained his tight grip until her heart stopped, then he dropped her.

The hitman then stepped over her body and walked back into the stateroom and opened the door. Eddie Bowman stood in the hallway holding two large trunks. Gutloff stepped aside as Eddie entered.

"There's only one of them here, in the bathroom," Gutloff told him.

Eddie sat one of the trunks on the bedroom floor, then carried the other into the bathroom. He stuffed Karen's body inside the trunk, breaking bones in her legs and arms to make her fit. He then tossed in the throw rug she was lying on and returned to the bedroom carrying the trunk. He then retrieved the other trunk and followed Gutloff into the hallway. Gutloff dropped back to let Eddie walk ahead of him, as they headed toward the elevator. He didn't want that psycho behind him.

Both men rode the elevator down to the lobby in silence, then they walked toward the parking garage, with Eddie carrying both trunks effortlessly. Once in the garage, they walked off in different directions, without a word spoken between them.

After discovering Karen Kiley was missing, Alexander Temple returned to *The Lucky Lady* carrying his suitcase, but left his Walther PPK in the car. He just hoped his identity wasn't blown.

Temple introduced himself to the boat's host, on the quarterdeck, using his mission's name, then added, "I believe you're expecting me."

Neither of the boat's hosts knew what he was talking about and each looked at the other, dumbfounded. One of the uniformed security guards walked over. "I'll take care of this one," he said. "Come with me, Mr. Briggs."

The guard led Temple into the casino. He looked across the room and pointed to a woman, seated at the cocktail bar with her back to them. "Over there," the guard said. "Talk to that woman, the one wearing the white evening dress. She'll take care of you."

Temple thanked him for his help, then crossed the casino floor to the bar area and stood behind the woman. He had recognized her even from across the room. She was the tall Mexican beauty who had flirted with him earlier in the casino. "Hello," he said.

Deep in thought, she turned around to dismiss the interloper, but upon seeing him, her face lit up. "Well, hello," she said, her voice raspy and seductive.

Temple asked, "Are you the person I'm supposed to meet with to get a room onboard?"

"That would be me," she said. "I've been expecting you, Mr. Briggs. Your room is ready. If you'll follow me, please."

When she stood up, her long dress rippled to the floor. It was a sleek, silk garment wrapped around her body like she was sewn into it.

It was common knowledge, tight dresses were best worn with nothing on underneath, to avoid the telltale lines of undergarments bleeding through. Some women, out of modesty, felt uncomfortable being so naked they usually wore panties or pantyhose underneath. Victoria apparently felt no such modesty.

When she turned from the bar to lead him to his room, her movement caused the thin material of her dress, to hug her shapely figure, in an almost indecent manner.

Temple gently grabbed her arm. "You can finish your drink first."

Victoria's sensuous eyes met his. "There's always another drink," she said.

"I'm in no hurry," he insisted.

Victoria regarded him for a moment, then sat back down. "Alright. I'll finish it if you have one with me."

Temple faked a smile, "Now that's the best offer I've had all day."

She gave him a seductive grin, "Your day is going to get a lot better."

"You sure about that?" Temple quipped.

"I can guarantee it, Mr. Briggs," she said with a wink.

Temple sat beside her. "Call me Tom."

"Alright, Tom."

Temple ordered a drink, then asked, "What's your name?"

"Victoria Rodriguez. But my friends call me Tori."

"Are we going to be friends?"

"I certainly hope so," she replied with a devilish grin.

Temple gave her a long look while taking a sip from his glass.

Victoria noticed his stare. "What?" she asked curiously.

"Funny how things work out," he said.

"How so?" she probed.

"I was hoping I'd see you again," Temple lied, thinking she might be a useful asset later, if the shit hit the fan.

"You were hoping to see me again?" she explored.

"I was."

"Why?"

"There's something about you. I was too busy when I first saw you to find out what."

"Are you still too busy?" she asked, in a seductive tone.

"I've got plenty of time now," he said.

"For what?" she teased, her eyes gazing into his.

"You tell me," he said, staring back at her.

Victoria smiled broadly, sat her half-finished drink on the bar and stood up. "Why don't we go see your room now?"

Temple gulped his drink down, then probed. "So, you work for Mr. Donnetti?"

"No, not really," she said, then hooked her arm around his and led him across the casino floor.

Temple frowned. "Not really? What does that mean?"

"It means, I don't *work* for anybody."

"Then why are you here?" Temple asked as they continued walking.

"Jim Donnetti and I have an understanding. You might say I'm an unofficial hostess."

"No," Temple clarified, "I mean, why are you here with me, now?"

Without slowing her pace, Victoria answered almost matter-of-factly. "I wanna fuck you."

Temple stopped walking and stared at her.

"Does my bluntness shock you?" she asked, with a probing stare.

"A little. Most women aren't so outspoken."

"I'm not most women."

"Why me?" he asked.

Victoria smiled. "A woman can tell when she first sees a man if she wants to fuck him. Most women won't act on it. They'll think about it. They'll dream about it. They'll fantasize about it. But they won't act on it. Like I said, I'm not most women."

"No, you're not," Temple agreed.

"I don't need romance or flowers or a commitment. I just want the sex, just like you men do." Victoria tugged at his arm and they continued walking.

"Since you don't work for Donnetti," Temple stated, "how'd you manage to insert yourself into this escort detail?"

"I heard Big Jim tell a security guard to have one of the hostesses' show you your room, so I simply made the guard an offer he couldn't refuse."

"You're a resourceful woman."

"I get what I want," she said with confidence.

As Victoria led Temple across the casino floor, toward the corridor leading to the staterooms, The Grim Reaper deliberately took a position near where they would pass. He wanted to give The Iceman another look at him, to be positive the American agent did not recognize him. If, however, The Iceman so much as blinked, he would kill the American right then and there – along with anyone else who got in his way, as he made his escape. Shooting his way out of a casino was not a big concern. Armed casino security guards are trained not to draw their weapons inside a crowded casino, for fear of accidentally shooting a paying customer. That kind of publicity, no casino wanted. Recovery from such a PR nightmare would be impossible.

As The Iceman walked past him, The Grim Reaper watched carefully for any sign of recognition. He saw none. The Soviet relaxed his grip on the gun, under the newspaper. He could always be wrong about the security guards. There was always a chance that a maverick guard, with a cowboy mentality, might not follow orders and start blasting away at an armed threat, guests be damned. No sense taking unnecessary chances. He would wait for a better time.

As Victoria led Temple into the inner corridors of the boat, The Iceman remained vigilant for danger. He wasn't ready to buy her story of how she was overwhelmed by his charms. He also couldn't shake the feeling there was more to this woman than what she outwardly portrayed. Whoever she was, whatever she was up to, Temple decided to let her play out her hand.

When they arrived at his room, Victoria opened the door without the use of a key. Temple was not surprised. With the clothing she wore, there was no place to put a key.

Temple followed her into the sitting area, of a huge two-room suite, and closed the door behind him. The sitting area was comfortably decorated with a two-sectional couch and an oval-shaped coffee table in front of it. Mounted on the wall, in front of the couch, was a 30" TV. A mahogany desk and leather chair lined the starboard wall. The door leading to the bedroom was partially open, the light inside revealed a dresser and what appeared to be a king-size bed.

Victoria glanced around the room. "It's way too bright in here," she said, then continued over to the light switch. She looked over her shoulder at him with a gleam in her eyes, then turned the dimmer knob down. "Much better," she said.

Temple disregarded her flirtation and entered the bedroom. He sat his suitcase on the floor next to the bed, then peeked into the closet and bathroom, in a seemingly casual manner, but really to make sure nobody was waiting to jump him. When he was assured there was no hidden danger, he gave her a nod of approval on the room.

Victoria sauntered over to him, her tall statuesque body on full display. "You like?" she asked.

Temple knew what she was asking had nothing to do

with the room. "Looks good to me," he smiled.

Victoria smiled back, then grabbed his belt and pulled him closer. When he didn't back away, she leaned in for the kiss, and was aroused when he accepted her tongue.

During their sensual kiss, Temple kept his eyes partially open. If there was danger, he wanted to see it coming.

Victoria moaned deeply, as their kiss grew more intense. When their lips reluctantly parted to take a breath, she purred, "I knew I was right about you." Victoria flashed a devilish grin, then ripped his shirt open, buttons flying everywhere. She admired the dense muscularity of his upper body, as his tattered shirt hung loosely over powerful shoulders. She locked her eyes on his and held his stare, then reached behind her neck and unfastened the one button that held up the top of her gown. When the button was released, the top of her dress dropped around her waist, exposing her full, magnificent breasts. Victoria then pulled her gown the rest of the way down, in a slow, deliberate tease, her eyes never leaving his. Finally, she let the gown fall to the floor and stepped out of it, her voluptuous, naked body demanded his full attention and dared him to look away.

Temple did not look away. Maybe she was just who she appeared to be, a horny woman. A beautiful, horny woman. And since he had a little time to kill, why not enjoy it. Temple pulled his tattered shirt off. Then his shoes and socks followed. He started to unbuckle his belt.

"I should freshen up first," Victoria said while caressing her right inner thigh.

As she walked away, Temple enjoyed the stimulating view of her naked body, until she disappeared into the bathroom. He continued to undress and, had just pulled his pants off, when he heard glass breaking in the bathroom. Temple bolted toward the noise only wearing his underwear.

When he ran into the bathroom, he saw Victoria standing by the sink, modestly covering her nakedness with a bath towel. The index finger from her other hand was up to her lips. Her facial expression had changed. The vixen was gone, replaced by cold seriousness. He saw the broken glass on the floor was an ashtray. Victoria made a motion with her finger for him to come closer. When he did, she whispered, "Your bedroom is bugged for sound and there's a closed-circuit camera hidden behind the two-way mirror, at the head of your bed."

Temple stared at her. Who in the hell was she? And why was she warning him? Temple stayed in character. "What are you talking about?"

"I'm with the FBI," Victoria whispered.

"You're what?" Temple exclaimed, the surprise in his voice was real.

She shot him a stern look, then whispered, "Keep your voice down." Then she moved her lips inches from his ear, "I'm an FBI agent," she repeated. "I'm on a special bureau task force. I know why you're here. We're after the same man, but for different reasons."

Temple wondered, who the hell was she, really? Even if she was with the FBI, why was she breaking her cover now and how did she know about him? D-branch didn't share mission details or agent information with anybody. He had to get to the bottom of this and fast. "Come on, Victoria," Temple said with a chuckle, maintaining his cover. "Don't go weird on me."

"My division director told me microdots, meant for the president, were stolen. He showed me a picture of you and said you'd be coming. He didn't give me any other details about you or your mission. Said it was above my pay grade."

Temple gave her a long look, shook his head, and

smiled, "You're kidding me, right?"

"We don't have time for these games, Tom, or whatever your real name is."

"Look lady," Temple began, "I don't know who you think I am, but you've made a mistake with —"

Victoria cut him off. "You arrived in Vegas with a CIA specialist named Karen Kiley. We know all about her, but you — you're the mystery man that my boss won't talk about."

Temple was still not convinced she was with the FBI. Delaware never mentioned her in the briefing, but he didn't mention his brother either. On the other hand, Donnetti could have gotten the information about him from Maxwell and passed it along to her. In any case, she knew too much about him and the mission, to let her live, if she wasn't who she said she was. For now, he would pretend to believe her story. He could always kill her later. Temple decided to play along. "Alright Victoria. You're right about me, but I had to be sure about you, you understand."

"Yeah, sure."

"You said my room is bugged. Are they on to me?"

"No. All new guests are initially assigned to one of these specially monitored rooms. Donnetti's not a very trusting man. He likes to observe his guests first, before giving them the run of the boat."

"Have you heard any recent chatter about Karen Kiley?"

"No. Haven't heard a thing. Why, did something happen?"

Temple ignored her question. "Do you know where the microdots are?"

Victoria noticed he avoided her question, but let it go. "No, I don't," she answered.

"Do you know what's on the microdots?" he questioned.

She shook her head no, "That's above my pay grade, too."

Temple's eyes narrowed. "Why are you on this boat?"

"I'm here for Donnetti. He's come up on our radar too many times to ignore. The FBI needed someone in his inner circle to take him down, so here I am."

"Then you're not here about the microdots?" Temple confirmed.

"No. I only heard about them when I was briefed about you."

"And you've been here how long?"

"Just over five months."

"Why the big mystery?" Temple asked.

Victoria was confused. "Huh? What mystery?"

"Why wasn't I told about you?"

"It didn't concern you," she quickly replied. "Your job is to —"

"I know what my job is. What's yours?"

"I told you."

Temple pressed, "They told you about me for a reason. Why?"

Victoria clutched the bath towel tighter in front of her, as she stared at him in awkward silence. She couldn't hide it from him any longer. He needed to hear the truth. Victoria exhaled heavily, then answered him, "If you get caught and have no hope of escape — my job is to kill you."

"I'd say that concerns me," Temple said sarcastically. Then he added, "Who does Donnetti think you are?"

"I'm supposed to be a high-priced call girl. Donnetti allows me to work on the boat as a — *special hostess* for his guests."

Temple considered her earlier demeanor toward him. "You're very convincing," he said.

"I have to be convincing," Victoria offered, "or I'm dead."

Without sharing too much information, Temple said, "When I was gambling earlier in the casino, I noticed that one of Donnetti's entourage took exception to you flirting with me."

"Yeah, that guy has been bird-dogging me for the last two days. He's one of Donnetti's hired guns. His name is Nick Marlow."

Temple nodded. "Why are you confiding in me now?"

"I had to warn you about your room being bugged and monitored. Besides, we felt it was safer for all concerned, if you knew who was on your side."

"*We* felt?" Temple probed.

"I've got a partner. He spoke to you earlier in the casino today."

"He spoke to me?"

"Remember the man who approached you in the casino, after you cashed in your chips?"

"That young blond guy?"

"Yes, that's him. He's new in the field, a little green, but he's a good, dependable agent. His name is Billy Shaw."

Temple momentarily thought about another rookie agent, Karen Kiley. She never had a chance. They never should have sent her out on a mission, with no training. Then he thought about himself. How they sent him to Vietnam with no training. It wasn't fair then either, but who said life had to be fair.

Temple glanced into the bedroom, then back to Victoria. "You said my bedroom is being monitored. Whoever's watching is expecting us to have sex. What do we do now?"

Victoria looked at him and said without emotion, "We give them the show they expect."

Temple wondered how many men she had to have sex with, on this mission, to solidify her cover identity. For undercover agents, sex was sometimes a part of the job. Some might say, for the female agents, it was an occupational hazard, but in reality, all agents do what they have to do to establish their cover identity or to obtain information. Covert male agents do it all the time, and nobody bats an eye. Sometimes, when female agents have to bed the enemy, they're looked upon as having low moral character. In the real world of undercover work, female operatives play by the same rules as the men, and sex is just a part of the job.

Now, to maintain her cover, Victoria was prepared to have sex with him, in front of the hidden camera monitoring his room. Temple considered her predicament. Maybe there was another way. "Do you know if the camera behind the mirror is set up for night vision?" he asked.

"No, they're not."

"Then we don't have to give them a real show," Temple said.

"Oh! I see what you mean," Victoria told him. "They can't see in the dark."

"That's right. We just cut the lights out before it gets too real."

Victoria tried to suppress her smile, as she was genuinely touched by his consideration.

Temple acknowledged her implied 'thank you' with a nod.

"We'll give them one hell of a sound show anyway," she said.

Temple looked down at the broken ashtray.

"I'll get it later," she told him.

"Alright then," Temple said, pulling his underwear off,

"let's do this."

Victoria's eyes widened for an instant at seeing the enormous size of his manhood. She quickly diverted her eyes up to meet his and played it off. "Showtime," she said, then dropped her bath towel and ran playfully back into the bedroom, giggling for the camera.

Temple got into character too, and ran after her, laughing as if there had been some sexual bantering in the bathroom. As he chased after her though, he couldn't help but notice the round firmness of her butt and how its muscles tightened and relaxed with each stride she took.

Victoria hopped onto the bed and Temple landed beside her. They quickly embraced. Temple was acutely aware of the camera. He was also aware of her naked body pressing against his. Victoria took the lead and straddled his body and, for the next several minutes, they put on an erotically stimulating show for the cameras, kissing, touching, and caressing. No body parts were off-limits. Their performance was so sensual Temple's manhood embarrassingly took notice, and more than once, he had to deflect penetration due to sheer proximity. A couple of times he felt she didn't want him to stop, but he resisted that overwhelming temptation.

In his private stateroom, Jim Donnetti quietly watched the closed-circuit feed from the hidden camera in Tom Briggs' bedroom. Donnetti had been watching the monitor ever since Briggs entered the room. He was not surprised to see Victoria Rodriguez with him. The guard, who was supposed to escort Briggs to his room, fearing reprisal for not following orders, went to Donnetti and told him of Victoria's request and sexual enticement. Donnetti thanked him for his honesty but assured him, if he ever overrode another order he would severely regret it.

Victoria's actions, Donnetti believed, were predictable. He noticed, earlier in the casino, how she reacted to Briggs when she first saw him. Knowing Victoria Rodriguez as he did, he expected her to make a move on him, as soon as she got the opportunity.

Behind Donnetti, two of his bodyguards were standing by the door, watching the monitor over Donnetti's shoulder with pretended disinterest.

Nick Marlow, sitting behind Donnetti, was not pleased with what he was seeing but contained his displeasure. He would settle up with that bitch later.

Donnetti concluded that Victoria's interference was not such a bad thing. Her presence in that room could serve a dual purpose. First, it allowed Donnetti the opportunity to watch Briggs more closely. Donnetti firmly believed observing a man during sex was the best way to learn something of his character. In bed, a man had no secrets. No phony self-projected image. His true self was revealed. And secondly, Donnetti glanced back briefly at Nick Marlow. If Briggs proved to be an adequate lover, maybe it would keep that Mexican slut out of that black bastard's bed.

Chapter 22

When Temple figured he and Victoria had provided enough entertainment for the hidden camera, he spread her legs and positioned his body between them.

Still playing her part, Victoria wrapped her muscular legs around him. For an uneasy moment, she wondered if he was going to take advantage and make penetration, on the pretext of playing to the camera.

Temple leaned close to her ear and whispered, "Now."

Victoria understood. She reached over to the bedside lamp and moaned, "It's way too bright in here," then flicked the light off, plunging the room into darkness. Victoria unwrapped her legs from around his waist. She felt him roll over onto his side next to her, his lips close to her ear.

Temple whispered, "This might be a good time for me to have a look around the boat. Can you keep up the show by yourself?" He felt Victoria roll over to face him. Her naked breasts pressed against his chest, as she leaned close to his ear.

"How long?" she whispered back.

"Maybe an hour. Maybe less."

"Sure. I can handle it. You ready?"

"I'm ready when you are."

Victoria rolled onto her back again and began moaning passionately, gasping, and crying out sexual obscenities.

Temple smiled as he slipped quietly out of bed. She was a good actress. He gathered up his clothing on the floor, in the dark, and collected the hardware items he had bought. He tiptoed toward the door to the sitting room. He knew Victoria had already turned the lights off out there, so, when he opened the door, he was certain whoever was watching them wouldn't notice it opening. Temple stepped into the dark sitting room and quietly closed the door behind him. He kept the lights off, as he put his clothes back on. The Walther went under his belt and he grabbed the paper bag of hardware items. A smile creased his lips at the sound of Victoria still moaning in erotic passion. He wondered how long she could keep that up.

Cautiously, Temple stepped into the hallway and headed toward the outside decks. It would be safer out there than using the inner corridors. When he got outside, he took the stairway up to deck level 03. He opened the door to a long narrow corridor and glanced inside. It was empty. Temple stepped in, closed the door behind him, and followed the path Donnetti had taken him on earlier. The door marked *Authorized Personnel Only* was up ahead. He opened it and stepped into the white corridor leading to the vault. Before proceeding to the white door at the other end, he stood his ground and visually scanned the passageway for security devices. Donnetti had previously described his security system in great detail, but Temple was not so gullible as to believe Donnetti had showed him everything. Once he was relatively certain there were no hidden devices on this side of the door, Temple continued forward. He opened the white door slowly, cautiously, looking for hidden security systems. He saw none — so far. Temple entered the security entryway and glanced at the phone used by Donnetti earlier, to have the interior security alarms shut off. He walked past the phone and approached the door. This one, Temple remembered, would be locked. When he stepped close to the door to examine the lock, an earsplitting security alarm sounded.

Temple whirled around and ran back the way he came. He had to get back to his room. He was sure Donnetti's people would eventually show up there looking for him, the new guy, despite Victoria's excellent performance. Temple rushed back to the starboard deck and down several flights of stairs. He started down the corridor to his stateroom, but stopped abruptly at seeing the door at the other end of the hallway being pulled open. There was no way he could make it to his stateroom, at the far end of the corridor now, nor could he make it back out of the door he just entered.

Just before the first uniformed guard stepped into the corridor, Temple quickly grabbed the closest doorknob to him. It was unlocked. He ducked inside. The stateroom had no sitting area – just a bedroom and bath – and there was no mirror at the head of the bed to conceal a camera. He could hear someone moving around in the bathroom and heard the faucet turn on and off, then on again. Temple turned his attention back to the noises in the hallway, as the voices got closer. When the voices faded, Temple cracked open the door and peeked out. He saw about a half dozen guards running out onto the starboard deck. When the last man was out of sight, Temple started to make a run for his room. That's when the bathroom door opened behind him, and he heard a familiar voice.

"What the hell are you doing in my room?" she blurted out. "Did you follow me here?"

Temple turned to see the woman, who had given him a ride when he was hitchhiking earlier. What the hell was she doing here? She told him she was in Las Vegas to visit her sister, then she dropped him off at the pier and drove away. She never said anything about coming back. Maybe she followed her sister onboard. Maybe everything she said was a lie. He hoped she wasn't a part of Donnetti's group. He hoped she wasn't somebody he was going to have to kill.

Her voice shook with a mixture of anger and fear as she confronted him. "I said, what are you doing here?"

Temple thought quickly. "Following you?" he scoffed. "I believe you've got that backwards, lady. This is my room. What are *you* doing here?" Temple saw the fear leave her face. She was starting to buy his lie.

"No, you're mistaken," she said. "This is my room. I've been here since I dropped you off this morning." Then she asked suspiciously, "Where have you been since then? Certainly not in this room."

"I've been in the casino. But I don't understand how this mix-up could have happened. I was told this room was — oh, wait a minute." Temple faked embarrassment. "Wait a minute. I know what the problem is. This room, it's the third room off the starboard corridor, isn't it?"

"Starboard corridor?"

"Right side," Temple clarified.

"Yes, it is."

"Well, that's it. My room is on the other end of the corridor, third room from the port side — ah, left side."

"So that's what happened," she said, the tightness leaving her face. "That port and starboard stuff gets me confused too."

"I'm sorry. I thought this was my room. I guess I'm little tired."

"Don't worry about it. No harm done."

"Well — Yolanda, it was nice seeing you again." Temple turned to leave.

"I'm surprised you remembered my name," she said. "Sorry, I don't remember yours."

"Tom Briggs," he said, then started for the door. When he got there, he heard voices in the hallway again. Temple turned back to Yolanda, stalling for time. "Oh, did you find your sister?" he asked.

Yolanda's eyes clouded. "I found her."

Temple walked back toward her, feigning sympathy. "What's wrong?"

"Nothing. Nothing's wrong."

In a soothing voice, Temple probed further, "It might help if you talk about it."

Yolanda returned a bewildered stare. He was a stranger to her. She had no reason in the world to open up to him or to even trust him — but she did. Somehow, she felt she could. She couldn't explain it even to herself. It was just a feeling.

"I'm a good listener," Temple added. In truth, he didn't care about her problems with her sister. He wanted to get back to his room, before Donnetti's people decided to search it. He knew he still had some time though, because the security guards were not knocking on doors in this corridor yet.

"I don't want to burden —"

"It's no burden," Temple cut in. "I want to help. Besides, you helped me earlier with the ride. It's the least I can do."

Yolanda plodded over to the sofa and sat down. She stared at the floor, gathering her thoughts. When she looked up at him, her eyes were full of tears. "My mother's dying," she said, her voice quivering. "She wants to see my sister, Edna, one last time before she —" Yolanda couldn't say the word again, so she skipped forward in her story. "I flew in from Seattle to try and make that happen for my mom."

The name 'Edna' rang alarm bells for Temple. One of Donnetti's hired guns was named Edna Jean Case. He wondered if Yolanda's sister was the hired gun. The fact that Yolanda is black and Edna Jean Case is white didn't matter – they could still be sisters. They could be the offspring of interracial parents, just as he was. On the other hand, maybe Yolanda just got caught in her first lie. Temple sat down beside her and probed further, keeping his radar tuned to the sounds in the hallway. "You said you were going to *try* to get your sister to go home with you? Are you thinking she might not want to go?"

"I honestly don't know."

Temple's brow drew tight. "Why would she refuse, after learning about her mother's condition?"

"They never really got along."

"But if your mother is — not well, surely that cancels out whatever disagreements they might have had."

"I hope so," Yolanda mumbled, with a faraway look in her eyes.

"It'll all work out," Temple offered, while glancing back at the door.

Yolanda noticed Temple's attention seemed elsewhere.

"You don't really want to hear this, do you?"

"Sure I do," Temple lied, as he continued listening to the voices come and go in the hallway, with more frequency. He was running out of time. He had to get back to his room.

Yolanda continued, "Until today, I hadn't seen or spoken to my sister since she ran away at age sixteen. She just dropped out of sight." Yolanda thought back. "She was such a lonely little girl then. Always kept to herself. She only had one close friend back then: Margaret. Margaret was kind of weird. Really sneaky. Always looking at you out the corner of her eyes. But she practically worshiped Edna, even though Edna took advantage of her, sometimes to the point of cruelty. Edna's mother was always after her about how she treated her friend."

"Edna's mother?" Temple questioned.

Yolanda gave him a long look. "I was adopted into the Crump family when Edna was ten. I think Edna always resented me for it."

Now Temple knew her sister was one of Donnetti's hired killers. And being adopted explained how she had a white sister. Temple probed further, not out of curiosity, but in an attempt to keep her talking, until he could figure out how to get back to his room without being seen.

"Did your father send you here to bring Edna back?"

"No. He died two years after my adoption, in a boating accident."

"I'm sorry to hear that."

"It was a long time ago," she mumbled.

"How did you know Edna was here?"

"Margaret told us."

Temple said, "Guess that was a shock, finding your sister after all this time."

"It was. Strange thing is, Margaret lives in my

neighborhood, but she never told us she'd been keeping in touch with Edna. She's never even come by for a visit. Then one day she shows up at our door saying she heard my mom was sick. I think she only came by to verify mom was ill before she told us about Edna."

Temple noticed it was suddenly quiet in the hallway. Now was his opportunity to get back to his room. Temple started to politely excuse himself, on some phony pretext, when suddenly he heard a knock at Yolanda's door.

The voice on the other side of the door boomed out, "Yolanda! Open up. It's Edna."

Yolanda stood up and started for the door. Over her shoulder, she said to Temple, "Maybe you can help me with her. I never could talk to her."

"Wait a minute," Temple insisted in a low but commanding voice.

Yolanda stared at him in confusion. She did not understand the serious tone in his voice. Very quickly though, the truth dawned on her, when this man – this stranger, really – hurriedly moved toward her bathroom to hide. He had been lying to her.

Edna pounded impatiently on the door. "Come on! Open up! I don't have all day!"

Yolanda glanced at the door then back at Temple. Their eyes locked briefly, as he disappeared into her bathroom. He pushed the door shut, leaving it open just enough so he could hear and see what was going on.

Yolanda opened the door for her sister.

Alexander Temple felt like a mouse, trapped in a box, with no place to run. Yolanda had no reason to keep his presence a secret. It was obvious to her now that he had been lying. The sensible thing for her to do was to run screaming to her sister. Temple, however, did not think she would do the sensible thing. He noticed the look in her eyes the moment she realized he had lied. Surprisingly, it was not the look of someone frightened or even angry, but more one of hurt, because she confided in him and he lied to her.

Despite the confusion on her face, Temple's every instinct told him she would not turn him in. But, just in case he was wrong, he had his Walther ready.

Edna Jean Case stormed into the room grumbling. "It's about time you opened the damn door." Noticing her step sister's puzzled expression, Edna barked, "What's the matter with you?"

Temple readied himself, in case his instincts were wrong, and considered scenarios on taking the two women out, if it came to that. Edna was the professional. Maybe Yolanda was, too. But Edna was the known threat so, he would have to take her out first.

Yolanda finally answered, "Nothing's wrong with me. I'm just worried about – mom."

"I decided not to go back with you," Edna announced.

Yolanda frowned in disbelief. "You can't mean that."

"I mean it," Edna countered, her face frozen in a granite stare.

"Your mother is *dying*. She wants to see you one last time. How can you say no to that?"

"Maybe I just don't want to see her. Did either of you ever think about that?"

"Why are you doing this? Surely you can put your personal feelings aside for a little while. Don't let your mother die, without her family by her side."

"Can't help you," Edna said dismissively.

"How can you be so cruel to your own flesh and blood?"

"My going back there won't keep her alive. She's gonna die. There's nothing anybody can do about it. Why should I inconvenience myself?"

"Inconvenience! Your mother wants to see you one last time before —"

"Yeah, yeah, I know, before she dies."

Yolanda sadly shook her head. "You hate her that much?"

Edna was truly astonished by the question. "I've been gone for over twenty years, for a reason. That old lady means nothing to me. I suggest you take your ass back home to *Mama* just as fast as you can. From what you've told me, I don't think the old gal has got much time left." Edna cracked a half-smile, then added, "Tell Mama I said, bon voyage."

Yolanda impulsively lurched forward to slap her sister's foul mouth, but Edna easily, caught her hand in mid-swing, then aggressively shoved her to the floor.

"Don't you dare get up," Edna growled.

Yolanda trembled in fear on the floor. She saw the cold rage in Edna's eyes and it terrified her. Fearing for her safety, she glanced at the bathroom door for help, but Tom didn't come out.

After a tense few moments, Edna's posture relaxed. She unclenched her fist and took a relaxing breath. When she spoke, her words were slow and deliberate, "This one time. I'm going to overlook what you did. This one time. For old time's sake. But don't *ever* try that again." Edna gave her one last menacing stare, then turned to leave, but stopped at the door. "Oh, yeah," Edna remembered, then looked back at Yolanda, who was still cowered on the floor. "Mr. Donnetti wants all of his resident guests to know there's a thief on board. The fool just tried to break into Donnetti's safe. We're pretty sure he's still on board. We'll find him. But, if you should see anybody lurking around — as you're leaving to go home *today,* be sure to alert security."

When Edna left the room, Yolanda stood up, still trembling from the encounter, as Temple stepped out of the bathroom.

Yolanda turned and faced him. "They're looking for you, aren't they?"

"I can explain."

Yolanda backed up and grabbed hold of the doorknob, like it was her safety net. "You can explain lying?"

"I can." Then he lied to her again. "I had to hide. I'm working undercover."

"You're what?"

"Mr. Donnetti hired me to do a job for him."

"I thought you were here on vacation, to do some gambling. That's what you said."

"I was. I mean, I am."

"Which is it? She snapped curtly.

Temple hadn't heard any sounds in the hallway since Edna left. But he couldn't leave now, with Yolanda being suspicious. She could still blow his cover. But, if he didn't leave soon, he could blow it himself. He needed to wrap this up.

"I am a freelance writer," he lied. "I came to Vegas to relax and gamble. Earlier today I met Mr. Donnetti. He offered me serious money to do an undercover job for him."

"What kind of undercover job?"

Temple gave her that *should-I-take-her-into-my-confidence-look*, then he said, "You understand this is just between you and me?"

"I understand," she said with apprehension, as her hand dropped from the doorknob.

Temple lowered his voice, as if he were telling her a secret, "Somebody has been systematically stealing money off this boat for the past couple of months. Mr. Donnetti hired a professional investigator, but he didn't have any luck, so he asked me to help."

"If a professional investigator couldn't find the thief, what good can you do?"

"I'm a mystery suspense writer," he clarified. "This kind of puzzle is right up my alley. Besides, Mr. Donnetti read my last two books, and he thinks I can do the job. Frankly, so do I."

"Why didn't Mr. Donnetti just go to the police?"

"He wants to keep this thing out of the press."

"Why?"

"He doesn't want to scare this guy off. He'd rather catch him in the act. Makes for a better case." Temple kept his ears attuned to the hallway, as he fended off her questions. It was still quiet out there. He still had a chance.

Yolanda looked at him with suspicion. "Why did you hide from my sister? There's no way she would have guessed you were working undercover for Donnetti just because you were in my room."

Temple suppressed his frown. This woman was sharp. She was asking all the right questions. He had to admire her for that, even though she just asked him the one question that he had no logical answer for. And since there was no logical answer, he needed a diversionary one. Something that would take her focus off why he hid in the bathroom.

Temple thought quickly. "You're probably right, but I couldn't take the chance. I didn't want to have to answer a lot of questions," he paused, then added the hook, "especially if your sister turns out to be the one I'm after."

Yolanda's eyes flashed wide. "You don't really think my sister is the thief?"

"I don't know," Temple replied. He found it interesting how Yolanda still defended her sister, even after the way

Edna treated her.

"But you do suspect her?" Yolanda challenged.

"I suspect everybody until I can prove otherwise."

"Do you suspect me, too?"

"No. I was here with you, when the last attempted theft occurred. Besides, the casino thefts started months ago. You weren't even here."

Yolanda paused. "I'm going to have to warn my sister that she's under suspicion."

"I thought we had an agreement. This conversation was supposed to be just between us."

"You can't expect me to sit back and say nothing?"

"I expect you to keep your word."

"I won't let her walk into a trap. I don't care what she's done. I don't want to further alienate her. There's still a chance I can talk her into going home with me."

In a soothing tone, Temple said, "You know she'll never go back with you. You know that. Go home, Yolanda. Tell your mother you couldn't find Edna. At least she'll have you by her side at the end. Go home. She may need you right now."

With a deep sigh, Yolanda had to accept that inevitable truth. "Alright, Tom. I suppose I knew all along that she wouldn't go with me. I just didn't want to accept it."

"You're making the right decision," Temple said and started for the door.

"You're leaving?" she asked.

"I've got some things I have to do." Temple listened as he approached the door. He still heard nothing in the hallway. Before leaving her room, he glanced back at her. "Seems like we're always saying goodbye."

Chapter 23

Temple hurried back to his room, at the other end of the corridor. The door was still unlocked, just as he left it. Temple slipped back into the dark sitting room and locked the door behind him. No sounds were coming from the bedroom. He wondered if Victoria was still there, or, if maybe somebody else was there, waiting for him. Temple eased cautiously toward the bedroom door, but stopped abruptly when he heard voices in the hallway getting closer. He couldn't understand much of what they were saying, but heard enough to know they were coming in. Three forceful knocks at the door boomed out, followed by the doorknob jiggling. There was no more time. He opened the bedroom door quickly and ducked into more darkness, hoping he wasn't running into a trap. Just as he was closing the bedroom door, his stateroom door was opening. Temple hopped onto the bed, fully dressed, and threw the covers over himself. He could feel someone else in the bed. Right away, he knew it was Victoria from the scent of her perfume. But he could not detect any breathing. He leaned in closer.

Victoria's eyes opened suddenly. "Tom?" she uttered softly in relief.

"They're coming in now," he whispered.

Victoria quickly flipped the covers off her naked body and rolled over partially on top of Temple, just as the bedroom door was pushed open. Three shadowy figures barged into the room. One flicked on the lights. Victoria looked up at them, but intentionally did not cover herself. Temple made sure he kept his clothing hidden by the covers, as he got up on one elbow, squinting his eyes as if the sudden light was too bright for him. "What the hell is this?" Temple cursed, as the three, armed security men glared down at them.

Victoria allowed the guards to get a distracting view of her naked body, to take their attention away from the fact that Temple was holding the covers up around his neck. Victoria then partially covered herself with the blanket and snapped sarcastically, "By all means come on in, but you'll have to excuse the mess. We weren't expecting company."

"Shut up, Victoria," one of the guards barked.

Temple frowned. "I said, what the hell is going on. Is this how you treat your guests?"

"Somebody just tried to break into a secured area," said the burly guard standing closest to the bed. "We've got orders to search all the rooms. Have you been in here since you came back aboard?" he asked Temple.

"Yes!" Temple snapped. "I've been right here. Now if

you don't mind, we'd like to have some privacy."

The burly guard ignored Temple. "What about that, Victoria? He been here the whole time?"

Victoria considered her answer. If they already knew the truth, she could blow her cover by protecting him. She calculated the risk, considered the odds, then slapped her butt with one hand and said, "Where else would he be?"

One of the guards peeked into the bathroom, then nodded to the burly guard.

"Sorry for the intrusion," the burly guard said with hollow sincerity, "but the guy we're after is armed and extremely dangerous. He severely wounded one of my guards already."

Victoria said with obvious sarcasm, "Oh, how awful."

The burly guard regarded Victoria with a contemptuous glare before leading the other two guards out of the room, intentionally leaving the lights on to benefit the hidden camera.

When the guards were gone, Temple flopped back on the bed in relief.

Victoria snuggled up close to him under the covers, her lips only inches from his ear. "Did you get it?" she whispered.

Playing to the camera, Temple put his arm around her. He couldn't help but enjoy the feel of her naked body pressing against him. Even with his clothing on, her smooth skin and full curvaceous figure felt amazingly stimulating. "No," he whispered. "Didn't even get close to it."

Victoria then said aloud, for the benefit of those listening, "Those assholes certainly spoiled the moment." She reached over to the nightstand, turned the clock radio on to a music channel, and snuggled back against him knowing the music would help drown out her voice. "That guard you seriously injured; did he get a good look at you?" she asked.

"There was no injured guard," said Temple. "He lied to you." Then Temple deliberately lied to her too, "Nobody saw me." He saw no reason to drag Yolanda's name into this. He believed Yolanda's story, and Yolanda accepted his lie. He didn't think she'd blow his cover story and was probably leaving town tonight or tomorrow morning anyway.

"So, what happens now?" Victoria asked, still pressed against him.

Temple tried to keep his mind on business, but damn, her voluptuous body felt so good and his body was paying attention. Temple refocused and answered her, "I'm making another run at his safe – tonight."

"Tonight?" Victoria questioned with surprise. "Do you have a new plan?"

"No. Same plan. Only this time I do it right. What about you?" Temple asked. "Did you have any trouble while I was gone?"

"No, it went smoothly," she whispered, then leaned partially on top of him and kissed him passionately on the lips for the camera.

When she pulled away, Temple resisted the impulse to hold her there for a few extra moments. Victoria, again, laid her head on the pillow close to his ear, and draped one of her legs across his. Temple hoped she wouldn't feel his growing erection. "So," Temple said, trying to shift his thoughts away from this naked Amazonian beauty, "when I ran back in here you were so quiet, I wasn't sure what to think."

Victoria did feel his erection against her thigh. It would have been impossible not to, given his ample size, but she pretended she had not, and casually moved her leg, while shifting her weight, before answering. "I saw somebody run in here, so I pretended to be asleep. If it wasn't you, I was going to need a cover story to protect myself." Victoria then confessed, "I was prepared to throw you under the bus. I was going to tell them you could have slipped out of the room after I fell asleep." Then she added, "Nothing personal, you understand."

"I understand," said Temple. Had he been in her position, he would've done the same thing.

"Will you need me anymore tonight?" she asked.

Temple ignored the ache in his loins. "No, I won't."

"Then I guess I'd better be going. Good luck," she said, then rolled back to her side of the bed and turned the radio off.

When she got out of bed, Temple's eyes trailed her magnificent, naked body, as she walked away. His eyes settled on her round hips and firm butt cheeks. Both swayed provocatively with each step, with a little bounce, and just enough jiggle to demand attention. Temple's eyes dropped just below her butt, to that tiny space between her full, firm thighs. His imagination overcame him.

"Wait!" Temple blurted out as she neared the bathroom.

Victoria turned to face him, surprised at his unexpected outburst and confused by why he was speaking so surveillance could hear him.

Temple displayed a devilish grin, "Do you have to go right now?"

Victoria could see his eyes openly admiring her body. Instinctively, she thought to cover herself with her hands but didn't. Modesty didn't fit her undercover persona. Anyone watching them would have picked up on that right away. So, Victoria just stood there, naked, before his probing stare, and suddenly she wasn't confused anymore. That look in his eyes, she recognized it. She'd seen that look before, from so many men, who wanted to have sex with her. She was stunned to get that look from him, but not surprised. After all, he was only a man.

Victoria knew his brazen proposition did not compromise her cover. She was sure he knew it, too. Even though she had faked a sexual encounter with him earlier, she still had the option now to say no, and it would sound perfectly reasonable, to anyone listening. They would just assume she was ready to move on to the next swinging dick. If she declined, she knew Briggs would understand, too, and they would merely go their separate ways. No harm, no foul. On the other hand, if she said yes, she was pretty sure he would turn the lights back off so nobody would see them, if they did it for real. It was a ballsy move on his part but damned presumptuous. Victoria stared back into his smile. How could she tell him, without shattering his fragile male ego, that she simply was not interested? This was a job, not a date. It had nothing to do with him personally. She'd been with so many men, in the past few months, in the line of duty, that sex was just not fulfilling to her anymore. For months now, she had not been able to achieve an orgasm, even with the one real date she managed to work into her schedule, and that was damn frustrating. But she was not going to be just another booty call, because of his fragile ego. It was a pity, though. He had such a charming smile and was not an unattractive man. In fact, he was quite good-looking and had a strong, powerful body and an *enormous* cock.

Victoria's eyes moved along the length of his body, to the spot under the covers where *IT* would be. How many times in a woman's life, does she get a chance at one of those really big ones? With the image of it still in her mind, a small grin crept across her lips. *Oh well, what the hell?* She thought. *Why not.* She was long past the morality issue, with all the frogs she'd slept with during field missions, and none of them were hung like this guy.

Victoria walked back to the bed and turned the room lights off and the radio on. She slid under the covers next to him and put her lips close to his ear, "I thought you were going to make another run at Donnetti's safe?"

"Later," he told her. "I need to let the heat die down first."

Victoria felt his hands around her waist pulling her closer. "You think this is a good idea?" she whispered.

Temple kissed her gently on the lips. At first, she did not respond. Temple kissed her again, this time slipping his tongue into her mouth, inviting hers to play. Gradually, she started to respond in kind, until finally, their tongues were exploring each other with frenzied lust. Victoria moaned, this time for real, as her sexual senses awakened, for the first time in a long time. She pulled back, for a moment, and stared at him in amazement. She couldn't believe how aroused she was becoming. They kissed again. This time she didn't pull away from the bulge swelling in his pants, and only then did she remember he was still fully dressed.

"Let's get you out of these clothes," she breathed.

Temple sat up in bed and slipped his shoes and socks off while Victoria impatiently went to work on his belt. When he started pulling his slacks down, she couldn't wait anymore. Victoria slid her hand inside his underwear and excitedly closed her fingers around a monstrous pole of throbbing flesh growing bigger and harder by the second. As he continued undressing, Victoria maintained her firm grip, as if she were afraid it might get away from her. When his underwear came off, she pushed him onto his back with her free hand. Then she anxiously engulfed as much of him as she could, and groaned like a starving woman in a hungered frenzy.

251

Temple held on as long as he could, then pulled away at the last second. Not yet, he told himself.

Victoria wasn't ready to stop, but when Temple abruptly lifted her and flipped her onto her back, she felt a new surge of excitement. Quickly she threw her legs apart, eager for whatever came next. Temple moved into position, his face just inches from her sex. Once his tongue touched her down there, her body quivered in spastic jerks. When his tongue probed deeper, she cried out, "Ooooh sssssshit!" and was soon moaning in delirious pleasure. Only when his lips moved to her inner thigh was Victoria able to catch her breath and speak. "I want that big dick," she breathed heavily.

Temple got onto his knees, lifted her legs up and back, until her feet almost touched the headboard, then he mounted her.

"Wait," Victoria blurted out, her voice thick and husky. "Let me get on top. I want to *fuck* you."

Temple stopped. His manhood was touching her down there, but had not yet made penetration. He considered her request for less than a second, then rolled over onto his back.

Victoria quickly straddled him and excitedly lowered onto his massive organ.

"*Hol — ly — Sssshit!*" Victoria cried out, as that throbbing animal squeezed inch by inch inside of her. Once she had taken in as much as she could, Victoria paused to savor its thickness. Then slowly, very gingerly, she began moving her hips back and forth. As her body adjusted to his girth, she leaned forward, rested both hands on his chest to steady herself, and gradually started whipping her hips more aggressively.

For a while, Temple didn't move. He just let her enjoy the ride. He enjoyed it, too. A lot. But, when he reached the point where he could no longer just lay still, he firmly grabbed her waist and began ramming his hips into her.

Victoria pounded her hips down to meet every thrust. She loved his roughness. After a while, she closed her eyes, wet her lips with her tongue, and rode him like she was atop a wild stallion. She could feel his hands gripping her tighter, his fingers digging into her flesh. Then she heard him groan. That excited her even more, and she began wiggling her ass furiously on top of him.

Then Victoria felt his body shudder. She knew what that meant and her heart dropped. She shouted in her mind, *Oh no! Oh, God, no! Don't stop now! Not now! I'm so close.*

Temple couldn't wait for her another second. His body tensed then released in a flood of pleasure.

Victoria's enthusiasm faded and she frowned in frustration, unable again to reach that elusive plateau. That briefly awakened fire in her body was already turning cold. Too bad. He had potential. At least she thought he did. Annoyed, with yet another man who couldn't get it done, she was about to get out of bed, when Temple shocked her. He got up on his knees again and positioned his body between her legs. She was totally surprised and practically giddy when she saw that his massive erection was back. Her heart began pounding even more rapidly when he drove that beautiful thing back inside of her.

Victoria was all smiles, as she started moving her hips again with his. This time they were like two ballet dancers moving in perfect erotic unison. For one enraptured moment in time, Victoria was lost in ecstasy, and could not contain the prolonged gasping whimper that flowed from her throat.

As Temple's physical pleasure spiked, he braced himself for better traction, and started pounding his hips into her with more aggressive intensity.

Victoria's eyes blinked wide. "Oooooh baby!" she shouted out loud. He was really getting in there. Every nerve ending in her body was on fire. Nobody had ever handled her like this. Then surprisingly, and with incredulous disbelief, she felt herself nearing that elusive sexual peak that had long ago abandoned her. The muscles in her legs and stomach and back started to tense up. Her breathing became short and labored. She felt incredible excitement and anticipation. She hadn't felt that in a long time. Simultaneously a wave of pleasure flowed through her body, making her tingle and throb between her legs. She could feel herself getting hot and wet. And, in that extraordinary moment, her breathing stopped. Her body stiffened — erupting in a powerful orgasmic tremor. All she could manage was a long, pleasurable moan. It had been so very long.

Victoria drifted off in erotic bliss, as the feeling of euphoria washed over her. While submerged in sensual fulfilment, she hoped the sensations would never end. Then she felt his weight shift on top of her, and her body started jerking in rapid spasms. He was still inside of her and she was extremely sensitive down there. "No. Don't." she breathed.

"Don't what?" Temple whispered back.

"Don't stop," she begged.

"Stopping never crossed my mind," he said, then slid his hands under her hips and grabbed her butt cheeks firmly with both hands.

Victoria made a whimpering sound as he started slamming his hips into hers again. Although exhausted, Victoria stayed with him, her hips now greedily meeting his. It was so damn good. He was going in so deep it hurt. But she loved it. She wanted it. She needed it.

Soon she began moaning in incredulous ecstasy. Her eyes glazed in exultant bliss. Then suddenly, her eyes popped open and she stared up at him in awe. *She was going to cum again.* Yes! YES! She could feel it. Victoria quickly flung both arms around Temple's neck and held on tight, as multiple convulsive orgasms rocked her body for the first time, each one more powerful than the next. And they kept coming in what seemed an endless uncontrollable flood.

In the midst of her spasms, Victoria heard Temple groan, then felt him explode inside of her. Although she was utterly exhausted, she instinctively continued grinding her hips against his, to take all he had left. When she felt his strength finally fade away, she surrendered to her exhaustion and collapsed on top of him. As her eyelids flickered shut, a soft moan of pleasure escaped her lips. Her only regret, as she drifted off to sleep, was not having enough energy left to put his waning manhood in her mouth, to taste how well she enjoyed it.

Temple was panting, to catch his breath, as he rolled her gently off his chest and onto her back and then her side. Once his breathing slowed, he scooted up behind her in a spooning position, and wrapped his arms around her, pulling her in close. Temple was tired too, but he did not go to sleep. He stared off into the darkness. Other things were on his mind. He estimated he could lay there three or four more hours before going at Donnetti's safe again. The heat will have died down some by then, and they'd never expect him to go after the safe again tonight. He just hoped the Alpha Data was there. He needed to recover the microdots before they were auctioned off. The proof that we were not alone in this vast universe, had to remain a secret. Not merely because alien life was the most significant discovery in the history of man, but because they obviously had technology and weaponry far superior to any known on earth. That kind of information could never go public. Mass hysteria would erupt around the world. Enemy governments would be in chaos. Even allies would become enemies, if that information wasn't shared. Temple knew he would have to get the microdots back before they realized what they had.

Temple glanced at Victoria. Even in the darkness, he could see her hair laid in disarray. He lightly brushed the loose strands from her face. He would have to keep his distance from her, as much as possible, from here on out. If Maxwell engineered Karen Kiley's disappearance, maybe Maxwell knew about him too, or would soon. He doubted one jump in the sack with Victoria would send out any alarm bells based on her cover as an escort. But no sense risking her cover any further by proximity. He would just have to stay away from her.

Eventually, Temple closed his eyes and set the internal clock in his head to wake him at a certain time. Approximately three hours later, Temple opened his eyes, alert to his surroundings. He woke Victoria, with a gentle shake. "Get dressed," he whispered.

Victoria got out of bed, without question or conversation, and went into the bathroom to shower. When she returned to the bedroom, she was still naked. The radio was off. The room lights were on. She knew if someone was still monitoring them, they could hear and see everything.

"You were great, baby," Temple said for the benefit of the hidden microphones.

"You were pretty great, yourself," she responded, then slipped back into the white evening dress she wore earlier.

Temple pretended he was surprised to see her getting dressed. "Are you leaving?"

"I'm a working girl," Victoria quipped. "I can't afford to

stay in one place too long. Time is money, and I can't make any, giving out freebies like this. It was fun, sugar, but I really need to go." Victoria knelt beside the bed to kiss him goodbye then whispered, "You still going after the safe?"

"Yes," he whispered back.

Victoria walked toward the door to leave, then turned back to him with a grin. "One more freebie won't break the bank," she said. "Why don't you stop by my room later tonight?"

Now it was Temple's turn to be surprised. If she was serious, what she was asking was totally out of the question. Once he got the Alpha Data, he had no intentions of stopping for anything. No piece of ass was so good that he would risk his life and the mission for it. Hell, chasing pussy was how Johnny Davis got himself killed. On the other hand, maybe she was just staying in character.

"If I have time," Temple told her.

Victoria gave him a flirtatious look, "Please come see me. Room 522A, deck level five."

"Alright," he lied. "I'll be there."

Victoria seemed satisfied with his answer. As she left the room, she said over her shoulder, "See you later, sugar."

When she was gone, Temple turned his thoughts to the more serious business of murder. He did not anticipate too much trouble with killing Donnetti, even though the fat man was heavily guarded around the clock. There were always ways of getting to your target; the problem was getting away clean, after the job was done. Now, however, without Karen Kiley, Temple had another problem to consider: what to do with the Alpha Data after he recovers it? Earlier he had toyed with the idea of letting Karen take the Alpha Data to the president and his people, while he stayed behind, to settle with Donnetti and the others. That way, if he were caught or killed, the Alpha Data would still be safe. But with Karen missing, everything changed. Temple needed a new plan, in case they caught on to him. Not knowing who Maxwell was or who he controlled, Temple didn't dare entrust the Alpha Data to Victoria or her partner, Billy Shaw. He certainly wasn't going to risk delivering it himself, not with The Grim Reaper somewhere out there waiting for him. The best solution, Temple decided, was to hide the Alpha Data somewhere off the boat. Another agent could recover it later.

Still pretending he was not aware of the hidden camera, Temple got out of bed naked. He picked his clothes up off the floor, along with some hardware items wrapped in them, and went into the bathroom. He took a quick shower then stayed in the bathroom and got dressed. The items from the hardware store, he left on the sink. Those common household items would go unnoticed if seen by anyone. He would collect them, when he got back to his room.

Right now, he had to go see Victoria Rodriguez one more time, but not for another romp in the sack.

Chapter 24

Nick Marlow was steaming mad. Sitting a few feet behind Donnetti, he had watched the live video feed, from the hidden camera, in Temple's room. Although he knew Victoria Rodriguez was a paid whore, it angered him to hear how much she enjoyed having sex with that nobody. Until now, Marlow had assumed she was simply not very vocal during sex, because when they were together, the best he could draw out of her was an occasional whimper. But, when he heard her screaming and swearing, like a drunken sailor while having sex with Briggs, it was a blow to his ego, to see another man do to her what he could not. What bothered Marlow the most was he secretly cared for that slutty Mexican bitch. He would never admit that to anyone, and he wished it wasn't true, but it was. She was so damn freaky in bed — he loved the way she made him feel. Damn that rotten bitch. That slutty, nasty, pretty bitch.

There was a knock at Donnetti's door. Eddie Bowman entered the room without being invited in. The two, armed guards at the door took an offensive posture when the door opened, but their bravado immediately shriveled when they saw who it was. Both guards greeted Eddie with a nervous nod. The blond giant ignored them as he crossed the room toward Donnetti. Nick Marlow discreetly moved his hand closer to his gun. He didn't trust that depraved maniac. Eddie was just too damn unstable – like nitroglycerin, ready to explode at any moment.

As Eddie closed the distance between them, Marlow braced himself in his chair and eased his hand just a bit closer to his gun. Eddie continued past Marlow, without even a glance in his direction. The big man then stood to the left of Donnetti's chair and waited to be acknowledged. Donnetti picked up the phone on the coffee table and dialed a number. When the line connected, Donnetti said, "Goodman, it's me. A man named Tom Briggs is staying at the Golden Nugget. I want to know what room he's in." Donnetti hung up, turned to Eddie and pointed a finger toward the floor. He enjoyed flaunting power and control over the big man.

Eddie Bowman lowered to one knee, without hesitation. "What can I do for you, sir?"

"I've got another little job for you," Donnetti told him. "I want you to go to the Golden Nugget and search Mr. Briggs' room. Let me know if you find anything I should be aware of. Take Jason Meats with you. Tell him to stake out that Kiley woman's room. If anyone shows up there looking for her, that's not with the hotel staff, I want them handled. Quietly," Donnetti emphasized.

"I understand," said Eddie.

"Make sure the Injun understands too, and tell him not to leave that girl's room, until I send someone to relieve him in the morning."

"Should I wait in Briggs' room to see who shows up?"

"No, just do what I told you, then hurry up and get back here this time," Donnetti barked.

Eddie made no comment.

Donnetti toyed with him further, "You sure you didn't have any trouble with the Kiley woman?"

"No trouble at all, Mr. Donnetti."

"You took a long time getting back. You sure there were no problems?"

Eddie was noticeably uncomfortable with the question, but did not waver in his answer. "No problems, sir."

Donnetti enjoyed watching Eddie squirm, and he was the only man in the world, who could draw that reaction from the giant. Donnetti, of course, already knew why Eddie was so late in returning to the boat. He had expected it.

Eddie Bowman had no idea Donnetti had long ago learned of his secret, nor was he aware that Donnetti's lawyer, William Penrod, discovered it quite by accident.

Penrod learned of Eddie's secret, shortly after Donnetti surprisingly, brought the blond giant into the fold two years ago. Late one night, Donnetti sent Penrod to deliver a message to Eddie, who at the time was living in a little rental house, owned by Donnetti, on the southwest side of town. Eddie's phone service had been disconnected, and the telephone company refused to reinstate it. Not only was the bill three months late, but Eddie had severely beaten one of their service representatives, when the tech initially went out to disconnect the line.

So, Penrod had the distasteful task of delivering

Donnetti's message to Eddie in person, at night. Penrod drove out to Eddie's house and found no exterior or interior lights on. Eddie's car was not in its usual driveway parking space, alongside the house. Although Eddie never parked in the back, as there were no paved roads back there, Penrod checked it anyway. The car was not there either. He considered the possibility that Eddie's car was in the shop and the big man was asleep, inside the house. Penrod walked back around to the front door. He was afraid to wake the big man, but gathered his courage and knocked anyway. When no one answered, after a few attempts, Penrod returned to his car at the curb, turned on a late-night radio station, and waited. Maybe he would be back soon. Penrod frankly hoped he wouldn't. He didn't relish the idea of making a surprise visit to this psycho's house anyway, especially at night.

After twenty minutes or so, Penrod was surprised to see a light inside Eddie's house come on, as Eddie's car was still not there. For a moment, Penrod wasn't sure what to do. If Eddie was in there, why didn't he answer the door earlier? If the big man just got home, why'd he sneak around to the back? Maybe he was doing something he didn't want anybody to know about, in which case, it would be hazardous to walk in on him now. Even under ideal circumstances, the thought of approaching Eddie was a frightening prospect, but this — this scared the shit out of Penrod. Eddie was a destructive force, subject to no real control. Penrod always wondered why Donnetti would want such a man around. But, even more puzzling, was the fact that Eddie Bowman obeyed Donnetti. Why would the big man do that? That was the big mystery, one that Donnetti had never shared with him.

Penrod stared at the lighted window. What if Eddie wasn't in there? *Who could it be? Burglars?* No, Penrod quickly dismissed that thought. A burglar would not break into a house at night and start turning lights on. At least, he didn't think a burglar would. In any case, he had to find out who was in there. Curiosity overpowered his fear. If he learned anything useful for Donnetti in the process – well, that was pure gravy.

Penrod drove a half block away, walked back to the house, creeping carefully through the bushes and over to the lighted window he knew, from previous visits, to be the bedroom. He peeked through warped window blinds and could see Eddie Bowman standing in the middle of the room. There was a woman with him – a tall, skinny blonde, maybe thirty-five years old. She was wearing a western shirt and jeans. There was a gag stuffed in her mouth. Her hands were bound behind her back. The right side of her face was severely bruised. One eye was swollen shut. She was crying heavily and looked absolutely terrified.

Eddie yelled something at her that Penrod couldn't make out. The woman abruptly stopped crying but began trembling uncontrollably. Eddie leered at her, with a sadistic grin, then shoved her backwards onto the bed. Penrod could hear her terrified screams through the wall, as she squirmed on the bed in sheer panic. Eddie pounced on her quickly and started choking her, with both hands. The woman began thrashing frantically, her eyes bulging in horror, as she struggled for air. When her body finally went limp, there was no doubt in Penrod's mind that she was dead — that he had just witnessed a murder. The brutality of her death did not shock Penrod though. These people he worked for and represented in court were all killers. That's what they do. Penrod had learned to live with it — for the money. In this instance, the woman's death was inevitable. She was not blindfolded. She had seen Eddie's face. She was in his home.

There was no other way this could have ended.

Penrod furrowed his brow in confusion, as Eddie rolled the dead woman over onto her stomach, then peeled her jeans off and ripped her panties away.

What the hell is he doing? Penrod pondered. It wasn't until the big man unbuckled his belt and unzipped his pants that Eddie's terrible secret dawned on him, like a slap in the face.

Penrod backed away from the window in revulsion, covering his mouth with his hand, to keep from crying out. He was stunned by the depth of Eddie's depravity. He had always known the blond giant was a twisted psychopath, but this perversion was beyond anything he could have imagined. Penrod pushed back through the bushes, cognizant he had to be absolutely quiet. He didn't want Eddie to ever know he had discovered his awful secret.

Penrod made it back to his car, shaken, and deeply disturbed by what he had learned. He drove hurriedly back to the boat and reported what he had witnessed to Donnetti. Penrod expected that Eddie would be immediately fired. Penrod was well aware that Donnetti was no choir boy himself and was responsible for a few unmarked graves in the desert. But, even Donnetti couldn't afford to have an employee committing random unsanctioned murders around town and then violating their corpses. It was bad for business, professionally and financially, and could eventually lead the police to his doorstep.

After hearing the sordid details, Donnetti mulled it over for a moment, then quietly replied, "I already know about that."

Penrod's eyes blinked once as he stood there dumbfounded.

Donnetti leaned forward in his chair and continued,

"You are not to discuss this ugly business with anyone else — ever. It will be our secret."

The subject was never mentioned again, nor was Eddie fired.

Long ago, Donnetti had learned about Eddie's necrophilia tendencies, after initiating a full-surveillance investigation on him when they first met. During a month-long stakeout, the Goodman Detective Agency observed Eddie commit a variety of misdemeanor crimes and three felony assaults, including one murder, which revealed Eddie's propensity for necrophilia. After releasing their findings to Donnetti, he still elected to keep the blond giant on the payroll. After that investigation, Donnetti was never surprised, when Eddie returned to the boat late, after some assignments that involved women. Actually, Donnetti expected it, and occasionally he even fed that depravity, unbeknownst to Eddie. Sometimes, Donnetti would intentionally assign Eddie jobs involving women, to satisfy his perversion in a controlled environment. Donnetti believed a sexually satisfied deviant was more easily controlled. That's why he sent Eddie along, when Gutloff went after the CIA woman, Karen Kiley. That's also why he chose Eddie to go after that mystery CIA agent, who spent the night with that black actress.

Just then the phone rang. Donnetti answered it, listened for a moment, then hung up and said to Eddie, who was still kneeling next to him, "Briggs' room number is 405. Search it and report back to me."

"Yes, sir," Eddie said.

When Eddie was gone, Nick Marlow relaxed. His thoughts turned back to the Mexican whore and that novelist, Briggs. He would settle with both of them, when this auction was over.

Jim Donnetti's thoughts lingered on the blond giant. Eddie had a lot of baggage requiring a great deal of special handling to keep him stable. The only reason he tolerated Eddie, over the past two years, was because everyone else feared him, which automatically made him a valuable asset. But, at the end of the day, Donnetti was confident of his control over Eddie Bowman, of that he had no doubt.

After Eddie left the room, Penrod wondered what Donnetti had on that blond freak to make him so docile, to make him show genuine respect, even admiration. Certainly, it wasn't blackmail, because of the murder and necrophilia of the kidnapped girl he had witnessed almost two years ago. You don't blackmail somebody like Eddie Bowman. It must be something far more terrible, but Penrod dared not ask.

William Penrod was never to learn that secret, but, had Donnetti confided in him, he would not have thought Eddie's behavior toward Donnetti such a mystery. After all, it was only natural for a son to show respect for his father.

Chapter 25

Jim Donnetti first met Eddie's mother, when he was nineteen years old and still lived in the home of Don Baresi. She was thirty-two years old, and only the second woman he had known sexually. Both sexual encounters ended disastrously, and both had a significant impact on defining the man he was to become.

His first life-altering experience occurred on his 19th birthday. The Don's eldest son, Antonio, who was then forty-two, took young Donnetti into the city to celebrate with a few drinks and to get him laid. They had done some bar hopping, before Antonio took Donnetti into his favorite bar, where there was always plenty of action. "See anything you like?" Antonio asked.

Donnetti, a bit embarrassed by Antonio's bluntness said, "Well, they're all very nice."

"Pick one. It's my treat."

"Are you serious?"

Antonio nodded. "Pick one."

"Suppose the one I pick is not a — well, you know — one of them."

"They're all one of them, for the right price. Just pick the one you want."

Donnetti glanced around the room, then said, "Over there. The brunette in the pink dress, in the corner. I like her, but —"

"But what?"

"You think she's one of them?"

Antonio grinned, then walked across the room toward the brunette.

Donnetti nervously stayed by the bar and watched Antonio, from the corners of his eyes, as his uncle approached the woman and started a conversation with her. Donnetti's embarrassment heightened when Antonio and the brunette looked back in his direction. It all seemed so crude to him, buying and selling sex, yet the prospect of having sex excited him.

He saw Antonio discreetly slip some money to her, then they both started in his direction. As they got closer, Donnetti got a better look at her. She had a nice slim body. Her face was a bit overly made up with lipstick, rouge, and eye shadow. There was a mole under her left eye he wasn't sure was real. Despite all of the make-up, he thought she was still an attractive woman.

Antonio told Donnetti, "Everything's all arranged. She's been paid for the whole night. All you have to do is enjoy it. Happy birthday, kid." Antonio sauntered over to a shapely redhead, who seemed to know him, and greeted him with a hug and a deep open mouth kiss.

As Antonio escorted his redheaded friend outside, he yelled back to Donnetti, "See you back at the house in the morning, kid."

Donnetti nodded at Antonio. but didn't quite know what to say to the woman standing next to him. What does one say to a woman bought and paid for? His uncle never should have left him alone with her.

"What's your name?" she finally asked, breaking the ice.

Donnetti was thankful she started the conversation. "Jim Donnetti," he answered. "What's yours?"

"Jamie."

"What's your last name?"

"Does it matter?"

"No, I guess not."

"Well?" she asked.

"Well, what?" Donnetti inquired with confusion.

"You want to stay here for a few drinks first, or do we go somewhere and get a room?"

It just occurred to Donnetti, he didn't know where they were supposed to do it. He assumed she had a room upstairs. "Ah, whatever is customary," he said.

"Whatever you want baby, you're paying for it."

What the hell was she talking about, Donnetti wondered. He thought Antonio had paid for everything. He decided not to make an issue of it though, because he didn't want to seem ignorant about how this process worked. "Do you live nearby?" he asked.

"There is a place close by that I use," she said.

"Sounds good to me," Donnetti replied.

As Jamie led him across the room, toward the door, it felt like everybody in the bar was watching him, knowing this woman was just paid to have sex with him. It was a little embarrassing. Once outside, she flagged down a cab, which took them about three miles away, to a dingy little motel courtyard full of single, one-story units set in a horseshoe pattern. After Donnetti paid the driver, Jamie led him to cottage number twelve. She took a key from her purse, unlocked the door, and they went inside. Donnetti was not too surprised to see the broken-down single bed and worn covers. Nor was he surprised to see the rusty, corroded, porcelain sink and walls badly in need of painting. The chipped stucco walls outside of the motel and the grossly unkempt grounds, around the buildings, didn't lead him to expect much more.

When Jamie sat down on the bed and started to unbutton her blouse, the door abruptly opened, but she did not seem surprised. A burly man. with a cruel face, walked in and closed the door behind him. "That'll be seventy-five dollars for the night," the man told Donnetti.

Donnetti looked down at Jamie, whose eyes were glued to the floor. Donnetti turned back to the intruder. "That's a lot for this room."

"The room is fifty bucks," the man said. "The seventy-five is for the girl."

"There must be some mistake," Donnetti argued. "She's already been paid."

"Whatever arrangements you made with her does not concern me. You owe me one hundred and twenty-five dollars for the girl and the room."

Donnetti looked down at Jamie again, who still had not lifted her stare from the floor.

The burly man bellowed at Donnetti. "Hey! I'm talking to you."

When Donnetti looked up at the man again, his hand

was extended for the money. Donnetti felt chills run through his body, as he sized up the situation. This was a shakedown and the girl was a part of it, which explained her silence now and lack of surprise. Donnetti doubted this guy had anything to do with the running of this motel. He was probably just her pimp. Jamie had signaled him in some way, after they entered the courtyard. The question now was, what could he do about it? He wondered how many men, at this point in the shakedown, went ahead and paid. Donnetti glanced back at Jamie again, who pretended to be oblivious to what was happening. Too bad. She was very attractive. Having his first sexual experience with her would have been nice, but Donnetti had no intentions of paying out any more money. Besides, he wasn't certain now if it was even safe to spend the night there, or for that matter, if she would even stay with him after the money was paid. Donnetti decided his best bet was to get the hell out of there. When he made a move for the door, the burly man stepped in front of it.

Oh shit. Now what? Donnetti thought. He sure as hell couldn't fight his way out, and he had no idea if others were waiting for him outside the door. It was apparent though, that this son-of-a-bitch wasn't going to let him leave without paying, whether he fucked the girl or not.

"Give me the money now," the man growled.

Donnetti succumbed to the only possibility left to him. It was probably the same decision many men before him had to make. He paid the money.

The burly man smirked, as he counted the currency. Afterward, he stuffed the wad of bills in his pocket, glared at Donnetti, and then stepped aside.

Donnetti promptly left the room, hoping no one was waiting to jump him outside. When he reached the parking lot, he noticed the burly man was following him at a distance. Donnetti continued walking at a regular pace, until he turned the corner, then he took off at a full run. He kept running until he reached a well-lighted street with plenty of people. Only then did he dare look back, and was relieved to see he had not been pursued. Donnetti checked his watch. It wasn't quite closing time for the bars yet, so he went into the first bar he happened upon and quickly downed two shots of scotch to calm his nerves. He ordered a third drink and sipped it slowly, as he pondered about the cluster fuck that had just happened. He was too embarrassed to tell his Uncle Antonio about this and too ashamed to go to his godfather. How could he tell anyone that a whore and her pimp played him and then sent him running scared? No, he couldn't tell anybody. He would handle this himself.

The bartender announced it was last call. Donnetti quickly downed the remainder of his drink and ordered another one. By the time the bar closed, he knew what he had to do. Donnetti got a room in town, for the night, to give support to the lie he was going to tell in the morning. He laid awake, in the darkness, thinking about his plan, not sure he had the guts to go through with it. He had never committed an act of violence before, never even been in a fight, where someone used his fists. Things somehow always worked themselves out. But this thing that happened tonight shamed him. He couldn't just let it go. It needed to be handled. He had to regain his self-respect.

Jim Donnetti planned to find that whore and get his money back – Antonio's money, too – and then rape that bitch to get what was owed to him.

That next morning when Donnetti got home, Antonio anxiously awaited him with a big grin. "How was it, kid?"

Donnetti put a hand on his uncle's shoulder. "She was great. Thank you. I want you to know I won't ever forget what you did for me. I could not have had a nicer present."

Antonio nodded and walked away, swelled with pride. Now his nephew was a man.

Later that evening Donnetti cruised the bar district, driving a Cadillac from the Don's extensive fleet of cars. For two hours, he drove up and down the streets where the whores congregated. He spent another hour parked across the street, from the horseshoe-shaped motel, where he was suckered. Prostitutes, pimps, and johns were coming and going, but there was no sign of Jamie or her pimp. Donnetti drove back to the blue light district and parked to watch some more. He wasn't there very long before he spotted her walking out of a grocery store and straddling a bicycle. At first glance, he almost didn't recognize her. She wasn't wearing all of the make-up or false eyelashes that she had on last night. Even her mole was gone. She also wasn't dressed like a hooker. Instead, she was wearing a baggy pullover sweater and loose-fitting jeans. Without high heels, she was much shorter than he thought and quite ordinary looking, but still cute.

When she pedaled off on the bicycle, Donnetti followed at a distance. At one point, he drove past her to get a better look, just to make sure he had the right person. After seeing her up close, he knew he did. It was Jamie. But seeing her up close in the daylight was a shock. She was not the mature woman he thought she was. She was a young woman – eighteen, maybe nineteen years old. Donnetti stopped his car ahead of her, in an area where there were no street lamps. He reached under the seat and pulled out the butcher knife he had taken from the Don's kitchen. The fact that she was a teenager did not change his plans. If anything, it bolstered his confidence that he could do this. Donnetti watched her through his rearview mirror, as she approached his car.

When she was close, he got out of his car with his back to her, keeping the knife well hidden. Just as she started to ride past him, Donnetti spun around and snatched her off the bicycle. He let her get a good look at the butcher knife. "If you scream, I'll kill you right now," he threatened, as convincingly as he could.

Jamie's eyes were more on the knife than his face, so she didn't recognize him right away.

"Get in the car," he ordered.

"Please don't hurt —"

"Shut up," he yelled, then swung the driver's door open. "Get in the fucking car."

That's when Jamie recognized him. "Jim!" she squeaked; his name caught in her throat. Then, with her voice quivering she pleaded, "I'm so sorry for what happened. It wasn't my fault. That damn fool brother of mine made me do it." Jamie looked into his eyes for understanding, but saw no warmth, no compassion, no mercy. "He's crazy!" she blurted out. "I didn't wanna do it, but he made me. And it's not the first time either. Whenever he needs extra money, he makes me —"

Donnetti grabbed her sweater, under her chin, and pulled her in close. "I said, get your ass in the car."

From the crazed look in his eyes, Jamie believed, if she didn't do exactly what he said, this man was going to kill her right there on the street. Jamie got in the car and slid over to the passenger side. For now, she would do what he wanted, until she could find a way to escape.

Donnetti got behind the wheel. "Put your seat belt on," he ordered. He didn't want her jumping out. Once she was strapped in, he drove off, still holding the butcher knife in plain sight.

"Look, mister," Jamie pleaded, "suppose I can get all

your money back for you – yours and that friend of yours who paid me in the bar. Would that square things?"

Donnetti did not answer her. He didn't even look in her direction.

Jamie continued, "I'm not trying to set you up. I'll get your money back out of my savings. It'll be just between us. My brother doesn't have to know." Jamie waited for some kind of response, but got none, so she tried again to reason with him. "I know you don't have any reason to trust me after last night, but you gotta believe me now 'cause I'm giving it to ya straight." Again, she looked for some understanding, but still, he ignored her. Jamie started to ramble, "You don't have to worry about my brother being at my place when I give you the money. He's got his own place downtown. It's just me and my mom. And she won't be there either. She'll be at work. It'll just be you and me. Nobody else needs to know about this. Whattaya say, mister?"

"No," Donnetti said.

Jamie tried to reach him with logic. "Why not? Why hurt me? I told you it was all my brother's fault. He's crazy. He made me do it. Listen, up till now, nobody's been hurt. You wanna go to prison for hurting me? Of course you don't." Jamie paused briefly to look for a reaction, then continued, "Let me help you. I'll get your money back. I'll even kick in a few bucks for your trouble and inconvenience. Then we both go our separate ways. Deal?"

Donnetti glanced at her for the first time since she got in his car. He was scared to death but was amazed at how easily he could conceal it. It was so strange. The things he was saying and doing and thinking, he never thought possible, not for someone whose life had always been so protected. Oddly enough though, this new adversarial role felt liberating. Donnetti glared at her and said, "If you say one more word, I'm going to cut your fucking throat."

Jamie sat back and remained silent the remainder of the drive. Once Donnetti figured he had driven far enough away from the populated areas of town, he pulled off the main street onto a dirt road and continued for a few miles before stopping the car. Donnetti got out and held the driver's door open. Jamie hesitantly slid across the seat and stepped out of the car. Donnetti shut the door then opened the rear door. "Get in," he said.

Jamie felt, for the first time, that Donnetti was not going to kill her, at least not right away. She at least had a few more minutes to live. But now she knew what he was really after, and that terrified her, too, as she got into the back seat of the Cadillac.

Donnetti leaned down and looked at her. "Take your clothes off. All of them."

"Please don't do this," she mumbled.

"Shut the fuck up and get on with it."

As Jamie pulled her sweater off, Donnetti felt his tender, virgin loins tingling with nervous excitement. Jamie started crying, as she held the sweater up in front of her body like a shield. Donnetti reached into the car, snatched the sweater from her hands and threw it on the floor, in the back seat. He crawled in next to her and pressed the blade of the butcher knife against her throat. Jamie stiffened, her eyes bulging wide. Donnetti leaned in closer, his face almost touching hers. "I want you completely naked in one minute. Any clothing left on after that, I'm cutting them off of you." Donnetti slipped the knife under her bra between the two cups and cut the small strip of material in the middle with one swipe of his wrist. Her bra popped open, and her breasts spilled out. Jamie let out a frightened shriek.

Donnetti backed out of the car and glanced at his watch.

"One minute," he warned and pointed the butcher knife at her. Jamie sniveled and fought back tears, as she begrudgingly removed her clothing. Donnetti thought it amusing to see the lying, little whore crying real tears. He didn't, for one minute, believe any of that bullshit about her brother forcing her to pretend to be a prostitute.

Jamie stripped down to her panties, but before pulling them off, she looked up at him, still crying, her voice almost inaudible. "I'm a virgin," she whispered. "My brother never forced me to go all the way with anybody."

Her admission stunned Donnetti. It was the last thing he had expected to hear, but surprisingly it had the ring of truth. He believed, by the look in her eyes, she was not lying. Donnetti took one step back from the car. "I believe you," he said.

Jamie's face timidly brightened with hope.

Donnetti glanced at his watch again. "Your minute is almost up, bitch."

Jamie's brief optimism shattered. Nothing was going to change his mind. He was determined to rape her no matter what. Jamie started crying again, as she pulled her panties off and dropped them on the car's dirty floor.

Seeing her cowering naked in the car, scared and helpless, made Donnetti feel an enormous sense of power. And he liked it. Cautiously, he looked around just to be sure nobody was driving down the road toward them, then he dropped his pants and underwear to his ankles and awkwardly climbed back into the car beside her, still holding the knife in plain view. He didn't waste time with foreplay. He just forced her legs apart and took her on the back seat of the car. After his twenty two-second assault, Donnetti backed out of the car on rubbery legs, trembling from incredible ecstasy. Jamie huddled in the corner of the car, in pain and bleeding, from the loss of her virginity.

Luckily for Donnetti, and for the sake of the Don's car, he had the good foresight to cover the back seat with a blanket, before he left that evening in search of her. He had anticipated some mess when they were done, although not to this extent.

Despite Jamie's searing pain, and the total humiliation she suffered, her mind was still clear and alert. Even now she was contemplating how to save her life. She was relieved to see he wasn't holding the knife anymore, but waited, with uncertainty, for him to regain his composure.

When his breathing slowed, he told her to get dressed.

Jamie's anxiety slightly relaxed. She didn't think she was going to die this day. If he intended to kill her, he would not have told her to get dressed.

Donnetti pulled his underwear and pants back up, then got into the driver's seat. He reached back to the rear passenger door and unlocked it. "Hurry up and get dressed, then get your ass back up here," he growled.

"I'm still bleeding," she mumbled in humiliation.

Donnetti looked back at Jamie. Her eyes were red and puffy from crying, and her hair was in disarray. She had already gotten her sweater and panties back on but had not pulled her jeans all the way up as the crotch of her panties was blood-soaked. She looked so pathetic and frightened and ashamed sitting there, with her hands cupped embarrassingly over the bloody spot between her legs.

Donnetti found it curious that he felt no shame or guilt for what he had done. He didn't even feel sorry for her as she sat there cringing in fear of him. Donnetti reached into his back pocket, pulled out a soiled handkerchief, and tossed it back to her. "Plug that hole up before you bleed all over the car."

As she tried to compose herself, Donnetti sneered, "Never mind. Stay back there on the blanket." Donnetti drove off. He did not care now that she might try to jump. If she was dumb enough to jump from a moving car, so be it. He already got what he came for.

Jamie didn't try to jump. She was too afraid to try.

Donnetti drove into town and back to where she left her bike. "Get out," he ordered.

Jamie hesitated, thinking he was making a cruel joke, to taunt her.

Donnetti barked, "Go on. Get out of here."

When she reached for the door handle, Donnetti warned, "You tell anyone about me, about what happened, I'll find you again, and I'll kill you. Now get the hell out of my car."

The following evening, the Don was told that one of the family's contacts, inside the police department, informed him police detectives were looking for a young man in his early twenties, named Jim, in connection with the rape of an eighteen-year-old girl last night.

"Was the last name mentioned?" the Don asked.

"No. The young girl could not remember his last name."

"Is she cooperating with the police?"

"No. But her mother, Erma Shaffer, is."

"I see," the Don answered.

"One other thing, this girl who was raped, has an older brother. A real hothead. He's looking for Jim, too."

The Don took a moment, then said, "Send some people out on the street. Find out exactly what happened. I want that information today."

"Should I talk to Jim?"

"I don't want him to know that I know."

"Alright, Mr. Baresi. I'll get right on it."

Four hours later, the Don knew all about the rape and why it happened and had already taken steps to satisfy everyone concerned. Erma Shaffer received a visit from a man who identified himself as Mario Tollini. He advised her it would be wise to forget this unpleasant tragedy. To help her emotionally heal, a generous cash amount would be transferred into her bank account. Tollini further explained that Don Baresi would consider her a valued friend, who he *hoped* would get over this tragedy soon, so she could go on living a long and healthy life.

Erma Shaffer recognized the hidden threat and accepted the Don's money and veiled offer of friendship. While the Consigliere sat in her apartment, she called police headquarters and informed them she and her daughter declined to press charges. Erma then assured the Consigliere she would talk to her son, but was afraid even she couldn't call him off.

Across town, Arnold Shaffer was fuming mad. He wanted to find that little prick, who violated his little sister, so he could tear his fucking head off and shit in the hole. He wanted to kill the miserable little fuck. How dare his poor excuse for a mother tell him to back off, to just forget it? No way. He was going to find this rapist and kill him, then dump his body in the gutter. But before he took this punk's miserable life, he was going to let him know he had fucked with the wrong family.

When Don Baresi received word of Arnold Shaffer's persistence, the Don dispatched two of his enforcers to see to it that Arnold had a change of heart, but left strict orders he was not to be seriously hurt. The Don had no desire to complicate his deal with Erma Shaffer at this point.

Later that day, two mob enforcers drove to the apartment where Arnold Shaffer lived, but he was not there.

They patiently waited in their car, spending the time playing cards, at a dollar a hand. Three hours and fifteen minutes later, Arnold Shaffer pulled into the parking lot in front of the complex. Arnold exited his car and was nearing the security gate, when the two enforcers approached him from behind. Arnold glanced back once and saw them, but did not sense danger. He just assumed they were there to visit the Murphy sisters upstairs. Those two nymphs were always entertaining men up there. The dumb bitches could have made a fortune selling that pussy instead of always giving it away.

So, Arnold Shaffer turned away from the strangers to open the gate. The bigger of the two men, a man even larger than Arnold, quickly wrapped his muscular arm around Arnold's throat, against his Adam's apple. The sudden crushing pain caused Arnold's legs to buckle, and before he knew what was happening, he was down on one knee and choking for air.

The other enforcer, a man much shorter than Arnold, grabbed a handful of Arnold's hair and jerked his head back forcing Arnold to look up at him. The shorter enforcer pulled out a .44 Remington Magnum revolver, in broad daylight, and forced its 7.5-inch barrel into Arnold's mouth, causing him to gag. "You Arnold Shaffer?" the shorter gunman growled.

Arnold's eyes bulged in absolute terror, as he nervously nodded yes.

The gunman said, "I hear you're looking for a guy named Jim."

Arnold started to nod yes again, but maybe that was the wrong answer. Maybe 'yes' would get his head blown off. His mind raced for the right thing to say, but it was impossible to focus, with the frightening realization a bullet might explode inside his mouth at any second.

The short gunman violently shook Arnold's head. "Well say something asshole. You lookin' for him or ain't ya?"

Arnold closed his eyes and held his breath and nodded yes. The next sound he heard was the gun being cocked in his mouth. Arnold's eyes popped open. Fear flooded his body and he lost control and wet his pants.

"Wrong answer," the gunman said. "But you know the right answer, don't you, Arnold?"

Quivering uncontrollably, Arnold quickly nodded yes.

"Good boy," said the gunman. "Just to be sure we're on the same page, I'm going to spell it out for you. I wouldn't want you to make any mistakes later." The man behind Arnold, tightened his stranglehold around Arnold's throat. The gunman in front of him said in a slow, methodical manner, "You are not looking for anybody, especially anybody named Jim. If you should happen to cross paths with anybody on the street named Jim, you are going to do your damnedest to avoid him. If I should hear, at some future date, that Jim met with some unfortunate tragedy, or even died in his sleep, you will see us again. Do you understand?"

Arnold nodded yes again.

The gunman decocked the magnum and pulled its long barrel out of Arnold's mouth. The big guy behind Arnold released his stranglehold, and Arnold dropped to all fours, gagging. Both men turned and walked calmly down the street. They got into their, car parked at the curb, and casually drove off, leaving Arnold a broken, humiliated man. Arnold remained on his knees sucking air and shamefully choking back tears. Those men did not fear him or his reputation. They did not fear the police, to have so brazenly assaulted him in public, in broad daylight. They didn't even wear masks to conceal their appearance. They didn't care who saw them.

Being openly attacked the way he was, shook him to his core. Arnold stumbled to his feet, still trembling. He didn't think about the urine stains on his pants, as he hurried back to his apartment. All he could think about was getting to safety. Once he was securely locked inside his apartment, he still did not feel safe. Being humbled, to such a disgraceful degree, left him completely demoralized, humiliated, fearful, and extremely paranoid. He was never the same after that. He quietly moved out of state and never again attempted to find the man named Jim.

The rape of Jamie Shaffer quietly died down and was forgotten. Jim Donnetti was never to learn what the Don had done for him. Weeks after the case had been filed away by the police department, Donnetti, still believing the case was active, continued to hide out at the Don's estate. He avoided leaving the property, for fear of being arrested or running into that crazy brother of hers, whom he was certain was still looking for him.

Chapter 26

Four months after the rape of Jamie Shaffer, Donnetti figured the heat had died down enough allowing him to venture outside the protective gates of the Baresi estate. He was careful to avoid those areas frequented by whores and pimps. He didn't want to run into Arnold or Jamie Shaffer. But ever since he lost his virginity to Jamie, he had awakened each day with morning wood. His need for more sex was almost overwhelming his good sense. But Donnetti was no fool, so he stayed away from the blue light district.

He eventually ended up at the Penthouse Bar in the Hudson Hotel, one of the more elegant nightspots in West Manhattan. He knew he would never run into the Shaffer's in a place like that. Upon entering the lounge, he could see the place was crowded. Several couples sat at tables lining the walls. Twenty or more people sat around the large horseshoe bar in the center of the room. There were slightly more women than men sitting at the bar. Many of the women were in conversation. Others seemed lonely, staring at nothing. Donnetti walked around the horseshoe bar, passing several women sitting alone, to a seat at the far end. He had wanted to sit beside a woman, but couldn't muster the courage, nor did he know what to say even if he did. He was not good at small talk. Women made him nervous. He never knew what to say to them to keep them interested, and he dreaded rejection. Paying a prostitute for sex was much easier. You get your pick of the litter. No refusal. Sex was guaranteed.

Donnetti ordered a drink and gazed across the room out the skyline window, overlooking Manhattan, Brooklyn, the Bronx, and Central Park. It was a magnificent view at night. Pity he had to enjoy it alone. As Donnetti ordered his second drink, a woman in business attire entered the lounge. She stood just inside the doorway and gazed around the crowded room. Several men noticed her. Donnetti guessed she was in her late twenties or early thirties.

The woman walked around to his side of the bar and smiled casually at him, as she scooted into the seat beside him, one of the few still available at the bar. Once seated, she attempted to light her cigarette, with a rather stubborn cigarette lighter. "Oh, darn it," she sighed.

Donnetti picked up a pack of matches from the bar, struck one match, and extended the flame to her. The woman took his hand in hers and guided the flame to her cigarette. She took a couple of puffs on it then said, "Thank you." Her eyes lingered on his for a moment, then she looked away and ordered a drink.

Donnetti shyly observed her from the corners of his

eyes. She was not what you would call a beautiful woman, but she was still attractive. Her appeal started with the way she walked into the room with confidence, her body erect with perfect posture, taking deliberate steps as she moved through the crowded bar, and glancing at selected people as she passed, offering a pleasant smile. Her glossy, brown hair was neatly trimmed down to her shoulders, and her soft features set off her striking hazel eyes. Those qualities made this otherwise ordinary-looking woman look very attractive indeed.

Donnetti wondered if perhaps he had imagined things. The way she held his hand, when he lit her cigarette. The lingering stare. *Was she flirting with him?* Nah, not possible. Stuff like that never happened to people like him. Still, Donnetti decided to order another drink. He wasn't ready to leave just yet.

After a while, he became acutely aware this intriguing woman, seated next to him had nearly finished her drink, but had not looked back in his direction since she sat down. Donnetti had been desperately trying to think of something witty to say since lighting her cigarette, but couldn't think of a thing. He felt awkward and ridiculous. What do you say to a woman, a total stranger, to get her interested in talking?

When Donnetti saw that she had finished her drink, panicked anxiety set in. *You're blowing it,* he told himself. *Say something to her, anything.*

Unexpectedly, the woman broke the ice first. "Are you okay?"

Donnetti was taken aback at the sound of her voice, and stumbled over his response.

"Oh, ah — yeah, I'm fine."

"I thought maybe you were ill. You look a little off-color."

"No. Ah, no, I'm fine." When Donnetti left it at that, she smiled politely and turned away again. *Dammit!* Donnetti thought. *Why didn't I say something else? She opened the door, and I slammed it shut.*

The woman reached for her purse.

Donnetti awkwardly blurted out, "Can I buy you a drink?" He wasn't sure if she was getting ready to leave or order something else.

The woman turned back to him. A delayed grin appeared on her face. "Sure," she said.

Donnetti got the bartender's attention and ordered a drink for both of them. He was still stunned she said yes. When the drinks were delivered, he asked, "What's your name?"

"Julia Bowman. What's yours?"

"Jim Donnetti," he said, then took several sips of his drink, as he tried to think of something else to say.

"So," she asked, "do you come here often?"

Donnetti took a silent breath to calm his nerves. "This is my first time. You?"

"I stop by whenever I'm in town."

"You're not from around here?" he asked.

"No. I'm from California."

"Where in California?"

"National City. Ever hear of it?"

"No, I don't think I have. Where is it?"

"It's a suburb just outside of San Diego. Most people on vacation from one of San Diego's suburbs, will just say, San Diego. It's much less complicated that way."

"So, you're here on vacation?" Donnetti asked.

"I am. I come to New York two or three times a year."

"Must be nice to be able to travel when you like."

"It is. I just love traveling." Julia paused and looked

directly at him, then added, "You meet such interesting people." She took a sip of her drink, then asked him, "What about you, Jim? Do you travel much?"

"I never travel too far from home. I'm curious, though. What kind of job do you have that gives you so much freedom to travel?"

"I don't work," she said. "I was left with a very adequate settlement."

"You're a widower?"

"Divorced. For a long time now," she said, matter-of-factly.

Donnetti glanced around the room. "This really is a cool bar. Nobody trying to hustle you here." As soon as the word 'hustle' left his mouth, he wished he hadn't said it. He didn't want her to think he hung out at dive bars.

Julia took a long drink from her glass, then asked coyly, "Does that happen to you a lot — being hustled I mean?"

Donnetti thought quickly. "No, but it did happen once," he admitted. "A few months ago, a call girl tried to pick me up in a bar. I turned her down."

Julia regarded him with squinted eyes, as if making up her mind on something.

Donnetti ordered another round of drinks. Later, after some casual conversation, Donnetti tried to make his next question sound as random as the rest. "When you visit New York do you stay with friends?"

"I travel to get away from friends," she said. "I like to disappear once in a while, and just get away."

"That could be terribly lonely," he suggested.

"Loneliness is a state of mind. I don't let it bother me. I'm perfectly content to spend my evenings alone."

Donnetti wondered why she was talking about being alone. Was she trying to tell him something? Was it possible he misread her signals? Did he waste all this time and money on drinks for nothing? Was he going to have to rape her too? Donnetti was tired of wasting time. "Is that what you want?" he asked.

"What do you mean?" she asked, with a confused look on her face.

"You said you were content to spend your evenings alone. Is that what you want — to be left alone tonight?"

Julia Bowman looked at him with the most startled expression. *What the hell was he talking about?* She had no intentions of going home alone tonight. How'd he ever get such a ridiculous idea? When she mentioned being alone, she only meant she was her own woman, and didn't need some man around all the time to look after her. But, by all means, she wanted this young stud to fuck her tonight. That's why she sat beside him. She loved them young and tender. She always did.

"No," said Julia Bowman softly, as she stared at him. "I don't want to be alone tonight."

Donnetti could not suppress the silly grin on his face. She wanted it as badly as he did.

As Julia finished the last of her drink, Donnetti nervously considered his next move. Having sex with a high-class woman like Julia Bowman, was going to be so much different than when he raped Jamie Shaffer. With that whore Jamie, it was strictly get in, get off, get out. But with Julia Bowman, it needed to be different. She was expecting him to make love to her. That worried him. He had never actually made love to a woman. He was afraid he couldn't satisfy her. Not because of his premature ejaculation with Jamie, but because he read somewhere, a man's first time was always premature. What worried Donnetti was his lack of experience. He was starting to wish he had just gone downtown and found a hooker; it would have been far less stressful. Whores didn't care about your quality of performance.

"Whenever you're ready," Julia Bowman said, putting her empty glass on the bar.

"I'm ready now," Donnetti replied, feeling less confident than he tried to sound. "How far away are you staying?"

Julia smiled. "I have a room right here in the hotel."

Donnetti followed her to her room. Julia didn't waste any time getting him into bed and Donnetti found his fears were unwarranted, primarily because of Julia's expertise. She proved to be a superstar in bed, greedily taking command, in an incredible one-woman act of erogenous titillation, which repeatedly drew him to the brink of explosion. She skillfully, however, never let him get quite there. A few times, when he was well past the point of no return, she somehow sensed it and gently pulled his testicles down with a little pressure, each time delaying his ejaculation. Incredibly, thirty minutes later, he was still in the game; during which time, she had positioned him into more erotic positions than he believed possible. And she didn't seem to mind doing all the work. Then, when she was finally ready for him to cum, she climbed off of him and gave him a blowjob. Just before he came, she flipped around and shoved his cock into her ass and let him explode there. After that Donnetti collapsed, totally exhausted. Julia let him rest a bit, then she started on him again.

After the marathon session, Donnetti woke up just before 11 pm and went home. Julia had tried to convince him to stay the night, but Donnetti declined. He told her some lie about having to pick somebody up at the airport. Donnetti just didn't feel comfortable sleeping there all night. He feared being asleep that long, when other people were present. It made him feel vulnerable, not just to vicious attacks, but to so-called harmless pranks. The bottom line was, Donnetti didn't like being fucked with when he was asleep. Even at Don Baresi's home, Donnetti locked his bedroom door every night.

So Donnetti went home and woke up in his own bed. That morning, he didn't speak to anyone about Julia Bowman. It was no one's business. Oddly enough though, he went through the day thinking not of Julia Bowman, but of that tramp, Jamie Shaffer. Even stranger, he had to admit he fantasized more about the uncooperative little whore, Jamie Shaffer, than he did for the eager, highly experienced Julia Bowman. That made no sense to him. Julia was, by far, better in bed, and he could even see a future with her, but there was something about Jamie. He couldn't quite figure out what it was. After a while, it occurred to him that taking Jamie by force, and feeling that sense of power over her, may have excited him more than he would like to admit. The only other possibility was that Jamie was a virgin. Maybe that's what excited him. Could that be it?

Later in the day, as Donnetti prepared for his second date with Julia Bowman, the Don's consigliere, Mario Tollini, brought word to him that the Don wanted to speak with him, in his study, before he left the grounds. Donnetti quickly finished dressing and went to see his Godfather. The Don was seated behind his huge maple desk, when Donnetti entered. Don Baresi set aside the papers he was reviewing and greeted Donnetti with a smile. "Come in, Jim."

Donnetti sat on the chair to the left of the desk. "You wanted to see me, sir?"

"Yes, and I'll get right to the point. It has come to my

attention that you met a woman named Julia Bowman last night."

Donnetti sat upright in his seat, surprised the Don knew about Julia and that he was even bringing it up. "Are you having me followed?"

"No," the Don replied. "But there are people in this city who tell me things."

"I'm nineteen years old," Donnetti muttered. "Why is it noteworthy when I spend time with a woman?"

"There are things about *this* woman I think you need to know."

"I don't care about her past. I know everything about Julia I need or want to know."

"Then go to her," the Don said without emotion and went back to reviewing the papers on his desk.

Donnetti rose quietly from his chair and left the office, wondering what the Don knew about Julia that he did not. When Donnetti arrived at Julia Bowman's room, she happily greeted him with a hungry kiss, that held the bittersweet taste of liquor and tobacco. He soon forgot about the Don's words of caution when Julia went to work on him, surpassing her sexual prowess from last night.

During one of their many breaks to catch their breath, she asked again if he could spend the night. Donnetti knew he couldn't keep using the airport lie, so he decided to level with her. "I can't stay," he said.

"Another airport pickup," she said flippantly.

"No. I lied about the airport pickup yesterday. The truth is, I can't spend the night, because I have this phobia about sleeping in someone else's bed. It makes me very uncomfortable. I wouldn't be able to fall asleep here."

Julia snaked her hand down between his legs and gently squeezed his balls. "You sure you can't stay the night?"

Donnetti trembled in erotic shivers. Her hand felt so good down there. He had to force the answer from his lips, although his body firmly disagreed. "I'm sure," he said.

"Well," she said, squeezing his balls tighter, "you don't have to go right now, do you?"

"Later works for me," he moaned, with a wincing smile.

Julia flashed an impish grin, then rolled over onto her back and spread her legs wide. "Here it is, baby. Come and get it," she said.

Donnetti got in position, but untimely lost his erection.

To Julia's surprise and dismay, even she was unable to get him hard enough again for penetration.

Donnetti was humiliated, but Julia comforted his ego by telling him it sometimes happens to all men. No big deal. He would do better tomorrow night.

Donnetti quickly accepted her rationale. It made perfect sense to him. It wasn't his fault. It wasn't his problem. Men were under all the pressure to perform. All a woman has to do is spread her damn legs.

During his drive home, Donnetti wondered about the dirt the Don claimed he had on Julia. He would ponder that mystery, on into the night, and much of the following day. It bothered him, not knowing because he detested secrets.

By eight o'clock that evening, as he dressed for his third date with Julia, he decided he had to know what the mystery was. He would just put the question to her – ask her point-blank about any dirt in her background that could be a problem for him. Of course, he would have to ask the question delicately. He had no desire to chase free pussy away.

Donnetti arrived at Julia's door a little after nine. He knocked but got no response. He knocked again. Still no answer. Donnetti went upstairs to the Penthouse Bar and described Julia to the bartender, asking if he'd seen her. The bartender hadn't seen her for a couple of days. Donnetti left frustrated. *Where the hell was she?* As he walked by the hotel desk on his way out, he considered one other possibility and stopped by the reception counter. "My name is Jim Donnetti. Do you have any messages for me?"

"What's your room number, sir?"

"I'm not a registered guest."

"Just one moment, sir. I'll check." The clerk looked through the outgoing message bin and returned with an envelope. Donnetti took it and walked outside before opening it. The letter inside was short and to the point. It read:

Sorry, Jim,
Something important came up.
I had to go home.
I won't be back.
It was nice while it lasted.
Goodbye, Julia

Chapter 27

During the first few weeks and months after Julia Bowman left town, Donnetti moped around the Baresi estate depressed and kept pretty much to himself. He missed Julia and wanted her back. Secretly, however, Donnetti feared his poor performance in bed the last time they were together had something to do with her sudden departure. Now with Julia gone, he would never get the chance to make it up to her. Often, Donnetti would return to the Penthouse Bar in hopes she might come back. She never did.

Three months later, Donnetti's Uncle Antonio and two of the Don's most trusted men were planning to go to California, on what Antonio described as a little business trip – but he added they would have some playtime afterward. Antonio invited Donnetti to come along for some much-needed R&R. Donnetti accepted and, a week later, they left by train. When they finally arrived at the Los Angeles train depot, they were met by a little old man, with a wrinkled face and tired eyes. The old man looked vaguely familiar to Donnetti.

Antonio made the introductions. "Jim, I'd like you to meet Darrel Laird. We'll be staying at his home while we're here."

Of course, Donnetti thought, *Darrel Laird*. He was a big name in silent films back in the '20s, but, like many of the stars in those days, Laird was unable to make the transition to the talkies, when sound pictures came along.

Antonio continued with the introductions. "Mr. Laird, I'd like you to meet Don Baresi's godson, Jim Donnetti."

Darrel Laird's eyes lit up respectfully, as he shook the hand of the Don's godson. "I've heard a great deal about you, Mr. Donnetti, from your godfather. I'm honored to finally get the opportunity to meet you."

After the introductions, they all piled into Laird's chauffeur-driven Rolls Royce Phantom VI. Donnetti sat beside Darrel Laird. They spoke briefly, but Donnetti was more interested in the sights, as they drove through Los Angeles, then along the Sunset Strip, and on into Beverly Hills. The chauffeur pulled into the long circular driveway of a magnificent mansion. They all got out and started for the house. Donnetti asked, Laird, "What about our luggage?"

"The servants will take care of the bags," Laird said over his shoulder.

Donnetti whispered to Antonio, "How can he afford all this? The house, the servants, the car? He hasn't made a movie since silent films were popular."

"He can't afford it," Antonio said.

"Then, how?"

"Laird lives here at the pleasure of the Don. He kind of watches the place. We say it's his house, because it makes him feel like he's still somebody."

"My godfather owns this mansion?"

"He does."

"Why Laird? There's plenty of broken-down actors out here."

"When Laird was big time, he did my father a service the Don never forgot."

"What service?"

"You ask too many questions," Antonio said, then walked away.

That evening after dinner, Antonio and the other two men, who accompanied them to California, left the house on business. They were gone for three days. During their extended absence, Laird showed Donnetti the city and introduced him to many people in and out of the movie industry, at various Hollywood haunts. In nearly every case Laird started the introductions by saying, "I'd like for you to meet a good friend of mine, Jimmy Donnetti. He's Carlo Baresi's nephew." Laird seemed to take great pride in introducing him that way. What surprised Donnetti was that these Hollywood people knew the Don's name and seemingly respected it. Apparently, his godfather had much more influence than he ever imagined. When Antonio and the other two men returned to the mansion, Donnetti was glad to see them. Donnetti asked Antonio, "How much longer before we have that R&R you talked about?"

"Tomorrow," Antonio said. "We're driving down to Tijuana."

Darrel Laird cut in, "Hey, that sounds like it might be fun. Mind if I tag along?"

"You're more than welcome," Antonio said.

The following day, Darrel Laird had his chauffeur drive them from Los Angeles to the Mexican border in the Rolls, but refused to let his driver cross into Mexico in the luxury automobile. Instead, the Rolls was parked on the U.S. side. They walked across the border and took a cab into Tijuana. Laird had protested boisterously when it was even suggested that they drive the Rolls into Mexico in style. "No way am I taking this beautiful machine into Mexico. Those tamale eaters can damn near strip a car clean when you stop for a red light."

Nobody put up an argument.

The first dive bar they entered featured nude women dancing, on an elevated stage, behind the bartender, who seemed uninterested in the naked bodies grinding and bumping behind him. The cocktail waitresses all wore tight, skimpy outfits and didn't appear to care when the customers grabbed and swatted their behinds, as they took orders and delivered drinks.

Donnetti and the others stayed long enough to have one round of drinks, then they moved on. The second club they visited also had nude dancing women, but the stage there was not elevated. In fact, it wasn't really a stage at all – just an area cordoned off with rope. Four naked women sauntered around inside the roped-off area, dancing teasingly just out of reach of the drunk men groping for them. One of the four naked women, modestly wore a short skirt but had no panties on underneath. The reason she wore the damn skirt at all was a mystery to Donnetti, because each time she moved or bent over, you got a clear view of everything she had. After a while, Donnetti did notice though, the customers seemed to favor the girl in the skirt. Even he had to admit he found her strangely more appealing than the other dancers, who openly bared it all, in the lewdest possible ways. It wasn't that the girl in the skirt was more attractive than the others. In truth, she looked somewhat homelier than the others. Donnetti reasoned her popularity stemmed from the fact that she wasn't completely naked, and customers had to steal glimpses of that hairy bush of hers. That's what made her different from the others, and it made her stand out.

After the girls had danced around awhile, the men in the front row seats and those others who could squeeze in close, began holding dollar tips out to the girls. For the tips, the dancers allowed the tippers brief liberties to fondle or kiss them on various parts of their body. Donnetti and his group watched for about twenty minutes, then at Darrel Laird's suggestion, they left to go to a club called The Hot Box.

On the way there, Darrel mentioned to the group that The Hot Box was one of the raunchiest in Tijuana, but he did not elaborate further. The moment they stepped into the club, which was actually a converted movie theater, Donnetti found out exactly what Laird meant. A naked woman was lying on her back, on a small bed, positioned caddy-corner on the stage to give the audience the best possible view. The woman held her legs up, with her knees drawn back to her ears. An old Mexican man, standing at the foot of the bed, held a big German shepherd on a taut leash and was barely able to contain the dog as it licked away at her vagina with great enthusiasm.

When the woman started to moan, some of the men in the audience began whistling and yelling, urging the dog on. Donnetti watched in amazement. He had never seen anything like that before. Sure, he'd heard the jokes about how rich women supposedly bought poodles for the sole purpose of getting their pet to lick them on lonely nights, but he never thought he'd see such a thing happen.

Antonio said, "Let's see if we can find somewhere to

sit."

Donnetti gazed around the room. The place was packed. Several people, ahead of them, were already standing and trying to find seats.

"Follow me," said Darrel Laird. He led them through the crowded room, down to the front row and the only vacant table in the theater. There was a sign on top of the table which read *RESERVED*. Laird placed the sign on the floor under the table. "We can sit here," he said.

"I don't think we'd better," Donnetti cautioned.

"It's alright," Darrel assured them. "I know the owner well. He always saves this table for his friends."

Antonio said, "I hope you know what you're doing, 'cause I sure as hell don't want to get thrown into a Mexican jail."

"Whattaya think, I'm crazy or something?" Laird blurted out. "Sure, I know what I'm doing. I ain't fool enough to go messin' with these beaners, not down here." Darrel sat down. "Trust me, it's okay."

Antonio nodded at the others, then sat down. The group followed his lead. Donnetti sat in the middle but never actually took his eyes off the stage. He was mesmerized by the show. When the woman's body started to shudder, Donnetti felt embarrassingly aroused. The dog became more excited too, and the old Mexican man had a hard time keeping the German shepherd from mauling her. After a while, the woman's moans got louder. Her hips convulsed and she cried out in a loud wail, with her orgasm gushing out like a fountain.

Darrel Laird jumped to his feet and began yelling right along with the crowd, urging the dog not to stop. Antonio and Donnetti laughed at Laird, whose animated gestures were quite amusing. When the woman pushed back on the dog's head, the old man holding the leash, pulled the dog off of her with great effort.

By this time, the crowd was clapping and yelling and whistling so loud the noise was almost deafening. Donnetti was grinning and applauding along with everyone else. He stopped abruptly, when Julia Bowman sat up on the bed, wiped her hair out of her face and smiled at the audience. Donnetti was stunned. He couldn't believe it was her. *No — it can't be her. It can't be.* But it was.

Julia Bowman hopped off the bed and walked close to the edge of the stage, bowing as if she had just performed in a successful Broadway show. The crowd applauded even louder when she turned her back to them and bowed again.

As she took her bows, some of the stagehands quickly pushed the bed off stage and replaced it with a specially constructed platform. Two other men escorted a donkey out onto the stage.

Upon seeing the donkey, the crowd went berserk, laughing and cursing and yelling the vilest things imaginable. They were eager to see if she could take it. Was it even possible? Gradually the audience started stomping their feet in unison, urging the act to begin.

Julia waited until the animal was standing by the platform, then she stepped up on the platform, in front of the donkey, with her back to the animal. The platform was constructed so her feet were about thirty-six inches apart. When she lowered her chest across the incline section of the platform, it left her knees bent and her buttocks up and out.

The two men holding the donkey moved the animal closer to the platform behind Julia. The donkey stepped onto the lower landing of the platform with his two hooves. With very little prodding, the donkey moved its two front feet up to the second, third, and fourth levels, until the donkey was standing upright on its hind legs behind Julia. The donkey brayed; his large erection was visible to everyone in the theater.

"Fuck that nasty bitch!" yelled a man sitting at the table next to Donnetti.

The suddenness of that man's scream so close snapped Donnetti back to the here and now, and he quickly looked to see if Antonio and the others at his table had noticed his recognition of the girl on stage. He was relieved to see that they had not. Their eyes were transfixed on the stage. But then he noticed something odd. All of the guys at his table sat erect in their chairs, but none of them seemed engaged in what they were watching. Then it dawned on him, the men at his table were not just detached from the performance; they were purposely avoiding eye contact with him. It was so obvious now, and apparently, they were all in on it – even Darrel Laird, whom Donnetti now remembered had insisted on their coming to this club, at this particular time, at this front-row table. Julia Bowman was what this whole trip was all about. They knew he had sex with her and that she worked here. They wanted him to know it, too. That's why this table was reserved. That's why he was invited to California.

Donnetti glared at Antonio. "Let's get the hell out of here."

Without a word, Antonio and the others rose from their seats and followed Donnetti back through the aisle, squeezing by throngs of wildly appreciative patrons, many standing and cheering the action on and shouting an assortment of vulgarities at the woman on stage. Despite the noise from the audience, Donnetti could hear the donkey braying excitedly and could hear Julia grunting in intense pain. As Donnetti's group continued toward the exit door, Julia's grunting splintered into a painfully, chilling scream startling everyone in the room. The boisterous crowd plunged into silence, and only the tortured screams from the stage could be heard. Voices of concern and fear swept through the room. Donnetti momentarily stopped but did not turn around. For a few seconds he felt a tug at his heart, but quickly buried the feelings and continued toward the exit sign. As they neared the door, Julia suddenly made a blood-curdling squeal that almost didn't sound human.

A horrified voice in the audience yelled, "Somebody oughtta stop this!"

Then Donnetti heard Julia yell at the audience, while choking back painful screams. "NO! DON'T YOU FUCKIN' DARE!"

Upon hearing her defiant cry, the audience roared back to life and was again in a frenzy of cheers and vulgarities. Donnetti exited the building, taking a much-needed breath of fresh air, but avoided eye contact with his crew. He was still upset at the length they went to in setting this up.

Across the street, he saw a taxi already waiting for them. He was not surprised. These guys thought of everything. The ride back to the border was in total silence.

During the long drive back to L.A., Donnetti considered his godfather's part in this. It seemed so clear now. Don Carlo Baresi was behind it all. Now that he thought about it, the Don was probably responsible for Julia leaving New York, suddenly, the way she did. Donnetti was glad he knew the truth about that whore, but at the same time, he hated Don Baresi for manipulating him so contemptibly. He hated Antonio and the others for being a part of it. He hated himself for ever having feelings for Julia, and he hated her because the slut tricked him, by making him think she was respectable.

Jim Donnetti never saw Julia Bowman again, and no

one ever spoke of her in his presence. During the years after that degrading revelation in Mexico, Donnetti tried to put that disgraceful episode out of his mind. But thirty-one years later, another Bowman walked into his life rather abruptly. His name was Eddie.

Chapter 28

Thirty-one years after the debacle in Mexico, with Julia Bowman, Jim Donnetti would meet her son in Los Angeles. Donnetti had just concluded a successful business meeting involving a plot to assassinate a Nevada government official. The Nevada councilman was leading the charge, in a supposedly secret meeting in Los Angeles, to revoke Donnetti's gaming license due to his perceived connection with organized crime.

After the meeting with the shooter, Donnetti headed back to his hotel, accompanied by his three beefy bodyguards. Once inside his hotel room, Donnetti decided to take a cold shower and get a good night's sleep, before flying back to Las Vegas in the morning. As he prepared for his shower, a knock rapped on the door.

ERNIE ADAMS

"Who the hell could that be at this time of night?" Donnetti snapped.

"Don't concern yourself with it, Mr. Donnetti," said the guard sitting closest to the door, as he backed away from the card table. "I'll take care of it."

The other two guards, confident the lead man could handle this minor interruption, continued with their poker game.

"Whoever it is," Donnetti yelled to his guards, from the bathroom doorway, "get rid of him. I don't want to see anybody else tonight. I don't care who it is."

"Consider it done, sir," the lead guard said.

"Damn right," one of the other guards interjected.

From inside the bathroom, Donnetti heard the knock repeated, this time more forcefully. Donnetti smiled as he closed the bathroom door. He knew if his guys were provoked, they would kick the crap out of whoever it was. And that was alright with him. Donnetti stepped into the shower stall and turned the cold water on high. He liked it that way.

Donnetti could hear some commotion in the other room, but ignored it. He assumed the late-night visitor had somehow talked himself into getting his ass kicked.

When the commotion got louder, Donnetti hoped they weren't killing the son-of-a-bitch. He didn't need that kind of trouble right now. Donnetti stepped out of the shower to reign his guys in. As he wrapped himself in a towel, the noise suddenly stopped. "What's going on out there?" Donnetti called out.

Nobody answered, but he could hear someone moving around out there. Donnetti started to open the door but decided against it. Something must be wrong for his bodyguards not to answer. Donnetti listened intently for some recognizable, hopefully friendly voice. He heard neither, but was nervously aware that whoever was out there was moving toward the bathroom door. For the first time in a long time, Donnetti felt fear, stark naked fear that left him utterly terrified. His three-armed guards had apparently been put out of action. Donnetti's mind skipped to the next logical conclusion. Someone out there had come to kill him. The realization that he was going to die numbed him. Donnetti quickly locked the bathroom door, cut the lights out then leaned back against the furthest wall, knowing none of this would save him. He heard the killer try the doorknob. Then there was silence. A moment later, there was a loud crash, as the door was kicked open, partially off its hinges. Donnetti crouched there in the darkness, looking up at the silhouette of the biggest man he'd ever seen.

The big man stared down at him and said, "I've been looking for you." Then he flicked on the light switch and added, "I'm Eddie Bowman." The blond giant said nothing else, as if what he did say was enough.

Trembling in fear, Donnetti looked up into the giant's cold, dark eyes, and mumbled,
"What do you want?"

"I want you," the big man said. "I'm your son."

His words struck Donnetti like a hard slap to the face, and it took him a few seconds to fully process what the man had said. "Y-You're what?" Donnetti stammered.

"My mother was Julia Bowman," he said.

Donnetti flashed back to the two nights he spent with Julia over thirty years ago. *But no, it can't be true. This man must be mistaken. No way could he be my son. Was it even possible that a donkey-fucking bitch could have born him a son? NO!* Donnetti overwhelmingly decided. *No way in hell. A tramp like Julia would have surely taken precautions against pregnancy. And even if she did not, that didn't mean he was the father. As much fucking as that bitch did, anybody could be the father, even one of those damn animals.*

Donnetti gathered his composure and cautiously stood up, keeping his eyes on the giant. When he spoke to the big man, he kept his voice in a calming tone. "What do you want with me?"

The blond giant looked surprised, as if the answer was obvious. "You're my father. A son should be with his father."

Donnetti took an anxious breath. Maybe this man was not here to kill him. With nervous apprehension, Donnetti asked, "What does that mean?"

"Where you go, I go," the big man said.

Donnetti involuntarily shook his head in denial, as he stumbled back into the wall. Why would his mother tell him such a lie? *Why did she pick me?* Donnetti's eyes momentarily shifted from the big man to the door hanging partially off its hinges, then back to the giant. Clearly, this guy had a fragile psyche and was hanging onto sanity by a thread. Donnetti did not want to set him off again, so when he spoke to the man, he did so in an overly subdued voice, "What happened to the men out there?"

"They told me I couldn't see you."

"What did you do to them?"

"I hit 'em," Eddie said with indifference.

Donnetti maintained a calming voice when he asked his next question, "Why don't we go into the bedroom? We'll be more comfortable out there." Donnetti felt an embarrassing relief, when the big man turned and headed for the bedroom. Donnetti gazed quickly around the bathroom for a weapon. He thought about the straight razor in his shaving kit but was too afraid to go for it. This blond giant had just taken out three-armed, badass security guards. Donnetti knew he wouldn't have a chance against this man with a razor. Donnetti followed the big man into the bedroom, with trepidation. Once there, cold fear crept back into his heart at seeing the brutal carnage.

All three bodyguards were dead. The lead guard's face was caved in and unrecognizable. The youngest guard looked like his right arm and back were broken, as he lay in a mangled heap on top of a shattered nightstand. The third guard was on the floor face down in a puddle of blood, just a few feet from the bathroom door.

Eddie Bowman nonchalantly stepped over that guard's body then sat down on a wooden chair beside the coffee table. The chair Eddie Bowman sat on looked undersized for his massive frame. He almost looked like a big child waiting dutifully for his teacher to speak, yet oblivious to the dead bodies around him.

As Donnetti stared at the blond giant, he was certain of one thing: this monster was no child of his. It occurred to him though, that Julia Bowman's lie may have saved his life. The big man seemed docile around him, even respectful. Donnetti started to believe that maybe he would get out of this mess alive after all. Donnetti sat on the bed across from Eddie and spoke in a monotone voice. "Do you have a driver's license or ID card?"

The big man nodded yes.

Donnetti extended his hand, palm up. "May I see it?"

Without hesitation, Eddie pulled his wallet from his back pocket, took out his driver's license, and handed it to Donnetti.

Donnetti reached slowly for the phone, but stopped, letting his hand hover over it. "I have to make a phone call. Afterwards, we'll talk." Donnetti picked up the phone with due caution, careful not to make any sudden moves. He didn't want Eddie to perceive it as a threat. Surprisingly, the blond giant didn't seem to mind at all, sitting there like a trusting son. Donnetti called the Goodman Detective Agency and gave them Eddie's information from his driver's license. "Get me everything you can on this man. I need it yesterday. Also, find out what you can about his parents. Call me back at this same number. If I don't answer on the first ring, hang up." Donnetti looked at Eddie and said, "One more call." The next phone call he made was to a man in Las Vegas, who he called the Cleaner.

"Yes?" the voice on the other end answered.

"It's me," Donnetti said. "I'm in Los Angeles. I have an untidy room. I need it cleaned."

"Where exactly are you, and is there a time issue?"

Donnetti gave him the hotel name and room number and added that there was most definitely a time issue.

"How dirty is the room?" the Cleaner asked.

"Looks like three frat boys went berserk in here," Donnetti answered.

The Cleaner said, "Doctor P is in your area. I'll send him right over."

Donnetti nodded to himself. He knew Doctor P was a skilled crime scene cleaner and very meticulous about his work. After the Cleaner hung up, Donnetti turned his attention back to the blond giant, his fear now starting to fade. The fool believed him to be his father. Maybe he could use that. "Tell me about your mother?" Donnetti asked, with more of an edge in his voice.

While Eddie talked about his mother, Donnetti quietly got dressed. Over the next twenty-five minutes, Eddie answered every question put to him. It was clear to Donnetti that Eddie didn't know about his mother's stage act, and

Donnetti certainly wasn't going to tell him. Donnetti also learned that Julia Bowman was dead. Four months ago, she was admitted to a hospital for a kidney infection and died on the operating table. Eddie Bowman had learned about Jim Donnetti from a letter discovered in his mother's safe deposit box, which named Donnetti as his father.

Donnetti paused the conversation, when he heard a knock at the door. "Who is it?" he asked.

"It's the Doctor," the voice on the other side of the door announced.

Donnetti turned to Eddie, "Do not speak to this man." Then Donnetti opened the door just wide enough for Doctor P to enter. After taking only two steps into the room, Doctor P stopped and scanned the bedroom a couple of times, noting the bodies, the blood, the damage, and he took a real good look at Eddie. "Is this the only room of concern?" he asked.

"Except for the bathroom door, yes."

"What time frame are we dealing with?"

"I have to check out by noon tomorrow."

"Alright. I have a crew en route. Is there someplace you two can go?"

Donnetti looked at Eddie. He had no intentions of taking that freak anywhere, but for Eddie's benefit, Donnetti said, "We can fly back to Las Vegas, but I'm expecting a call here in the next few minutes."

Doctor P stared at Donnetti, "Before my crew gets here, he needs to clean up. Have him leave all of his outer clothing on top of one of the bodies. I'll get him something to wear. I just hope I can find something big enough for him. Be back in a minute."

Just after Doctor P left the room, the telephone rang. It was the Goodman Detective Agency. "I've got some information on Eddie Bowman."

"Tell me about his parents first," Donnetti asked.

"Nobody seems to know who his father is, but his mother's name was Julia Bowman."

"Was?" Donnetti inquired, looking for confirmation of her death.

"She died about four months ago. I'm surprised she lived as long as she did."

"Why do you say that?"

"It seems Mrs. Bowman has been doing bestiality acts in Mexico for decades, long before she got pregnant with Eddie. That's ultimately what killed her."

Donnetti was confused. Eddie told him she died of complications from an unsuccessful medical procedure. "What do you mean, that's what killed her?" Donnetti asked.

"At her advanced age, one of those animals was too much for her. Split her in two. She bled to death on stage before a doctor could save her."

Donnetti looked over at the blond giant. Goodman's version of how Julia died was much different than what Eddie told him, but Donnetti doubted that Eddie lied. It was more likely the people around Julia lied to Eddie, to keep him from going berserk.

Goodman added, "Give me a little more time and I'll try to ID the daddy."

"That won't be necessary," Donnetti said. "Tell me about Eddie."

"Alright. This guy Eddie Bowman is a real winner. He's an ex-con. Been in and out of prison most of his adult life, on a variety of charges, including burglaries, robberies, assaults, a lot of felony batteries, and one attempted murder, plea-bargained down to a felony battery. Word is he's got a hair-trigger temper and is extremely antisocial. I found this interesting, too. A psychologist at his last prison wrote that

Eddie was capable of empathy and forming an emotional connection, but only in extremely rare cases. That same psychologist also wrote that Eddie was dangerously psychotic. I got a copy of his report here." Goodman paused. "I won't read the whole thing, but here are some of the highlights. He called Eddie a predator with a paranoid personality disorder. He said Eddie was also bipolar, easily agitated and prone to emotional outbursts, including uncontrollable fits of rage. He said something about Eddie showing signs of sexually deviant behavior, but I'm not sure where he was going with that. He also said Eddie has no respect for the law or the rights of others. He is capable of unimaginable cruelty and violence, but incapable of feeling remorse or guilt. Overall, he concluded Eddie was a brutally vicious sociopath."

Donnetti looked at Eddie when he asked Goodman the next question, "What does he look like?"

"He's a big guy. He's listed at 7 feet tall and packing 380 pounds of muscle. He's got blond hair and black eyes. Hell of a combination," Goodman said. "Anyway, this guy is a real monster. If you ever cross his path — run."

"Is there anything else?" Donnetti asked.

"That's all I have right now."

"Alright, thank you." Donnetti hung up and stared at the sociopath sitting across from him. He needed to decide on what to do about Eddie. The man was too much of a wild card to leave on his own, especially with the lie he was carrying. A bullet to the back of his head would solve the problem. But what if the prison psychiatrist was right? What if Eddie was able to make an emotional connection? If Eddie really thought he found his father — that might be the answer. Someone as volatile and imposing as Eddie could be good for business, if he could be controlled. As for Eddie

Bowman being his son – not a chance. He could never have a child with a whore like Julia. Donnetti believed it was more likely that Eddie was the spawn of one of those animals that she was always spreading her legs for. No wonder Eddie was so fucked up.

When Doctor P returned to the room, Donnetti instructed Eddie to change clothing and to clean up.

When his private plane was about to land at LAX, Donnetti headed for the airport with Eddie in tow. Along the way, Donnetti made it clear to Eddie that he was never to mention their father-son relationship to anyone. He convinced Eddie, for financial reasons that had long ago been established, it was best that nobody knew he had a son.

That financial story was, of course, a lie. It had nothing to do with finances; Donnetti just wanted to keep this whole Bowman mess a secret. He didn't want it getting out that he once had sex with a woman who fucked donkeys, and that he may have had a kid from that union. After all, he didn't believe he was the father and he didn't want anybody else to believe it or even consider it. As it stood now, everyone that knew of his brief fling with Julia was dead, except for his uncle, Antonio, who was so old and feeble-minded now, that he had trouble at times, even remembering his own name.

So, by the time Jim Donnetti's private plane landed in Las Vegas, he felt secure his relationship with Julia would remain his secret.

Still, despite his stern self-denial of Eddie's ridiculous claim, deep inside Donnetti's subconscious mind, he feared and believed Eddie Bowman *was* his son – though he would never admit it, not even to himself.

Chapter **29**

Alexander Temple hurried to Victoria's room, hoping to catch her before she left. He figured she'd go straight there to do her makeup and whatever else women do before they step out in public. He had questions about her rookie partner, Billy Shaw, which he forgot to ask. Namely, how much did Shaw know? Temple worried if Shaw was as lackadaisical with security as Karen Kiley was, his knowledge could be a problem.

Temple arrived at her room and started to knock, but stopped when he heard Victoria coming up behind him fast. She was still wearing the same white evening dress she had on earlier. She looked worried.

"What's wrong?" Temple asked.

"It's Billy. He's in trouble."

"What happened?"

"Donnetti's people are after him. Billy blew his cover, now he's on the run."

"Are they on to you, too?"

"No, I'm good."

"What does Shaw know about me and the mission?"

"Billy knows what I know."

"How the hell did he blow his cover?" Temple snapped.

"I don't know, but he said —" Victoria paused to look around cautiously, then leaned close to him and whispered, "He said he found the microdots."

"Wait," Temple cautioned, "let's get out of the corridor. Is your room bugged?"

"No. My room is clean."

"Are you sure?"

"Yes, I'm sure," she answered, with a hint of irritation.

Temple followed her into her stateroom, which looked just like Yolanda's room. Victoria then continued, "Billy said he knows where the microdots are. He wants to meet you back at your downtown hotel room before he slips out of town."

"Did he say he found them or he has them?"

"I didn't get a chance to ask. He left this information in a note for me, at one of our emergency drop spots onboard the boat."

"You sure it was Billy who left the note?"

"I'm sure," she insisted, looking annoyed again.

"Why are you sure?" Temple pressed.

"The note was in code. Billy and I worked out a unique code when we were first assigned here, so we could communicate with each other, if verbal communication became impossible or too dangerous."

"He could have been coerced," Temple suggested.

"He wasn't," Victoria stated with confidence. "We also had a backup code, which meant danger, in case we were under duress."

At that moment, Temple and Victoria both turned simultaneously to see Edna Jean Case step from her hiding place in the bathroom, with a pistol in her hand. "That code thing was pretty clever, Victoria," said Edna.

Victoria was startled by Edna's unexpected appearance. Temple was already in attack mode, but he held back. Edna was too far away; he couldn't get to her before she pulled the trigger. At that distance, he would take one bullet, maybe two, before he reached her.

Victoria seethed with anger, for making such a rookie mistake. She should have checked the bathroom before she started talking. It was careless and inexcusable, and now, quite possibly fatal.

Edna maintained her safe distance from them, holding her .38 caliber snub-nose revolver close to her body. "You," she said, pointing her gun at Temple, "get down on your knees. Put your hands behind your head. Interlock your fingers and cross your feet at the ankles."

After Temple assumed the position, Edna aimed her gun at Victoria. "Turn around and put your hands up on the wall. Now take two steps back. Spread your feet. That's right, you know the drill." Edna walked behind Victoria and placed the barrel of her gun firmly against the base of Victoria's head. "Move one inch and I'll blow your fucking head off." Edna patted Victoria down for weapons, but was soon running her hand along Victoria's body in an invasive caress.

Victoria tensed up in revulsion but did not resist. She didn't want to give this cold-blooded assassin any reason to pull the trigger. Edna moved her hand to Victoria's breasts and openly fondled them. Victoria blocked out her feelings, as she had so many times before, with all the faceless men she had to give herself to in the line of duty.

"All right," Edna said, finally backing away from her. "Now let's see if your boyfriend here is packing any weapons." Maintaining her distance, Edna ordered Temple to strip down to his underwear. When Temple did not immediately comply, Edna snarled, "That was not a request. Do it now."

Temple stood up, keeping his eyes on Edna as he began to undress. He had to get closer to her somehow. But Edna was smart. She was staying clear of his kill zone. When Temple was down to his underwear, Edna ordered, "Give me a 360."

After Edna was sure he was not armed, she told him to get dressed. Temple knew now that Edna wasn't planning on killing them, otherwise, why bother letting him get dressed.

Once he had his clothing back on, Edna said curtly, "Alright, let's go."

"Where to?" Victoria asked.

"Just start walking. I'll tell you where to turn."

Victoria intentionally moved away from Temple to get more separation between them as she started for the door. By increasing the kill zone, it might give one of them a chance to take Edna out. Before opening the door, Victoria stalled for time.

"How'd you know about me?" she asked Edna.

Good girl, Temple thought. *Talk to her. Get her talking. Get her distracted.*

Edna displayed a dull smile. "I didn't know about you. I just never liked you. Strutting around here all the time shaking that big ass. Thinking you're all that. I came in here looking for some dirt on you. I just happened to be in your bathroom snooping, when you walked in here and gave me all the dirt I needed." Edna turned to Temple. "And then there's you. You must be that super spy that Donnetti's been talking about. He says you're a very dangerous man." Edna looked him up and down with disdain. "You don't look so dangerous to me."

Edna pointed her gun at his head from across the room. "I could kill you so easily, dangerous man."

Temple didn't think she would shoot unless provoked, so he just stood there quietly watching her, poised and ready, waiting for her to make that one mistake.

Edna saw Victoria sneak a peek at the coffee table. "If you're thinking about that little .22 hidden under the table," Edna patted her jacket pocket, "I've got it." Then Edna pulled a six-inch folding knife from her back pants pocket. "I also found this," she said, flipping the blade out with her thumb.

Victoria casually looked in Temple's direction. It was only a glance, but he saw it and understood it. Victoria then suddenly lunged toward Edna.

Edna quickly aimed her gun at Victoria and was about to fire.

Victoria abruptly stopped after one step. She had no intention of reaching Edna; she only wanted to distract her, hopefully giving Temple, who was closer, a chance.

The moment Edna's gun turned away from him, Temple sprang forward with the quickness of a jungle cat. Edna immediately swung the gun back in his direction, her finger already tightening down on the trigger.

Temple closed the distance quickly and jammed the barrel of her gun back toward her chest, neutralizing her trigger finger and fracturing her wrist. In the middle of her scream, Temple connected with a right cross, fracturing her jaw and knocking her off her feet. On the way down, both weapons fell out of her hands, but when she hit the floor, she rolled instinctively toward the .38 revolver, grabbed it, and reared up ready to shoot.

The Iceman had already dropped to one knee and had the folding knife Edna dropped in his hand. He threw the knife a millisecond before she could pull the trigger. The blade slammed into her heart. Edna grunted like the wind was knocked out of her. Blood oozed out of her chest. She dropped the gun and grabbed for the handle of the knife with both hands, as she toppled over onto her back, her eyes open in a blank stare.

Temple recognized death when he saw it, but knelt and checked her pulse anyway.

Victoria came up behind him, "Is she dead?"

"She's dead," he said, standing up.

Victoria glared down at her. "What a bitch."

Temple looked at Victoria. "You took a big chance, drawing her attention that way."

Victoria shrugged her shoulders. "We do what we have to do." Then she gazed at Edna's body again. "What do we do about her?"

"We have to hide her. You know the boat better than I do. Any ideas?"

"We can weigh her down and dump her overboard. The water's deep here."

"No. Somebody might see us dropping her overboard."

"We sure as hell can't leave her on the boat," Victoria argued.

"Why not? By the time the body starts getting ripe, my mission should be over."

Victoria gave it some thought, then said, "Alright. We can dump her in the laundry room on deck 2. They won't do the laundry again for another two days."

Temple nodded. "How do we get her down to deck 2 without being seen?"

"Each floor with sleeping quarters, has an in-wall laundry chute that drops into a huge bin in the laundry room downstairs. We can stuff her in a laundry bag and drop her down the chute. All we have to do then is go down to the laundry room and make sure her bag is not on the top of the pile, just in case someone goes down there and gets nosy."

"Can we get a big enough laundry bag?"

Victoria opened the cedar chest at the foot of the bed and pulled out a huge laundry bag. She removed the few soiled items and passed the empty bag to him.

"This will do nicely," Temple said, then squatted next to Edna's body and laid the bag at her feet. He handed Victoria the .38 caliber revolver Edna dropped, but left the knife in her chest. Then he patted her down for anything of value. He found the .22 caliber and handed it to Victoria, too. After the pat-down, he put Edna's legs in the bag, pulled the rest of it up over her head, and tied it off.

"You ready?" Victoria asked, taking hold of one end of the bag.

"This is as far as you go," Temple told Victoria. "I'll handle it from here. No sense risking your cover further. Just tell me where the laundry chute is and the exact location of the laundry room downstairs."

"Alright," Victoria agreed, and gave him the directions. She started for the door, but stopped and looked back at him, with a look of concern. "Help Billy if you can," she said.

Temple nodded at her, then asked, "You gonna be here when I get back?"

"Yes. Why wouldn't I be?"

"If Shaw has the information I need, I'll deliver it, then

I'm coming back here to finish this. It might be safer if you're somewhere else."

Victoria smiled. "I do appreciate that. But I can't go. I don't get paid for being in the safe place. Don't worry about me, I've been to a few rodeos."

"Of that, I have no doubt," Temple said.

"Besides," Victoria added, "if you're not successful, I have to still be here to protect my cover." Victoria stepped out into the corridor to check the passageway, then leaned her head back in and said, "It's clear. You be careful." They exchanged glances, then she was gone.

Temple grabbed the laundry bag, with Edna's body in it, and let the entire bag dangle over his shoulder, as he held onto it with one hand. It was an incredible strain to support her full weight that way, but he had to make it look like he wasn't carrying anything heavier than laundry, in case the hallway surveillance cameras were being monitored. When Temple stepped out into the corridor, Victoria was gone. He continued down the passageway, found the laundry chute, dropped the bag inside, and heard it skid down the slide. He waited until it hit bottom, then went downstairs and located the laundry room. He peeked inside. Nobody was there. Temple hurriedly located Edna's bag, then threw other laundry bags on top of hers. If everything went as planned, he'd have the microdots and be long gone before her body was found.

Temple headed back through the ship, through the casino, and down the boarding brow, to his car at the pier side guest parking area. He took his Walther PPK out of the rolled towel in the back seat and stuffed it under his belt. He had to find Shaw before Donnetti's people did.

During the drive downtown, Temple's thoughts centered distastefully on the rookie FBI agent. Not only had Shaw succeeded in blowing his own cover, but he may have blown Temple's as well. Arranging this meeting in Temple's downtown room, was a stroke of pure stupidity on Shaw's part. Anybody could have followed him there, maybe even killed him there. The killer could still be there waiting to murder whomever else showed up. But Temple had no choice; he had to make the meet. If Shaw was still alive, Temple had to find out what he knew about the microdots.

Temple turned the air conditioner off in his car and rolled down the windows. The cool breeze felt good and refreshing on his face. He had always preferred *free air,* as he called it, over the cool, stale, artificial air from an air conditioner.

After driving for several miles in deep thought, Temple suddenly realized, at the last moment, that he was about to miss his turn. He swerved sharply across two lanes of traffic and took the off-ramp leading to Fremont Street.

"FUCK!" The Grim Reaper spat out, as he was unable to change lanes quickly enough, to follow the American. The Grim Reaper took the next off-ramp and headed back to the boat. He would reacquire the American when he returned.

Temple returned to the Golden Nugget Hotel and entered the casino, on full alert. When he stepped into the elevator, he hesitated, before pushing the button for his floor. He considered going to Karen's room first, but that thought was only fleeting. Karen was most likely dead, and her room was probably being watched. He pushed the button for his floor and patted the grip of his Walther PPK, as the elevator rose. He got off on his floor and moved cautiously toward his room. He noticed the hair on his door frame was gone. Someone had been in there. Maybe it was the maid. Maybe it was Shaw, or Shaw's killer. Maybe the killer was still there. Temple listened at the door, but heard nothing. He pulled his Walther out, held it close to his side, and unlocked the door as quietly as he could. He took one last look over his shoulder, pushed the door open suddenly and went in fast, with his gun extended at arm's length. The room was dark, with only the hallway light providing illumination, but that lighting only lasted a couple of seconds. He had pushed the door open with such force, it bounced off the wall, then swung shut behind him, plunging the bedroom back into darkness. Temple dropped to one knee, with his arm still extended, his Walther searching for a target.

He couldn't see a damn thing, but was acutely aware, if a gunman was there, his eyes were most likely already adjusted to the dark. Knowing a bullet might be fired into your brain at any moment was extremely disconcerting. Still, The Iceman remained motionless, waiting, listening, not breathing, for fear he might miss some barely audible sound that might cost him his life.

Gradually, when his eyes began to penetrate the darkness, it didn't appear that anybody was there. Quietly Temple sucked in new air, as he stood and backed against the wall, still holding his gun extended and ready. He reached back and flicked the light switch on, without turning to look for it. The sudden brightness made him squint, but he kept his eyes open. His eyes and gun moved together, as he scanned the room. It didn't appear that anyone had been there. Nothing had been moved. Nothing searched. He peeked into the bathroom. Nothing had been disturbed there either. So where was Billy Shaw? Maybe Donnetti's people already had him. If that was true, they'd soon be coming for him, too. If they didn't have Shaw, but followed him to this room, they would still be coming for him. Either way, this room was going to be a kill box. Temple decided his best option, if Shaw was still alive, was to try to intercept him in the casino before he reached the elevator. He would need some kind of disguise, though. If Shaw was being followed, he didn't want to be recognized contacting him. Temple went to the closet for a ball cap and sunglasses. It wouldn't be a great disguise but, if he pulled the brim down low, just above his eyes, it just might work. When Temple opened the closet door, a shadowy figure burst out bellowing wildly and hit him with a devastating punch.

Chapter 30

As awareness rushed back into Temple's numb limbs, he awoke with a start. Immediately, he rolled onto all fours, his body taut and ready, his eyes sweeping the room for danger, his fingers reaching for his Walther PPK.

After a quick scan, Temple realized his attacker was gone. So was his Walther. When he stood up, he felt mildly dizzy, and only then was he aware of the throbbing pain in his head. Possibly a concussion, but he couldn't worry about that now. Temple ignored the pain and walked around the room to survey the damage. Both the bedroom and bathroom were in total shambles. Some of the furniture and all of the lamps were overturned and smashed. The TV was on the floor, its frame was cracked and the 25-inch screen was shattered. Covers, sheets, and pillowcases were needlessly ripped and scattered about. Towel racks were torn from the bathroom wall. The pockets of his pants were pulled inside out and his wallet was gone.

Temple was fairly certain it was Eddie Bowman who attacked him and vandalized the room. Donnetti's other assets were all professionals; they would not have wasted time, unnecessarily, trashing the place. Temple also knew it wasn't The Grim Reaper, because he was still alive. It had to be Eddie. The big man was probably sent there to snoop, which meant Donnetti didn't know about him yet, otherwise, he'd be dead. It also meant Shaw was either still on the run, or they had him, but he hadn't talked yet. That uncertainty put Temple in an awkward position. He didn't know how much time he had left, before they caught Shaw or broke him. Temple sat on the edge of the bed and considered his options. Shaw told Victoria he knew where the microdots were. He didn't say he had them. So, Temple decided to stay with the plan, to make another run at Donnetti's safe. If he found nothing, he would grab Donnetti and force the information out of him. Excruciating pain was an excellent motivator, but that would have to be his last resort, because once he revealed himself, there was no going back.

Temple packed up a few of his things then left his room at the Golden Nugget for the last time. He went down to his car and retrieved his .357 double-barreled derringer, then went back into the casino, toward Karen Kiley's room. Going on the assumption that she was dead, her killer was possibly in her room right now, waiting to kill whomever showed up. Temple smiled. He hoped it was Eddie Bowman.

Temple pulled out his derringer, as he reached Kiley's room. He listened at the door, and gently tried the doorknob. He felt a twisted pleasure, as the doorknob turned freely in his hand. He continued turning it until it stopped, then he abruptly pushed the door open. Temple stayed in the corridor, just to the right of the doorway, in case bullets started flying.

The room was brightly lit, and Temple saw right away his cautiousness was not needed. Two men were waiting there alright, but both were dead. Now he knew what happened to Billy Shaw.

Shaw's body was on the floor seated upright, leaning against the wall. His legs were spread, his head down, and there was an enormous amount of blood on his lap, having dripped from a wound under his chin. On the floor, next to Shaw's bloodstained hand, was a .32 caliber revolver fitted with a silencer. The other body on the floor, was sprawled on his back alongside the bed, a neat little hole in his forehead. The dead man's eyes stared blankly up at Temple, his mouth slightly open, a butterfly knife still in his hand. Death came to Jason Meats as a surprise.

Behind Temple, Billy Shaw's head slowly rose, and his hand reached for the revolver on the floor. Shaw was vaguely aware of movement in the room. He didn't know who it was, but in his weakened condition, he couldn't wait to find out. Shaw closed his trembling fingers around the handle of the wheel gun and aimed at the blurry figure standing across from him. Gradually, he recognized the man standing there. "I've been waiting for you," Shaw said, letting his arm drop to the floor, his voice weak and almost inaudible.

Temple spun around, with his double-barreled derringer cocked and aimed at Shaw. Now Temple could see the gaping gash across Shaw's throat. It was incredible that Shaw could talk at all. It was a miracle he was still alive.

Shaw's face twisted in pain, as he forced his next words

out, "That son-of-a-bitch killed me, didn't he?"

Temple could see Shaw was mortally wounded, but he unwittingly prolonged his own life by remaining calm and holding his head down, which placed pressure on the wound and formed a blood clot that kept him from bleeding to death. Now, with his head up, the blood clot was broken and the blood was again flowing.

Temple grabbed a pillow off the floor and ripped the pillowcase off of it. He bunched it up and packed it against Shaw's throat, then tilted the man's head back down to reestablish the clot, though he knew it was much too late for that now. Temple answered Shaw's question honestly. "Yes, you're dying." Then Temple leaned in close and asked, "Where are the microdots, Billy?"

"The microdots," Shaw echoed. "Yes. I remember. Almost forgot." Shaw raised his head and looked to his left, then right. "My glasses. Can't find. Lost..."

"Don't worry about your eyeglasses," Temple said. "Tell me about the microdots."

Billy Shaw began to choke on the blood in his throat. He coughed uncontrollably while thick red blood emptied into his lap. Shaw's body tensed, as he struggled to stay alive, but he had nothing left to fight with. After one final exhale, Shaw fell forward into Temple's arms.

Temple lowered Shaw's head gently to the floor, looking at the man for whom he had previously held in such little regard. Temple had gravely misjudged him. Shaw had guts and the makings of a top-notch agent — had he only been given the time.

Temple hurriedly searched both men and the room but found nothing. Whatever Shaw knew, he took it with him. Temple went into the bathroom, washed Shaw's blood off his hands, left Karen's room and caught the elevator down.

Only then did he let himself think about Karen Kiley. Her death was now confirmed. Jason Meats' presence in her room proved that.

Temple left the hotel and drove his rental car back toward *The Lucky Lady*. Along the way, he was seething mad, thinking about Jim Donnetti. Too many good people had died because of him. The fat man may not have been the one who pulled the trigger, but he was responsible. He ordered it done. Temple believed, when the time came, he would enjoy killing this man.

Upon Temple's return to *The Lucky Lady*, he found Victoria Rodriguez, draped on the shoulder of an elderly gent at the roulette wheel.

"Hey, baby," Temple said, walking up behind her.

When Victoria saw him, her face lit up. "Hey, sugar," she said, running her hand flirtatiously along his chest to stay in character.

"Got a minute?" Temple asked.

Victoria looked at her companion, "You don't mind do you, sweetie? I'll just be a minute."

"No, I don't mind," the old man lied, as he glared at the young stud trying to move in on his woman.

Victoria kissed the old man on his cheek. "Be back in a bit, honey."

Temple led Victoria toward the cocktail lounge. He didn't notice the man at the craps table, staring intently at him from across the room. The Grim Reaper passed his roll of the dice and gathered his remaining chips, from the chip rack and moved to a position closer to his prey.

"Did you find Billy?" Victoria whispered as they walked arm in arm.

"I found him."

"Did he tell you where the microdots are?"

"Shaw's dead," Temple said.

Victoria's face went blank. "What happened?"

"Jason Meats killed him."

Victoria looked at him wide-eyed.

Temple answered her unspoken question. "They killed each other," he told her.

Victoria was silent for a few more steps, then whispered, "What now?"

As they stepped up to the bar, Temple changed the subject. Too many people were milling around. "What do you want to drink?" Temple asked.

"Scotch and water," she replied.

Temple relayed their drink orders to the bartender, then led Victoria to the far end of the bar, where it was less congested. "I'm going after the microdots now," he said.

"But you don't know where they are."

"I have a plan."

"Can I help?"

"No. I want to keep you out of it." Temple sipped his drink and noticed that the elderly man, Victoria was just with, was staring jealously at them from across the casino. "You gonna be alright?" Temple asked.

Victoria saw where he was looking and guessed what he was thinking. "When the time comes," Victoria told him in a reassuring tone, "I'll slip him a couple of pills. He'll sleep all night. He won't even get up to pee."

"Won't he be suspicious in the morning?" Temple asked.

"Maybe, but he won't ask any questions. Not after I tell him how great he was. He'll be too embarrassed to admit he couldn't remember giving it to me good," she said with a smile.

Temple nodded. "I see your point."

Victoria kissed him softly on the corner of his lips.

"Good luck," she whispered.

As Victoria started to walk away, Temple asked, "Did Edna's sister leave yet?"

Victoria was surprised by the question. Why was he asking about Edna's sister? She didn't think they even knew each other. "Yes," Victoria answered. "She left about a half-hour ago."

"Good," Temple said, feeling relieved.

Victoria grinned. "Yeah, she certainly did me a favor."

"What favor?"

"She got Nick Marlow off my back — at least for a little while."

"Nick Marlow?

"He's one of Donnetti's hired guns."

"I know who he is. But what's he got to do with Miss Case?"

"He's got the hots for her. Ever since she came on board, he's left me alone."

"But now that she's gone, he'll come after you again."

"Probably. But he doesn't give up that easily. I think he followed her to the airport."

"Why do you think that?"

"I was in the casino, when Edna's sister left with her luggage for the airport. About twenty minutes later, Marlow showed up. He asked the door security guard if he knew what time she left. When the guard told him, Marlow left the boat. Looked like he was in a real hurry."

"Why would he follow her to the airport?"

"He's obsessed. That's how he gets when he's fixated on a woman."

"Did she encourage him?"

I heard she rejected him. But I also know, from personal experience, he doesn't take rejection well."

"You think he'd hurt her because of that?"

Victoria saw concern in his eyes. This woman, this stranger, apparently meant something to him. "He's capable of it," Victoria acknowledged, "but in this case, I don't think so. I doubt he'd attack her in a crowded airport."

"Then why is he following her?" Temple said and started for the exit door.

Victoria grabbed Temple's arm. "You're going after her, aren't you?"

"I have to."

"Why?"

"I have to," he repeated.

"What about the mission?"

Temple glanced at his watch. "I've got four hours before the bidding starts. I'll be back in plenty of time."

"Look, why don't you stay here and do your job. I'll go to the airport and make sure she gets on the plane safely."

"I have to do this myself."

"But Tom —"

"Do you know what flight she's taking?"

"No, I don't."

"I'll be back," Temple said, then rushed to his car. For the first time in his life, Temple went against his training and instincts and put the mission second. He had to protect this woman. She reminded him so much of his former fiancée. He felt compelled, even obligated to keep her safe.

Chapter 31

The endless flow of cars on I-215 was typical in the Las Vegas area, but Temple still made pretty good time zig-zagging in and out of traffic. When he arrived at McCarran Airport, he pulled into the parking lot, stuffed his derringer into the glove compartment box, then sprinted across the lot toward the terminal. He hated leaving his derringer, but he couldn't very well take a loaded gun in with him. Airport security was really touchy about things like that.

Inside the airport, crowds of people moved through the terminal like cattle, many of them pulling their luggage in seemingly never-ending caravans. Some sat along the walls reading books and magazines. A few people were going in and out of the various snack shops, while others waited impatiently in long ticket lines. It was a common sight at every major airport.

Temple moved through the terminal quickly, glancing at each ticket line, looking for Yolanda or Marlow, but he didn't see either. He rushed over to one of the monitors displaying airline departure times for Seattle. If Yolanda told him the truth about where she was from, then Seattle is where she was headed. The earliest flight out for Seattle was Air Western's flight 401, which had a one-hour stopover in Reno. It was scheduled to depart from gate A21 in nineteen minutes. The next plane to Seattle wouldn't leave for two more hours, on a different airline. Air Western 401 was probably the one.

Temple ran to the airport screening area and made it through security without incident. He then ran up the stairway, to the second level where many of the boarding gates were located, taking the steps two at a time. He jogged down the corridor, sidestepping all of the slow-moving, *I've-got-all-day* walkers. When he got to gate A21, the passengers had already started boarding flight 401 through the access tunnel connecting the building to the airplane. He did not see Yolanda, amongst those few still filing on board, but did see Nick Marlow at the back of the boarding line. He was wearing a phony beard and mustache and had a ball cap pulled down low, just above his eyes. Marlow's presence there, in disguise, confirmed Temple's fears. Nick Marlow wasn't ready to let Yolanda go. Temple glanced at his watch. He had fourteen minutes left before flight 401 took off. Temple bolted back down the corridor. He had to get a ticket for that flight. Whatever Nick Marlow had in store for Yolanda, Alexander Temple knew he had to stop it. When Temple reached the ticket counter there were about twenty people in line and only four ticket stations open. He glanced at his watch again. Now he had eight minutes left. Temple went to the head of the line. An elderly man was standing there with a walker. Temple said aloud so that everyone in line could hear him. "Excuse me, sir, my flight is boarding right now. Flight 401 to Seattle. Do you mind if I cut in?"

The old man looked at him oddly, then said in a feeble, high-pitched voice, "What did you say?"

Temple spoke louder, with a bit more urgency, "My plane is boarding now. Can I cut in?"

The old man frowned as he strained to hear what the young man was saying. He shook his head. "Can't hear you, sonny. What did you say?"

Temple was normally a man of extraordinary patience, but his patience now was at an end. He was running out of time and was ready to explode. One of the ticket clerks overheard the conversation and called to Temple. "I'll take you here, sir."

The old man looked confused, as Temple stepped up to the counter ahead of him. The people in line behind the old man, tried to tell him what was going on. They were still trying to explain it to him, when Temple bolted back down the corridor with his ticket.

When Temple got back to gate A21, he was relieved to see that flight 401 had not yet pulled away from the building. According to his watch, the plane should have left a couple of minutes ago. He still had a chance to make it. Temple shoved his ticket into the startled boarding agent's face. "Can I still make flight 401?"

"I think so, but you'd better hurry," she said and quickly processed him through.

Temple grabbed his boarding pass and ran through the jetway. At the other end, he could see a boarding agent pushing the door to the plane closed. Temple yelled, "Hold it! You've got one more."

At first, the boarding agent looked back at him startled, but then politely said, "Sorry, sir. I thought we had everybody on board." The agent pulled the door back open, to the surprise of the onboard number 1 stewardess. Initially, the stewardess looked flustered, but when she saw Temple with a boarding pass, she switched into hostess mode. "Gee, that was a close one," she said smiling, then looked at Temple's ticket as he stepped on board. "The plane isn't crowded, sir. Take any open seat you want in coach."

Temple walked through first class and into coach. He could see Yolanda sitting toward the middle of the plane, on the left side, in a window seat. She was staring aimlessly out the window in deep thought. The one seat beside her was empty. Marlow was at the rear of the cabin, in an aisle seat. There was no one in the seat to his left, nor the three seats across the aisle from him. Marlow had positioned himself well. It was a good tactical position; from there he could observe everything. Marlow had eyes on Temple the moment he started down the aisle, but Temple pretended not to notice him.

Yolanda was still facing the window when Temple sat down on the seat beside her. "Mind if I sit here?" he asked.

Yolanda's eyes widened when she saw him. "Tom, what are you doing here?"

"I've got business in Reno."

Yolanda gave him an anxious look. "Are you here about my sister?

"No. I really do have business in Reno," he said. "But since you're here, I might as well tell you — your sister's been cleared. One of the cashiers did it. He confessed," Temple lied.

Relief washed over her face. "I knew she didn't do it."

At that moment, a voice boomed across the P.A. system.

"This is the captain speaking. There will be a short delay in takeoff, due to a minor instrument problem. Since we do not anticipate a long delay, I'll ask you to please remain seated and refrain from smoking, as we will be taxiing out once the adjustments are completed. Thank you."

Yolanda nervously looked at Temple. "I wonder what that was all about."

Temple noticed her overwhelming anxiety and tried to calm her. "Probably just a faulty control board panel light."

Yolanda looked apprehensive. "You think so?"

"Sure. If it was anything serious, Air Western wouldn't let this plane get off the ground."

Yolanda grinned, "You're right. They wouldn't."

Temple smiled back at her, but he was thinking about Nick Marlow. Why did the gunman follow her onto the plane? Surely not because she rebuffed his advances. What would be the point in that? She's leaving town. It also made no sense that Marlow would leave Las Vegas this close to the auction. Donnetti would never allow it at such a critical time, unless – it was Donnetti who sent him. That's the only thing that makes sense. It had nothing to do with Yolanda rejecting Marlow. But it did have something to do with Yolanda. That's why Marlow rushed to get on this particular plane. That's why he was in a disguise. He was going to do something and didn't want to be recognized. But what? And when was he going to do it?

When one of the stewardesses reopened the door inside the plane, Temple did not think it strange. Probably one of the technicians wanted to recheck his work from the inside. Temple realized he was wrong when an older man, wearing thick eyeglasses, shuffled onboard carrying a medium size tote bag. The head stewardess greeted the man with a gracious smile, which he acknowledged with a nod. As she closed and secured the door behind him, the old man sat in the seat across the aisle from Temple. The two seats to the right of the elderly man were occupied by a young couple holding hands.

As the aircraft backed away from the building and started toward the runway, the stewardesses walked up and down the aisle making sure the plane was ready for takeoff. Temple glanced at the old man. He wondered who he was. Clearly, the plane had waited for him to board. That business about the aircraft having instrument trouble was just a pacifier to justify the delay. The old man must have been somebody important to the airline because Temple did not recognize him as a celebrity.

The elderly man caught Temple staring at him and simply nodded. Temple returned the nod, then turned back to Yolanda, unaware the old man was now staring at him.

The head stewardess noticed the elderly man had his tote bag on his lap. She politely told him he would have to put it in the upper storage bin or on the floor, under the seat in front of him during takeoff.

"Yes, ma'am," the man acknowledged, then leaned forward and stuffed his bag under the seat. When he sat back up, his eyeglasses had been knocked slightly off-center and drooped at an undignified angle on his nose. The old man smiled awkwardly at the stewardess as he adjusted his eyeglasses. The stewardess smiled back, then continued attending to other passengers. After she left, the old man stared at Temple again. *It would not be long now*, The Grim Reaper thought.

For a while back there, The Grim Reaper feared The Iceman had eluded him again. And he would have too, had it not been for a lucky chain of events. Earlier, while following the American through the streets of Las Vegas,

The Grim Reaper had lost him in traffic. The Iceman had made a sudden turn in front of a big rig truck, zig-zagged between three slow-moving cars, and raced through a yellow light just as it turned red. The Grim Reaper would have run the red light, but saw a police car waiting to go at the intersection. All the Reaper could do was watch his prey disappear into the traffic ahead. When the light finally turned green, the Soviet proceeded with the flow of traffic, resigned to the frustrating reality that he had lost the American again. He was about to head back to *The Lucky Lady* when he noticed the airport up ahead. On a hunch, he continued to the airport and drove toward the terminal entrances. He was surprised to see the American agent sprinting across the parking lot toward the terminal. The Grim Reaper parked his car, by the closest terminal entrance and watched the American run right in front of him and into the airport. The Soviet's initial thought was to ram his car into the American, but he did not. He knew his chances of escape would be extremely difficult, if not impossible, if he had. Armed airport police were milling around the terminal entrance. Baggage handlers, outside with walkie-talkies could call for help. Every passenger, walking in and out of the terminal, was a possible witness. His description and car information would be broadcast to every law enforcement officer in the area, before he could clear the congested airport. No, he would wait for a better opportunity.

The Grim Reaper exited his car at the curb and followed the American inside the terminal. He wasn't concerned about leaving his vehicle in a no-parking zone or that it would eventually be towed. The rental car wasn't in his name, and he had no intentions of returning for it, anyway.

After some observations, the Soviet was a bit amused to discover that the American was following somebody, too.

He could not tell, just yet, who the American was following, but apparently, the person had just boarded flight 401 to Seattle. When he saw the American run back down the corridor the way he had just come, The Grim Reaper did not give pursuit. He knew where the American was going and where he would be later.

The Grim Reaper approached two boarding agents at gate A21 and presented his phony FBI credentials that he carried at all times. He asked to use the phone. Both clerks snapped to attention at seeing the FBI card. "Sure. Go ahead, sir."

The boarding agents backed away from the desk, as the man from the FBI dialed the in-house operator and asked to be transferred to the airline station manager. The connection went through immediately. The Grim Reaper identified himself to the station manager as an FBI agent and explained, it was a matter of extreme importance that flight 401 to Seattle be delayed for fifteen minutes, to await the arrival of an FBI special agent. He assured the station manager there was no danger to the plane or its passengers. The FBI was merely following someone of interest in an ongoing case. After a brief discussion, the station manager confirmed the FBI agent's credentials, with the on-site boarding agents, then agreed to hold the plane.

Stupid fools, the Reaper thought. *These gullible Americans just took him at his word. That and phony FBI credentials was all it took.* The Grim Reaper hurriedly rushed back to his car, hoping it was still there. When he got outside he saw that it was, but there was a parking ticket on it. He balled the ticket up, dropped it on the ground, and drove across the street to a private charter flying service. He knew the business would be closed. He circled the building looking for the best point of entry. When he saw the full plate glass window at the rear of the business, he drove through it, shattering glass everywhere. He quickly searched the store for what he needed. When he found it, he stuffed it into a canvas tote bag he had snatched off the counter. The Soviet then drove back across the street to catch flight 401 to Seattle.

The moment the Aircraft began to taxi away from the terminal, Yolanda's entire demeanor changed. She stopped talking, in mid-conversation, and her fingers locked onto the armrest. She stared straight ahead and looked paralyzed with fear. Temple tried to calm her anxiety, but she didn't answer him. She didn't even hear him. Not a word. She was only aware that this huge coffin was moving, and it was too late now to get off.

As the aircraft moved into takeoff position, Yolanda's grip on the armrest tightened. Her breathing became more erratic. A moment later, the engines roared, and the plane accelerated quickly down the runway. Yolanda made whimpering sounds, as the aircraft moved faster and faster. She caught her breath and held it, as the tires lifted off the ground and the aircraft soared upward, seemingly in slow motion. Yolanda remained in an almost catatonic state until the plane reached a cruising altitude of twenty-eight thousand feet and leveled out.

When Yolanda regained her composure, she peeked at Temple with embarrassment. She dreaded the sarcastic remarks she knew were coming. The jokes about her fear of flying. She'd heard them all before, and she hated being the butt of those hurtful jokes. But Temple surprised her. He said nothing about how she had reacted. Instead, he asked her how her mother was doing. Yolanda stared at him with intense appreciation, and for the next several minutes they talked about a variety of things, including the regular rainy seasons of Seattle to their favorite restaurants, in their respective cities. Gradually, Temple shifted the conversation to what he really wanted to know. Why was Marlow after her and did she even know it? Temple slyly began the probing questions. "You didn't get a chance to see much of *The Lucky Lady* when you were on board, did you?"

"No, not really. I stayed pretty much in my room."

"I figured that. I never saw you roaming around the boat."

"I did see you once in the casino," she said.

"Before or after I went into your room by mistake?"

"After."

"Why didn't you stop by and say hi?"

"I started to, but you rushed past me so quickly, I didn't get a chance. I tried to catch you, but you left the boat in a hurry."

Temple's expression didn't change, but he knew exactly when she must have seen him. It was just after he killed her sister, and then rushed off the boat to meet Billy Shaw. "I'm sorry I didn't see you," he said.

"Me too," she confessed. "I wanted to talk to you about a guy onboard who I was having trouble with. He was very persistent. Wouldn't take no for an answer. With you working for the casino owner, I figured you could help."

"He didn't get physical with you, did he?" Temple asked.

"No, he didn't. But he was really creepy. Kept following me around and coming to my room."

"He went to your room?"

"At least a half-dozen times, but I never let him in. Most of the time I didn't even answer the door. He didn't stop stalking me, until I finally went to the casino owner."

"What did the owner say?"

"He apologized that this happened on his boat and asked who it was. I told him the guy's name was Nick. I didn't remember his last name."

"What did the owner do about it?"

"I'm not sure what he did. He just told me he would handle it. And he did. I had no more trouble after that."

"Great. That kind of thing should never happen." Temple wasn't getting what he wanted. He needed to probe deeper. "So, were you nervous about approaching the casino owner?"

"No. I was pissed," she said. "I confronted him right in his stateroom."

"How'd you get past his security people?"

"I didn't see any security people. When I got to his room the door was ajar, and I could hear him inside talking business. Since he wasn't doing anything, you know, personal, I just walked right in."

"You walked right in?"

"I did," she said. "I was so angry. All I got was the run-around from the security people downstairs, when I told them about Nick. They didn't help me at all. But I knew the owner would have to do something."

At that moment, one of the stewardesses walked by taking cocktail orders. "I'd like a bourbon and soda," Yolanda said. Then, remembering where she was, Yolanda blurted out, "Make that a double."

"Yes ma'am," the stewardess acknowledged, then turned to Temple. "And you, sir?"

"I'll have a rum and coke," he replied.

The stewardess wrote their drink orders down, then moved on to other passengers.

Temple continued his probe with Yolanda. "So, you were saying that the owner was nice to you?"

"He was very nice. I was surprised because I went into his stateroom steaming mad, and expecting an argument."

"But you didn't get one?" Temple acknowledged.

"No. We had a nice talk," she said. "He was intelligent, gracious, and a perfect gentleman. His association with that other man didn't make sense to me though."

"What other man?"

"There was another man in the room with him. He was a really big guy. Real mean looking."

Temple guessed that the big guy was Eddie Bowman, but he displayed no reaction to her description. Temple probed further, "You said they were talking business when you walked in?"

"Yes, ah, no. I mean, the owner was talking business with someone on the phone, not with the big guy."

"What makes you think he was talking business?"

Yolanda thought back to the conversation. "Well — he said something about being glad when this business with the Alpha Data was completed."

That's it! Now Temple knew why Nick Marlow was on the plane. Donnetti was afraid Yolanda might repeat what she heard, or may have heard in his stateroom, so he wasn't taking any chances. He sent Marlow to kill her.

Temple was fairly confident Marlow would not make a move against Yolanda until the plane had landed. Then the gunman could isolate her somewhere. Temple considered several options on how to take Marlow out. Then he made up his mind. He would do it before the gunman ever left the plane. But to do it right, he would need a weapon. A kill like this, on a crowded plane, had to be quick, silent, and unnoticed.

At the front of the aircraft, two stewardesses, working coach, stepped from the galley with a rolling aluminum cart full of drinks. The cart was almost as wide as the aisle. One stewardess stood in front of the cart, the other trailed behind it, and together they rolled it down the aisle, delivering drinks to the passengers.

Temple waited until they moved the cart beyond his seat. "I'll be back," he told Yolanda, then stood up and headed toward the forward lavatory. Casually, he glanced back to see where the stewardesses were in the aisle, then he adjusted his stride accordingly. When he got to the lavatory door, he glanced back again and saw the stewardesses were in the perfect position, with their cart and bodies blocking Marlow's view. Temple took advantage of that blockage and peeked into the galley, looking for a weapon. Right away he spotted an ice pick. He palmed it, entered the bathroom and locked the door. Temple hid the ice pick in his sock, and waited a reasonable amount of time before returning to his seat.

The Grim Reaper watched Temple emerge from the restroom. He knew the American had a weapon now. He saw him grab something from the galley. The Soviet had a pretty clear picture now of what was going on and was amused by the charade unfolding before him. He was able to deduce, from The Iceman's lame interrogation of the girl, that the black American gangster, whom he recognized from his mission briefing, was after her. The girl didn't seem to be aware of it, but The Iceman was and was there to stop him. It didn't appear though, that the gangster knew who the American agent really was. Yes, it was all very amusing indeed.

When the American agent returned to his seat, The Grim Reaper leaned back in his chair and closed his eyes. He was reasonably confident that the American would not make a move against the gangster, until the plane had landed; most likely during the rush and anticipation to disembark the aircraft. It would be relatively easy, at that point, for The Iceman to isolate and eliminate his target. It was a good plan. Very logical. The Grim Reaper smiled to himself. Only one thing could ruin The Iceman's plan: if the plane never landed.

Chapter 32

The Grim Reaper considered his plan. He had done it once before, a long time ago, and it worked perfectly then. It should work again, except now he had to overcome a tactical error on his part. In his haste to get aboard, he failed to realize this aircraft was a DC-9. The cabin exit doors, on the DC-9, opened in front of huge turbofan engines. If he parachuted out any of those doors, he'd be sucked into the engine. He also couldn't use the rear, ventral airstair. Ever since the D.B. Cooper skyjacking, airlines have installed the Cooper Vane security device, which prevented the airstairs from being lowered in mid-flight. His only jump option now was to disable one of the engines before he bailed out. Or, he could always just wait until the plane landed and then take The Iceman out. The Grim Reaper considered his options, as he glared at the American sitting across the aisle from him.

Temple sat back in his seat finalizing how he would proceed against Nick Marlow. It would require split-second timing. Once the plane landed, he would remain seated while Yolanda safely exited the aircraft. He would then stand up and accidentally bump into Marlow in the aisle, whom he figured would exit last. Temple would then pretend to notice him, for the first time, and reach for a handshake. It didn't matter whether Marlow shook hands or not. Almost simultaneously with extending his hand, Temple would quickly bring his other hand up and stab the ice pick into Marlow's ear, deep enough to puncture his brain. For this to work, death had to be instant and silent. A struggle of any kind would be disastrous. He could not afford to be seen fighting this guy in the aisle. Authorities would have him detained before he got off the plane. Temple figured, after the ice pick attack, he'd dump Marlow's body across a row of seats. Then he would merge in with the unsuspecting, departing passengers ahead of him, and disappear into the terminal, before the body was discovered. By the time airport police arrived and secured the plane, he would have already booked himself onto another flight back to Las Vegas. The police would be busy sealing the airport exits, looking for someone trying to escape, not someone booked on an outgoing flight.

Temple turned his attention back to Yolanda and re-engaged her in casual conversation. He had given up the notion that she was somehow related to his former fiancée.

Yolanda appreciated talking with him and genuinely enjoyed his company. He was very easy to talk to, and unlike a lot of men, he didn't try to steer the conversation toward sex, after the first few minutes. He seemed sincerely interested in her as a person. It was a refreshing change.

Secretly though, she had to admit, it would have been nice if he wasn't *such* a gentleman.

As Air Western 401 continued its gradual descent toward Reno, some of the passengers excitedly peered out the window, eager to get to their destinations, while others continued their normal conversations.

Again, Yolanda sat shivering in her seat, her eyes glued on the wing. She just knew it would fall off at any moment.

Alexander Temple was perhaps the only passenger who noticed something on board was not quite right. He looked up and down the aisle. Where were the stewardesses? Why hadn't they picked up the drink glasses and food trays? They should be walking the aisle now, getting the cabin and passengers ready for landing, ensuring seats were in an upright position and seat belts were fastened. Temple also noticed the *Fasten Your Seat Belt* sign had not been turned on, and the pilot had not made the customary speech to the passengers, over the P.A. system, to prepare for landing.

Temple visually checked the aisle again. Nobody was servicing the plane. He looked back at Nick Marlow, who was busy getting the last few drags on his cigarette. Marlow did not seem to be aware that anything was out of the ordinary.

Temple casually unbuckled his seat belt, so as not to alarm Yolanda, and started walking forward in the aisle. He walked past the privacy curtain and entered the first-class section. A man and woman were sleeping with their heads together. Another man was wearing headphones and reading a magazine. The only other person was sitting in the first row near the flight cabin door. He had a confused look on his face even before he looked back at Temple. *Not a good sign.* Temple stopped at the flight cabin door, then gingerly pushed the door latch up to see if it was locked. It was not.

Definitely not a good sign. Temple considered going in with the ice pick in hand but decided against it, just in case there was nothing wrong. He didn't want to frighten the crew or be detained by authorities upon landing. Still, he suspected something was wrong and he had to find out what.

Temple exhaled quietly, then opened the door quickly. Like the lens from a camera, his eyes instantly captured everything in the flight cabin at a glance. It was much worse than he expected. The two pilots were dead, still strapped in their seats. Each had been shot in the head. One of the stewardesses was on the floor. Her dead body was pushed in a corner by the co-pilot's chair. The other stewardesses were probably dead somewhere else on the plane. Their killer was still there. He was wearing a backpack and leaning over the co-pilot, going through his pockets. Temple concluded the autopilot must have been switched on, since the plane was not flying erratically. He also noted the .25 automatic handgun, with the 2" silencer screwed into it, on top of the instrument console.

The killer's head snapped around instantly when the door opened. Temple recognized him. It was the old man who boarded the plane late. But when their eyes locked during that fraction of a second, Temple had a second realization. Although never having seen his face, Temple instinctively knew this man was The Grim Reaper.

Simultaneously, both men made a move for the gun. The Grim Reaper, moving surprisingly fast for his age, reached the gun first.

The passengers in first class were roused to their feet, the moment Temple rushed into the flight cabin. The confused man, who had been sitting closest to the flight cabin door was now terrified and standing with the other first-class passengers backed up against the privacy curtain.

The door to the cockpit had been pushed partially shut from the commotion inside, but no one dared open it. As the noise in the flight cabin grew louder, the frightened chatter in the first-class section alerted the passengers in coach. Talk spread quickly that something was wrong. Rubberneckers tried to see what was going on from their seats. Others unbuckled their seatbelts and started walking toward the flight cabin.

Inside the flight cabin, The Grim Reaper had started to spin toward Temple, with the gun in his right hand.

Temple rushed up behind him, hooked an arm around the man's waist and reached blindly for the gun with the other. When Temple grabbed the Reaper's right hand, the gun wasn't there. Maybe he dropped it. No. Now it was in his left hand. The gun barrel was peeking out just under the Reaper's right arm, aimed at Temple's belly. The Iceman rolled away from the barrel's line of fire and grabbed the Grim Reaper's gun hand.

Both men struggled for control of the weapon. The Soviet felt Temple's breath on the back of his neck and instinctively whipped his right elbow back into Temple's face.

A flash of light arced before Temple's eyes and, for a second or two, he was disorientated, but he didn't let go of the Soviet. If he did, he was dead.

When the Reaper couldn't pull his gun hand free, he drew his right arm back again for another elbow strike.

Temple felt the Soviet brace to attack, so he shoved the man's head into the wall and heard him groan. Temple then ripped the gun from his fingers, but couldn't hold onto it and heard it skid along the floor.

The moment the gun left the Grim Reaper's hand, he stomped on Temple's toes and drove the back of his head into Temple's face.

Temple felt the explosion go off in his brain and his senses were momentarily rattled.

The Soviet spun around to face the American and knocked him off balance, with a fist to the jaw. Before the American could regain his footing, the Soviet shoved him back and lunged for the gun on the floor.

Temple saw the move and quickly rammed his knee up into The Grim Reaper's face. A sickening thud cracked the air as his head snapped back violently.

The Grim Reaper groaned as he reeled backward, a grotesque hematoma already forming above his left eye. His face warped into a hateful scowl, as he charged at Temple again.

Both men engaged in a barrage of rapid-fire punches and elbows strikes, which the other defended with equal skill. Temple then threw a feint at the Soviet's head, to divert his attention, then stomped into his kneecap, hyperextending it.

The Grim Reaper screamed and his body leaned awkwardly forward.

Temple threw his body weight into his next punch and drove his fist hard into the Soviet's jaw and felt bone give way.

The Reaper's hands went up to protect his face.

Temple went low, with a crushing right fist to exposed ribs.

The Soviet doubled over, sucking air and dropped one elbow to protect his ribs.

Temple reached forward and pushed down on the man's head then rammed a knee up into his face again.

This time The Grim Reaper's nose and lips were busted and bleeding profusely, his mouth full of blood. He stumbled backwards into the co-pilot's chair in a daze, his eyes unable to focus. But even in that condition, the Soviet held his fist up and tried to stay in the fight, but his knee gave out and he fell to the floor.

Temple knelt and picked up the Soviet's gun.

At that exact moment, one of the passengers pushed the cockpit door open. Upon seeing the gun in Temple's hand and the bloody carnage inside the flight cabin, the passenger shrieked, "They're hijacking the plane!"

Temple's head snapped toward the door when it was flung open.

In that instant, The Grim Reaper sat up quickly and grabbed for the gun.

Temple saw the move and fired off one hurried round into the Soviet's forehead.

Panicked screams from passengers, outside the cockpit, erupted into total chaos. Mass hysteria quickly engulfed the entire plane, like a brush fire out of control. More people had pushed and clawed their way toward the cockpit and saw the unthinkable: the flight crew dead and a man with a gun.

Temple realized the passengers probably thought he killed the flight crew. He had to say something convincing, fast before the passengers rushed in and overpowered him. Temple yelled above the crowd noise in his most authoritative voice. "Listen to me! Everyone please — quiet down and listen to me! I'm an FBI agent," he lied, hoping they were too terrified to ask for credentials.

The crowd gradually quieted down.

"I just broke up a skyjacking attempt," Temple said, nodding toward the Soviet. "He killed the entire flight crew before I could stop him."

Nervous chatter spread quickly through the crowd. Someone yelled out in panic, "Then who's going to fly the plane?"

Temple could see Nick Marlow pushing his way forward. He looked just as wild-eyed and scared as the other passengers. The fact that Temple had just claimed to be an FBI agent didn't seem to faze Marlow. Maybe he didn't hear it. Maybe he was only interested in saving his own butt. Either way, Temple couldn't worry about that now.

"I'm a certified pilot," Temple yelled over the resurging screams from the passengers. "We're going to make it. I can fly this plane. Listen to me. I can fly this plane."

That revelation calmed the passengers. Temple had just given them the hope they were looking for. They were too terrified not to believe him or even challenge him.

"Anybody out there have a pilot's license?" Temple shouted. "I could use some help."

When no one answered, Temple said, "Alright. I'll do it myself, but I need you all to go back to your seats. There are too many people standing upfront. Your weight is not properly distributed throughout the plane. You're causing the nose to dive. Please, everyone, get back to your seats. Hurry, we don't have much time." Temple didn't know if that weight warning was true, but he had to get them away from the cockpit.

As the passengers rushed back to their seats, Temple yelled after them, "Fasten your seat belts. Put your head between your legs." Then to himself, he whispered, "And kiss your asses' goodbye."

Temple had no idea how to fly a large jet aircraft. He had been checked out in a single-engine Cessna and had about seventy hours solo. It was a required course during spy training. But that seemed a long time ago, and this wasn't a Cessna.

Temple noted the plane appeared to be flying straight

and level, so the autopilot had to be on. He knelt beside the Reaper and took a quick peek inside his tote bag, to ensure he was not carrying a bomb. All he found inside the bag was a parachute. *So that's how the Soviet was going to make his escape.*

Temple pulled the pilot from the captain's chair and sat behind the wheel. He was immediately overwhelmed with sensory overload, as he stared at the complexity of the flight control panel. There was no way in hell he could fly this plane. Then he noticed something else, too. The plane was not flying level anymore. It was descending.

After a few seconds of panic, Temple took a deep breath to calm himself. He knew, if he didn't get it together fast, the plane would crash, killing everyone on board. He slowed his breathing to a normal pace and focused on the problem at hand. The aircraft seemed to be flying in a controlled descent. He didn't know if this descent was a normal autopilot function or an instrument failure. Either way, Temple saw the ground getting closer. He scanned the vast panel of gauges, levers, and knobs, until he located the autopilot switch on the center control pedestal, just below the thrust levers. It *was* engaged. Whether it was working or not, he didn't know.

Temple gave the control panel a more focused look. Only a few things looked familiar to him from his Cessna training days. He recognized the control wheel, throttles, airspeed, altimeter, and altitude indicator. He also knew if he touched the wrong control, his mistake could be unrecoverable. He needed help. Temple reached back and grabbed the pilot's radio headset off the floor. He hoped the radio was still set to the air traffic control frequency they were in, because he was not sure how to find the correct frequency if it wasn't.

Temple barked into the mike, "Mayday, mayday, mayday," and felt a rush of relief when the area air traffic controller responded.

"This is Oakland Center. What is your emergency?"

"This is Air Western 401," Temple said. "We've been skyjacked, but have retaken the aircraft. The skyjacker is dead, but so are the pilots and crew."

"What?" Say again 401."

"We've been skyjacked. The skyjacker is dead. So are the pilots and crew. We need help."

There was a short moment of silence, then Oakland Center said, "Understood Air Western 401. Who am I speaking to?"

Remembering the name he saw on an Army Sergeant's nameplate aboard the plane, Temple replied, "My name is Sergeant Holloway, United States Army."

"Are you a pilot?"

"I trained in a single-engine Cessna years ago. Got 70 hours solo, but haven't flown in years."

"Roger that. We have you on our screen. You have good altitude, but you're in a slow gradual descent and a little off course. Are you familiar with the control panel of a DC-9?"

"No, I'm not, but a few gauges look familiar."

"Do you see the autopilot?"

"The autopilot is on," Temple told him, anticipating the question.

"Alright," the controller said. "Do you know how to dial in a radio frequency?"

Temple had already spotted the radio; it looked somewhat similar to the Cessna radio. "If I know which frequency I'm looking for, yes," he responded.

"Good. I'm going to have you change to a discrete frequency so it'll be just us. Go to frequency 121.5 MHz now."

"Standby," Temple said and turned the radio knob to the requested frequency. "Air Western on frequency 121.5," Temple replied. "Are you here?"

"I'm here, Air Western. You did fine. Do you know approximately how many passengers are on board?".

Temple knew exactly how many people were on board. Keeping track of people around him was just something he did subconsciously, as a matter of habit and survival. But Temple decided not to give Oakland Center an exact number. It might seem odd that he knew it so precisely. "About 60 people," Temple said, then asked, "Can you talk us down?"

"Give me a minute. I'm patching you through to a DC-9 pilot flying nearby. He'll get you down."

"Affirmative," Temple said, feeling hopeful now.

"Don't worry about air congestion," the ATC controller told him. "We're clearing all traffic between you and the airport."

Another voice joined them on frequency 121.5. "TWA 394 to Air Western 401."

"Air Western 401. I'm here."

"I've been briefed on your situation," the TWA pilot said. "I'll get you down. What's your name, son?"

"Sergeant Holloway," Temple told him.

"What is your altitude, Holloway?"

Temple glanced at the altimeter. "18,300 feet, but slowly descending."

"I was told your autopilot is on."

"It is," Temple replied.

"Okay. In a moment I'm going to ask you to turn it off. Don't worry, I'll help you land. You're about thirty-five minutes from the airport, but we're going to have to make a couple of course corrections. Do you see the heading and course display?"

"I see it, just below the artificial horizon screen."

"Yes, that's it. In a moment, I'm going to ask you to turn the left heading knob, at the bottom of the screen, to two nine zero. Understand?"

"Yes, sir."

"O.K. Turn to heading two nine zero now."

When Temple did what he was told the plane started to bank. "We're turning," Temple said.

"Good. That's what it's supposed to do. We're going to stay on that course for a little while but, in the meantime, I want to familiarize you with some of the controls."

"Understood," Temple said.

The TWA captain continued, "If you look down at the control pedestal you will see the words, automatic pilot."

"I see it," Temple said.

"Just below it is a black knob. Turning that knob left or right will also turn the plane. It won't steer you to a precise direction like the heading and course knob, but it will turn the aircraft using the autopilot."

"Good to know," Temple said.

"To the left of that knob is a little pitch wheel," the TWA captain added. "You can increase your speed by rolling that wheel forward or decrease it by rolling it back. Do you understand?"

"I understand."

"Do you know where your airspeed indicator is?"

"Yes, it's to the left of the artificial horizon screen," Temple replied.

"That's right. What is your current airspeed?"

"Three hundred and fifty knots."

"What is your altitude?"

"14,900 feet."

"Alright. Now we're going to make another course change. Turn the heading knob to two four zero."

Temple turned the knob. "Done," he said.

The TWA captain then said, "Look down at the control pedestal again. The lever furthest from you is for the flaps and slats. During the approach, I will direct you to move that lever back, one notch at a time, to help slow the plane. To engage that lever, just lift it up and back. Once you're about six miles from landing, I will tell you to pull the landing gear lever down."

"Where is it?" Temple asked.

"Just to the left of the co-pilot's airspeed indicator gauge."

"I see it," Temple acknowledged.

"During this whole procedure, you may hear some automated warning commands and caution buzzers. I'll hear them, too. Ignore them unless I tell you otherwise."

"Copy that," Temple said.

"Just before you touch down, I will tell you when to flare the nose up, so you'll land on your main wheels first. It's similar to landing a Cessna, except you're sitting much higher off the ground."

"Understood," Temple told him.

The TWA pilot continued, "Your landing speed should be between 120 and 140 knots. Once you touch down, you're going to have to slow her down. You do that by pulling the thrust levers all the way back, then you pull the reverse thrust levers back. The reverse levers are located on top of the thrust levers."

"I see them," Temple told him.

"After that, you put your flaps and slats all the way down, then apply the foot brakes. You do that by gently pressing down on the top portion of the rudder pedals, being careful not to drag the plane into a skid. If you see yourself veering away from the centerline of the runway, use the rudder pedals to steer back to center. That's pretty much it. I'm going to keep this landing simple, and I'll talk you through each step until we have you safely on the ground."

"Sounds like I'm talking to the right man," Temple said, a big smile crossing his lips.

"You're doing just fine, Holloway. You ready to get this bird on the ground?"

"I'm ready, but first, can you tell me how to brighten the control panel lights? They're starting to dim."

"Which gauges are getting dim?"

"All of them," Temple said.

After a moment, the TWA pilot said, "Sounds like the skyjacker may have disabled the constant speed drive to both generators."

"Ok, so how do I re-engage them?" Temple asked.

"You can't," the TWA pilot said. "Once it's disengaged it can't be re-engaged."

"So, what do I do? These panel lights are almost out."

"Forget about the panel lights. They're going to go dark when the batteries die. But that's o.k. I'll talk you through the landing. As long as the engines are running, you've got power. We don't need the batteries to land the plane."

With some anxiety, Temple asked, "Alright, so what's the plan?"

"I want you to disengage the autopilot switch now. It's the big yellow button on the control wheel."

Temple disengaged the autopilot and heard the warning horn notification that it was turned off. "Done," Temple said.

"How does it feel?" the TWA pilot asked.

Temple could feel the heavy control forces on the

wheel. "A little heavy, but I can —"

Suddenly, both engines stopped.

"Oh shit!" Temple cursed.

"What happened?" The TWA pilot asked.

"Sounds like both engines quit."

Through the headphones, Temple could hear nervous chatter in the background. After a moment, the TWA pilot came back on the air and said "The skyjacker must have turned the fuel pump switches off, too. Alright. New plan. Just try to keep the plane level and the nose slightly down. I'll talk you through this."

"Why don't I just turn the fuel pumps back on?" Temple asked.

"The procedure to try an engine restart is too complicated and we don't have the time. We're going to have to glide you to a landing."

"What? You want this airliner to glide down? Is that what you said?"

"We don't have a choice. Your fuel has been shut off. You have no engine power. The plane *is* going down. But I can still get you on the ground safely. I'll talk you through the landing. Just fly the plane and keep the nose slightly down. That's important."

"Alright. Alright. O.K., I can do this." Temple glanced at the panel display. "Alright. The nose is down. A little. Now what?" Temple asked.

"Now we land the plane," the TWA pilot said. "And remember, ATC has cleared the traffic below you, so you don't have to worry about that."

Temple gathered his wits, and with emotional control, he growled, "Alright. Let's do this." With a tight grip, he held the yoke in one hand and the thrust levers in the other. His eyes instinctively moved back and forth between the darkening airspeed indicator, the artificial horizon, and the altimeter gauges. His former flight training was kicking in. Now his primary focus was to control the jet during descent. Nothing else mattered. Not even the screams from the passenger cabin behind him. All he could hear now was the wind outside rushing by.

With some concern, however, Temple knew, once the battery power was drained, he would most likely lose communications with the TWA pilot.

"Are you still there?" Temple uneasily asked.

"I'm still with you," the TWA pilot responded.

Temple sighed uncomfortably. "Looks like I'm not going to make it to the airport. Where can I land this thing?"

"We're already checking. Standby."

The yoke responded much stiffer in Temple's hands than the Cessna he trained in. He gripped the yoke tighter. He could feel his heart thumping in his chest. Sweat dripped from his brow as he struggled to control the aircraft and keep the wings level. His ears eagerly waiting for more instructions. After what seemed an eternity, but in actuality was only a few seconds, the TWA pilot announced, "We found a landing site."

"Where is it?'

"Close. How are you doing over there?"

"We're going down fast," Temple said

"I know. But that's o.k. You're doing fine."

"How do I get to the landing site?"

"I'm going to need you to turn the plane right, to three-five-zero. Can you do that?"

"I can do that," Temple acknowledged, feeling a little more in control.

When Air Western 401 completed the turn, the TWA pilot said, "You should see your landing site just ahead."

Temple looked ahead for the landing site but didn't see anything long enough or flat enough to land on. "What am I looking for?" Temple asked.

"Do you see that long stretch of freeway at your one o'clock?"

"I see it."

"Turn toward it. Line up with the freeway on your nose. That's where you're going to put her down."

When Temple didn't respond, the TWA pilot cut back in. "Do you copy, Holloway?"

Temple was staring at the freeway off in the distance. He was still too far away to tell how much traffic was down there, and couldn't help but think about the innocent drivers he was about to crash on top of. He was also concerned about overpasses, billboard signs, and power lines, and wondering if that stretch of highway down there was really long enough and straight enough to land on.

"Did you copy my last, Holloway?" The TWA pilot repeated.

"Affirmative. I copy. Are you sure about this?"

"We don't have a choice. The sand dunes are too soft and hilly to make a landing. What's your altitude now?"

"One-thousand four hundred feet."

"What's your airspeed?"

"240 knots."

"Alright, I want you to slow to 200 knots."

Temple complied. "Done," he said.

"Good. We show you about 10 miles from touchdown. It's a six-lane highway, three lanes in each direction. We are going to land you with the flow of traffic, in the northbound lanes. Do you copy?"

"Affirmative." The enormity of what he was about to attempt weighed heavily on him, as he could now see the large amount of traffic on the freeway ahead. For an instant, doubt, as to whether he could land safely, gripped his mind, but he pushed that uncertainty aside. He had to get this done.

The TWA pilot cut in, "I'm here. Just off your left wing. You're about 8 miles out. Lower your speed to 190 knots."

Temple complied again. "Done," he said.

"Do you see a handle with a round knob on top of it on the co-pilot's side?"

"Yes."

"That's the landing gear. Push it all the way down now."

The TWA pilot saw the landing gear go down, but he couldn't tell if they locked into place. The TWA pilot kept that concern to himself. No sense adding that concern into Holloway's thoughts. "Now slow your speed to 160 knots and keep it there through the flare," the pilot told him.

"Done," Temple said.

A moment later, the aircraft's automated altitude warning system announced 1000 feet, but its prerecorded monotone voice was full of static and breaking up.

The TWA pilot cut in again, "Alright, I want you —"

Suddenly the cockpit radio went silent. The lights on the control gauges flickered then went dark.

"Say again," Temple urged, although he knew no one would answer.

And nobody did.

Temple stared at the freeway getting closer. Now he was on his own. His mind raced feverishly with catastrophic thoughts. The aircraft was speeding toward the ground at 160 knots. The radio was dead. The engines were dead. He was behind the wheel of a commercial jet aircraft, gliding, with no power, toward a freeway full of cars. He only had seconds to get it right. There would be no do-overs.

For an instant, confusion clouded his mind. The TWA pilot earlier recommended a landing speed between 120 and 140 knots. The pilot also recommended flaring the plane at 160 knots. That meant landing the plane at a faster speed than was recommended. Is that really what the pilot wanted? Or was he about to recommend a slower landing speed just before the radio went dead? Temple had no way of knowing now, but the Army taught him to obey his last order first, so he kept the speed at 160 knots. He hoped he was right.

As the large DC-9 approached the freeway, its enormous wingspan stretched over several lanes, like a gigantic bird of prey swooping down to attack.

The drivers in the southbound lanes were the first on the ground to notice the giant aircraft's erratic descent. In that horrifying moment, they realized the plane was going to land on the freeway. Dozens of cars swerved and slammed on their brakes, and then collided one after the other. Some of the drivers avoided the massive vehicle pileup by veering off the highway and driving across the dunes, until their tires dug too deep to move. Others abandoned their cars on the highway and ran.

Drivers in the northbound lanes watched this scene unfold on the other side of the freeway in utter shock. Something horrific must have happened in the southbound lanes to cause the massive pileup.

A moment later, a sudden rush of air enveloped the northbound lanes as the huge aircraft rapidly descended. A loud whooshing sound flooded the ears of the northbound drivers, as the aircraft swept low over the tops of their cars, leaving a high-pitched turbulence in its wake.

Temple held the yoke and thrust levers in a death grip. His eyes stretched wide, unblinking, adrenaline surging through his veins. His heart pounded so hard it hurt.

Just moments before touching down, Temple pulled the yoke back to raise the nose of the aircraft so the plane would land on its larger main wheels first. He only hoped he had not pulled the wheel back too much, or too late, as he braced for impact.

The big jet stayed in the air just long enough to fly ahead of the main body of cars on the freeway. When it finally dropped out of the sky, the main landing wheels slammed into the highway at 150 knots and severely jolted the plane. As the aircraft leveled out, the smaller, nose wheels crashed down hard on the pavement. The entire aircraft shook violently, as it continued barreling down the freeway, quickly overtaking the few vehicles still ahead of it, and scattering them like bowling pins.

Suddenly remembering what the TWA pilot told him, Temple pulled the thrust levers all the way back. Nothing happened. Then he pulled the reverse thrust levers back. Still nothing. The aircraft continued to bounce and shimmy along the freeway without slowing down. Temple pressed both feet firmly on the top edge of the pedals trying to slow the aircraft. The nose of the plane began vibrating even more violently than before. Temple backed off the pedals, but the nose gear still buckled below him and collapsed anyway. The nose of the aircraft dropped to the pavement and skidded out of control. Its great body creaking, whining and threatening to fall apart at any second. Temple depressed the center part of the foot pedal, trying to steer the aircraft, but it was a useless effort, since the nose gear had collapsed. The aircraft careened down the freeway, then crashed through the concrete center divider and slid into the oncoming southbound traffic lanes, where it slammed into three abandoned cars, one of which burst into flames. Two of the larger main landing tires, on one side of the aircraft, blew out. Then the entire main landing gear warped and broke off. The aircraft dropped to its belly. The sound of metal scraping radiated throughout the plane, as it skidded across the freeway. One wing took out several billboards. The plane slid off the freeway and across the dunes, where it finally heaved to a merciful stop in the soft sand.

Chapter 33

Although the nightmare inside the aircraft was over, the passengers aboard Air Western 401 were still too afraid to accept it. For several seconds, there was absolute silence inside the aircraft. The stillness was finally broken by a lone cheer, then the entire cabin burst into spontaneous applause.

Alexander Temple took one deep, calming breath but released it quickly, then slid out of the pilot's seat. He was mentally and physically drained, but he ignored his own discomfort. Time was critical. He had to find Yolanda Case before Nick Marlow did.

Temple opened the flight cabin door. The passengers were all standing and pushing toward the exit doors. He had to stop them. He needed all of them to use the front exit door so he could keep track of Marlow. Temple stepped out of the flight cabin and yelled, "We have to all exit out of the front door, to my right. The other doors are wired with explosives." Temple knew this story made no sense, but he also knew, in their fragile mental state, the passengers would believe it.

Nervous chatter circulated throughout the plane. Temple yelled again, "We need to get off as quickly as possible. The jet fuel used in this aircraft could still catch fire and explode."

That was all it took. Passengers started shouting, and pushing, and fighting to get to the left side forward exit. People, who had only a moment ago, thanked God for bringing them and their fellow passengers safely through this terrible ordeal, were now cursing and clawing at their fellow passengers' throats.

Temple intentionally threw a little more fuel on the fire. "Hurry up! Get that forward door open!" he yelled. "We've got to get off this plane now!"

Temple watched the fear he created spread like wildfire. *Good.* He wanted them in panic mode, so he could do what he needed to do unseen. What he told them was a lie. Since there was no fire in progress, he really didn't think the aircraft was in any danger of exploding. It was unfortunate how he had to intentionally panic the passengers, but he had to get them thinking about themselves and not him. He realized some of them might be injured in the rush to escape the plane, but it couldn't be helped.

Two of the passengers got the front door open and promptly exited the plane, without offering assistance to anyone behind them. Others, who had congregated by the door, quickly followed. In the maze of tangled bodies pushing their way through the aisle, Temple could see

Sergeant Holloway helping Yolanda. As Holloway led her past him, Temple could see her eyes were glazed over in shock. She almost seemed catatonic in her movements.

In the rear of the line, he saw Marlow. As long as Marlow stayed in the rear, Temple knew his new plan could still work.

Temple returned to the flight cabin and knelt alongside The Grim Reaper's body. He conducted a quick, but more thorough search, occasionally glancing up to keep track of Marlow's location in line. The first thing he found was an orchid bloom in the Soviet's front pants pocket. It was The Grim Reaper's calling card and confirmation that he was right about this man. Temple put it back in his pocket and continued the search. Next, he found the usual things: a pocket comb, a pack of gum, a hotel key, car keys, and a wallet. The wallet held at least a thousand dollars, most of it in new, crisp one-hundred-dollar bills. There were also family photos, credit and identification cards, and a New York City driver's license with the name Seymour Goldstein on it. They were very good quality forgeries. The Soviet's breast pocket contained a small, flat, leather wallet. He opened it and, for a moment, was taken aback. Inside was an FBI identification card, also with the name Seymour Goldstein on it. Temple took a second look at it, then realized, it too was a fake. Had it not been for his familiarity with various agency ID cards, he would not have spotted it as a phony. This FBI card, however, explained a lot. He had wondered how the Soviet got a commercial airliner, to wait for him, how he got through airport security with a gun, and how he got inside the flight cabin. Now Temple knew. Posing as an FBI agent gave the Soviet the clout to do just about whatever he wanted.

Temple heard a woman scream at the exit door. He

looked up just in time to see a man push an elderly woman out the door, angry that she was holding up the line and not jumping out. Luckily, due to the broken landing gear, they weren't too high off the ground, but for an older woman, a five-foot drop could still break bones.

The remaining passengers in line were still yelling at each other, as they pushed and shoved their way toward the forward exit door. Marlow was still at the rear.

As the line got shorter, Temple hurriedly put everything he found back in the Reaper's pockets. He would leave it for the real FBI to find. Once they found the phony credentials and the orchid bloom, they would eventually put it all together.

Temple removed the ice pick from his sock and slipped it inside his left sleeve. He stuck the sharp, pointy tip into the cuff of his shirt, so his hands would be empty, when his arms hung at his side. He glanced down at the .25 automatic but decided to stick with the ice pick. It was easier to conceal and just as good for silent, close-up killing. As Marlow neared the cockpit doorway, Temple walked out to the edge of the galley and encouraged the passengers to settle down. He didn't want anybody else injured exiting the aircraft. He was careful not to make eye contact with Marlow, although he could tell Marlow was intently staring at him.

As the two men in front of Marlow walked by the cockpit door, Temple looked up into Marlow's eyes, allegedly for the first time, and then looked away, pretending not to recognize him. The handshake scenario wasn't going to work after a plane crash.

Marlow's eyes instinctively went to Temple's hands, checking for weapons. It was a casual glance that would have gone unnoticed by the average person, but Temple expected it and made sure his body language did not present a threat.

The two passengers, who preceded Marlow, squatted to jump off the plane, Temple stepped behind Marlow, as if to follow him out.

Nick Marlow had decided to kill them both. Yolanda, because he had orders. Tom Briggs was personal, for taking Victoria Rodriguez from him. Once they were both off the plane, he would isolate them. Then he'd kill them both and fade away like dust in the wind.

As Marlow started to kneel down to jump off the plane, Temple reached around, grabbed him by his throat with a one-handed vice-tight grip, and pulled him back into the aisle. Once he dragged Marlow away from the door, Temple let the ice pick drop into his other hand.

Marlow tried to pry Temple's death grip loose.

The Iceman extended his other arm around Marlow's body and stabbed the stainless-steel ice pick into the hitman's chest, all the way in, to the handle. Marlow groaned and reached for the ice pick with both hands. His knees buckled and he was suddenly dead weight in Temple's arms. Temple stepped back and let Marlow fall backwards. His head bounced off the floor, his eyes open, staring at nothing.

Temple stepped over his body and started to exit the plane, but remembered something he almost forgot. Lincoln Delaware wanted a picture of The Grim Reaper. Temple went back into the flight cabin and pulled the pen camera from his breast pocket. He hovered over the Soviet and snapped the shutter release three times. He did not think it odd that his boss asked him to take pictures of this man. After all, there were no photographs of him on file anywhere, and no one had ever seen his face. For well over thirty years, The Grim Reaper had been the invisible, seemingly invincible man. Now he was dead. Obviously, Delaware wanted to see what this man looked like. It was, for those reasons, Temple misread the intensity in Delaware's eyes when the request was made. Temple had no way of knowing that Delaware, too, had once been hunted by the Reaper, and nearly died in a plane skyjacked by him. He didn't know that the news of The Grim Reaper's death would touch his boss in such a personal way, or that it would be to the old man, once called The Fisherman, a justice long overdue.

Temple put the pen camera back in his pocket, then started for the exit door. He didn't bother wiping his fingerprints off anything. They were untraceable anyway.

As Temple prepared to jump out of the plane, he saw most of the passengers running off into the dunes, trying to get a safe distance away, in case there was an explosion. A few others only made it a short distance from the plane, before they flopped down exhausted in the sand. Several motorists, now on foot, were flooding the area. Some tried to help the wounded. Others were there just to see the carnage. No police or other first responders were on scene yet, but he could hear sirens in the distance racing toward them.

Temple spotted Yolanda walking around in a daze, about 75 yards from the plane. Sergeant Holloway was no longer with her. Temple jumped to the ground and ran to her. She looked up at him, with confused eyes, but didn't say a word. He scooped her up in his arms, like a baby, and took off running, pretending he, too, feared the aircraft might explode. He carried her to a point beyond where most of the passengers stopped running and sat her down on the sand. Kneeling beside her, he stared into her empty eyes. Somehow, he had to get through to her. He needed her help. She was the only one on the plane who could lead authorities back to him in Las Vegas. He didn't want the police or the

FBI, tracking him back to Donnetti's gambling boat before he concluded his mission. Temple tried to communicate with her. "Yolanda, you're safe now. Do you hear me?"

Yolanda stared right at him, but her eyes still held a faraway look. Temple tried again. "Can you hear me, Yolanda? Do you understand what I'm saying? Nod if you understand me."

Yolanda held eye contact with him, but still made no indication of understanding.

The first Highway Patrol car pulled up and a young officer got out, heading toward the main body of passengers. More sirens could be heard in the distance getting closer. Temple knew his time was running out. He had to slip away before more police showed up and somebody pointed him out as the man who landed the plane.

"Listen to me, Yolanda. This is very important. Try to understand what I'm about to say." Temple gave her shoulders a gentle shake when she looked away. "Are you listening?" he said.

Yolanda's eyes turned toward him again, but with that same blank expression. Temple didn't know if she was paying attention or even understood what he was saying, but at this point, he had no choice. He had to chance it. Temple stared into her blank eyes. "Yolanda, listen to me. Nick Marlow was onboard the plane. He followed you. He was there to kill you."

Yolanda's right eyebrow rose just a bit.

Yeah, I think she heard that, Temple thought. Somewhere in her subconscious mind, she must have been listening. But how much of it would she retain? How much would she believe? And most importantly, if she believed him, would she lie for him?

Temple continued, "Donnetti sent him to kill you,

because of something you overheard. Don't worry though, Marlow can't hurt you anymore. He's dead." Temple paused, then added, "He tried to kill you after the plane crashed. I fought him. He died. Now I'm in trouble."

Yolanda's blank eyes shifted away from him. Temple grabbed her shoulders and shook her harder than he had intended. "I need your help. Are you listening to me?"

Yolanda's eyes floated back toward him. Her facial expression drew tight. She appeared frightened.

Temple didn't know if that fear in her eyes was of him or Marlow. "I stopped Marlow when he tried to kill you," Temple repeated. "I had to kill him. Do you understand what I'm saying?"

Without any facial expression, she mumbled, "You killed him."

"I had to," Temple explained again. "He was trying to kill you."

Yolanda just stared at him.

More Highway Patrol officers were arriving on scene. One of them was heading in his direction. Temple only had a few seconds to brief Yolanda on what to say to the authorities.

"The police will be here soon," Temple said. "They are never going to believe my story about why I had to kill Marlow. They're going to call it murder. They're going to send me to jail — unless you help me."

As other passengers from the flight wandered near them, Temple leaned in closer to her. "Don't tell the police that I was on the plane. You don't know who the man was that sat beside you on the plane. We never exchanged names. Will you do that for me, Yolanda?" Again, he got no response. He wondered how much of it Yolanda heard, how much she would remember, and if she would back his story.

Highway patrolman Frank Heston wasn't looking at anyone in particular when he walked over and, therefore, didn't notice one man walking away. Heston needed to clear up some conflicting information. So far, the people he talked to gave different accounts of what happened. The only fact most of them agreed upon was that an FBI agent landed the plane, but their descriptions of him varied. However, according to the code-three call Heston was responding to, an Army Sergeant named Holloway landed the plane, after killing a lone skyjacker. But that didn't check out, either. When Heston talked to Holloway, the Sergeant claimed he had nothing to do with flying the plane or killing the skyjacker. Holloway's story was verified by the people who sat beside him. So, who was flying the aircraft, and why did he use Holloway's name?

Officer Heston approached a small group of people milling around, many of whom eagerly had something to say about the crash. Shortly after Officer Heston began taking their statements, he received an all-units alert call on his walkie-talkie. It was from his supervisor, who had boarded the aircraft upon arrival.

"Everybody, watch your backs out there. There's something else going on here. We just found an FBI agent on board with a bullet hole in his head. Another guy has an ice pick in his chest. Be careful out there. Whoever did this is probably still close by."

Officer Heston gazed around the crash site and wondered what the hell was going on. It was then that he noticed the young black woman sitting alone in the sand. Heston approached her. "May I speak to you for a moment?" he asked, standing over her. When the young woman did not respond, Heston asked again, his voice more commanding. "Miss, I'd like to talk to you about the crash."

Still, the woman ignored him.

Heston squatted beside her. "Hey lady, don't you hear me talking to —" Heston noticed her pale complexion, her dilated eyes, and her shallow and irregular breathing. Although it was a warm day, she had chills. He took her wrist and found her pulse, rapid and weak. He placed his open palm on her forehead. It was cold and clammy. Her symptoms were unmistakable: she was in shock. Officer Heston put his hands gently on her shoulders and eased her down onto her back. He built a small sand mound under her feet, to keep her legs elevated at a higher level than her head. He looked over his shoulder and yelled, "I need a doctor over here."

Chapter 34

As Alexander Temple debarked from Western Airlines Flight 71 back in Las Vegas, he was thinking about Yolanda Case. Ever since he left her, at the crash site, and hitchhiked a ride to the Reno airport, he wondered how she was doing. The last time he saw her, she looked nearly comatose. He also wondered if she kept his secret.

Temple rushed through the airport and back to his car, in the parking lot. He had a little more than an hour before the auction. It was going to be tight. But just in case something went wrong, Temple made a brief stop, at a closed post office, and broke in through a back door. He stole a small packing box, a roll of tape, and some stamps. He put the pen camera, which contained photos of The Grim

Reaper, inside the box and mailed it to Lincoln Delaware.

Temple drove back to the marina. He parked at the far end of the dock then boarded The Lucky Lady and went straight to his room. In the bathroom, he collected the items left in plain sight: two small mirrors, one roll of tape, and a small flashlight. Then he left his room and headed for the security area. When he got there, he found, like before, there were no guards on duty. He opened the door to the security area and went inside.

He did not see the man, in the shadows of the corridor, watching him.

The first security device he had to defeat was the sensing mat that tripped him up the first time he attempted to get into the safe. The mat was 3 by 5 feet, not very large. This time, Temple simply leaped over it and went on to the next obstacle, the so-called pick-proof lock. He knelt in front of the door and studied the lock. After only a few seconds, he selected the proper pick and tension bar, from the little black case in his pocket. He wasn't worried about the lock. What gave him some concern was the mirror affixed to the other side of the door. He knew the mirror was positioned to reflect a light beam, coming from the far side of the room. As long as the light beam reflected back into the source, the alarm was armed. But if the door was opened, the light beam would be broken and the alarm would go off. It was a simple but clever system and would have worked, had Donnetti not told him about it. Temple had noticed, when he was first shown the alarm system, the hinges on the door were on the outside. That meant the door opened toward him. The construction error there was obvious. Had the door opened inward, he would have had no chance of opening it, without setting off the alarm. The only question now was, how much leeway was there to open the door toward him, without breaking the light beam.

Temple went to work on the pick-proof lock and had it open in less than thirty seconds. He then opened the door just a crack, pressed his ear against the wall and peeked between the small opening. He needed to confirm that the mirror diameter and position on the door had not changed since he last saw it. Temple could not see the mirror enough, from that limited view, so he eased the door open just a little bit more, hoping it wasn't too much.

Now he could see the mirror, three inches in diameter and about three feet down from the top of the door. Temple backed away from the door and selected the larger of the two mirrors he brought with him. He tore off a four-foot strip of tape, which he wrapped around the handle of the mirror, so it dangled like a yo-yo on a string. He slid the mirror over the partially opened door and lowered it gingerly down the other side, until it hung in front of the security mirror. He affixed the other end of the tape to the ledge above the doorway. Now his mirror reflected the light beam, instead of the mirror on the back of the door.

Temple opened the door and proceeded to the next obstacle, another locked door. After a glance, he selected a different lock pick. With this one, he would not need a chamber tension bar. Temple pushed the pick into the keyhole, as far back as it could go, then applied upward pressure on the pick and raked it out. It only took one swipe and the lock was open. Temple opened the door but didn't go in. He stared across the long narrow corridor leading to the room with the safe. He could see the safe from where he stood. It sat there dark and ominous, as if daring him to proceed further. Temple scanned the long hallway. There was a fifteen-foot-long mat in the middle of the floor. He figured it was either pressure-sensitive or possibly wired for electrocution. He already knew about the infrared crisscross security beams in front of the safe. What gave him caution were the security devices he didn't know about. Temple's eyes traveled cautiously from wall to wall, ceiling to floor. Nothing. He got down on his hands and knees so he could view the corridor from another angle. That's when he saw it. A tripwire stretched tautly across the hallway, just beyond the doorway about ankle-high. It was such a very fine wire, even now, with it only inches from his nose, he could just barely see it.

Temple looked beyond that wire for a secondary trip line. He didn't see any, but that didn't mean they weren't there. Temple stood up and switched his attention back to the floor mat. It was too wide to straddle and too long to jump, but he could probably tiptoe, along one side of the mat, as it did not fit snuggly against the bulkhead.

Temple gazed again at the tripwire. If there were more, he wouldn't see them unless he was crawling on all fours. But crawling across the floor wasn't possible. Temple considered the problem, then pulled the strings from both his shoes and tied them together at one end. He stepped over the first tripwire and snuggled against the wall on his toes. Then he proceeded carefully along the narrow edge, between the mat and the wall, while holding the shoestring dangling just ahead of him. If there was another tripwire, the shoestring would come into contact with it first.

Slowly, cautiously, Temple inched forward, his eyes glued on the shoestring. He got a little more than halfway, before the shoestring came into contact with another wire. Temple stepped over the wire then continued the rest of the way without incident. He stuffed the shoestring in his pocket. Now he was less than ten feet from the safe. The only thing blocking his way now was the crisscross light beams.

Temple took the flashlight from his pocket and switched it to the infrared mode. The security light beams, across the doorway, were now visible. The crisscross pattern was so tight not even a small child could get through it. After careful study, a smile crept across Temple's lips. As he suspected, there was really only one light beam, originating from a lens in the left wall, about three inches off the floor. The beam ricocheted off several carefully positioned mirrors on both walls, creating the crisscross pattern that ended up shining into a photoelectric eye on the upper right sidewall. That electric eye was the key to defeating this system. All he had to do was redirect the beam. This type of security system was incapable of distinguishing one continuous light beam from another. As long as a light of equal wattage, or better, was shined directly into it, this system would continue to register all clear. Using the masking tape, Temple firmly secured the flashlight from the ceiling and aimed it directly at the photoelectric eye. He held it steady then turned it on, successfully neutralizing the crisscross beam.

Temple walked over to the safe and knelt in front of it to get a better look at the locking mechanism. It was a Group 2 combination lock with a dial. Temple put his ear close to the dial and went to work. Slowly, he turned the dial and listened for variations in the clicking sounds. He combined that effort with the tactile techniques he had some success with in the past.

Within a minute, he started hearing the tumblers click into place. After the third tumbler had locked in, Temple started turning the dial slowly to the right. He felt some resistance on the dial pad but continued turning it until it clicked on the final number. Temple opened the safe.

The man in the shadows, who had been watching Temple, turned away and hurriedly headed back down the corridor.

After a quick, but thorough ransacking of the safe's contents, Temple realized the Alpha Data was not there. He checked his watch. There was no time left; the auction had already begun.

As Temple made his way out of the security area, he made up his mind. He would kidnap Donnetti. Even though the auction had already begun, Temple believed he still had time. He didn't think the fat man would be foolish enough to bring the Alpha Data to the auction. Donnetti would most likely wait, until there was a winning bidder, then he would deliver the merchandise in a private setting.

All Temple had to do now was snatch Donnetti out from under his bodyguards. Maybe Victoria could help him there. With her time on board, she might have some good intel on how to isolate him.

Once clear of the security area, Temple took the time to quickly re-thread his shoes. He didn't want loose shoes to be a problem later, if he had to run.

When he was done, he began his search for Victoria in the casino area, then he checked the lounge. After that, he walked along the outer decks. Finally, he headed toward her room. He just hoped she wasn't — entertaining.

Chapter 35

Temple listened at Victoria's door. He didn't hear anything, so he knocked.

After a short delay, Victoria called out, "Who is it?"

"It's me, Tom."

"Just a minute," Victoria said. A few seconds later, she partially opened the door but stood blocking the entrance. Her face was slightly flushed and her hair was in disarray. "I'm not alone," she whispered.

Temple couldn't help but notice the tight fit of her dress, a green, low cut, mini that teasingly hugged the curves of her voluptuous body. Temple leaned close to her ear, "It's not in the safe."

"Are you sure?" Victoria asked.

"I'm sure."

"So, it's over?" she probed.

"Not yet," he said.

"What are you going to do?"

Before he could answer, an impatient voice called to Victoria from inside the room, "Come on Victoria! Hurry up!"

Victoria looked back at the man in her room. "I'll be with you in a minute, darlin'." Victoria stepped out into the hall and closed the door behind her, then whispered, "You know the auction is already in progress?"

Temple nodded. "I'll just have to grab Donnetti as soon as it's over."

"What good will that do?"

"I doubt Donnetti will bring the microdots to the auction. So, if I grab him afterward, I'll persuade him to give them to me."

"What if you're wrong? What if he wants to showcase the microdots for the bidders?

"I don't think so. Too many things could go wrong, if he brings the microdots out in the open. No, he'll wait until the losing bidders leave the boat, then he'll go get them."

"Well, that does make sense," she admitted.

"You know the boat. Is there a secure location onboard where I can take him?"

"I don't think so," she told him.

"Then I'll have to find a way to get him off the boat." Before leaving, Temple glanced at her room door, then back to her. "Are you going to be alright?"

Victoria nodded, then said, "I have to go."

As Temple started to leave, a man stepped out of the shadows into the corridor. "Hold it right there!" Alvin Gutloff growled.

Temple saw the S&W .45 Auto in Gutloff's hand, his finger on the trigger. "What is this?" Temple demanded, feigning outrage.

Victoria, too, pretended innocence. "Apparently, you two have something to talk about," then she started to go back into her room.

"Don't you move, Victoria," Gutloff growled, walking toward them.

"What the fuck's going on here?" Victoria snapped.

Gutloff ignored her. "Both of you. Inside. Let's go."

"What's this all about?" Temple protested.

"Get your asses in that room, now," Gutloff ordered, and followed them in.

Once inside, Temple was surprised to see the lawyer, William Penrod, sitting on the edge of Victoria's bed, fully dressed, with an erection sticking out of his unzipped trousers.

William Penrod jumped to his feet and stuffed himself back into his pants, when they walked in the room. He tried to pull his zipper up, but it was stuck.

"Well look-a-here," said Gutloff.

Penrod stopped fumbling with his zipper, when he saw the gun in Gutloff's hand. "What is the meaning of this, Mr. Gutloff?" Penrod demanded, covering his open fly with his hands.

Gutloff said, "Why don't you tell me, lawyer."

"What's that supposed to mean?" Penrod challenged.

"It means, you'd better have a damn good reason for being here."

Penrod misunderstood. "I'm sorry, I didn't know this was your woman."

"The bitch means nothing to me," Gutloff snapped.

"Then what's the problem here?" Penrod barked.

"Yeah," said Temple, "I'd like to hear the answer to that myself."

"So would I," Victoria spat out.

Gutloff pointed the gun at Temple. "This man is a spy."

Temple faked a laugh. "I'm what?"

Victoria stared at Temple, pretending to be shocked.

"That's right, Miss Rodriguez," said Gutloff. "He's a government agent. You look surprised?"

"Of course I'm surprised!" she snapped.

Gutloff looked at Penrod. "What about you, lawyer? Are you surprised too?"

"Yes, I'm surprised," said Penrod. "But are you sure?"

"I'm sure."

Temple started to protest, "Now, wait a minute –"

"Shut up!" Gutloff shouted as he aimed the gun at Temple's head. "And keep it shut. You open your mouth just one more time, and I'm gonna blow your fuckin' head off. Do we understand each other?"

Temple nodded yes.

Gutloff glared at Temple a moment longer, then continued his conversation with Penrod. "Like I said, lawyer, I'm sure. I just watched him waltz through Mr. Donnetti's security system like a pro. No vacationing writer could do that."

Penrod turned to Temple. "No. A vacationing writer couldn't." Penrod started toward the phone. "We'd better call Mr. Donnetti right away."

"Hold it right there," Gutloff growled at Penrod.

Penrod stopped, with his hand inches from the phone. "What?"

"Get back over there with the others."

"What is this?" Penrod questioned.

"Get back with the others. Now!" Gutloff ordered, with

the .45 now leveled on Penrod.

"Alright, take it easy," Penrod said nervously, as he rejoined the others. "But what's this all about?"

Gutloff said, "I need to find out who everybody really is. You could all be partners, for all I know."

"Partners?" Victoria scoffed. "You must be kidding. I'm just here to have a good time."

"I don't kid," Gutloff growled, with a chilling stare.

Penrod pointed to his open zipper. "Surely it's obvious why I'm here."

"That don't prove shit!" Gutloff snapped. "Maybe while you and Victoria were waiting for your partner here, to show up, she gave you a blowjob to kill some time."

"No! That's not the way it was," Penrod protested.

"But I don't know that — do I?"

"If you let me call Mr. Donnetti, he'll straighten all of this out," Penrod offered.

Temple let the derringer up his sleeve slide into his hand.

"Alright. Give him a call," said Gutloff, then he glanced down at his watch.

The moment Gutloff's eyes moved, Temple brought his arm up and squeezed off two rounds, before Gutloff ever knew what hit him. Both bullets slammed just above Gutloff's right eyebrow. The first one went in clean. No blood, just a neat, little entry hole. The second one was messy, with blood exploding out the back of his head. Gutloff dropped like a rag doll, his gun bounced across the floor, to a spot between Penrod and Victoria.

Calculating that Temple's derringer was empty, Penrod made a grab for Gutloff's .45.

Victoria saw Penrod make his move and knew she couldn't beat him to it. For a split second, she wondered if she should even try. Helping Tom now would clearly blow her cover.

Before Penrod could grab the gun, Victoria took one leaping step forward and kicked the gun toward Temple.

Temple scooped it up and aimed it at Penrod.

"Well," said Penrod, as he stood back up, "now we know who everybody is."

"Check the corridor," Temple told Victoria.

Victoria left the room and returned a moment later. "It's all clear," she said. "What about him?"

"I don't see that we have much of a choice," said Temple.

"W-wait," Penrod stammered, as he stumbled back against the wall. "Don't shoot. I can help you. I know where the government microdots are."

"Where are they?" Temple asked.

"If I tell you where, you'll kill me," said Penrod.

"You think you're any safer if you don't?"

"It's onboard," Penrod told him.

"Where?"

"In Donnetti's private safe."

"Bullshit. I looked in his safe."

"No, not the floor safe. Mr. Donnetti has another safe. A private safe. Nobody else knows about it but me."

"How do you know about it?"

"I make it my business to know what goes on around here. Even Mr. Donnetti's not aware that I know."

"You sure the microdots are there?"

"I've seen them," Penrod told him.

Temple lowered the gun. "Alright. Let's go get them."

"Wait," said Penrod. "Let's deal first."

"You got nothing to bargain with. Let's go."

"You're forgetting the microdots."

Temple raised his gun again. "Look, you little bastard, either you show me where the safe is, or I'll fuckin' kill you right now. That's the deal."

Trembling nervously, Penrod stuttered, "If you s-shoot, I p-promise you'll never f-find it."

"Then I'll turn this boat into firewood, and nobody else will find it either."

Penrod mumbled, "If you do that, you'll never really know if the microdots were here."

Temple lowered the gun again. "Keep talking, lawyer."

"My life for the microdots. That's the deal."

"How do you propose we do this?"

"I'll tell you where the microdots are and I'll give you the combination. But you have to leave me here, alive. You can tie me up so I can't warn anybody."

"You're not concerned I might go back on our deal, once I get the combination?" Temple asked.

"I'm gambling you won't shoot me, before you verify that my information is correct. Once you see that it is, it would make no sense for you to walk all the way back here, just to kill me, after you have what you want. You can just walk away. By the time I'm found, you'll be long gone."

Temple considered his proposal. "Alright, but not here. Let's go find a place a little more private."

Penrod felt relieved, as he walked ahead of them toward the door.

Victoria gave Temple a hard stare.

Temple knew what that look meant. She was telling him, in no uncertain terms: *you may be willing to risk your cover by dealing with this creep, but not me. He dies when this is over.*

Temple motioned for Victoria to proceed ahead of him. As they left the room, Temple wondered how Penrod and

Victoria could both be so gullible, to ever believe he would honor that deal. Penrod was a key player in Donnetti's organization. That, in itself, was enough to seal his fate.

As they rounded the corner, in single file, the elevator door ahead of them opened. Half a dozen security guards poured out with guns drawn. The corridor exploded in gunfire. Temple saw Victoria fall. He managed to squeeze off two rounds, hitting two of the guards, before several bullets tore painfully into his body and neck. Temple reeled backwards and struggled to stay on his feet. He wanted to keep shooting, to take more of them with him, but he was hit by another volley. Several to the body and one to the head. Temple staggered and fell. He opened his eyes, only once, and saw the security guards cautiously approaching him with guns drawn. He heard laughter somewhere above him and rolled his head toward the sound.

Penrod stood triumphantly above him with a smirk on his face. "And you were going to kill me," Penrod snarled, then spat down on him.

Temple felt saliva splatter on his face. He also felt the .45 still in his hand. With his last bit of strength, Temple brought the gun up suddenly, to the surprise of his tormentor, and fired. The bullet caught Penrod in the throat. Temple smiled, then slipped into a black void of darkness.

Chapter 36

When Jim Donnetti returned to *The Lucky Lady*, Eddie Bowman met him at the brow. The two bodyguards accompanying Donnetti followed at a discreet distance. Donnetti looked up at Eddie questioningly.

The big man shook his head no.

Donnetti frowned, then asked, "What about Penrod?"

"He's dead."

"Did he say anything about it before he died?"

"He never regained consciousness."

Donnetti dismissed the two bodyguards, who had accompanied him, then headed toward his stateroom. Eddie Bowman followed him without being told. When they got to

Donnetti's door, Eddie walked in ahead of him and did the customary premises check. Donnetti then entered, sat in his favorite chair and gave Eddie a look. Eddie walked to the wet bar and mixed his father his favorite drink. After giving the cocktail to Donnetti, the giant turned to leave.

"Just a minute," Donnetti said, as the big man neared the door.

"Yes sir, what can I do for you?" Eddie hoped his father would offer him a drink. Maybe ask him to sit down and just talk for a while.

Donnetti took a sip from his drink then said, "Turn the lights off on your way out."

Without any outward sign of emotion, Eddie Bowman simply replied, "Yes, sir."

Donnetti sat there alone, contemplating his next move. He was running out of time. Fifteen minutes later, Eddie Bowman returned. "It's time sir."

Donnetti followed Eddie to the boat's barbershop. A uniformed armed guard was standing outside the door when they approached. The guard nodded at them and opened the door. A burly security guard in plain clothes, appeared in the doorway, but stepped aside upon seeing who was coming in.

Eddie entered the shop first, Donnetti followed. Inside the spacious three-chair shop was another uniformed guard. He stood behind the center chair, guarding the man seated there. The man had been stripped of all his clothing and was strapped securely to the barber chair, with thick leather straps bound tightly around his wrists, ankles, and waist.

The man looked up as Eddie and Donnetti entered.

Donnetti whispered something to the two guards, after which they both left the room. Eddie shut the door behind them. Donnetti sat down on the barber chair, to the right of the restrained man. "Now that you are awake — Mr. Temple

— that is your name, isn't it?"

Temple didn't answer.

Donnetti continued, "It doesn't matter. But we do have some business to discuss."

"I'm guessing your men shot me with tranquilizer guns," Temple said. "Why?"

"I think that should be rather obvious, Mr. Temple."

"I'm afraid it's not," Temple replied.

Donnetti's features turned hard. "No more games. Where is it?"

Temple stared curiously at him. Could he be talking about the Alpha Data? Did somebody else get to it first? Or maybe it was something else. "Where's what?" Temple asked.

Donnetti exhaled wearily and shook his head. "Wrong answer." Donnetti turned toward Eddie Bowman and nodded. The big man pulled a .357 Magnum from under his jacket and handed it to his father. Donnetti flipped the cylinder open and made sure Temple saw it was fully loaded with real ammo. Then he said with no emotion, "Unless you tell me what I want to know, I'm going to kill you. Right here in this room." Donnetti stood up and walked around to Temple's left side. He put the 8- and 3/8-inch barrel against Temple's head and asked again, "Where is it?"

Temple did not think Donnetti was ready to pull the trigger. The fat man had gone to too much trouble, with the tranquilizers, to just shoot him now. "If you shoot," Temple gambled, "you'll never find it."

Donnetti cocked the trigger.

"Alright," Temple cut in, thinking he may have misjudged the situation. "I'll take you to it, but before I —"

"No deals. Tell me now or you're dead."

"It's in my room," Temple lied.

"No, it's not," Donnetti snarled, then pressed the Magnum harder against Temple's head.

Temple caught his breath and prepared himself for the explosion. There was nothing else he could say or do to stop this, but he kept his eyes open. He wanted to see death coming.

After what seemed an eternity, the gun barrel was removed from his head. Donnetti glared down at him. "No, I'm not going to shoot you. At least not yet. We still have things to discuss." Donnetti gave the gun back to Eddie and whispered something to him. After the blond giant left the room, Donnetti sat back on the barber chair beside Temple. "I'm going to make my position and your predicament perfectly clear. The auction is over. The Chinese now legally own the microdots."

"Legally?" Temple taunted.

"Legal or not, it belongs to the Chinese. They paid for it. They want it. They don't know yet that the microdots are missing, and I assured them they would have their purchase within two hours. So, you see, I don't have much time left. You have even less."

Eddie Bowman walked back into the room, with a pair of large industrial pliers.

Donnetti continued in a steady tone, "I have found it saves a lot of time, with the back-and-forth discussion, if we thoroughly understand each other at the outset." Donnetti glanced at Eddie.

The big man did not attempt to hide his sadistic grin, as he moved toward Temple, with the pliers. Eddie crudely shoved his hand down between Temple's legs and lifted his genitals.

Temple grunted, then tensed his body to get ready for the terrible pain he knew was coming.

Eddie fitted the pliers around Temple's left testicle.

"Not too hard," Donnetti cautioned. "I still have questions."

Just as the words cleared the fat man's mouth, Eddie squeezed the pliers.

At first, there was only pressure. An instant later, the pain was unimaginable. Temple's head snapped back and his mouth opened wide, as he screamed in pain. His entire body stiffened, every muscle bulging and straining to its limits. Then he began jerking violently in uncontrollable spasms.

After nearly a full minute, the intensity gradually waned. Temple collapsed, exhausted, his body still shuddering as arcs of pain continued to throb in his groin. Slowly, the fog in his mind lifted and Temple could hear Donnetti's voice.

"How much pain you receive, before you die, is up to you. So, I'll ask you again, where is it?"

With contempt in his eyes, Temple glared up at the fat man with a defiant sneer.

"You must answer promptly, Mr. Temple," the fat man said.

Temple saw the glimpse from Donnetti to Eddie and, in that twilight of thought, Eddie squeezed the pliers again. Temple's body flew into a spastic frenzy of excruciating pain. This time his body jolted more violently than before, and his groan was gut-wrenching.

Shuddering uncontrollably, Temple clenched his teeth and made a growling noise trying to contain the rupturing pain. Slowly, the debilitating aching in his groin lessened, to a severe deep throbbing. Temple opened his eyes, while still breathing, heavily trying to catch his breath.

Donnetti repeated the question. "Where is it?"

Temple had to tell this madman something, anything, to

stall for time. He didn't know how much more he could take. In a strained voice, Temple lied again, "I hid them. In my hotel room downtown. I'll show you where, if —"

"I will not bargain with you," Donnetti interrupted, and nodded at Eddie again. The big man squeezed the pliers once more and again came unimaginable pain. Temple's scream barely sounded human, and his body flew into violent convulsions.

When his spasms lessened, Temple slumped raggedly in his chair, groaning, his body still withering in agony. After a moment, he looked up at Donnetti, through bloodshot eyes. It was hard to focus, to think, his mind still reeling in a thick fog of disorder. One thing was clear though: he didn't see any way out. This bastard was going to kill him. He always knew one day it could happen. So be it. Temple resigned himself to that fact, then clenched his teeth in defiance and forced a smile.

Eddie Bowman flew into a rage. "Let me crush his fuckin' balls. He'll talk then."

Donnetti leaned toward the giant. "You must learn to be patient, Eddie. Patience is the key." Donnetti glanced at Temple's quivering body and calmly told Eddie, "Before we're done with him, he will talk to us." Donnetti nodded at Eddie again and the torture continued. After repeated assaults with the pliers, Jim Donnetti could only stare at Temple in silent disbelief. This man had been reduced to a quivering mass of flesh, and still he refused to talk.

When Temple finally passed out, Donnetti's jaw tightened in frustration, as he glanced up at the clock. "Give me the pliers, Eddie," he said.

The big man did not immediately respond to his father's request. He wasn't done with this man yet.

"Give me the pliers, *now!*" Donnetti ordered.

Reluctantly, Eddie surrendered them.

"Now wake him," Donnetti said.

Eddie slapped Temple's face hard, but the agent did not wake up.

Donnetti sat erect in his chair. Panic suddenly gripped him. He feared the man might be dead. Hurriedly, he grabbed the agent's wrist and felt for a pulse. He was relieved to find one. This government man was not allowed to die his way out of this, before he revealed the location of the microdots. The Chinese were not the sort to tolerate any delays in receiving their property, especially after the enormous investment they made. Donnetti told Eddie again to wake him.

Eddie grabbed a hand full of Temple's hair and jerked his head back, then slapped his face repeatedly. He continued the slaps, even after Temple was visibly awake.

"Enough," said Donnetti.

Eddie raised his hand to deliver another backhanded slap.

"I said that's enough!" Donnetti roared.

Eddie stopped his assault in mid-swing but still had rage in his eyes.

"He's awake. You can leave us now," Donnetti ordered with a chastising stare.

Eddie held Donnetti's stare for a moment, then backed down and started for the door.

Donnetti watched the big man as he left the room. When the door shut behind him, Donnetti breathed a little easier. No other man had ever unnerved him so. Donnetti understood, even with his control over Eddie, the man was still highly volatile and could blow at any moment. Of late, it seemed Eddie was becoming more resistant. Perhaps his usefulness was coming to an end.

Donnetti heard a deep painful groan come from his captive and he turned toward him.

"You are a fool," Donnetti began. "A stupid, ignorant fool. Look at you. Your nerves are shot. What's left of your manhood is in question. And you're taking all this punishment, so your agent buddies can say you died a brave, and loyal man." Donnetti stood up and walked around Temple's chair. "The truth is, they'll never know. Nobody will know except you and me, and the executioner. All your foolish heroics will never be known. So, the real question is, how do you want to die, Mr. Temple? More pain? My man Eddie enjoys inflicting pain. Or would you rather die quickly? No more pain. No more suffering. You choose right now." Donnetti paused, then asked the question again, "Where is it?"

Temple's eyes blinked shut, as he edged near unconsciousness again.

Donnetti grabbed a clump of Temple's hair and jerked his head back and forth. "Tell me now!" Donnetti yelled.

It took all of Temple's energy, but he forced another smile, as he sank back into unconsciousness.

Chapter 37

When Temple's eyes opened again, he was still naked and strapped in the barber chair. His groin was swollen and throbbing painfully. Donnetti and his henchman were gone. Across the room, an armed security guard was standing by the door. Strapped in the chair beside him was Victoria Rodriguez. She was still wearing the same green dress she had on, when they were shot with tranquilizers.

When Victoria saw Temple was awake, she asked, "Are you okay?"

"I've been better," he said, choking back the pain. Then noticing the fresh bruises on her face and left arm, he asked, "What about you?"

She offered a weak smile, "I've been better too."

When the guard saw Temple was awake, he picked up a phone and called someone.

Temple felt slightly embarrassed, sitting there naked like that, but he ignored the discomfort. He knew his problems were about to get much worse. But maybe he could salvage her cover. "Why did they grab you?" he said, aloud, pretending she was not involved.

Victoria said under her breath, "They know who we are. They think one or both of us know where the microdots are."

Temple started to speak but grimaced from the searing pain in his groin.

"Tom? You don't look so good."

Temple waited until the intense throbbing waned. "I'll be alright," he breathed.

Victoria gave him an inquisitive look. "Did you tell them anything?"

"No," Temple said, and hoped his answer might keep him alive long enough to kill them all.

Victoria nodded. Then she whispered, "I'll figure a way to get us out of here."

Before Temple could reply, Donnetti and Eddie re-entered the barbershop. Eddie stayed by the door, as Donnetti continued over to Temple. "It has become obvious to me," Donnetti began, "you have no regard for your own life. You are mentally prepared to die. The question is, do you care about anybody else?"

Donnetti walked over to Victoria. "Pretty girl," Donnetti said, stroking her hair.

Victoria jerked her head away from his hand.

Donnetti laughed, then turned to Temple and asked again, "Where is it?"

When Temple didn't answer, Donnetti looked back at Eddie. "Kill this bitch."

As Eddie moved toward her, Victoria frantically jerked at her wrist restraints, trying to pull her arms free.

The big man took a position behind her chair and locked his massive forearm around her neck. Victoria's eyes bulged wide, as the pressure grew tighter. She opened her mouth to scream, but no sound came out. As the pressure increased, she squirmed wildly in the chair. A few seconds later, her body began jerking violently and her eyelids started to flutter.

Temple saw Donnetti watching him for a reaction. That told The Iceman a lot. He didn't think Donnetti was ready to kill her, not with the microdots still missing. Temple gambled that he was right. If he was wrong, Victoria was going to die. They both were.

"Wait!" Donnetti blurted out to Eddie, then he stared at Temple in astonishment. This agent didn't give a shit about his partner. What was it going to take to break him? Donnetti knew he couldn't kill either one of them yet, not until he got one of them to reveal the location of the microdots. Donnetti looked back and forth between the two of them. Maybe there was another way.

Donnetti turned to the security man at the door. "Have the guard standing outside come in."

When the guard entered, Donnetti said, "Why don't you two take Victoria to another room and keep her entertained. Get some of the other boys in security to help you with that."

Both guards knew what he wanted them to do and looked at each other with silly grins, as if they had just hit the jackpot. Both eagerly started undoing her security straps.

Victoria stared at the guards, with a hateful sneer, as they worked on her restraints.

Temple said nothing. He knew he couldn't stop what was about to happen. Showing any emotion now would make it worse. Donnetti would exploit that weakness and hurt her more, to try to force him to talk. Hopefully, Victoria could save herself.

As the guards stood Victoria up and handcuffed her hands behind her back, Temple gave her a look, and she returned it. Neither one showing emotion. Both of them understood they were on their own.

Donnetti said, "When you boys are done with her, let Eddie have a go at her. If she's not in a talkative mood after that, I'll have Eddie get a hammer and change her mind."

As the guards dragged her toward the door, Victoria struggled, trying to break free.

"Last chance, Victoria," Donnetti's voice boomed. "Where are my microdots?"

"Kiss my ass," she spat out.

"When these men are done with you, you'll talk to me, and then you'll beg me to kill you. And only then, will you have my permission to die."

After the guards hauled Victoria out of the barbershop, Donnetti turned to Eddie Bowman. "If she's still not talking after the hammer, then she really doesn't know anything, so get rid of her."

Temple's fist clenched tightly, as he sat there helpless.

As soon as Eddie left, another man entered the shop.

Temple couldn't tear his eyes away from the man walking in. It was not possible. How could Nick Marlow still be alive? That ice pick had gone all the way in.

Nick Marlow returned Temple's stare, as he crossed the room toward Donnetti. With each step, Marlow appeared to be in considerable pain, and he kept his left arm close to his body.

Donnetti frowned. "What are you doing in here?"

"I was told you wanted to see me," Marlow explained.

"In my office. Wait for me there."

Marlow mad-dogged Temple, as he left the room.

Donnetti turned to Temple and chuckled. "You look like you've just seen a ghost."

Temple didn't know what to say. Marlow was supposed to be dead.

"You know, you almost killed Nick on that plane," Donnetti said.

"I don't know how I didn't," Temple confessed.

"You came close. When Nick told me, that you had stabbed an ice pick into his chest, frankly, I didn't believe him, not until my boat's doctor confirmed his story. Amazingly, you missed all of his vital organs. Can you imagine the odds of something like that happening?" Donnetti paused to hear Temple's response. When Temple didn't answer, Donnetti continued, "Anyway, when the medics took him off the plane, they were surprised at how good his vitals were. He was in a lot of pain—still is—but not critically. They bandaged him up and took him to the hospital, but old Nick skipped out, when their backs were turned. He's one tough boy. Anyway, he caught the next flight back. Needless to say, he's very upset with you. Nick's only request was that we let him kill you." Donnetti let that sink in, then added, "I can control Nick. What I want you to think about is Victoria Rodriguez. You may not give a shit whether your partner lives or dies, but I can promise you, her death won't be quick. You know what those men are doing to her right now. By the time they're done, if she still refuses to give up the microdots, Eddie is going to take a hammer and start breaking bones in her fingers, her hands, her feet, her face—you get the picture. She's going to die slowly in horrible pain. You can stop it. You know what I want to hear."

Temple knew he had to get out of this chair, for either of them to have a chance. He tried a bluff. "Alright. Let the girl go and I'll take you to it. There's nothing she can say to her bosses that'll hurt you. It'll be her word against yours. In a court of law, her word is not enough to —"

"This is not a give and take, Mr. Temple. I take. You give. That's it. I will not bargain with you."

Temple stared back at his captor; he had no cards left to play. In a low rumble, Temple growled, "I'm going to kill you, fat man."

Donnetti laughed. "I'm sure you would try, if you had the opportunity. But as you can see, you do not." Donnetti started for the door, then said over his shoulder as he left the room, "When Eddie's done with your partner, we will conclude our business with you, one way or another."

Twenty long minutes later, Nick Marlow hobbled back into the barbershop with two armed uniformed guards in tow, one of whom was carrying a bundle of clothing. Marlow pulled out a German Luger automatic and aimed it at Temple from across the room. Then he told the guards to untie him.

Temple noticed the guards appeared nervous, as they approached him. Neither one of them would hold his stare. Temple shifted his gaze to Nick Marlow.

Marlow did not look away. He owed Temple for that ice pick attack and was hoping the agent would try something now. A furtive move, a flinch, anything, so that he could justify to Donnetti why he had to kill the spy, instead of delivering him to the boss as ordered.

As the guards unshackled Temple, he could barely move without feeling excruciating pain. Even with his extensive training in State of Mind Control, it was still extremely difficult for his mind to ignore the crippling pain in his body. His physical injuries were just too severe. But he was, at times, able to minimally reduce his pain, to a level just above unbearable. Not much, but it was something. And as long as he had something left, he would resist and keep fighting.

When the restraints on his wrist were taken off, he kept his head down. He did not want them to see the rage in his eyes. Once all of his restraints were removed, the guard carrying the clothing tossed them at him.

"Get dressed," Marlow ordered.

When Temple tried to stand, the crippling pain in his groin radiated through his body, and he fell back into the barber chair wincing in agony.

"Hurry up and get dressed," Marlow growled, impatiently.

Temple looked up at Marlow with weary, painful eyes, then deliberately taunted him with a smirk and said, "Didn't think I'd be seeing you again."

Nick Marlow fumed in anger. He wanted so badly to shoot that cock sucker in his big mouth. But that's not what Donnetti wanted. At least, not yet.

The two guards pulled Temple to his feet. They helped him get dressed, then wrapped his arms around their shoulders and walked him out of the barbershop and down the corridor ahead of Marlow, who followed at a safe distance. As they moved through the winding passageways, Temple was consumed with guilt and rage over what was happening to Victoria Rodriguez. He also thought about Yolanda Case. She must have made it, since nobody was talking about her. At least she was safe.

After traveling through several corridors, they stopped at a lone door. Temple sensed the guards were starting to feel more confident.

Enjoy it while you can, Temple thought.

Marlow knocked on the door, then entered without an

invitation and closed it behind him.

The guards patiently supported Temple's weight while waiting for Marlow to return. When Marlow opened the door a couple of minutes later, he looked boiling mad. "Bring him in," Marlow snarled.

The guards walked Temple to the center of the room, which was set up as an office. Jim Donnetti was seated behind his desk, puffing on a cigar and holding a cup of coffee. He studied the government agent as they brought him in. Temple looked weak. He could barely stand, and his head slumped forward. "You can leave us now," Donnetti told the two guards.

"He may fall down if we let go, sir," one of them said.

"Then let him fall," Donnetti replied.

The guards released him.

Temple stumbled forward a bit but didn't fall.

The guards left the room, but Marlow maintained his position by the door, behind Temple.

Donnetti blew on his coffee to cool it, then took a cautious sip. He nodded his approval, then took another sip. Afterwards, he gazed over at Temple. "We are both out of time," Donnetti said. "The Chinese will be here soon to pick up their property. I don't have it. Which means, minimally, I'm going to have to give them their money back, plus a 10% bump for their inconvenience. But even with that generous gesture on my part, they're not going to be happy. I'm going to have to convince them I didn't make a side deal with the Soviets or one of the other bidders."

Temple mumbled through gritted teeth, "And you're telling me this, why?"

"Because I do have something that will help me smooth this mess out — you."

"What's that supposed to mean?"

"You are an anomaly," Donnetti began. "My source assures me that you don't exist inside any known American intelligence agency, yet here you are. I think the Chinese might find the existence of a shadow organization inside U.S. Intelligence intriguing. With the intel they can beat out of you and the cash settlement that I'm going to offer; I think that might be enough to get their minds off the microdots."

Marlow blurted out, "Let's just kill him like we planned!"

"You don't get a vote," Donnetti said, without looking at him. Then to Temple, he said, "I will have to rebuild credibility with the Chinese. Using you is how I do that." Donnetti took another sip of his coffee, then leaned back in his chair. "The Chinese will have better luck with you than I did. They won't be rushed. They'll have all the time in the world to find out all about you and your organization."

Temple's head rose slowly. His eyes met Donnetti's, for the first time since entering his office. When Donnetti saw the rage, he looked to Marlow. But before he could call for help, Temple ignored his own pain, made a Superman dive onto Donnetti's desk and locked his fingers around his tormenter's throat. Temple was not concerned that Marlow might shoot him in the back. He was probably going to die anyway, but not before he took the fat man with him. As Temple squeezed Donnetti's fat, sweaty throat, he could hear Marlow rushing up behind him, but he didn't let go. Squeezing the life out of this vile man was all that mattered.

Marlow hooked his hand under Temple's chin and jerked his head back, causing Temple to lose his grip on Donnetti's throat. Jim Donnetti fell back into his chair. The chair rolled backward, then tipped over and crashed to the floor, with Donnetti choking and gasping for air.

With his adrenalin pumping, Temple rolled toward

Marlow and rammed an open palm strike to the gunman's chest, aiming for the same spot where he had stabbed him earlier.

Marlow screamed and stumbled backward, his face twisted in agony, as he clutched his chest with his one good hand.

Jim Donnetti yelled for the two guards in the hallway as Marlow laboriously pulled his 9mm Luger, from under his belt.

The two guards reentered the office. Realizing now the scream they heard was not from the captive agent, cold fear flushed through their veins. Both guards clumsily pulled out their semi-automatics.

Marlow glanced back over his shoulder and saw terror in the guards' eyes. He also saw that he was about to be in their line of fire.

Temple sprang forward, grimacing in nearly unbearable pain, and twisted the Luger out of Marlow's hand.

When the guards saw that the agent now had the gun, they panicked and opened fire.

Chapter 38

A hail of gunfire erupted in the room. Jim Donnetti ducked behind his desk, when the shooting started. Temple grabbed Marlow by his shoulder and spun him around, then held him up as a shield.

The guards were in full panic mode. The prisoner had a gun. Blind fear clutched at their hearts, as they fired at the threat, in a reckless frenzy, with no thought of Marlow and Donnetti being in their line of fire. At fifteen feet away, most of their shots went wild, shattering items all around the room. But some got through.

Temple felt the impact of three rounds slamming into his shield. Marlow grunted and his body went limp. Suddenly Temple was holding up dead weight. The Iceman peeked around Marlow's body, with the Luger ready to fire. As soon as he stuck his head out, he heard one round zip past his ear. Almost simultaneously with that sound, The Iceman fired one round. The bullet pierced through one guard's forehead. A red mist burst into the air and the guard dropped at his partner's feet. The second guard turned and ran. Temple dropped his shield and fired two rounds into the running man's back. The second guard staggered, dropped to his knees, and fell face down in the hallway.

Temple glanced down at Marlow. There was no doubt this time. Nick Marlow was dead.

"Now it's just you and me," Temple growled at Donnetti, as his adrenalin-rush faded and the pain resurfaced. "Come out from behind there," Temple ordered, gritting his teeth to control the pain in his body.

When Donnetti did not respond, Temple fired a round through the desk.

Donnetti yelled out, then popped up quickly, with his hands raised. "Alright! Alright! Don't shoot!" he pleaded. "You need me. I'm your ticket off this boat."

Temple glared back at him. "I'll take my chances." As Temple squeezed the trigger, a hand reached from behind him and deflected his aim, just as the bullet left the barrel. The Luger was then jerked from his hand and he was violently shoved to the floor. Temple landed hard and moaned from the severe throbbing in his testicles. While still grimacing, Temple rolled over onto his side and looked up into the cold black eyes of his attacker: Eddie Bowman.

Instead of pursuing Temple, the blond giant worriedly turned to his father, who was leaning across his desk, wincing, and holding his hand against his left side where the deflected bullet grazed him.

Breathing erratically, Donnetti snapped, "I'm okay,

dammit! Now kill that son-of-a-bitch!" *To hell with the Chinese,* Donnetti thought.

Eddie Bowman turned back to Temple but let the Luger, in his hand, drop to the floor.

Donnetti yelled out, "What the hell are you doing?"

Temple knew right away what Eddie was doing. It was a challenge. *Mano a mano.* Clearly, this man was not a professional. A professional would not have given up the advantage; he would have just pulled the trigger and walked away. That's certainly what Temple would have done.

Temple tightened his jaw, fighting back the terrible pain in his groin, as he struggled to stand up.

Impatiently, Eddie grabbed him by his collar and jerked him to his feet.

Temple came up swinging and drove his fist into Eddie's jaw.

The big man grunted, as his head snapped back, but he immediately responded with a punch of his own.

Temple saw the huge fist coming, but couldn't move his head out of the way. He only had time to turn his head sideways, in order to avoid a straight-on punch. Eddie's giant fist landed with the force of a sledgehammer. Temple felt bone fracture in his cheek. His ear went numb. Throbbing pressure radiated behind his eyes and, for a few seconds, he could not see. But he could smell Eddie's stale breath in his face, and knew the big man was close and facing him. Temple sprang forward, without regard for his own injuries, and whipped his knee up between Eddie's legs. Temple growled deeply, through clenched teeth, as his sudden movement ripped at every nerve in his groin.

Eddie hunched over moaning like a wounded animal.

Temple reached out blindly and found Eddie's head and held it down, then brought his knee up into the big man's face. Again, Temple's nerve endings were on fire, but he knew his knee landed solidly, when he felt something in Eddie's face break and heard the big man groan. Temple started to knee him again, but Eddie reared up bellowing wildly and exploded forward, ramming Temple back against the wall. The Ice Man felt like his chest had just caved in. He couldn't catch his breath, without feeling the excruciatingly disjointed movement of ribs ripping at his insides. Still, Temple tried to push the big man back, but his body was too weak and his knees buckled.

Eddie wouldn't let him fall. He held Temple up and pinned him back against the wall.

Through blurred vision, Temple could see blood flowing from the big man's broken nose.

Then Eddie hit him again. And again. He must have passed out, because he didn't remember falling, but the crash to the floor somewhat revived him to a groggy, disorientated state. He could feel deep bruising and multiple fractures in his face. Temple forced his swollen eyelids open. Blood, from his facial injuries trickled into his eyes, further obscuring his already blurred vision. Temple felt Eddie grab his collar, and he was jerked to his feet again. Instinctively Temple clawed for the big man's eyes.

Eddie jerked his head back, out of the way, and grabbed Temple's wrist. He twisted the arm over so Temple's left elbow was down, then Eddie dropped to one knee and slammed the agent's outstretched arm down across his thigh, breaking the elbow with a devastating crack.

Temple screamed and withered on the floor in agony.

Eddie Bowman stood up and glared down at the spy man, then raised his foot to stomp on his skull – but stopped, when he heard the sudden wail from the boat's fire alarm.

The voice over the intercom, following the alarm,

reported there was an emergency on board and all guests and crew had to leave the boat immediately.

Eddie turned to his father.

"FUCK THAT ALARM!" Donnetti shouted. "He's getting away!"

Temple had already started crawling across the room, dragging his broken arm, like a useless anchor. Each crawling motion severely straining the damaged nerves in his ruptured groin and swollen testicles.

Eddie Bowman grabbed Temple's foot and pulled him back.

Temple kicked his foot free, and sprang forward, yelling in horrific pain, as he lunged for the gun on the floor.

Eddie rushed up behind him, grabbed Temple's left shoulder, and yanked him to his feet again.

When Eddie spun him around, Temple pushed the barrel of the Luger against the giant's chest and squeeze the trigger. The blast blew a hole into the big man's chest, knocking him several feet back, but it was Alexander Temple, who dropped to his knees as crippling pain ravaged his body.

Though reeling in agony, Temple could still see, through eyes now nearly swollen shut, that the big man was coming after him again. Temple brought the Luger back on target, with his right hand, and repeatedly squeezed the trigger until the clip was empty. Each round slammed into Eddie's chest, jolting his massive frame, but the big man kept coming.

Eddie Bowman grabbed Temple's neck, with both hands, and lifted him until his toes dangled just off the floor.

Temple started gasping for air and clawing at Eddie's grip. The lack of oxygen to his brain was overwhelming. He was about to pass out, when Eddie's grip suddenly loosened, and both men fell to the floor. Alexander Temple landed hard, coughing, and gagging, as air painfully rushed back into his lungs. The first thing he was cognizant of was the giant's cold black eyes staring at him. Temple started scooting away from him, but quickly realized, his haste was unnecessary. Eddie Bowman was dead.

Temple glanced around the room for Jim Donnetti, but he was gone. Temple rolled over onto his knees and started to stand up, but stopped, when he felt a sharp pain in his side – broken ribs. His left arm was also broken. Breathing was difficult and his chest felt like shit, but he wasn't sure what the full extent of that injury was.

Temple clenched his teeth and groaned, as he tried again to stand up. His testicles felt like they were about to burst. He paused, took a ragged breath, then grunted loudly, and pushed himself to his feet. Once he was up, he felt extremely lightheaded, almost to the point of losing consciousness, but he braced himself up, on a chair, and gazed across the room. He needed some air. There was a porthole behind Donnetti's desk. If he could open it, get some air on his face, maybe he could stay conscious. Temple stumbled over to the porthole and worked frantically unscrewing the six bolts, so he could open it. When he got the screws undone and the porthole open, a refreshing breeze rushed in. Temple stuck his face through the hole. The cold air felt good, but he still teetered on the verge of passing out. Temple took more deep breaths, as deep as his broken ribs would allow. It was then he noticed; the boat was no longer moored alongside the pier. Temple turned from the porthole and staggered toward the door. He had to get off the boat before it got too far into the lake. He needed medical attention and was too weak for a long swim. As for the mission, he was in no shape to complete it, if that was even possible now. Temple stumbled out into the corridor, weak and disoriented. He hugged the wall for support, as he staggered aimlessly down one corridor and then another, not sure he was even heading in the right direction. Suddenly, the room started spinning and everything went black.

When Temple's eyes opened again, he was on the floor, not sure how long he had been there. In the distance, he could hear footsteps. Instinctively, he reached for his gun but remembered it wasn't there. Temple staggered to his feet and continued stumbling through the corridor. The footsteps were getting closer. He heard his mission's name called out. At least, he thought he did. He was too dizzy to concentrate.

As Temple started to round another corner, someone grabbed his right shoulder. The last thing he clearly remembered was a hand quickly patting him down. Everything after that, came in flashed sequences, as Temple drifted in and out of semi-consciousness. He remembered someone pulling him along through the passageway. He also remembered walking down a stairway, maybe two, and going through a door hatch. A cold stiff breeze suddenly smacked him in the face. He realized he was somewhere on an outside deck. He was being pushed toward the safety railing. Temple tried to break free from this person but was too weak. When he felt himself being lifted over the railing, he grabbed the line with his only good hand, and held on as tightly as he could. Then, quite clearly, he recognized the person's voice, who was trying to push him over the rail.

"Let go of the line, Tom," Victoria Rodriquez shouted. "We've got to get off the boat. I've set some explosive charges. The whole boat's gonna blow."

Temple turned to her with an incensed stare.

"It's ok," Victoria insisted. "Only Donnetti and his boot lickers are left onboard. We have to finish this."

Temple let go of the line.

Victoria reached down, between his legs, from behind and flipped him over the lifeline. When Temple hit the water, a couple of decks down, he was knocked out cold.

When Temple woke up, he was lying on his back, in an inflatable life raft. Pain still consumed his body. He felt dazed and disjointed. One of the first things he noticed was the long black dress Victoria was wearing. He didn't think she even noticed he was awake. The raft was still floating close to the boat, and Victoria was squatting down, busily getting out the oars, with her dress draped high above her knees. Temple could see the .38 caliber pistol and holster strapped to her thigh. He tried to speak to her. He wanted to help but slipped back into unconsciousness.

During his next flash of awareness, he could see they were now about thirty feet away from the boat. Victoria was rowing frantically, trying to get more distance between them and the impending explosion. Temple noticed her dress was now pulled down to a respectable level. On the deck of the boat, he could see Jim Donnetti standing at the railing, pointing a finger toward them and yelling at someone behind him.

Victoria looked back at the boat, to see what had caused Temple to stir. She could see Donnetti glaring at them and she heard Temple mumble something. "What? What did you say?" Victoria asked.

"Shoot him," Temple said.

"What for? The boat's going to blow up any minute now."

"We gotta be sure," Temple insisted while struggling to stay conscious.

"He won't live through the explosion," she protested.

"Shoot him—before he—gets away."

"Tom—"

"Shoot him, dammit!"

"With what?" Victoria replied. "We don't have a gun between us." She glanced at Donnetti, then back to Temple. "Wait," she said, "there should be a flare gun in the survival kit on this raft. I can shoot him with that—maybe." Victoria located the flare gun, loaded it, and aimed it at Donnetti, who was frantically waving at someone behind him to hurry to his location.

Donnetti was not looking at the raft, as Victoria got him in her sights. When he turned back to her, Victoria squeezed the trigger. The gun fired with a loud boom but not much recoil. The flare struck Donnetti in the chest and knocked him back, away from the railing. His clothing ignited instantly, and he burst into a human torch.

Instead of dropping to the floor and trying to roll the flames out, Donnetti panicked and took off running. Three uniformed guards rushed onto the deck to save him, but they were too late. The flames had totally engulfed him.

Victoria put the flare gun down and continued rowing to get more distance.

Two of the guards, on the boat, rushed to the deck railing and fired several rounds at the raft.

With bullets zipping all around them, Victoria started rowing at a more energetic pace. All of a sudden, a powerful blast exploded aboard the gambling boat, hurling bits and pieces of the upper decks high into the sky. A moment later, a second and then third explosion blew *The Lucky Lady* apart. The force from the last blast was so powerful that the raft overturned. Temple remembered hitting the water and hearing Victoria scream.

Chapter **39**

When Temple woke, he was back in the raft. Victoria Rodriguez was in the process of setting a splint and sling on his left arm. Temple made no attempt to stir. He was physically drained and his entire body was in excruciating pain. When Victoria noticed he was awake, her worried expression turned to relief and she gave him a broad smile.

Temple watched her silently as she attended to his arm. Even now, soaking wet with stringy hair and smeared makeup, she was a stunningly attractive woman.

Victoria's smile faded. "I thought I was going to lose you, Tom. You've lost so much blood. How do you feel?"

"Like shit."

"I'm not surprised," said Victoria. "You took one hell

of a beating."

"How long?" Temple asked.

"You've been out for about ten minutes," she said, finishing off the sling. "There, that should hold, until you can retrieve the microdots. Then we can get you to a doctor."

"The microdots?" Temple blurted out, with a confused look. "How do you know you didn't blow them up with the boat?"

"I found another note from Billy," Victoria said, as she started rowing back toward the docks. Then she looked at him. "He said he had the microdots and was going to give them to you."

"He never had a chance to," Temple answered. After watching her for a while, Temple asked her something he had been wondering about. "How'd you get away from Donnetti's men?"

Victoria cast her eyes downward. "I didn't," she said quietly. "Not completely."

Temple understood her meaning, but she didn't answer his question. For now, he would let it ride. He was tired. His body needed the rest, but he couldn't get that vision, from earlier, out of his mind. Strapped to Victoria's left thigh was a .38 caliber snub-nose revolver. When he told her to shoot Donnetti, she told him she didn't have a gun. Why did she lie? Temple could only think of one reason. She was hiding something from him, and that gun was her insurance policy. Temple hated what he was thinking, but he had to face the real possibility that this woman, whom he had trusted, could be a traitor, perhaps even a foreign agent. If either were true, she was probably after the Alpha Data, too, and was only keeping him alive because she believed he knew where it was. Once she got her hands on it, he was expendable. Of course, this was mostly speculation. Victoria could be just who she presented herself to be: a deep-cover FBI agent trying to help a fellow intelligence officer. Unfortunately for Victoria, speculation was all he had, because he just might have to kill her, with nothing more than that.

Victoria smiled down at him. Temple returned it and closed his eyes, for some much-needed rest. Whoever she really was, he knew he was safe for now.

It seemed he had just drifted to sleep, when he felt a gentle shake. He opened his eyes and saw Victoria bending over him. She looked tired.

"We're back at the docks," Victoria said. "How do you feel, Tom?"

"Lousy," Temple admitted. He started to stand but felt dizzy and fell back down.

Victoria leaned over to help him up.

Temple suddenly pitched forward and punched her in the jaw. Victoria fell back in the raft, and Temple snaked his hand under her dress and pulled the revolver from its holster.

Victoria sat up dazed, holding her cheek and looking confused. "What the fuck was that for?" she cursed, her eyes moving between him and the gun in his hand.

"You told me you didn't have a gun," Temple said.

"I lied. So what? You don't tell me everything."

"We were under fire. Under those circumstances, there was no reason to keep the gun a secret."

"I didn't see any reason to waste a bullet on Donnetti. He wasn't going to survive the explosion, anyway. What's gotten into you?"

"I think you're a double agent."

"What?" Victoria stood up looking dumbfounded. "You must be kidding."

"Does it look like I'm kidding?"

"Is this all because of that damn gun?"

"Not just that. You never should have told me about the first note from Billy Shaw."

Victoria looked confused. "What's that supposed to mean?"

"It made no sense that Billy didn't tell you where he hid the microdots but was willing to tell me. The only logical answer is that Shaw didn't trust you. Maybe he—" Temple grimaced, as he felt a sudden intense throbbing in his groin.

Victoria took one subtle step toward him.

As his pain gradually eased, Temple continued in a strained voice, "Maybe he even found out you were a foreign agent."

Victoria had the most amazed look on her face. "You can't really believe that?"

"You look too damn good," he told her.

Victoria's face drew tight. "What?"

"The last time I saw you, you were being dragged off to be raped and tortured. Now here you are, without any new bruises and wearing a different dress."

"After they were done with me, I killed the bastards," she said. Then she glanced down at her dress. "They pretty much tore off the dress I was wearing, so I had to change."

"That all makes sense," Temple admitted.

"But you don't believe me, do you?"

"I think you're working for Donnetti," Temple said.

"You *think*! All this because you *think* you're right?"

"In our business, sometimes that's all we have."

"So, what are you going to do, Tom, kill me on a ridiculous hunch?"

Temple briefly considered the possibility that he was wrong, but knew his indecision wasn't enough to save her.

"I'm not the enemy, Tom," Victoria said. "What can I say to convince you?"

Temple shook his head and moved his finger into the trigger guard. "There's nothing you can say."

The raft abruptly rocked, when a wave rolled roughly underneath it. Temple groaned from the ripping pain in his groin, as the boat jostled him around.

Victoria moved in on him, with the quickness of a cat and kicked into his broken ribs. Temple screamed and doubled over groaning.

Victoria snatched the gun out of his hand, pushed him down, took a step back, and pointed the revolver down at him.

Temple had fallen back on top of the oars, then crashed into the first aid kit, scattering its contents along the bottom of the raft. While lying there withering in agony, Temple forced his swollen eyelids open in search of a weapon. On the floor of the raft beneath him, he remembered seeing a mixture of gauzes, sterile pads, bandages, and one pair of surgical-style scissors.

Victoria lowered the gun. "I'm sorry about that, Tom, but I had to get the gun back. You were going to kill me, for Pete's sake." Victoria moved closer to him and her voice softened. "Hope I didn't hurt you too much." She extended her left hand. "Let me help you up. We've got to get you off this raft and to a doctor."

Temple noticed the gun still in her right hand, her finger next to the trigger. He reached up to her, and she helped him to his feet.

The raft was tied to a ladder, on the dock, leading up to the pier. In Temple's current condition, he knew it was not going to be an easy climb.

"You go first," she told him. "I'll follow you up to make sure you don't fall off."

Temple glanced up the length of the ladder. "Alright,

let's do it," he said.

The climb up the ladder was grueling, but he could feel Victoria below him, pushing him, supporting him, and urging him on. Even with her help, it took all his reserves to continue climbing. Once he got to the top of the ladder, he crawled onto the pier and collapsed, trembling from the intense pain between his legs.

Victoria rested her hand on his back. "You okay?" she asked.

Temple didn't answer. His cumulative injuries had caught up with him and he felt like he had nothing left.

Victoria said, "We have to get out of here. Can you make it, Tom?"

Temple looked up at her and grimaced. "I can make it," he said, trying to convince himself. "Just give me a minute."

"We need to go now," she urged.

"Alright," Temple said, breathing painfully. "Give me a hand up."

Victoria paused, gave him a wary look, then helped him to his feet and supported his weight, as they walked down the pier, but Temple was staggering badly and Victoria had great difficulty holding him up. "This is not going to work," she said. "You're not going to make it to the hospital like this. You're too banged up. And you've already lost so much blood. Hell, you're still bleeding now. It's a miracle you're still alive." After a few more steps, Victoria added, "I know in your present state of mind, you don't trust me, but I am not the enemy. I'm on your side. Let me help you complete your mission. Tell me where the microdots are. I'll call an ambulance for you, then I'll go get them."

"The gun first," Temple mumbled.

"Tom, please, we don't have time to—"

"The gun first," he repeated more forcefully.

After a long pause, Victoria giggled curtly, then dropped him to the ground. "No, I can't give you the gun," she said, the empathy in her voice gone. "For a moment there, I was *almost* tempted to give it to you, to prove my, loyalty," she added with sarcasm. "But no, I couldn't do it. Not with you. You're much too dangerous, to put a loaded gun, in your hands. Even in your weakened condition, I couldn't chance it. You were going to kill me earlier on a hunch."

"So, you *are* a traitor?" he said, moving his hand slowly, cautiously toward his sling.

"Oh, I'm so much more than that, Tom. Or should I say, Alexander Temple? Yeah, I know who you are."

Temple looked at her, with surprise, as he pieced it together. "You're the double agent everybody's been looking for."

"That's right. I'm Maxwell. But you—you are still somewhat of a mystery. You work for a black ops division, inside the CIA, that doesn't exist. You're here to recover microdots, containing information so secret, not even my source knows what's really on them."

"Your source?" Temple questioned, as he rolled onto his injured left side, easing his right hand inside the sling, to retrieve the surgical scissors he had stashed there.

Victoria smiled broadly. "Your President's chief of staff. The fool doesn't know when to shut up. He always wants to impress me with what he knows." Victoria laughed. "Good pussy can make a man do just about anything. But enough about me." Victoria aimed her gun at his head, her facial expression suddenly serious and the tone of her voice chilling. "I will only ask you this once. Where have you hidden the microdots and what's on them?"

Staring down the barrel of a gun was something you

never get used to, but how you respond to it can be the difference between life and death. In this instance, Temple's instincts told him that she would not shoot, at least not until she got her questions answered. That's why she helped him get off the boat. That's why he was still alive now. She wanted information. Temple ignored her threat and just stared back at her, while moving his fingers casually toward the scissors. He knew his attack would have to be explosive. One powerful stab, to her chest, just left of center, should drive the blades and shaft into her heart. But he would have to wait until she was closer. He was only going to get one chance at this.

When Temple's fingers reached the back of the sling, the scissors weren't there. No! They had to be there. Temple controlled his panic and kept his fingers moving.

Victoria glared down at him, her eyes cold and her finger tautly on the trigger. After a few anxious moments, a restrained smile crossed Victoria's lips and she lowered her aim. "No, I'm not going to kill you, but I will put a bullet in your knee cap if I have to. Maiming you won't diminish your usefulness."

"What's that supposed to mean?" Temple probed.

Victoria's lips curled into a sneer. "I may not have the microdots," she said, "but I do have you. You're going to be the consolation prize. The people I report to should be here any minute now. And I assure you, when they're done with you, they'll know all about you, your organization, and the microdots."

Temple's fingers found the scissors. They had slipped down in the sling, along the backside of his broken arm, where he couldn't feel them. Unfortunately, Temple no longer had the luxury of waiting for her to move into striking range. She had people coming for him. He had to act now, before they arrived.

"Why'd you blow up the boat?" Temple asked, stalling for just a little more time, as he pulled the scissors casually out of the sling.

"Those fool guards were going to rape me. I had to tell them that I was Maxwell. They told Donnetti and he made them back off. After that, I didn't have time to hunt each one of them down. Besides, I didn't know who else they talked to, so I blew the boat to make sure I got them all." Victoria paused, to give him a once over, with appreciative eyes. "You know," Victoria said, shaking her head in regret, "in a way, I'm going to hate to have to turn you over to them. It'll be a long time before I find another man, who can satisfy me the way you did." Victoria shrugged her shoulders, "Oh well, business is business."

Temple got a firm grip on the blade of the scissors as his hand cleared the sling. He calculated Victoria was standing just over six feet from him. Despite his broken ribs, Temple took a deep breath then suddenly snapped around, like a released tightly-coiled spring, and flung the scissors toward her heart.

Victoria's superior reflexes kicked in immediately. She had already started to duck, but her quick reaction caused the blades of the scissors to miss her intended chest and slam into the right side of her throat, into the trachea. Victoria grunted on impact, then made a gagging sound. The gun in her hand fired wildly and struck the pier close to Temple's head.

Temple, however, barely noticed it. He had already rolled into a fetal position and was convulsing, in spasms, from his own internal injuries. Moving so aggressively had again amplified every nerve ending in his body.

It took several moments before he could focus. The taste

of blood was thick in his mouth. The pain in his upper body and groin was almost unbearable. Still, he forced himself up on one elbow and looked for Victoria. He spotted her lying motionless at the edge of the pier. Blood was spurting from her neck, like a geyser. The Iceman struggled to his feet and staggered toward her. He had to finish this. By the time he dropped to his knees beside her, the geyser had stopped, which meant her heart was no longer pumping. The scissors were still gripped in her blood-soaked left hand, the revolver tightly clenched in the other.

Temple rolled himself into a seated position, diagonally to her, then using his feet, he pushed Victoria's body off the pier into the water. Again, he struggled to his feet and made his way groggily down the pier. If he could just make it to the street, to get some help. Just a few more steps. Keep moving. Just a few more steps.

Up ahead, he could see blurred headlights from cars on the street, outside the dock area. Just a few more steps.

By the time Temple made it to the street, he was barely conscious and moving on sheer will alone. He stopped in the middle of the roadway, reeling in a daze. Where were the cars now? There were no cars. No people. Nothing. The streets were deserted. Temple turned and tried to make it back to the curb, but collapsed in the middle of the street.

In the distance, an old Chrysler Imperial approached the intersection. The driver, an elderly man in his mid-seventies, was being berated by his wife, about his terrible driving. Neither of them noticed the body, in the middle of the street, until it was almost too late. At the last moment, the elderly man saw something big in his path and veered off just in time. He slammed on his brakes, causing the Chrysler to spin out of control across the center divider, finally coming to rest in the oncoming lanes.

Chapter 40

Alexander Temple was wheeled, from the Memorial Hospital recovery room, to a private room on the third floor. Approximately one hour after he was taken to his room, a long black limo pulled up in front of the hospital, where an unknown elderly couple had earlier dropped off a severely battered, unconscious man, whose driver's license identified him as Tom Briggs.

Of the two men in the limo, only the passenger in the rear seat got out and entered the hospital. He rode the elevator up to the third floor and went straight to room 315. He paused, at the open doorway, before going in. The man, he was there to see, was heavily bandaged and sitting up in bed gazing out the window. He was alone.

Alexander Temple turned toward the man, as he entered the room. It had been a long time since he'd seen Dickerson Allen, the CIA special agent whose mistake, years ago, caused him to lose his real identity, his family, and his fiancé.

Dickerson Allen spoke first. "Hello, Al."

Temple gave him a stern look because Allen did not use his mission's name.

"Don't worry," Allen said, "the room is not bugged. We checked." Allen sat on the hardback chair beside the bed. "Did you get it?" he asked.

"No," Temple answered. "But I've had a little time to think about it since I've been here. I think I know where it is. Shaw's last words to me were to find his lost eyeglasses. At the time, I thought he was asking me to find them in his room, so he could see."

"What does this have to do with the Alpha Data?" Allen asked.

"I think the microdots are on them."

"But you said his eyeglasses were missing?"

"No, Shaw said they were lost."

A perplexed look crossed Allen's face. "I'm not following you."

"His eyeglasses were never in his room, but, if they were lost anywhere else, it would be impossible for me to find, right?"

"It would be — difficult," Allen conceded, not sure where Temple was going with this.

"Where would you look for lost property in a hotel?" Temple asked.

Allen considered the question. "In the lost and found department," he said.

"That's right. I think Shaw dropped his glasses off there,

as found property, so he wouldn't be caught with them. That's why he told me they were lost."

Allen smiled. "We'll check it out. Is there anything else I should know?" he said standing up.

"I found Maxwell," Temple said.

Allen's eyebrows rose.

"I killed her," Temple added.

"Her? Maxwell was a woman?"

"Victoria Rodriguez was Maxwell. I'm sure you know who she is."

"Is your cover intact?"

"No. Victoria knew who I was. She had inside help."

"From who?" Allen asked.

"The President's chief of staff. Apparently, he talks a lot between the sheets."

"I'll take care of that," Allen said, then gave Temple a long, hard look. "So — your identity was blown. Too bad." Allen turned and started toward the door, but stopped and looked back over his shoulder. "You're sure Maxwell is dead?"

"I'm sure," Temple told him. As Allen reached for the doorknob, Temple frowned and asked with disdain, "Aren't you going to ask me about Karen Kiley?"

"We already know about Miss Kiley," Allen said, then he left the room.

About two hours later, the same black limo returned to the hospital. Dickerson Allen exited the vehicle, from the front passenger seat, and walked into the lobby. He called Temple's room, from a payphone, and spoke to him briefly. "This is Allen. You were right about the eyeglasses."

Dickerson Allen got back into the long black automobile, which pulled around to the side of the hospital. Two burly men, dressed in black, exited the limo from the rear seat. Both wore brimmed hats pulled down just above their eyes. The two men entered the hospital through the service entrance. They took the service elevator, up to the third floor, and went directly to the room of Alexander Temple. They paused at the doorway, when they saw a nurse changing one of Temple's bandages, then they continued down the hallway and waited until the nurse left. After she was gone, the men in black entered Temple's room and closed the door behind them.

A short time later, a stunned and horrified group of people, outside the hospital, saw a man in a hospital gown, jump to his death from a third-story window. A crowd gathered around the dead man's body.

Before the two men in black left Temple's room, the nurse, who was there earlier, returned. The taller of the two men turned away and put his hat back on. The nurse was momentarily startled, by the two sinister-looking men in black, but regained her composure quickly. She noticed her patient's bed was empty. "What happened to Mr. Temple?" she asked.

"He just stepped out," one of the men answered.

"Stepped out!" she exclaimed. "He was told to stay off his feet for a few days. How does he ever expect to get better?" she ranted. "Look, you tell him for me — no, never mind, I'll tell him myself when he gets back here." The nurse stormed out of the room flustered.

The two men waited a moment longer, then caught the service elevator back down to the lobby. They left the hospital through the service entrance and got back into the limo. As the sleek black automobile pulled back into traffic, the sound of approaching sirens could be heard.

Not long after driving away from the hospital, Dickerson Allen and the two men in black boarded a private plane at McCarran Airport. Allen was busy in conversation, with the man in black who had spoken to the nurse. The other man in black, who had remained silent, was still silent now. He had much on his mind. He wondered who the dead man was and why his identity was kept a secret from him. What was the big mystery? He was certain Dickerson Allen knew the man, but Allen wasn't talking. He didn't think the other man in black knew any more than he did, which was practically nothing. He was only told the man was terminally ill and had agreed to die in that fashion, for the good of the agency and some unspecified compensation to his family. There was never any mention as to who the man was or who he worked for. He did not think the man was a fellow agent. He was quite sure he had never laid eyes on him before he walked into that hospital room.

So, who was that guy? What was the big mystery? He pondered that question throughout most of their flight enroute to San Diego. When the light aircraft hit a rough air pocket, he cradled his broken arm and sat back in his seat, considering his own fate. He was now a man with no name again.

Alexander Temple wondered who he was going to be tomorrow.

Thank you to all those who contributed to the success of this book

PILOT CONSULTANTS, thank you for taking the time. Your expertise helped me greatly with portions of this story.
> *George Ramirez*
> *Garrett Hartsuker*

BETA READERS, thanks for your invaluable insight. Your comments gave me a lot to think about and ultimately made my story more grounded.
> *Jen Rauscher*
> *Colleen Williams*
> *Suzi Smith*
> *Harry Curry*
> *Diane Curry*
> *Kim Bieda*

EDITOR ASSISTS, very knowledgeable at what they do.
> *Sande Hall*   my longtime friend
> *Editornancy*   from Fiverr
> *Kristencolv*   from Fiverr
> *Brookewrites*   from Fiverr

BOOK COVER DESIGNER FROM FIVERR, I loved it at first sight.
> *Pro_ebookcovers*

ORIGINAL TYPIST, she took handwritten scribble and made it readable
> *Arlene Kurban*

ABOUT THE AUTHOR

Ernie Adams is a retired San Diego Police Sergeant and first-time author of the new novel, *President's Eyes Only*. After decades of reading action-adventure novels, this is Ernie's first attempt at writing his own full-length novel. His many years in police work has given him a unique perspective in developing memorable characters and intriguing plots, with real world conflicts that are both challenging and disturbing. Ernie served in the U.S. Navy. After his four-year enlistment, he worked a few other jobs before embarking on a career in law enforcement. It was, during his Navy time, that his writing impulses began. Intrigued by action thrillers, he whetted his writing appetite with the creation of numerous action-packed short stories, allowing him to actualize his own characters and plot lines. *President's Eyes Only* is an adult thriller. It is edgy, hard-hitting, and nail-biting, engaging your imagination with each turn of a page. You will not want to put it down. *Scott McEwen, bestselling author of American Sniper says, "Exciting plot with twists and turns of masterful skill."*

Made in the USA
Las Vegas, NV
20 October 2024

10173852R00260